THE FIRST CHURCH OF
THE NEW MILLENNIUM

BRYAN APPLEYARD

THE FIRST CHURCH OF THE NEW MILLENNIUM

Doubleday

LONDON · NEW YORK · TORONTO · SYDNEY · AUCKLAND

TRANSWORLD PUBLISHERS LTD
61–63 Uxbridge Road, London W5 5SA

TRANSWORLD PUBLISHERS (AUSTRALIA) PTY LTD
15–25 Helles Avenue, Moorebank, NSW 2170

TRANSWORLD PUBLISHERS (NZ) LTD
3 William Pickering Drive,
Albany, Auckland

Published 1994 by Doubleday
a division of Transworld Publishers Ltd
Copyright © Bryan Appleyard 1994

A catalogue record for this book is available from the British Library

ISBN 0–385–404859

Typeset in 11½/13pt Sabon by
Chippendale Type Ltd, Otley, West Yorkshire.
Printed in Great Britain by
Mackays of Chatham, PLC, Chatham, Kent.

FOR CHRISTENA

ONE

THE DARKNESS BEHIND took shape and followed. Panic told me I could maintain my steady walking pace no longer, yet I fought against the pressure to run. I was being pursued by nothing more than my own rising terror. What had been there had gone, or it had never been. I stopped breathing and looked back to see an empty black space. There was nothing there. The walk resumed, I breathed again and concentrated on the lights ahead, the way they bounced with each steady step. Strange how they bounced, how everything moves because we move. But, unobserved, the space behind me was rushing to coalesce into numberless new impossibilities. The great hand of my fear pushed me forward. I surrendered, stumbling clumsily into a run, tripping on the rock-strewn track, my legs twisting and jarring painfully on the rutted surface.

Then the broken track gave way to the smooth stones that wound across the last of the meadows. It was still raining, the drops cold against my cheeks. I slithered on the wet surfaces that shone with the spiked, orange reflections of the approaching lights. Finally I ran through the narrow alley, the walls amplifying the thumping of my shoes. I stopped as the walls ended and I found myself on the pavement of the village street.

The orange lamps made a long shelter of visibility against the raging darkness beyond. This lit space was filled with streaks of slanting rain, the ground shone and shimmered and there was a cold, abandoned stillness. The street was empty but for an old woman walking away from me on the far side. She was clutching a hat to her head and dragging a small dog. Beyond them the lights of the pub cast golden rhomboids over the wooden tables on the cobbled front yard.

Slowly I crossed and passed into the yellow light and the drifting blue-grey smoke of the Three Arches. Here I would be safe; here nothing impossible ever happened.

'Hello, stranger! Hello indeed! Thought you were always working, old man, that's why you come down to our part of the world. Isn't it? Not for pubbing with the boys. Oh, no. Not our Mr Rix. Not our Mr Architect Rix. Well, well, well. Quite a surprise. Quite a surprise.'

This was Jack, landlord of the Three Arches – check shirt, cravat, corduroy trousers and a local accent modified by alien jocularities.

'I needed a break, Jack, you know we all need a break. Even you must need a break sometimes.' I returned the smile and then drank quickly from the beer he had already drawn. His gaze held.

'Oh, yes! Often feel the need of a break myself. Not easy. Not easy, Mr Architect Rix, I can tell you. Not in my line of business.'

'Not in mine either, Jack, ask any architect. But just thought tonight would be an evening off.'

I hated my deferential slippage into his manner, my readiness to become each person that I met. The only motive my instincts ever allowed me was to get on, to get away; to give them all whatever they required and get on to the next thing. But, now, could there ever be a next thing?

'A whisky too, Jack. A double.'

'A double whisky! Well!'

He regarded me with a renewed wariness, considering that second drink, the shaking of the hand that held the beer glass, the soaking, matted hair and the pale, streaked cheeks. In my panic I had been in too much of a hurry to do anything about my crazed appearance, and Jack cared about appearances. With his grey quiff and horseshoe cufflinks, he was a man who lived to be 'dapper'.

'I see. I see. You don't look too well, Mr Architect Rix. Not been . . . ' he paused, ' . . . overdoing it, have we?'

He slid the whisky towards me, but held on to the glass as if vetting my suitability for hard liquor.

'I'm fine, Jack. No, I don't think I've been overdoing it. Don't worry about me.'

It was early evening and the pub was almost empty. There were a few young farmers drinking by the bar, hunched and inexplicably tense, also there was Jim, the watery-eyed old drunk who always sat in the same corner, beneath a clock formed from a mirror that had once advertised a cough cure. At intervals Jack would signal to Jim who would at once rise and shuffle slowly about the pub collecting glasses and grumbling.

The scene was neither pleasant nor friendly, but it was familiar enough, changeless, curative of the extreme ailments of the dark spaces outside. It was warm and I needed warmth. As the surface flush generated by my running faded, the cold returned, biting deep into my body. It was the cold of shock, an interstellar, unreachable cold, colder than anything the weather might provide, a superlunary chill that could neither be avoided nor shaken off. This was why I wanted drink. Alcohol heats the invisible interior tubes and cisterns and pricks the white skin with red warmth, denies the cold within for a while. But it is always there. Absolute zero: complete cold: the cessation of movement: journey's end.

My mind rushed and screamed to be away but, just, my nerve held and I outstared Jack, pulling the whisky away from the pressure of his fingers.

'Thanks, Landlord Jack.'

'My pleasure, Mr Architect Rix.'

I took both my glasses to one of the dark tables that stretched in a carpeted sea away from the pink flooring around the bar. I sat at the one nearest the old gas fire, its white, pierced columns like skyscrapers, the red of heat rising up them like the flames of hell. From my seat I looked cautiously around. Above the bar Jack's enormous new hi-def television shone, a wide, grinning mouth, colourful with exotic disorders. A blonde woman was talking breathlessly about the preparations for the New Year, the New Millennium. Huge silver spheres would float above our cities, great ships would be seen on our rivers, a space-shot would colour the upper atmosphere, the last thousand years would be recorded in twenty-four-hour pageants across the nation and, on a single, seven-day television programme, the next thousand years would be covered the following week. It was still almost a year away, but we spoke of little else these days. Once in a thousand years! We were special.

In a far corner was one of Jack's earlier innovations – a big VR booth, a black cubicle with helmet and gloves inside and a red and gold curved sign – 'Super Virtuality: Step into Another World'. People had once queued to play, now it was seldom used.

The young farmers were drinking beer from bottles with gold foil around the tops. They stood by the bar, flexing their legs and torsos. Four of them were dressed almost identically in jeans and shirts; I may have seen them before, but I was sure I had not seen the fifth. He was an outcast in the group, wearing tight black leather trousers with silver chains hung about the hips. More chains decorated the high-heeled metal-tipped shoes that curved upwards from sole to pointed toe. His shirt was black, baggy and decorated with a variety of silver devices – skulls and snarling mythical creatures – and he wore a leather jacket draped over his shoulders. His features were thin and embittered as if expressive of some great betrayal that had inspired this aggressive armour. He talked less than the others; instead he gazed around the bar. He caught my eye. I looked away but, to my embarrassment, felt him hold his gaze upon me. I opened a notebook that I kept in my coat pocket, hunched myself down in the chair and attempted to sketch.

The hi-def had moved on to news from the Mars mission. It was going well, on schedule to land in time to mark the Millennium. In the spacecraft men and women dressed in vests and shorts floated happily, turning somersaults and showing off their muscles to allay the fears of some dissident scientists that they would suffer and die horribly from the prolonged period of weightlessness required by the mission. Dale, the captain, stepped towards the camera and delivered a speech to the world. His face appeared to float as it filled the big screen.

' . . . the first human feet to step on the Red Planet, the world of ancient canals and our new dreams. We are proud to have been asked to make your history. From Mars Mission 2000, we say: peace, the dream continues.'

He concluded with a firm, floating smile while his crew stood waving in a wobbly zero-gravity semicircle behind him. In my notebook I sketched their waving hands, receding poignantly into a starry background.

The boy in leather was still staring at me and I grew conscious of my sketching. It was more eccentric, less acceptable in the Arches than merely sitting. My skin prickled with the fear that I was even more out of place here than I had realized. I grasped, my thumb underneath, the thick, dark wood of the table and saw a fine mist form on the polished surface around the outline of my fingers. Perhaps what I had seen in that field an hour ago was reflected in my appearance. I looked mad, dangerous and disgusting, inspiring thoughts of violence in honest folk.

I put away the notebook. A shudder at once ran through my body as those soaking walls slid again before my eyes with such dragging, granular horror that I actually yelped softly in an effort to banish the hallucination. I looked up, dizzy and sick with the moment of perfect recall.

I thought nobody had heard my cry, but then I noticed that the leather youth was watching me with a renewed curiosity. He held this look for a moment longer and then began walking towards me, carrying his glass.

'Join you, yeah?' he suggested.

His voice and accent were grotesquely amiable – the customarily cocky local mix of charm and sarcasm. I said nothing, afraid that if I opened my mouth I would at once vomit. I knew that he must now see how pale my face was, the sheen of cold sweat on my skin, the hand clutching the table, the faint halo on the varnish.

'Seen you round here quite a bit, yeah?'

He sat down and leaned back, the better to organize his thin legs around the unfamiliar geometry of the table. Jack, polishing a glass with a checkered cloth, had moved to the nearest end of the bar and was watching. He leaned over the food counter with its circular tray of squat, cylindrical stainless steel salt and pepper pots. Here was an event, something to replenish the wells of his malice. Above him on the hi-def an animation was showing the curved, looping route to Mars and back.

'I'm sure you have.' I spoke coolly, fighting the pressure of my nausea.

'Ralph.' He extended his hand across the table. It was tattooed along the outer base of the thumb with a writhing snake. I took it, it was warm.

'Stephen Rix.'

'Yeah. You've got that old farmhouse up on the Pasture.'

The tentativeness of his initial approach had clearly been a game. He knew me well enough.

'That's right.'

'Me and the lads,' he gestured at the drinking friends, 'we go shooting up there sometimes. Rabbits or crows. You're an architect. Seen your drawing board and your big CAD screen through the window.'

This came out flatly. The detail of the drawing board implied a threatened intrusion, but that of the computer showed interested knowledge. I was observed. I was known.

'Rabbits, eh? Yes, an architect. My firm's in town. But I do quite a bit of my work up here. Why, incidentally, do you shoot crows?'

'For the farmers. They hate 'em. Crows eat anything, you see. Peck out the eyes and tongues of new lambs.'

This casual detail of rural horror triggered yet again the vision of the soaking walls. Then there was a pause as if something significant was about to be said. Jim in his green suit and thick woollen waistcoat shuffled up to our table, breathing heavily. He stared at us for a moment apparently about to level a dreadful accusation, and then dropped his eyes to the table.

'These dead?' He nodded to indicate the empty glasses.

'Yes,' I said quickly, pushing them towards him, all too obviously encouraging him to leave at once.

'I'll bury 'em . . . ' he laughed wheezily, ' . . . they'll be bury-
ing me soon enough.'

At this he roared, then, focusing painfully, his tongue projecting between his wet lips with the effort of concentration,
he reached out arthritic hands and slid his nobbled fingers into
the empty glasses, bringing them together with a brittle clatter.
He turned and shuffled back towards the bar.

Ralph snapped convulsively out of his baffled gaze. 'Yeah,
hang on a minute.' He stood up and, hunching one shoulder,
slid his flattened hand into the tight pocket of his trousers. With
some effort he prised a few coins out and turned towards Jack.

'Two more pints,' he called as he walked towards the bar,
his eyes fixed on the hi-def.

Jack kept his eye on Ralph, took the glasses and edged along
the metal counter, feeling his way to the pump handles like a
blind man and, finally, pulling one to spurt a beige vortex.
Only at the last moment was he forced to look down as the
glass filled. Ralph carried the two glasses back, placing one in
front of me.

'An architect. Well I'm not a farmer like this lot.'

He did not appear to be about to say anything more. Yet
this was why he had approached me, to distance himself from
the others, not to be as easily understood, to show his life had
a different end. Perhaps I was an aspirational figure for him, a
cosmopolitan type with the keys to the big city. His face was
young. The skin, white, blemished and flaring red around his
throat, suggested vulnerability.

But still he said nothing more. He watched a small girl in
heavy black shoes singing about Mars on the television. He
watched her dancing among red craters with a number of
small fat men dressed in green.

Then I could no longer bear the silence. I needed to get on
to the next thing. I asked him what he did.

'An artist. Must be the only one for miles. Drawing and
painting. But the big thing is the sculpture.'

'What kind of stuff?'

He looked wounded.

'Conceptual, of course. But the sculpture's more mainstream
– carving stone and so on. Like it, but it's not important, is it?'

13

'That depends, I don't know. Do you make a living out of it?'

Jack, still at the end of the bar and evidently listening, snorted and moved away to murmur something to the farmers.

The little girl had started on another Mars song. Ralph absentmindedly sang along as if taken over by the habits of a normal night in the Arches. Then, suddenly, he switched his attention back to me.

'Hardly a living. Sold a bit of stuff last year after art school and the carving still sells round here – walkers passing through seem to like the easy stuff. Marshalls . . . ' he gestured across the street at the light blue shop selling jams, tea-towels and local cheeses, ' . . . they sell a few pieces. But the drawing and painting's no good for them. A city gallery's interested, but they have been for over a year. Interested!' He laughed to establish his healthy scepticism.

'You live here?'

'Yeah, a room above the garage. Anyway, don't want anything to do with those big city art people. Better here. Making quite a bit now by copying gargoyles of the Minster. They love that.'

The sudden coincidence of that detail startled me and jerked the damp walls and the great cloth back to my mind's eye. My muscles tensed and my head sprang up to stare at Ralph's face. Was this why he had come? Had he been sent? Ralph could be some kind of messenger, some inhabitant of this other world.

'Something wrong with that? Can copy gargoyles if I like.'

'No, no. Sorry. It wasn't that. Just a coincidence.'

'Oh.' He seemed to consider asking for an explanation. 'What sort of thing do you do then?'

As he said this he reached into the inside pocket of his jacket and brought out a small, hardbacked, wine-red book. He flicked through its pages, revealing a number of drawings of faces, until he came to a clean sheet. He took out a pencil, crossed his legs, rested the book on his thigh and began to study my face.

'Nothing in particular. Everything really – offices, flats. We're in business, big business, we've got a staff of more than a hundred architects to support. Rix–Cummings, you might

14

have heard of us. But I think we're still a bit too radical for most people. We frighten them. I'm just working on this block of flats at the moment. I have to finish it by next week. That's why I came up here this time – for some peace and quiet to get it out of the way. There's a lot of money involved.'

'Yeah, but is it any good?'

'Sorry?'

'The flats.'

'I . . . well . . . '

I was overcome for a moment by a juvenile pang of aesthetic conscience. I looked hard at Ralph. He had been sent. He was telling me to change my life. He was the voice of what I had just seen.

'Are you going to draw me?'

'Yeah. Don't mind, do you? Do it a lot. Kind of a diary.'

He flicked through the pages to show me. His style was spare. There was no shading, just a thick, wavering line and some curious blobs to suggest contour. Each drawing was dated and timed. The faces were all contorted in violent expressions of laughter, pain or nausea. I laughed at them.

'Prats, aren't they? Work, drink, throw up. For what? Just puking. Turn 'em into gargoyles, hanging in the air, fixed to nothing. Oh, sod this.'

This moment of disgusted revelation made him suddenly grow impatient and his eyes flicked around the room to find some release. He settled on the farmers and jeered and gestured at them. They grinned and sneered back at him. Even his anguish was a message.

I bought some more drinks – more beer for him, more whisky for me. He drew. We were silent.

With time and alcohol this arrangement was replaced by indulgent, mutual concern. Our talk became warm and animated. He lived in this place, he explained, because it was where he was born and, for the moment, he could see no reason to move. He repeated his attack on big city art. He spoke familiarly in the critical jargon of the schools while casually flicking with his pencil at the surface of the paper. He had been sent, I knew.

'The thing that draws everything together . . . ' he waved his tattooed hand, ' . . . everything is touching everything else.'

15

'Why the gear?'

'What?'

'The leather, the chains – all that. Why?'

'Always worn leather. Used to have a bike. Can't afford it any more and can't afford new clothes. Leather goes on for ever. But get the right stuff to start with and it lasts. Warm too, you need that here.'

'Yes, you do. You need to keep warm. Nothing worse than being cold.'

'Nothing? Maybe. And anyway, warm or not, you don't end up looking like those puddings over there!'

He shouted the last four words over his shoulder at the farmers. One responded: 'Or that poof over there!'

But the violence had gone from Ralph. His ornaments and clothes now hung from him as no more than signs to be discussed or as value for money or interesting memorabilia. This inspired in me a new affection, a sentimental sense of a common humanity. He had been sent to show me all of this as well. And he had this longing to be away, here in body but distant in mind, at some point far away from the banal, sacred rural rhythms to which his farmer friends were enslaved. The end offered by their lives was the satisfaction of having maintained a cycle of normality. He required the extraordinary because he felt the pressure of that awful knowledge that he, in the end, would only be Ralph once. He had something to tell me. Give him time.

These plangent, moistly emotional thoughts signalled drunkenness. Events were taking on an alcoholic acceleration. The Arches was filling up with more farmers and a few girlfriends. One girl, wearing one of the silver imitation spacesuits that had been in vogue since the Mars mission had blasted off, was swerving desperately about in helmet and gloves inside the VR. She giggled and screamed, punching at the monsters only she could see. Finally she crashed heavily to the ground, sending an earring skidding along the black plastic of the booth. The farmers laughed and then switched to lascivious encouragement as the girl struggled to rise.

I too was drunk. There had been more pints and whisky. Any rapid movement of the eye produced a dragging effect as the images of Jack, bar, new people and strange golden

16

lights rushed to keep their places. On the television a blind-folded man was being asked to find the bare-breasted girls concealed in a room of misleading plastic and rubber shapes. The compère called on the audience to help him out by crying, 'Warm, warmer, hot!' or 'Cold, colder, freezing!' The man shuffled helplessly, his arms outstretched, his hands cupped, his mouth hanging sadly open.

'God!' Ralph suddenly exclaimed, gulping slightly from his last swallow of beer. 'How do we do it? It's a wonder we don't see more people sobbing in the street. It's so difficult. What are we supposed to do?'

'Sculpt?'

'Or build. Oh, yeah, sure. But we wouldn't be doing this if it all worked properly. Would you build? No. I wouldn't sculpt. Why doesn't it work?'

He seemed close to hard, bitter, drunken tears and I had begun to feel the wet pressure of the drink behind my own eyes.

'Don't know. Why not move to town?'

'Get a feeling of choking there. Suffocation. At least there's air up here, not like town. But those bastards are pretty suffocating.'

'But you're talking of an attitude, not the reality. Look at it differently, it's all in here . . . ' I leaned forward and tapped his head.

He fell silent. I stared at the worn carpet, a swirling pattern of dark reds matted with shiny black patches. The drink enfolded my head – a mounting haze, a metallic sensation rising like a column in the centre of my skull.

As we held our silence the tumult outside drove me to nurse my inner terrors with a new affection. What I had seen was, at least, my own, something bigger and better than the movement of the seasons or even Ralph's conceptual art. Drink had transformed it into a possession of ultimate per-sonal value, beyond the calculation of actuaries, beyond hi-def television, the seasonal virtues of the farmers, the VR and Jack. The farmers had now finally relented, picked up the girl and unfastened her helmet and gloves. Her face had gone pale and she seemed about to vomit.

17

I remembered being told of the caves beneath these hills – this landscape, it was said, was bigger below ground than above. I laughed at the thought that perhaps, for me, this underworld had simply leapt into sight before returning to where it belonged. It was only an accident, an embarrassing failure in the organization of things.

But no. Ralph had been sent to tell me something. Then I felt the crushing inevitability of being forced by the drink to tell Ralph first. This frightened me. But also I felt relief that disclosure was now out of my hands and in those of my drunkenness. I wanted to impress him, to signal that I was ready, up there in the peaks, clutching my brow, correctly anguished. And then, when I had told him, he would tell me.

TWO

So I TOLD him, beginning with this trouble I have with the matter of consciousness. I have always been subject to fainting fits. Every few months I simply pass out and there is a brief flurry of concern about my health. There are no typical circumstances that might indicate a pattern, though restaurants are often involved. Once, over lunch, I paused in the middle of a conversational point and flopped into the stew, my eyes and mouth gaping. I lay there, it was said, for some twenty seconds before rising, monstrous and drooling, from the gravy swamp and continuing my monologue as if nothing had happened. Of course, for me, nothing had until I became aware of the frozen shock on the faces opposite, the uproar of the waiters, the irritated glances from neighbouring tables and the brown juices running down my shirtfront. At another restaurant I had to be retrieved from the basement toilet where I had crumpled gracefully to the marble floor like, said the man who led me back to my table, a dropped silk scarf. Otherwise I have blacked out in corridors, at desks, in meetings or, most dangerously, on staircases. Once I discovered by careful self-examination that I had fainted while reading in bed. Jill, my wife, was sceptical, pointing out that, given the venue, I was most likely to have fallen asleep.

Science has proved inadequate to the case. When I have passed out in the company of anybody unfamiliar with my history they have invariably feared the worst and rushed me to hospital. On a dozen occasions I have been through the same ritual of examination, each time to be told that I was, within the tightly drawn parameters of medical wisdom, well. Patiently I explain to doctors, anxious lunch companions or saintly, concerned strangers that brief passages of oblivion are, for me, natural. To promote them from an inconvenience to a problem is unnecessary. That is the way I am made. My consciousness is not robust, it teeters always on the edge of extinction. Stephen Rix is a fact that flickers and fizzes like a faulty light fitting.

Only this time it had not been like that, it had not been like that at all. This time I had not slipped briefly out of the world to return chatting and smiling, unchanged and unimpaired. This time I had stepped through a door and could not step back. The light still flickered, but now to cast its light on a world that only looked the same. In reality it could no longer be relied upon for its old soothing qualities of mute lumpishness, predictability and boredom. I could never again be sure, as I had always been so sure, that nothing would ever really happen.

It was late afternoon when it began. The darkness was closing in. I had been working all day. The Sempri lamp above my drawing board and the CAD computer screen projected a bright cone that enclosed my hunched figure. Outside this cone the darkness of the house was shaped by the tiny red and green lights that glowed on the machines – fax, answering machine, hi-fi, television, computer, all little doors through which the chattering plenitude of the world entered without troubling the empty valleys outside. A cable from the big computer processor was attached to the helmet and gloves of the VR set that I kept up here for distraction. A light glowed there too; I had deliberately forgotten to turn it off. The truth was that I loved these lights obediently ready, yet pursing a logic that had no need of me. They provided the same comfort I obtained from driving over those big, white arrows painted on the road. This is what it was to be a machine.

20

All day my concentration had held. Then came the usual moment of slippage; some passing difficulty wearied me beyond the effort of solution. I leaned back and the work at once vanished from my mind. In the ensuing pause I dreamt for a moment, amidst all these consoles, panels and displays, of being some space traveller, alone and impossibly distant with only these for companions. The galaxies swam lazily by my portholes and I slid backwards into a stiff, horizontal stretch, my hands driven hard into my pockets.

My back, my 'bad' back, emitted a sharp pain to bring me home. This is my other big problem. This bad back aches and occasionally sends pain darting up my spine and down my legs. So, there we are, there is the fainting and there is the back. All the time my body is telling me: listen, I am here, rubbing, straining, wearing, sometimes even blankly refusing to nourish your brain. In one awkward motion my body and I are slipping away from the world; locked together we are dying.

The pain subsided and I looked back at the work on my drawing board. It was a balcony cleverly, vulgarly designed to add market value to a big, expensive block of flats. By my drawing Rizzoli's *Spirit of the Moderne* lay open at an elaborate detail from some nineteen-twenties extravagance. I had stopped just short of plagiarism, borrowing primarily a certain trick of the steelwork which made it look, for a moment, unsupported and then, by a cunning double curve, revealed its logic. It was nasty but pretty enough to charm the buyers and smart enough to convince the arty end of the trade that I was still 'serious'. Sleep crowded in and, in an almost-dream, Jill and Francesca dressed in long white gowns stepped out on to the balcony and entwined themselves in the steel.

Irritated with myself, I shook off the moment of sleep. I would go for a walk. It was pouring with rain but still just light enough. I let the sandals drop from my feet and slid from the high stool. In the hallway I dug my calves into cold rubber boots, clad and hooded myself for the weather and stepped outside. As I did so I heard the phone ring twice and then the intercepting click of the answering machine.

Outside I disturbed two rabbits that raced away from a low mound by my fence. I stepped carefully over the slippery, mossy stones beyond the door and strolled around the house into the tall, swaying grass behind. The land was rough and sodden, clutching and then releasing my boots. I felt puny and expendable, trapped between the fury of the air and the soaking weight of the earth. I climbed the shattered gate, secured pitifully by orange nylon rope, and crossed the first meadow, a dome of grass and reeds surmounted by a small barn. Over the wire fence I turned sharp left to bring myself on to a direct line to the valley bottom. I walked steadily for a few moments and then paused.

I was standing on a narrow path running along the edge of the meadow that undulates across the floor of the valley. My back was to the meadow and I was staring down at the deep ditch that separated the path from the dry stone wall. Grass had grown thickly on the banks of the ditch, so the racing water was only partly visible as a deep brown gleam. That day it was almost inaudible as well behind that deafening, deadening noise of the rain on the grass, mud and myself. The sight of the water – rushing, almost underground – shocked me into stillness. I stared for a while and then timidly dipped the toe of my boot into the water and waited for the cold to penetrate. I reached downward and the water pressed against the sides of my boot forming rubber concavities that closed about my calf and sucked at my weight. Then I felt the deep cold of the stream that spread at once like a wave through my body. But I could find no footing and I had to draw back.

The cold persisted and my body had now grown heavy with some foreboding, some threat that I could no longer deny. This fear seemed to be involved with that dark noise. Water, rushing below and falling from above was sucking me in, blurring me into the landscape. I saw myself as if from the top of the furthest ridge that was silhouetted against the grey sky. I was a dark stump dissolving beneath this immense pressure, the outline softening, growing indistinct and finally becoming no more than a spot on the retina induced by the strain of peering through that darkening, streaming air.

And then whatever I am stopped.

I could not think. I could not act. I could neither move myself nor cause movement in the world. All that I then knew

22

was what I saw or heard or felt or smelt or tasted. Inside the transparent shell of my senses was nothing and no reason for anything. I felt neither well nor ill, happy nor sad, neither anxious nor at peace. Nothing would happen, nothing had happened, nothing need happen. I had stopped and for that moment I could not know I knew.

It was like falling asleep except that, afterwards, the only dream I could remember was of the world as it was. Perhaps all that stopped was my consciousness. I merely stopped watching myself and, for that interval, I became my senses, a single, thin, animal awareness.

There was the feeling of the hood over the head, the clothes against the skin. There was the sound of the hiss and clatter of the rain, the high roar and whine of the wind, the smell of the wet earth and the taste of the water that streaked down the face and crept over the rim of the lips. There was the sight of the fading light of an early evening in winter at that moment when the sky seems to draw brightness from the land. Above was hard, grey, undifferentiated, unchanging illumination, below a rapidly blackening landscape, inhabited by shapes grown mobile, viscous, rounded and unclear beneath the weight of the gathering dark, the dissolving pressure of the rain and the bitter erosions of the wind.

I had become part of that melting land. I was a husk, an animal body or a dead tree that was being slowly reabsorbed by the earth, its living function ended and only the mute fabric – a few fibres, bones or a stubborn, hollowed trunk, spongy with rot – vainly resisting for a little while longer. This was the land: crushed, impacted layers of unrecorded, unrecoverable, unconscious history. And then this was me: a shell of sensations without reason or past, an awareness without meaning, a being that could blink out of existence between one heartbeat and the next and leave nothing changed, nothing to recall, no magnetic trace of memory.

Soon I was to think of this pause as a preparation; everything stopped so that this next thing could start. But later I would doubt this. I would begin to think it was my moment of choice; I had decided to sink into my desires. Or, again, this was the onset of my illness. I broke down, cracked, succumbed to

23

the stress or to some virus. Finally I was to decide that such explanations did not matter. What happened next, happened. Why make a liar of experience? Even of my experience?

Then the moment – or was it hours? – passed. Thought returned like an awakening. I turned away, screwed my eyes tight shut and pressed my right hand into the back of my neck, as if by muscular strain I could recover the sense of the conscious day. Warm, then cold waves washed through my skull. I pressed my head back, taking mild pleasure from the pain this caused and hoping it would restore my purpose, get me back to work. Slowly, luxuriously, I allowed the tension to release itself, brought my head forward and opened my eyes.

All seemed, for that instant, to be unchanged: the ridge of the valley, outlined at its western end against the paler sky that marked the hidden sunset, the shallow sweep of fields and their walls and barns rising gracefully from the valley floor and the meadow, green but bristling with reed clumps and marshy with neglect. I began to relax, grateful that nothing real had happened, only some odd, physiological interlude, an effect of age maybe, just another chemical contingency.

Then I took a pace forward and was at once brutally deprived of the comfort of this illusion. For, this time, something had happened. Out there, beyond the far wall of the meadow, something *had* changed. At first I only felt this. I sensed an ominous discontinuity so frightful that a racing of my pulse at once signalled the onset of panic. It was like the feathery touch of death in a dream or waking with the sudden certainty that there was a stranger in the room. I began to reason that the stopping episode must have been serious, a failure or malfunction in my brain. What had changed was in me.

But then I saw that it was not. I saw that the world had changed. A black mass rose from the next field; impossibly huge, it concealed the valley's slopes and the ridge behind and rose into the grey sky to culminate in a series of incomprehensible blocks and spikes, a silhouetted clutter of which I could make no sense. As if in some dim memory of a device usually employed in children's stories, I rubbed my eyes to ensure that this was no defect of vision. But, opening them again, the intrusion remained, as, by now, I knew it would.

I stared and waited in fear as the logic of these shapes began to become undeniable. I did not see them any better, but my mind started to accept what it could no longer reject. Finally I recognized what I saw with perfect certainty. To my left two western towers terminating in clusters of pinnacles and castellations and surmounted by spires; a central tower and another spire rising to three, maybe four hundred feet; the long ridge of the nave roof; a south transept with rose window, lancets and, just distinguishable, great showers of saints over a south entrance; the choir and apse ending in a hunched clutter of flying buttresses. A cathedral had sprung into being while I had been staring into my ditch.

With my mind's formation of the word 'cathedral', there was a terrible hiatus. I did not breathe. I felt surrounded by a silence and a new, still coldness. I waited. Then the shock of the spectacle turned back on me and seemed to rush across the meadow, winding me and forcing a sudden intake of breath. I was left sick and empty, choked by the conflicting fears that I was mad beyond recovery or dead or damned. The sensation of the proximity of this vast, dark, enclosed, impossible space brought me close to fainting and I felt blindly about for something to hold myself upright. But there was nothing and I sank to my knees, my eyes, forced to record, still taking in more details of this monstrous church.

In this position I found myself possessed of a curious, intense rationality. Still the panic rose but, even as it did, I observed one part of my brain engaged in an astonishingly cool attempt to give this building a place, a date, a critical assessment. Kneeling in that soaking meadow, I catalogued what details I could make out, compared and contrasted its forms with others that I knew, analysed its composition, its structural logic, considered its proportions. And so it went on. As the critique lengthened in my mind, the sickness receded. I rose, the coldness of the wet grass had now oozed through to meet the coldness of my blood, and I began taking a few steps towards the church.

It was limestone, probably a pale fawn colour when dry, but today darkened by the rain. Today! Had there been any other day for this building? Certainly it appeared old, but cathedrals do and I had walked this field yesterday – it had not been there then. Logically, therefore, it must be younger than a day. I stopped walking and began wondering if I was witnessing some stupendous reversal of physical law: the cathedral had transported itself here, slipped through the eye of a dimensional needle and would, soon enough, slip back. For now, some distant city had only a gaping vacancy where its pious climax should have been. But the building was in darkness and looked closed-up, so at least it had been night wherever it had come from and its temporary absence might not immediately be noticed.

Fear returned, accompanied by a hard gust that turned the streaming air into a shot-filled vacuum. My exposed skin was flayed by the flung drops. With this came the conviction, the certainty, the faith that this was for me alone: thousands of tons of stone, glass, lead, iron, wood plunged into being here and now for me to see . . . and then whatever was inside . . .

At the thought of an interior I shuddered so violently that I felt as if my bones had clashed and scraped. Opening doors into dark, huge enclosed spaces had always filled me with sick apprehension. It was a sensation both alluring and repellent. The pure terror was always concentrated in that first moment when the usual heavy door – most horribly a double door, the inner covered in green baize – swings to admit me to all that emptiness, that knowledge. Then the uninterrupted nave hurtling away from the fragile figure at the entrance . . .

How much more horrible, then, was this to be? Unconsciously, I had resumed walking towards a point midway between the west towers and the south transept and more detail was emerging from the darkness. The length of the nave was punctuated by deep buttresses that rose to gently stepped piers capped with elaborately crocketed pinnacles. From these leapt double flyers, the lower, I guessed, meeting the springing of the vault and the upper the topmost point of the lateral web. The aisle windows were double and topped by cusped *oculi*, those of the clerestory doubled this pattern again and added a third, enlarged *oculus*. Most were dark, due either to the conditions or to the depth of colour of the stained glass. But, with a few further steps, one of the clerestory windows became transparent. Through it I saw the northern wall of the nave, a fragment of darkening sky crossed by tracery and, I thought, the shadowed curvature of the vault.

The impression of the nave wall was of a grand, demonstrative simplicity. This might have been a text-book diagram of some exemplar of Gothic cathedrals. The visible side of the south-west tower was, in contrast, intensively decorated, flamelike ogival tracery curved upwards amidst a frenzy of spidery carvings. The discontinuity suggested something more specific than merely a generalized, ideal vision of the great Gothic church. The contrasting styles indicated a history, an existence independent of mine. This was a particular church built for a particular place at a particular time.

But, as ever with Gothic, all of its warm particularity was consumed by the mad refinement of the style and its impossible demands – no walls, only supports; no stable matter, only energy; no volumes, only lines; no fact, only symbol; no things, only ideas. All clear and yet all concealed. These buttresses hid the true structure from the interior and yet that interior was composed as an expression of structure – perhaps of a lighter, finer, more heavenly structure than man could build. Such churches were built by people to whom the world did not mean something, rather it was what it meant. The real was an idea. Heaven was not symbolized by this building, it was modelled. And, in its niches and convolutions, were little homes where all of us incomplete, twisted ones could find rest.

To my right the transept was now enclosing me in its sharp, dark angles. I stepped back a few paces to try and see through the gloom. The main door inside its tremendous saint-strewn portal looked quite obviously closed – massively hinged, a great metal plate with a daunting keyhole and, across the whole thing, a heavy, rusted iron bar was crudely but decisively padlocked. On the side of the transept now facing me was a smaller entrance. A double arch divided by an exquisite, slender pier opened on to blackness. Clearly this was some form of porch. I walked towards it, a sickness amounting to pain in my stomach. The position of the porch meant that I was obliged to walk directly into that terrible angle between transept and nave where all the tons of masonry and the bounding, soaring equilibrium of the building seemed to be focused.

The stone of the arches was polished up to shoulder level, apparently by the passage of thousands of bodies, another sign that this was a real, used church. Yet the opening was wide so the sheen suggested a crush of people, jostling and forcing their way into the cathedral. The church was not just for me. But it was *here* for me.

I passed into the porchway. Inside stone benches ran round the small, square area and delicate columns rose to heavy and elaborate fan-vaulting. The stones of the floor were damp and a small pool had collected in one corner. Ripples from the draught that was all the porch admitted of the gale outside ran across the dimly reflecting surface. There were none of the usual printed signs about this being a place of worship, the typed notices giving times of services, the guides, postcards or warnings. Before me was a high double door, again locked. But this time the left-hand door contained a smaller entry which stood ajar by perhaps an inch. The doors were aged, silvery oak, deeply moulded and, as I laid my palm against the smaller one, the wood felt cold, ridged and hard, almost metallic.

My breaths came quicker and shallower. I closed my eyes and let my head fall forward for a moment, feeling the prickly damp cold that is the usual prelude to fainting. The fear of unconsciousness urged me onwards, I might wake afterwards with no more than the suspicion that this had been a dream. Fearing such a loss even more than that interior, I leaned with my full weight and pushed the door open. Stepping over the wooden sill, its surface protected by another iron bar, I closed my eyes again and entered the church. Inside I felt the air, still deeply cold but now calmer, of an interior. It felt as heavy as water and eddied gently as if I were in some vast tank inhabited by grave, slow sea monsters. In my private darkness I pictured currents swirling about the piers, shafts and arcades and forming strange vortices in the aisles. There were always these movements in such spaces, nothing seemed to cause them, yet they were there. Nothing was ever quite without movement.

My eyes still closed, I felt this drifting air connect me to the whole great volume of atmosphere within as it hung in the nave and aisles, filling the interior up to the terrible vaulting, through the crossing and up to the altar. At first I felt sure there was no sound, but then, horribly, I heard a distant noise, far away to my right from close to where the altar must have been. It was impossible to decipher – a cracking and booming alternated, the two blending and separating.

At last I opened my eyes to see the stone floor at my feet and then I raised my head slowly to take in the transept. I did not dare look to my right, in the direction of the noise. The expected piers launched their clustered shafts up through the clerestory to fan out into flawless sexpartite vaulting. The work was austere, scarcely decorated, and precise. Above me a huge rose window glowed darkly, barely illuminated by the darkening sky. Beneath the rose there was a sudden outburst of carved exuberance – double-blind arcading swirling upward in three-dimensional ogives and then rising into five slender lancets. Within the arcading were slate and marble tablets, haphazardly placed, some containing reliefs of the dead men they celebrated, others abstract compositions of obelisks, pediments and columns with sheaves of arrows, broken staves or lowered banners. There seemed to be no words, only a general celebration of mortality. I smelt the rank, still, frozen scent of the long dead.

I turned and saw the opposing north transept – another rose window but in a contrasting design and, this time, no lancets. The crossing was empty between the four piers that supported the central tower. To the right was a wooden screen from which rose an organ surmounted by clusters of pinnacles, angels and pipes. The screen itself looked black, but odd varnished points glowed, catching what remained of the evening light and indicating the intensity of the carving. I walked towards the crossing, keeping my eyes firmly fixed on the centre of the far rose window. Then, as I passed the two nearest piers, I looked downward. To mark the centre was a circular labyrinth, the sign of the master, carved in black and white stone.

I looked up to see the uncountable ribs of the crossing springing smoothly from their piers to a single huge central boss. From there hung a heavy brass chain whose length induced in me a strange, reverse vertigo. At the end of the chain was an enormous censer which swayed slightly in sympathy with the ambient motion of the air. The movement of this heavy brass

29

container with its smoke-blackened voids and filigree so close to my head sickened me. The vertigo washed through me and I stumbled. Fearful of collapsing, I walked towards the screen and sat upon one of the two steps that led upward towards the arch. When my balance returned after a few seconds, I rose and turned to go through the iron gates. These protected the entry into the choir and were now swung back to line the wooden passage with their bars.

Through the arch was the empty choir. Again I studied the walls. In the nearest bays exotically formed strainer arches leapt the gaps, indicating more ambitious spacing by the master mason. Here the detailing was luxuriant, constantly breaking and restoring the lines of the structure with leaves, fruit, trees and twisted, dwarfish faces. I looked up and followed with my eye the ridge rib of the high vault down towards the eastern end. My gaze was interrupted by a sudden darkness. At first I thought this was a trick of the light, but the interruption was too abrupt. I then wondered if the entire impossible building was now unravelling itself, leaving this blackness behind. But finally I realized that this darkness was the explanation of the strange noise I had heard. For a huge black sheet hung from the vaulting, across the entire width of the choir and down to the flat, gleaming stone floor. Some wind seemed to be causing this great cloth to belly out and its lowest corners to leap and crack. But there was no noise of wind, only this cracking and booming and a distinct hissing as the edge of the cloth swept across the stones of the floor.

The size of the cloth and the possibility of what lay beyond caused my agoraphobic sickness to return. I stood still for some time, unable to run in terror and yet paralysed by the impossibility of approaching that blackness. At last an acceptance of the fact that I was taking part in a ritual which I was obliged to complete forced me onward. I approached the cloth. In my mind it seemed to billow, hiss and crack in mounting, defensive anger as I drew nearer.

I made for the right-hand side, hoping to catch the edge and simply turn it back to look behind. But, as I came within touching distance, my eye was caught by a great wave starting in the top left-hand corner of the cloth and curling slowly downward towards me. I stepped back but it was too late. The upward movement of that wave caught me in the face, the cloth rushed over my nose, mouth and forehead, burning me as it did so and filling my throat and nostrils with choking dust and the acrid scent of age. The pressure increased, now on my chest as well as my face and I was deafened by a roaring as the cloth wrapped its corner around my back. I twisted violently but the movement coiled me in yet more cloth. I strained to look upward and found myself in an immensely tall, black cone, a huge wizard's hat, whose point seemed to be as high as the vaulting itself. This cone swirled wildly about its base and then toppled. I fell slowly, the cloth pushing me forward on to the cold stones of the choir.

There was a rushing noise, a tide of voices crying their recognitions and lamentations, some calling my name, some warning me, some wailing over my loss. And then I awoke with the rain from above and the sodden grass beneath soaking into my clothes. I rolled over to feel the spots sting my face with their cold. A sharp pain stabbed at my back. I breathed with deliberate steadiness and waited. But there was nothing to wait for. I sat up and looked about me. The cathedral had gone.

THREE

'A CATHEDRAL?'

'A cathedral.'

'Wow. Never heard of that one before. What are you going to do about it?'

'Do?'

'Yeah, do. You can't just pass up on this one.'

I stared at Ralph. 'You mean get treatment – psychoanalysis, tranquillizers, hypnotherapy, that stuff?'

'No, man. This is something you've got to use.'

He had been sent. I could never, unaided, have arrived at the idea of using this church.

'How on earth can I use it?'

He looked thoughtful and then suddenly drained his glass. 'Come and see the studio. Might give you some ideas.'

'OK.'

I finished my drink and rose. Jack, absently polishing a glass as if instructed to look busy by some invisible director, watched me stumble against the side of the table and set up a musical tinkling of glasses.

'Good night, gentlemen,' he sneered.

'Good night, Jack,' I called back, spitting out his name like snake venom sucked from a wound. 'A very good night, Landlord Jack. You have a really good one, Jack, you hear me?'

'Thanks, Mr Architect Rix, I will.'

We left unsteadily. I felt the eyes of the pub upon our backs as a patch of intense heat between the shoulders. Had I become a middle-aged queer picking up the local pretty boy? Outside I looked up to see the sky had cleared. The stars shuddered as if vibrating with the pressure of the hard wind that coursed through the valley. I felt an immense elation. Ralph was going to explain everything. In the meantime I would explain everything to him.

I clutched Ralph by the arm and attempted to fix his eye with a fierce stare.

'We are all', I spoke with a weird urgency that even I noticed was weird, 'dualists. Have you ever wondered why everything manifests itself or can be explained in twos? Good–bad, hot–cold, of course, but also mind–body, beauty–morals, awake–asleep and so on. Every problem is the failure to resolve into one, to live with opposites. Look up – look down, swing left – swing right . . . What do we want? We don't know. With three choices or more we can always eliminate the terms until we get down to two, then we stick. We choose one. Remember, say the therapists, you can't make a *wrong* decision, choose one and make it right. Crap. The truth is we can't make a *right* decision. Choose one and regret the loss of the other for the rest of your life . . . '

This was not, of course, explaining anything. I was raving stupidly, but it did not matter. Ralph was not listening and neither, in a sense, was I. The automatic rhapsody of my drunkenness had begun. All I wanted to do was convince Ralph of the glorious landscape of the Rix mind.

'Yes, yes, a cathedral with this bloody enormous black cloth concealing the altar. Vast. At least I assume there was an altar. I never saw it . . . the cloth . . . '

Ralph's hands were jammed in his trouser pockets, his shoulders hunched about his neck. He walked with an odd delicacy on his curved, pointed soles as if avoiding the cracks in the paving stones. The pavement narrowed here and the wall of the churchyard rose. I released his arm and dropped back. For a moment he vanished in shadow to appear seconds later in the pale orange glow of the streetlight. I reached the same spot and missed my footing. My feet sheared to my left. The nearness of the wall saved me from falling as I put out my right hand flat against the cold stones.

'Shit!'

Ralph walked on unnoticing. My wrist felt sprained, a sensation that at once blurred in my mind with a sudden glimpse of Orion over the White Hart.

I glanced into the shop window we were passing. An ancient, chipped dummy was modelling a woollen hat, a thick, ribbed pullover, thornproof plus fours, socks and walking boots. The painted eyes were glazed as in death, the pale brown lips were flecked with white where paint had fallen off and the two arms gestured hopelessly, their palms facing outward. At the feet were aluminium pots and pans that fitted ingeniously into each other, compasses, piles of more woollens and guidebooks to the region.

Ralph looked back to see what had happened to me. I gestured to indicate that I was following. He led me across the battered tarmac of the petrol station. The shabby little office was in darkness. Ralph took me round the side where there was an open flight of stone steps that I had never noticed before. At the top was an old, partly rotten, black door. Ralph opened this. Inside we stood for a moment in total darkness amid strange smells – adhesives, plastics, a certain sharp, metallic scent. Ralph was groping for something that turned out to be an immensely long string which operated the switch for the three naked bulbs that ran the length of the room and had now burst painfully into life.

He wandered in, leaving the string swinging from the switch it controlled at the apex of the steeply pitched roof. The room ran the length and breadth of the building. Three arched windows looked to the rear and one to the front. On the walls were posters of motorbikes, all ripped through the middle and stuck alongside similarly ripped tourist office pictures of hills, streams and farms. Objects, sculptures littered the floor, but I failed for the moment to take them in. I sat, a theatrical palm once more to my forehead, on a rumpled bed pushed against the wall.

Ralph was wandering about the sculptures which, I now saw, consisted of rocks strangely attached to fragments of machinery – washing machines, televisions or nameless industrial tools. The machinery was coloured to tone in exactly with the rock and the points of junction between the two were carefully modelled to defy a precise distinction. The pieces were possessed of an ugly energy as if they had been found below ground and now resented their exposure in the thin air.

Ralph had stopped wandering and was now staring out of the window into, from my perspective, complete blackness. He massaged the back of his neck and twisted it occasionally as if freeing some mechanism. I heard a soft moan, though whether from Ralph or from within the roaring voices in my mind I could not tell. Conceivably I had moaned.

After some minutes it became clear that I was here only to be in the presence of his work. There were to be no further drinks or talk. Perhaps these works would explain how I was to use my cathedral. I felt relieved. Clearly I would not have to provide a commentary and yet, equally clearly, there was the unspoken assumption that I would be impressed. I was, but in no condition to explain the fact.

Time passed. A twinge in my wrist, sprained on the churchyard wall, caused me, at last, to make a movement. I shook my hand, causing a dart of pain up to my elbow. There was another moan and this time the bed upon which I was sitting creaked and moved slightly. I jumped to my feet. Beneath the tangled pile of blankets and sheets a thin, dark-haired girl was sleeping. A dream was now provoking her into rapid flicks of a hand across her face and angry mutterings. Ralph had turned round at my movement.

'That's Sally.'

'Oh.'

'She lives here with me. Met her at college. She hardly ever goes out. Even in the village they scarcely know she exists.'

Sally twisted angrily in bed, tying the blankets into hard bonds about her body. Now on her back, she suddenly began to punch rapidly at the air with her fists and to emit a long, continuous whine of anger.

'She's always doing that. Don't know why. She can never remember any of her dreams. She sleeps so much. It's like she's never really awake.'

Her face had the unfinished look of a baby's – blurred about the nose and mouth – and her neck, rising out of a white T-shirt, was smooth and slender. The eyebrows were thick and her lashes long. Her hair was heavy and so smooth that it remained untangled by all her movements. For no reason that I can recall and certainly none that made sense I bent across the bed and kissed both her closed eyes. They opened. Large, almost black pupils stared back at me for a moment in shock, then closed again and she rolled away with a murmur of irritation. I rose and turned to find Ralph looking at me with a steady smile.

'Like Sally do you?'

'I don't know. She's just . . . '

'Yeah, she's just . . . never could finish that sentence myself. Let's see your place,' he said, turning and plucking at the light cord. The click announced darkness interrupted only by the curling, dancing, bulbous shapes left in my eyes by the raw glare. I looked briefly back at Sally, but I could only make out an indecipherable pile of bedclothes.

We walked up the steep lane towards my house.

'I liked the work . . . a lot.'

'Thanks. It's hard. To do anything like that. You have to start thinking about everything. But you don't know everything so what you do seems smaller, never enough.'

'Yes, yes. But what is everything?'

'Well, everything. If everything is touching everything else . . . '

'Then you can't touch anything without touching everything.'

'Yes.'

'And you can't know anything without knowing everything.'

Pointlessly ambitious, drunken rhapsodies. He began singing to himself, the words sounded like: 'This is the beginning of a new age.' We struggled up the lane. A crescent moon had appeared to supplement the orange glow from the village that was fading the further we walked. Finally, we made it and I let him into the house, noting the number one glowing on the answering machine but failing to take the action silently

36

demanded. We debated for a while about drinks and then settled on cans of beer. Ralph flicked through the drawings of the flats on my board and glanced quickly at the books, briefly turning the pages of Rizzoli.

'So this cathedral . . . '

'Yes,' I said eagerly. 'It appeared in a field over there. I walked into it, looked about, walked towards where the altar should have been, was wrapped in this bloody big black cloth that seemed to have a life of its own, almost suffocated, and then came to lying in the field soaking wet. I have to say this kind of thing does not normally happen to me. I just thought I ought to say that.'

'No. What do you think it means?'

I shrugged. 'I should tell myself it was a dream, but I know it wasn't. Maybe I'm going mad, but I don't think I am. What I actually feel is that I saw – was shown perhaps – something impossible that was intended to direct me away from the merely possible. A sign. I saw something that said things were not even remotely as they seem. Something you can't speak about. Something that stops you just moving on to the next thing.'

'But we do speak about things like that.'

'Oh yes, we do. Pointlessly, fruitlessly, issuelessly. Until suddenly this thing appears and then vanishes. You see, it wasn't something *like that*, it was the thing itself.'

'You've got to speak about it.'

'Have I? To say what? Describe it? Draw it?'

'Yeah, yeah, that's it. Draw it. Get it down on paper.'

'There's a thought.'

I took my small notebook from a table and began to sketch. It came easily, detailed and convincing. I cackled happily. This was how to use it.

'I can do it! I can bloody do it! Hoo, hoo, hooo!'

'See!' Ralph rose with this approving exclamation and walked over to a shelf of books. 'Got anything to read?'

'Well, yes.'

I drew and he read. After some time he reached into an inside pocket and, without looking up from his reading, passed me his sketch book.

'Have a look at your picture.'

37

I took it and flicked through the pages until I reached mine. This drawing was different, heavily shaded and the background blackened by parallel lines like rain. From this my face emerged, hardly recognizable, the eyes staring and the mouth pursed and open in a violent O. My neck was stretched backward from my head into a wall of heavier shading. I was a gargoyle in the wind and rain, forever staring from high on the apex of a pointed arch.

FOUR

'WELL!' ORLANDO EXCLAIMED. 'Well! So *this* is where we are going. I did wonder . . . '

He had silently entered through the front door, picked his fastidious way through the boots and coats in the hallway and was now standing in front of me. His usually sleepy eyes were dramatically widened by the sight of the sheets of paper scattered about the floor. Like a vast white flower with black veined petals, the drawings lay in a ring around the stool, the drawing board and me. I was resting with my cheek flat against the sloping surface of the board. Orlando regarded me. I stared back, unresponsive. He raised one eyebrow, all that was necessary in his repertoire to cover: What is this? Have you gone mad? Then, plucking carefully at the creases of his trousers, he crouched down stiffly and, between thumb and forefinger, lifted a corner of the nearest sheet with exaggerated care. He rose, holding the paper, closed his eyes, reopened them and tilted his head the better to study the drawing.

' . . . the practice has drifted so, rudderless. I blame myself. No. Don't say a word! I have simply slaved away without a thought to the wider issues of form and content. You, Stephen, were always the visionary one, the one who saw through the daily grind to our tormented souls beneath. Now at last I see – Gothic, where we should have been all along. Of course! But one tiny query: can we actually get fifteen square metres of bathroom into a . . . ' he tilted his head to the opposite side, ' . . . a pinnacle? I mean the bidet alone . . . My imagination is, as you know, unremittingly trivial. And these crockets – the cost! And *such* a finial! Never mind, if there is a way, count upon me, we shall find it.'

This was Orlando Cummings, my partner, the other, more colourful half of Rix–Cummings. Large, grandiloquent, homosexual, he had delivered such speeches on my shortcomings and eccentricities for over twenty years. It was the house style – a burst of withering irony from him, patient justifications from me. His grandeur was reductive, bringing us back to the real world; my patience was explosive, affecting to aspire to the heavens. We had worn these masks of the noisy cynic and the quiet visionary for so long now that we could not be bothered to take them off.

We met at architectural school and formed an insular, aggressive team that specialized in pouring scorn on the competitive efforts of our contemporaries. Orlando targeted the pale dreamers, I the ruddy careerists. He was known as Orlando the Great. His grand, dandyish homosexuality made me uneasy in those days. It was too finished, every response was too certain. But the unease was really envy and it was out of envy that I cultivated a similarly flamboyant form of heterosexual life. I was thought by the gullible to spend my nights in languorous revelries of unimaginable extremity with powerful and exotic women. In reality I was no more than routinely promiscuous. Orlando found this dull and frequently attempted to persuade me to sample his tastes by suggesting 'amenable, biddable boys'. But I declined. I liked the idea of our aristocratic difference from the shabby masses, but I drew the line at the sexuality he insisted was required for the full flowering of the dandy pose.

We were universally assumed to be geniuses. We cultivated inexplicable but significant impulses. Once we painted ourselves – along with his boyfriend and my girlfriend – lime green and held a lime green picnic with lime green food, plates, cutlery and a bunch of lime green flowers in the midst of a park. A lime green line drawn on the grass indicated we were not to be disturbed, only to be discreetly contemplated. We were, in the event, very indiscreetly disturbed by a number of threats of violence and some, I thought, rather convincing abuse. As architecture, however, the picnic was a complete success since, angry as these onlookers had evidently been, none had crossed that line.

Education completed, we went into partnership, lived for some years on our avant-garde reputation, publishing sparse, exquisite and always unbuilt schemes in the professional press. Our infrequent joint lectures attracted dissident and malodorous audiences, one of which wrecked the lecture theatre and thereby put an end to our academic career. I was blamed for the wreckage because of my revolutionary remarks about indeterminacy.

Finally, almost undetectably and certainly without catching each other's eyes, we made our peace with the real world. The schemes loosened up, clients appeared, we made money and then more money and then a lot of money. There were big office blocks, ingenious housing and one stupendous theatre. Our staff swelled to over one hundred. I told myself Orlando was leading me down this road, but I suspected I was making a liar of my conscience. Over the years the house style had been modified slightly. My self-protective conviction that Orlando was the leading compromiser has encouraged in me a more arty, eccentric persona and he, in reply, has become ever more ruthlessly practical.

As he stared at my drawings, he succeeded in incorporating all of this history in an unspoken commentary. He took in my dishevelment and exhausted posture with a quick movement of his eyes. He looked betrayed and yet honestly requiring help; he was with me and yet, for my own good, against me.

I laughed nervously, raised my head as if in all innocence and ran a hand through my hair in an attempt to re-establish our mutually normal roles: me interestingly wayward, brought to book by his eloquence; him tolerant, organizing, personally unencumbered by the unforgivable mess of the heterosexual life.

'Orlando. I wasn't expecting you.'

41

He looked weary, closed his eyes and shook his head.

'I see. You weren't expecting me. Failing to expect me is more like it.'

He strolled over to the answering machine, its red one still glowing, and turned the switch to play. The tape raced, squealing, backwards.

'I shall be arriving', said Orlando's recorded voice with the slow solemnity he adopted to indicate that he regarded these machines as revolting and unreliable, 'tomorrow, mid-morning. There are things to discuss, we shall consult and have lunch. See you soon, partner.'

He turned the switch back, the tape squealed again and he looked at me.

'Ah. I hadn't actually played that back. I was distracted.'

'Evidently.'

'Good drive?'

'Simplicity itself. I always expected much more traffic after they did away with the trains. But I suppose the little people just decided not to move about so much.'

'Has to be good for them. Has to be. Tea? Coffee?'

I spoke brightly, but felt at once awkward as I noticed from the continued irony of his expression that he was all too aware of my attempts to draw him away from the embarrassment of the drawings. I waved him towards the kitchen, intending to talk while I made the drinks. His size gave me the familiar sense of crowding and slight danger as he stepped into the smaller room. He was wearing a self-consciously 'country' suit in green tweed with hugely welted brown brogues, a soft shirt and woollen tie. Orlando always dressed the part. In town he would wear a pin-striped 'city' suit, this in the country and corduroys and slippers at home. He baffled the more colourfully dressed, creative homosexual types with whom we had always mixed.

'The boys', he would explain, 'prefer it. It makes them feel secure . . . normal in spite of everything. Ultra-normal, in fact. Nothing for their mummies to worry about at all.'

His hands were now thrust hard into his jacket pockets, indicating a rare touch of angry determination. He knew I would not have done the necessary work on the flats and he was considering his approach.

'Tea, I think. Stephen . . . ahm, now let's see, where shall I begin? How goes it with you?'

The voice offered a momentary hint of real concern and he dropped the drawing he was still carrying on to the table as if signalling we were to move on to the more important matter of the state of my soul.

'Fine. Well, as you've seen, a bit odd, actually. Nothing to worry about though. I'll have the job finished soon enough.'

The feebly apologetic note made him look at me, his staring, bulbous, ugly face faintly weary, the lips pursed.

'Soon enough? Really? I hope so. You have been a bit odd. Of course. How else? Never anything less than odd. We can usually rely on you for odd. Good old, odd old Stephen.'

He took out one of his tins of small cigars and studied the beige lid for a moment. Then he flipped it open and removed a small, roughened brown tube from the curl of parchment wrapping. He lit it while I noisily organized the equipment for tea. The smoke rose, billowed and then settled in grey-blue planes in the dim light of the kitchen. I had not opened the pale cream blinds and the room felt like the inside of an egg. Orlando smiled, his head seeming to drift above these gaseous levels, reminding me of the distorted, floating head of Captain Dale addressing us from Mars Mission 2000. My intended conversation had left me and suddenly I felt we were stuck in that room, trapped by the moment, by his irritation, by my guilt and by the smoke. I was further oppressed by the sense of Ralph asleep somewhere, the need to explain him, to explain everything.

I felt also, behind me, the sullen pressure of the long, dead time of the morning, before that a tide of voices and waking, before that sleep, the night, the evening, the afternoon, the rain. The past had a new potency. It contained a time when I had lost contact. Oh, Orlando, you were so wrong, these dozens of insanely detailed drawings were not where we were going, they were where I had been. Someone had come back from that field, but not the person who had left the house.

Waking had been an unwelcome birth. I was thrust, resisting, down a corridor of echoing whispers and cries into real light, the eyes and mouth drained of all moisture again, the head

43

clogged. But this time also the terrific fatigue, the weight of knowing I could only climb back to the day after the day before. Seldom could tomorrow have failed so miserably to be another day. Visions of huge flat walls sprouting terrible creatures stayed with me from my dreams. Stones gesticulated in anger and furniture attacked me. Spreading planes of light. A ginger cat was dying in terrible agony, foam encircling its mouth, a fox-like creature was screaming and curving its back as if to bend its body away from the pain. A dark-haired girl slept on, staring now and then, wide-eyed but unconsciously, at my streaked and shadowed face.

In the pale, curtained light of the bedroom my eyes had opened to see a lion crouched on the table. Its lower jaw had moved slightly. It was waiting to strike. Familiar with such effects of half-light but aware that I could no longer rely even on the stability of illusion, I tried to work out what the real cause of the silhouette might be. I wanted to keep the lion rather than face its transformation into something explicable. I did not want my cathedral to collapse into madness. The vision once gone could never be regained.

But the effort of recollection – attempting to decipher the shape through memory alone – proved impossible. I turned on the light. The lion was a pile of books, a pencil and a silk scarf, one corner of which was caught by an intermittent draught.

Having frightened away the lion, I rose and plucked at the cord of the blind on the bedroom window; the spring unhitched and the fabric leapt to reveal the valley beyond. The sky was a hard blue interrupted by high, white clouds. On the distant hillsides shadows and sunlight chased each other like arguments. Interacting wave fronts: nothing untoward there. Today I need not read these dull, dappled things for significance. Today, perhaps, they were more sharp, more clear, more hurtful because of the pain behind my eyes, the hardened consistency of vision, the daze of alcohol and other memories. But that was all.

In the bathroom I turned on the cold tap and let the water run over my wrists, the arteries pressed together. It sent a shiver through me and started an ache in my stomach. The field – *that field* – of course, was empty. Above it, the cool air moved unobstructed by masonry. The sun cast no broken shadows on neighbouring fields. Birds were not surprised by new, high perches.

Could one call it a cathedral if it had this habit of appearing and disappearing? Cathedrals do not do that. Is there a word for an infrequently – perhaps once only – existing church? But all things exist once only, come into being and vanish, leaving, perhaps, ripples in the water, but then they too fade and die. In this case only the timescale was wrong. It was a small matter, only a minor disturbance on the plane of the acceptable. Nothing to fret about. These things happen.

The lion had been at ten o'clock. I had never in my life slept so late. Struggling down from the bedroom I tried to attach some sense to the day that lay ahead. I was confronted by an impossible choice. There was Orlando and his flats – urgent, very urgent, angry clients, missed deadlines, hours of work still to do. But there was also the cathedral – urgent, but why? Because it needed work – my work. The choice was made.

I drank water, tea, anything I could organize and, erasing all practical considerations from my mind, began once again sketching the church, trying to work from the real memory rather than from easy reconstructions of my limited, amateur's knowledge of Gothic. I sketched furiously, covering the paper with details and working so quickly that I could not bear to expend time on changing sheets, finding instead new corners and spaces to fill. Among my music I found some monastic chants which I played as loud as I dared. I feared waking Ralph. He had, uninvited, found himself a spare bedroom. His presence had become a nuisance. I had to get on.

The drawings began to remind me of the logic of Gothic. I saw how those travelling architects and masons had aspired to eliminate the sullen immobility of the wall, how they had fought with the extremity of the demands their interiors placed upon their exteriors, the lucidity and yet complexity of their structures. Modern buildings were structurally solved after the initial aesthetic decisions had been made. Classical buildings required a denial of effort, there could be nothing precarious and therefore unsettling. But in Gothic the structural solution and the aesthetic could hardly be distinguished. There was no discontinuity between the refinement of the idea and the brute matter of the world. The world was an idea. The precariousness and the disturbing energy were the point.

I worked most intensely on the tracery of one of the windows of the nave. With each attempt to recreate what I had seen, the sculpting of the stone became more absurdly elaborate. How had they dreamed of these shapes? In plan the sections of the stone acquired globules and clusters that locked together to form, in elevation, slender shafts that rose and branched through the glass. The chamfered, concave forms of the *oculus* dipped and swooped to include the glass in the stone, the materials brought together rather than framing each other, the stone becoming glass, the glass stone.

The truncated forms grew, changed, reproduced, filling the paper with their impatient, amputated demands. I shaded them to signal their weight, sketched fragments of texture to indicate their grain. I was seized by the idea of a complete, self-consistent style – no longer that irate self-examination, that insistent puzzle about why this should be that shape or that colour. Nothing here need be arbitrary or undecided.

The phone rang. It was Tina, my lovely, disinterested secretary.

'Hello, Stephen. How yooooo?'

'Tina. Right. Tina. Fine. Any messages?'

'Weather nice? It's lovely here. Messages? I'll say. Should I fax them?'

'Sure. Anything urgent?'

'Your wife says don't forget your back appointment and Francesca rang . . . '

She paused deferentially. Was she filing her nails and chewing gum?

'Right . . . right. Look, Tina, there's a book on my shelves, a big green one, called *The Origins of Gothic* by W. D. Wimsy. Near the front there's a big double page diagram titled something like "The Genesis of the Gothic Vault". Could you fax a copy of that as well? And as many of the other big, detailed drawings as you can manage.'

'OK, sure. Anything else?'

I felt a surge of affection for her. No questions, simplicity itself. I was her boss, I did inexplicable things. But they demanded no more from her than did the weather or some alien war or famine. You wear a coat, you slip some coins in the box, you fax things – this was nothing to her. Even the deferential pause after the name of Francesca, my lover, was no more than the proper thing to do. I was just what happened at work.

'No, no. Right . . . right. See you soon.'

'OK, Stephen, be good,' she laughed. 'Don't do anything I wouldn't do.'

I had been given an excuse to interrupt my work, an excuse that worked because I wanted to do it. I did it. I rang Francesca . . . engaged. I rang Francesca . . . engaged. I rang Francesca . . . no answer. Impossible. I rang Francesca . . . no answer. I howled in agitation and rested my forehead amidst the pens and pencils on the cold marble top of the table next to the drawing board.

The faxes began to come through at the familiar sliding, reptilian pace. A long list of names and phone numbers and then the Gothic diagrams. These I stared at for some twenty minutes, trying to accustom myself to their means and methods. I wanted to draw as a Gothic architect without effort, without reference. It had, I was sure, to come naturally or not at all. Then the fax machine beeped again and a blank page slid through.

Superstitiously I took this to mean: *now* ring Francesca. She was nervous about leaving evidence so she said or faxed nothing. Perhaps she was now faxing a form of nothing that could act as a message. So I rang her again . . . no answer. But a paragraph of Wimsy's caught my eye. It concerned one of the more rational justifications of Gothic – the resolution through pointed arches of the problem of the differential heights of intersecting tunnel vaults. The burning to ring Francesca was cooled. I returned feverishly to my drawings. Finally I had paused and rested my cheek against the cool smoothness of the drawing board. Then Orlando had walked in. 'Well! Well!'

In the kitchen Orlando had abandoned his mock-fatherly tone and was now slumped against the wall, rubbing his eyes. The expression on his face indicated we were to slip into plangent fatigue, the despair of the dandy on confronting work. It was, finally, so hard just to live.

'The flats, Stephen,' he said vaguely. 'We really must move on . . .'

Feeling lighter for his apparent relaxation and grateful for his silence, I carried the wooden tray of tea and biscuits into the living room only for my agitation to return. Ralph was plugged into the VR machine. His helmeted head swivelled and his hands waved. I turned to see Orlando looking startled and then wearily questioning – not more stuff to deal with, more distractions from work.

I put down the tray and caught one of Ralph's flailing arms. He stopped in shock, turned off the machine and took off the helmet. He acknowledged me with a friendly smile.

'Good game that,' he said and then froze awkwardly when he saw Orlando looming behind, nibbling at a shortbread with eyebrows raised. Ralph rubbed his palms nervously on his thighs. This made him remember the gloves which he now removed.

'Oh,' said Orlando, lowering the biscuit, 'I see. You have a . . . friend. How nice. A friend. Everybody should have a friend.'

The repetitions of the word seemed to drift lazily, balloon-like, around the room, acquiring, as they did so, the intended connotations.

'Ralph, this is Orlando, my partner. Ralph's a local sculptor . . . er, rather good. I met him in the pub last night.'

'How nice! How nice! And good too, you say, wonderful! Particularly nice to be good.'

Orlando held the biscuit in his mouth and shook Ralph's hand warmly, placing his own left over their two joined rights and holding on too long. Finally he stopped and turned to me.

'And, naturally, in your cups the conversation turned to . . .' he waved the shortbread airily at the drawing board, ' . . . churches and stuff.'

Ralph smiled, having regained his composure. Orlando turned back to him and studied this expression closely for a moment.

'A sculptor eh? And what do you work with? What sub-stances just seem to grow under your hand? Don't be shy.'

He raised his eyebrows and smiled encouragingly.

'Oh, anything. But always with stone. Mix things up. You'd like it. It is good.'

'I'm sure I would and I am sure it is.'

Orlando looked knowingly at Ralph, pretending, for my benefit and embarrassment, to have reached some awkward conclusion. I put the tray down and went mindlessly back into the kitchen to get another cup.

By the time I returned from the kitchen, Orlando was assiduously working on forming an alliance against me, his customary pastime. The rule that Orlando must plot against me had always been part of our game.

'Often see cathedrals,' Ralph was asking with a note of confident irony I had not previously heard, 'does he?'

The story had been told. Orlando, now seated on the arm of Ralph's chair, turned and beamed triumphantly at me, so broadly, I noticed, that his eyes were closed by the effort. I was shocked by Ralph's tone. Was this to be his part – to side, sneering, with my critics?

'I'm not sure I can answer that on his behalf . . . Who can tell? He may just have decided to come clean on this one, having lived with others daily. Or this may be his first. Or perhaps all the others were classical or baroque. He only felt the need to mention this one because it was Gothic. The mystery . . . But here he is, let's ask the man himself. Stephen, often see cathedrals do you?'

I said nothing. Orlando shrugged, his palms raised. 'No answer. Well I can at least tell you that he has never told me about any cathedrals.'

'This is, indeed, my first,' I said at last, trying to keep my voice steady and urbane, 'and I didn't just see it. I went inside it and touched it. It was there.'

'You don't think this may be what is vulgarly termed a mid-life crisis – hot flushes and so on. The realization of mortality, finding yourself crouched on all fours before the horror of the discovery that this is no dress rehearsal.'

Orlando had for some time been trying to convince me that my age – forty-two – was a particularly dangerous one. He was forty-three and claimed to have navigated his way around the worst pitfalls. 'The important thing', he would say, 'is not to say or do anything boring.'

'Suppose it is. I still saw this cathedral. Whether I was having a hot flush at the time is immaterial. The church, in contrast, was very material. You'd probably have suffered a hot flush if you'd seen it.'

'Yes. Good answer. We shouldn't rush to the conclusion that, because there is an apparent cause, it must also be a sufficient cause. Mid-life crisis makes church, but, on the other hand, it really did make it. World stuff, not just mind stuff.'

I realized, for the first time, that 'stuff' was Orlando's favourite word. 'It's hard to imagine what kind of cause could be sufficient – at least from the point of view of the one person – me – who knows perfectly well that I wasn't hallucinating.'

'Well, we can only take that line so far. Perhaps we ought to switch our attention to effect. What do you intend to do? Chalk it up to experience? Embark on a retreat? I only ask, you will appreciate, as your partner in Rix–Cummings. These things have certain practical implications, but, alas, very few practical applications. Would that they had. Would that we could . . . soar.'

Orlando spoke with the obvious expectation that I would eventually succumb and dismiss the whole affair as a passing aberration. Twice he rolled the word 'practical' with heavy irony and smiled at Ralph in an attempt to reinforce a sense of conspiracy. Something odd had happened, he wanted me to understand, nothing more. Odd things were not our business. They happened, but you could ignore them and all would be well. I realized I was being drawn towards a choice between the great leveller of Orlando's irony or something from a different, more contoured order of things.

'Well . . . '

'I knew it!' Orlando burst out, drawing grand conclusions from my moment's hesitation. 'I blame it on his mother, in-sufficient discipline. He ran wild. Or that Francesca. Adultery gives people the vaguest notions. I always knew Rix would get religion or something. Now he's got adulterer's Gothic.'

'I did not run wild.'

'Francesca?' enquired Ralph.

'Oh, I'll tell you about *her* later.'

'Why do we always look backwards for explanations?' I asked, dimly aware that I was not fully paying attention to any of this. 'Because of cause and effect, we accept anything chronological. But maybe we shouldn't. What if something happened now that was explained by the future?'

'Tedious sci-fi, dear boy. What if we could reach the stars, talk to aliens, float above the motorways at a thousand miles an hour? You are always trying to make life more exciting than it actually is. We determinists always like to insist that it is, in reality, far duller. All we can do is smooth the path towards what is going to happen anyway.'

'No, it's not that. What if we simply switched the language round and explained forwards. This mug is full here because it is at one end of a process. It is full because it will be empty . . . '

'And your damned church was there, I presume, because it will be built.'

'Quite. Well possibly.'

'Except it's not there now.'

The theory needs some work, of course, but perhaps some kind of hint was intended. A sign . . . '

I looked at Ralph. Orlando stood up and grew agitated, whether genuinely or not I was, as usual, unable to tell.

'It's just what you wanted this, isn't it? An excuse – some crazy stuff. Other people fall ill, get bad backs, hernias or whatever – you have to see a damned cathedral *and* you have a bad back.'

'And I faint.'

'*And* you faint.' He turned to Ralph. 'He does these things from time to time. Not cathedrals necessarily. Every so often we have a little Stephen episode . . . What was the last one? Ah yes, the animal clock that never told the right time. Nearly lost the job on that one, didn't we, Stephen? Only six months ago, the frequency of your hot flushes is rising.'

'It's perfectly understandable you should say these things, Orlando. Perfectly understandable that you should insist it is dismissible as a function of some enduring character defect. Unfortunately I *did* see it. I walked about inside it. I touched it. That doesn't deny what you are saying, of course, it just makes

51

it slightly difficult for me to accept as helpful or definitive.'

'Oh, very good. Too good to be true, I think.'

'Look, if I'm going to talk to you, we have to escape from this. On my terms, if you like.'

'Amazing. The nerve.'

'Seriously. I'm changing myself and everything else because of what I saw . . . did. It's the change that counts, not the banal issue of whether you believe me.'

'Ah! The Change! What did I say?'

These thoughts – this decision – had only just come to me as the fog of the morning had cleared. This thing had, I realized, happened. What could I do? It walked with me now and had greeted me when I woke. Here was a new kind of nuisance, a novel way of interrupting the conduct of ordinary life – like falling in love, or a terminal illness. And, like both of those, it waved some flag of significance at me. *Do* something! Here is something unavoidably huge, specifically for you to deal with. There is no next thing. You cannot turn away. To do so would leave you a traitor for the rest of your life – but a traitor to what?

I had hardly been looking for it. Quite the reverse: an ordered, neatly relative and very affluent existence was mine after all the noisy, posturing, aspiring years. I had settled for good rather than great and had proved myself capable of convincing myself that I was, indeed, good. It was enough. The need for smart trickery had subsided. Even the adultery was nicely controlled. I had grown up. Death wasn't so bad. I had only one life, but, on the other hand, only I had to bother about regretting it. And then this, intimating what? Immortality? Maybe.

The word 'change' had prompted Orlando to examine Ralph again with cool theatrical suspicion. Ralph had turned away to study the books.

'Well, perhaps I ought to have a word with Jill about these . . . changes,' he curved his mouth downward suggestively.

'Oh, don't be absurd. I went to the pub last night in a state and met Ralph. He is, I suspect, a genius.' Ralph looked over his shoulder and smiled coolly. 'He lives with this girl called Sally . . . '

I added this last to establish the general manliness of the

proceedings, but the name unnerved me for a moment. I remembered, for the first time that day, kissing her eyes and the memory drove out all else from my head. Here was another sudden girl to distract me from my sudden church. There were always sudden girls.

'Does she always sleep?' I asked Ralph, again losing touch with Orlando. He looked round again, blankly at first, evidently startled to be included. Then he understood.

'Sally, yeah, most of the time. Said she should see a doctor. But she just said that was her, take it or leave it. She says she enjoys sleeping more than anything, sex included. Suppose the thing is to fuck her while she's asleep.'

Orlando looked irate at the coarseness and the digression, but I could not immediately leave the subject.

'She lives here,' I explained to him, 'but even in the village hardly anybody knows of her existence. Strange . . . '

'Good,' said Orlando, rubbing his hands. 'Strange, an excellent summary of the themes of the morning. The virginal sleeper, the phantom church. Strange, very. However, strange means out of the ordinary and it is only out of the damp, lumpish loam of the ordinary that strangeness, an exotic but less than hardy crop, can grow. And ordinary also requires cultivation. Then there is the matter of this block of flats – prosaic I know, unsoaring I am fully aware, yet having its own satisfactions. What I suggest is that to make you feel you are doing something – er – relevant, we should take a walk, you, me, Sculptor Ralph, examine your field, check on what cathedrals might be lying about there and return here to get on with these drawings. OK? Deal?'

He finished with a clownlike, innocent grin, his palms invitingly, hucksterishly spread. I agreed, while dreading my side of the contract – the prospect of facing the flats again. But, oddly, this was the first time that the thought of returning to the field had occurred to me. Ralph also seemed keen, walking to the door the minute the suggestion had been made. So I found myself retracing my steps of the day before, climbing over the gate and picking our way through the clumps of rushes that grew in the sodden field beyond. The land sloped quite steeply and Orlando slithered and fell as the leather soles of his brogues skated across the wet grass. He said nothing, but picked himself up, closed his eyes, sighed and marched on. On the far side we climbed the remains of the stone wall and turned to walk along the half-buried stream, now flowing less rapidly than the day before. The rains had gone and the ancient water courses were calmly guiding away the excesses they had left behind. I found my spot.

'I was standing here.'

I demonstrated my pose to Orlando. Ralph had his hands thrust flat into his pockets and was standing hunched and staring at the distant ridge. There were two orange dots, rain-proofed walkers heading down towards the village.

'Really,' said Orlando, '*just* fancy.'

I looked coldly at him to indicate I required a certain gravity. 'I became aware of something behind me, turned, and there it was.'

I gestured at the field. Orlando looked at me, then the field, and began marching about with an elaborately conscientious air.

'What are you looking for?'

'I don't know. Fragments, the odd crocket perhaps, a touch of tracery, a bewildered priest, searching for his lost church . . . '

'How on earth could there be anything like that?'

'I don't know, but why on earth did we come here? Perhaps in these situations – whatever they are – we should expect scorch marks left by the huge rockets that propelled the Cathedral Church of St Stephen the Wet back into the cold interstellar vacancies whence it came.'

'It was cold, but, if I felt it came from anywhere, I think I would say it was from *below*. This land is virtually hollow with subterranean caverns. I was once told some were big enough to hold a cathedral.'

Orlando looked despairing and then began pacing the field again, this time apparently measuring its dimensions. From some distance he launched into a series of hand signals trying to establish the edges of the building. Finally he returned to my side, panting slightly and glowing about the cheeks.

'Big i' faith,' he muttered, 'but not, as it were, present. Not present at all. And, I'm afraid, no evidence, not a shred.'

'Good place for it, though.'

Orlando and I both swung round at this suddenly authoritative remark from Ralph who was still staring at the distant ridge. He turned to meet our eyes. 'It's a good site. Like to place something here myself.'

I felt there was some welcome urgency in this sliver of outside encouragement. Had he glimpsed something, some fragment of my cathedral, some logic?

'Why exactly?'

'It just looks prepared. This field is the flattest thing for miles . . . and the way the valley opens out. It's a stage set. A natural plinth.'

After some disappointment that there was nothing more, I found myself wondering whether the suitability of the site had somehow forced the church upon me. I had unconsciously designed it and then created it for a few moments. There had been times in my more ambitious days when, at the point of waking, I had half-dreamed I was walking through a building that I had been working on the day before. It was a phenomenon that had promised so much, a vocation. But it went nowhere, declining over the years into a mild pleasure.

'A natural plinth,' said Orlando. 'Exactly so. Well time's up. Plinth it may be, but to the less sensitive eye it remains a field like any other.'

I started as Orlando put an arm around my shoulders and began to push me back towards the house and work, claiming his side of the deal.

'Look,' he said as I fell into step with the pressure of his arm, 'I hate to sound utterly boring, but do you think you have a little too much stuff going on in your life at the moment?'

I said nothing and felt a kind of gloom at the necessity of going through this most obvious ritual – the application of the overwork hypothesis. Already I had heard this from Landlord Jack.

'We have been busy – all to the good, of course, but you can lose perspective. And this thing about Francesca and Jill. I mean I know I have sort of encouraged it, lying about your whereabouts and so on, but it's hardly the sort of thing that keeps a boy . . . balanced.'

I sensed that he had immediately regretted this last word –
it had been too clear a statement. In any case, the imbalances
were encouraged by him, just as during our student days the
flamboyance of his sex life had encouraged my pretences. He
hurried on to cover the tactical error.

'I think, maybe, a rest. We have to finish these sodding flats,
but I'll take over the work after this bit and you can go off
somewhere. On your own, I think, but I suppose you'll end up
with one of your women. You have to watch this stress thing. It
creeps up on you. Most of the time you don't even know you're
under stress and then suddenly . . . ' He clapped his hands.

I clapped back derisively, impatient with the banality of all
this. I broke angrily away from his arm, picked up a large,
contorted branch from the ground and sauntered back to Ralph
who was walking silently behind us. I stripped twigs from
the branch as I walked. Putting my arm round his shoulders,
I raised the branch in the air.

'Orlando,' I shouted, 'there's one thing I forgot to mention.
I'm going to build it.'

This is what Ralph had been sent to tell me. The site was the
final clue. Now I understood.

'Yeah!' cried Ralph with sudden animation. He picked up a
stone and hurled it into the field. Its arc took it straight through
where the south transept had been . . . would be.

I squeezed Ralph's shoulders and smiled at Orlando so
broadly that my eyes closed. Then, our arms locking us
together, Ralph and I began to dance towards him, kicking
our legs and singing tuneless nonsense.

'Balloo, ballooo, ballaballally loo. Honky, wonky, donky,
fereeeee!'

Orlando watched us coolly.

'And a Happy New Year to you both,' he said, turning
away.

'Gerdoing, gerdoing, cha cha cha!'

'Oh, Stephen, Stephen, what are we going to do with you?'

FIVE

I HAD THAT dream again. Once more the dying cat, the howling
fox-like thing, but this time they were inside – in a kitchen
where I was trying to cook a meal. Pans bubbled, filling the
air with steam, and hot fat spurted, stinging my hands and
staining my clothes with dark spots. The food was urgent, we
were expecting people. I struggled, breathlessly. But this time a
man was there too – grey-haired, pointed nose, a horribly thin
face. He muttered in some unrecognizable language and ran,
crouching, around the room in a long black coat streaked with
egg and grease. On every third circuit he would break off and
gabble stories of returning kings, defeated bastard sons, boats,
witches, all the time pushing and snatching at me with a yellow
hand, his long fingernails catching in my clothes. I screamed at
him to let me get on with the cooking and he would rush off
on another three circuits of the kitchen.

Then there was another room.

Then it was the room in which I was.

Finally it was me, sweating and conscious, the taste of fat in
my mouth. The pale light admitted by the thin yellow curtains
revealed that I was safe in the calming, innocuous scenery of

home. On a white table in the window bay was a spherical glass vase of pink carnations, the flower heads arranged in an open circle and the stalks crossing at the meniscus to form an underwater wigwam. Next to the table was a single turquoise cane chair with a yellow cushion. That side of the room appeared to be waiting to be occupied; it could be a painting of a hotel room, expressing vacancy or idle wealth. On the far wall a heavy wooden mantelpiece bore a sculpture of a reclining woman made of thousands of fragments of coloured glass. Another table – round and oak – was covered with magazines, flawlessly aligned, overlapping like fish scales, their titles visible: *Dream Homes, Different Worlds, Interior Life.* I had awoken into Jill's world, styled and perfect, the air vibrating with her remote presence. One familiar part of my soul was at once soothed by all this organization. Another part screamed that it was no longer for me.

Aware of a pricking at my eye as I blinked, I plucked a crust from the inner corner of the socket and examined the grains that clung to my nail. A liquid had oozed out of me in the night and dried in the cool air of the bedroom. In nursery language this was 'sleep', as if the loss of consciousness was a brown oil inside you. Perhaps wakefulness was a cloud of white gas. I flicked the nail against my thumb and the grains disappeared into the air and the sheets to be lost for ever.

Twisting awkwardly, I picked up the drawing pad that I kept by the bed and started sketching. The lines would not come with their usual early morning fluency. My pencil skidded and rambled of its own accord. Mildly annoyed, I abandoned my attempts at the north transept and began to draw monsters, slavering creatures with beak-like mouths, horns and spiked tails. At last even these collapsed with the effort of representation and I resorted to scribbling frantic cross-hatchings, swirls and vortices.

I put the pad down and raised the bed cover to look down on my naked body. Not bad, as I always concluded, for forty-two. Certainly it was pale and rather soft, but not hairy and not so fat as to deserve the adjective. From here even the genitals looked about as right as such things could ever do. But a general scattering of moles reminded me of what I assumed would be

58

my cancerous destiny. I had attempted to count these stipples, but the contortions involved as well as the difficulty of working out which I had already counted made the task impossible. My moles must have a number, but I could not find it. I stared for some time at the body, framed by the radiating ripples of the lower sheet and shrouded by the tent of the upper. This was me. Yesterday it had also been me. Tomorrow it would be me. Then, one day, it would not. What, then, would it be?

I rose, pulled on a dressing gown, crossed the landing at the centre of which another table bore an extravagant arrangement of dried flowers. The breeze of my passing dislodged a few spikes and petal shards. On the staircase Jill's grainy black-and-white photographic collection stepped grimly down beside me. Some showed thrust-jawed women, others scenes from jungle wars, one a dead man on a mortuary table and one a peasant wedding. All were framed in thick, polished walnut.

In the enormous kitchen Jill was sitting at the table writing a letter while Tom and Elizabeth whispered. My wife is a handsome woman, somewhat large with broad shoulders, her face long and intellectual. On this template is superimposed her style of rather sensible glamour – her hair is tended and subtly coloured, her clothes calculated and expensive. This would not be vanity to her, simply an aspect of the purposeful project of herself.

'I need a strong woman,' I would tell myself.

'Why?' I would reply.

I just do.

She was always engaged in projects of arcane complexity and massive social demands, all of them executed in this room. She liked to move among the shabby and the dowdy inhabitants of the world of charity, crushing them by being both groomed and virtuous. Her phone and fax were on a trolley that followed her about while she cooked or ate, a computer slid out from one of the cupboards. Like most of the rest of the house the kitchen was hers. But here her style was less diluted by the traces of others. So the kitchen decor was more intense: dark wooden shelving and furniture were artfully enhanced with rich fabrics, fragments of tapestry, piles of plates and pans, more dried flowers and a large, stone statue of some tribesman with a severe face and folded arms. A row of marbled box files ran along one wall to be intercepted by the one feature I could regard as wholly mine – a bricked-up door.

'Don't you see?' I would ask her with an air of bright, encouraging frustration. 'It is a *memento mori*. A door through which we cannot pass but to which we all must come. Or maybe pass through as something different – vapour, unthinking vapour.'

'Vapour is on the right lines, but a cooker hood would have been more appropriate. The kitchen is not about symbolism. The kitchen is real.'

'Symbolism . . . symbolism. Where better than the real belly of the house? Like gargoyles and tombs in a cathedral – a reminder of the last great negation of all things – in this case children, tarragon, avocados, files, artichoke hearts, split peas . . . Anyway the kitchen is hardly the place for a computer.'

'The kitchen is the place for what I put in it.'

We had met at some unusually serious party soon after Orlando and I had started Rix–Cummings. Being drunk and impressed by her large, glamorous solidity, I had launched into a series of vacuous, supposedly intriguing generalizations. Jill had looked at first bored and then angry. Finally, she witheringly pointed out a number of mistaken facts, discredited interpretations and logical blunders in my discourse. She had been right about all of them. I fought back, deploying a degree of humble charm. And then I saw dawn in her eyes a look that was quite indecipherable, a look of fierce understanding and conviction. Thereafter I would always recognize it as the sign that a new project, an interesting case, a worthy cause had been identified. That night, the what were to her preliminaries completed, she began to explain to me how she could help. I looked at her long face and considered her background of suburban squirearchy, good works and brassbound common sense. I concluded that this was just what I needed after the long, posturing debauch of my student years and our fate was sealed.

But this morning she offered me no more than the barest acknowledgement. I suspected I might be next on her schedule after the letter. Unable to do much else but wait my turn, I sat down and watched the soft undulations of my children's faces. My breathing faltered. Love, love, love calling me to enter in, calling me to surrender myself. But the distances are immense. We are flying apart at the speed of light. And children are made to be impermeable. Those features that appear so soft, in reality resist everything, observing, when they happen to think of it, my decay with a conclusive indifference. I touched Elizabeth's hair.

'Daddy! Don't do that!'

Scorn. I am a natural hazard for which she feels a fleeting tenderness.

Tom spoke without looking up from his reading, a children's newspaper. 'Dad, did you know they've got VR machines on the Mars mission? They thought the crew would go mad in such a small space. So they use the VR to pretend they're, you know, outside, in somewhere bigger. Great isn't it?'

'Good idea. It's like you using the VR machine to pretend you're on a spaceship.'

He thought for a moment and then laughed at the cleverness.

'Oh yeah! And they're bringing out one of the games they're using. A motorbike game. It's called Captain Dale's Red Rider. Can I have it?'

'As ever, we shall see.'

My own father had died when I was twenty-five and I had married soon afterwards. He was an almost absurdly vivid man. His hair was perfectly silver and his shoes perfectly shined. He was a curious blend of yeoman and patrician. Tall, beautifully spoken and ironic, his conversational style would swing from classical reference to obscure ethnic expressiveness – 'Let the dog see the rabbit,' was one standard drawn from some memory of hunting. It meant a space was to be cleared for his concentrated attention. As a child I had always misheard it as 'Let the duck see the rabbit,' and, consequently, filled pages of drawing pads with pictures of ducks, some with glasses, intently examining rabbits.

He was an engineer of the heroic kind, designing fabulous structures with impractical spans and of improbable height. His projects were all wars of nerves between himself and his architects. Invariably, the architect would crack and admit he had no faith in the structure at which point my father would purse his lips and confess that it was indeed unsound but he had been 'just testing'. He travelled, taking with him, we always knew, old girlfriends and, occasionally, younger ones.

My mother did not seem to mind. She stayed in their strange house whether he was at home or away. Large and baffling to visitors, the house overlooked a flat and waterlogged landscape through its immoderate expanses of plate glass – a substance loved by my father and, therefore, subjected to the same kinds of extreme demands as his wife, his girlfriends and his clients. A strong wind once blew in one of these windows. He replaced it and attached a vibration device that would supposedly react to and counteract the effect of wind pressure.

My mother lived her last years alone in that house. The window was still intact as was the device, but she still gloomily expected its demise every autumn. I visited her when I had to and we talked bleakly of our separate lives as if avoiding the subject of some nameless, terrible mistake we had made. Then she died as if losing interest.

My father died in his bed, but returned to me three nights later. I dreamt I was sitting in the kitchen with my mother in an immobile tableau of expectancy. There was a knock at the back door. I answered it. It was dark and sharply cold. A dog ran in. I looked up and there stood my father, smiling apologetically and wearing a red pullover he had never, to my knowledge, possessed in life. Languidly he stepped inside and the dream ended. The sweater, I later concluded, was my sleeping mind's emblem of his failed and punctured heart.

'Let the duck see the rabbit,' he said. 'Let the duck see the rabbit.'

The local paper – the *Pointed Park Post* – lay on the table. 'It makes you wonder why anyone bothers to care,' began a page one editorial. 'Make no mistake. Who do these people think they are?' A headline announced: 'Star resigns from Millennium Committee'.

'Daddy,' Elizabeth asked, 'who do you like best? Wilbur?'
'Dilys.'
These were the heroes of a jerky television puppet show.
'Why?'
'She's funny.'

62

'She's a bit sad.'

'Yes. But we love her, don't we? We want to make her happy. Wilbur and Wilfred want to make her happy.'

'They give her presents.'

'That's right: a cake and a pot.'

'Yes!'

She laughed violently and began to hiccup. Tom hit her roughly on the back and she howled. The sound caused the dog, Dandy, to look up from his basket and bark briefly. I threw him some toast which he caught with a quick downward snap and chewed rapidly in case more was to come.

Jill gave me a weary look.

'Don't get them excited just before school, Stephen, it ruins their concentration. Why do I have to say that every morning? And don't feed the dog.'

The children and the dog retreated, knowing my brief anarchy had been suppressed. The rain had stopped and a pale sun cast oblique rhomboids about the kitchen. Elizabeth began to snatch at the yellow air.

'What are you doing?' demanded Jill. The movements meant another distraction from her letter. She sighed pointedly, shook her head and heroically forced herself to carry on with her writing without waiting for an answer.

'The sunshine has made dust all over. Look! I'm going to catch it.'

'It was there before, you just couldn't see it. Now stop that and eat your breakfast.' Jill spoke, while still writing, with flat authority.

'How do you know?' I asked. 'It could come from the sun.'

'Stupid!' Tom whispered malevolently at Elizabeth.

'It could. It could. There was dust round the sun, Miss Havers told us. She said five billion years ago the earth did not exist, there was just a big cloud of dust and gas spinning round the sun.'

'Even more stupid.'

'Miss Havers is right,' said Jill to calm the row, 'but the sun didn't make the dust.'

One of each, ten and eight, that's how we summarized these two when asked. They were part of the single web of work and

life, life and work. Conceived as a solution of the problem —
what one, under the circumstances, did — but ending up as a
separate assertion of something else entirely. Out there, they
are out there. Most things you deal with are in here, but
they are out there like nothing else.

'How do we know Miss Havers is right?' I asked. Jill gave
me a cynical look. She finished her letter, enveloped, addressed
and stamped it and looked at me again, this time with an
upward flick of her head and her long, straight, dark hair.
Such looks were planned, intended to indicate progress with
her agenda. I was next to be dealt with.

'Orlando is furious,' she said with slow, measured intensity.

I glanced at the children to imply that this should not
really be discussed in front of them. This was an old habit
of evasion; I knew it would not work.

'He is not, he is frightened, which is not the same thing.
He thinks I have cracked up. And, if I have, he is worried
there will be no more work. Happily I have not cracked up,
so there should be no problem.'

'Cracked up . . . cracked up,' murmured Elizabeth wonder-
ingly. She was ignored.

'To me he says he is furious and I think he talks more frankly
to me than to you. Either way, what *I* want to know, Stephen,
is why you *need* to believe in this damn church.'

This was the style that had once convinced me that she
knew something that I did not. Since then the conviction has
occasionally left me, but never for long. The question for her
now was not: had Stephen seen a cathedral in a field? It was:
why did Stephen need to see a cathedral in a field?

'Let us say, for once, that this is not the issue. Let us say
this church briefly existed. This would seem to be an event of
what you would describe as momentous masculinity. It was out
there, unarguable, external to and unaffected by your causes,
lives, feelings . . . '

'Feelings, Stephen, are all we have. Women can at least face
up to that. Men seem to find it a bleak prospect, they just want
to witter on about machines, nonsense like that.'

Whatever the fight, we always fired the same ammunition.
She began to gather papers together and clapped her hands twice

to indicate to the children it was time to leave for school. The dog leapt expectantly out of his basket, but paused and padded round the kitchen when it heard no follow-up command.

'Are you going to the office?'

This was the way we were: the outlines of an argument loosely stated and then Jill's sense of a timetable ruling out further debate.

'Of course, Orlando has some big developer coming in.'

'Yes, yes. He told me about him. They knew each other at school.'

The degree of consultation between my wife and Orlando was always alarming. I had been back in town for a day and a half and already Orlando must have briefed Jill. What was the point? Was constant surveillance necessary to monitor and contain my eccentricities?

He had left soon after the walk around the field. We had arrived at some compromise which would involve him putting off the client and the details of the flats being completed in the office. I had driven back that evening after promising Ralph I would give him work on the church if anything happened.

'What are your movements then?'

'Well I've got my back appointment first. I think I've got to see somebody this afternoon.'

I should, of course, have invented a name, a watertight alibi for my visits to Francesca. But, somehow, I always felt a not-quite-lie was more acceptable, as if vagueness gave it credibility and imprecision allowed of a later retraction.

Tom and Elizabeth finally scrambled out of the room followed by Dandy, barking. Jill paused on her way out, probably struck by the transparent perfidy of my last remark. Gazing down at me, she was dressed, made-up, broad-shouldered and in charge, her correspondence held primly under her arm.

'It's not just me and Orlando you know. It's the children, it's even those hippies who work for you. You don't just exist in your head, you chose to have responsibilities and you can't unchoose.'

'Yes and I meet them, I meet them all. I am responsible. But what if I have really been given a sign? Aren't you supposed to throw all that aside? Isn't that a responsibility too?'

'Some think so. I don't. I think you're supposed to have the balls to go with your real feelings. Stop pretending there's something else. You are a classic case – art in youth, churches in middle age – always have to have something grander, some private little mysticism. Just let's get on with things, real things.'

Leaving that demand ringing in the air, she walked out, calling to the children to follow. They did, of course, appearing magically ready at her side as she swept grandly out of the front door, swinging it shut and projecting a gust of fresh air along the hall to the kitchen. Dandy yelped as the slammed door excluded him from the adventure and returned sadly to his basket, habit telling him he could expect nothing from me.

I slumped forward to rest my head on the knotted and veined pine of the table. Turning to feel the wood on my cheek, I gently spun a knife and watched its shape change at each moment of the rotation. The way the mind meanders: I play with things – a pen most often, making of its form a rocket, a building, some arbitrary type of weapon, boyish things. This occupies moments, then minutes and, in aggregate, weeks, months of this life. What is happening here? I am pretending I am doing something else or being somebody else. Then I start guiltily and return to what I was doing. But I always pause again, pick up a ruler which becomes a beam, a bridge, an impractically slender skyscraper.

I dozed for a moment, then woke, shivering with anxiety as I realized that my back appointment was in ten minutes. I rushed up the stairs to dress, fighting a dizzy moment that could have become a faint.

Outside the weather had changed again. The sun had gone and the sky was a featureless grey, the air motionless. It was neither cold nor warm. It would be spring soon enough. In sunlight or wind buildings felt poised for movement or actively resisting it. Today nothing was happening. Objects were enrobed in the still air in anticipation of nothing, filling their spaces without effort or concern. The street looked like one of those shots in a film where nothing moves and, as each second passes, you wonder: is this a still? Then, suddenly, a brief ripple of air causes a branch to shift, a car passes or the eyes of the stationary watcher blink and you know we are still in motion, though once again nothing is moving.

As I walked I plucked leaves from the hedges and folded and crushed them between my fingers. I anticipated the best hedges, looking always for the thicker, more greenly crushable leaves. It is a kind of answer from the world, the sensation and the rank, vegetable smell on my fingers. But best of all was to spot a ripe flake of stone or brick on a garden wall and break it off as I passed, a violent acceleration of the weathering process.

Cars were parked on either side of the road and a single lane of traffic was stopped down the middle. There was some problem at the crossroads and everything felt cluttered, jammed. The houses were held back from this confusion by small, square gardens, all heavily and self-consciously planted, some with thick screens of vegetation to keep out noise and fumes. In one, I noticed an old woman in bulky disordered clothes. She was known to have been an actress of note in her prime, but some kind of madness had taken hold. Now she was bent over, plucking at the soil. I laughed briefly for no good reason and she looked up and stared angrily at me. At her windows, several cats pressed their heads against the burglar-proof grilles. She was not a subject for anger or laughter, she was being wonderful, doing what old ladies did. I walked another fifty yards and looked back. She had gone. I had put her off her gardening.

Scenes from the wealthy inner city suburb of Pointed Park: a nineteenth-century fantasy town. Bright white villas laid along whimsical street plans – mandorlas, sinuous roads of Yin and Yang – and brick elves' houses with carved barge boards, finials, gables and turrets. A triangle between two converging main roads, a railway station at its apex, a street of expensive shops at its base. Horatio Wilfred Argent built it; oval, sepia portraits with blurred edges show a dissident, self-made type wearing whiskers and a crumpled, cantankerous suit. They said it couldn't be done, he would run out of money. They attacked his version of Gothic. But he went ahead and built it. Swags of foliage burst from his bastardized columns. Ogees yearn up his façades. He built it.

I turned into a humbler street of three-storey houses with

deep basements into which you could peer over the heavy iron railings covered with tiny, globular, fruit-like encrustations from years of black overpaintings. In one of these basements lived Gerald, my back man.

On the face of it this back was a simple engineering problem, simple but not soluble, a result of the fine, fragile tolerances required for an upright animal. Left to my own devices with this defective mechanism, I would have died, panting in the open grassland waiting for a predator to finish me off, becoming, after the vultures, a dark stain on the verdure, dissolving into the soil, washed away by rain, a few particles carried off by the wind. From each you could reconstruct me, given time, given money. But nobody would. Away they would fly – little blown slivers of my potential consciousness. Here and there perhaps a brief pocket of remembrance of being Stephen Rix.

As the problem grew worse pain darted down my legs and locked my spine. My body had shifted over into a curious lopsided gait that had entertained the physiotherapists as quite exemplary. Then they had tried their gimmicks, their tricks, machines and convivial pep-talks employing a plastic model of the human spine to explain the mechanics of my disability. With each talk and each trick my condition grew worse. They were baffled but cheerful. I suggested their mechanics might be a misinterpretation. I'm an architect, I said, I know about these things. They gave me pitying looks, the pain was clearly fogging my mind. Doctors tried other devices, injections into my spine, more elaborate forms of physiotherapy and then, quietly, began talking of surgery. Stepping round the pools of their reticence, I learned that this involved recovering, prone and immobile, on a board for weeks. The thought of those hundreds of hours of stillness became, in my mind, worse than lifelong pain. I fought for breath at the prospect. Finally, a divorced friend of Jill's had suggested Gerald. He had cured her bizarre range of muscular and skeletal disorders and reformed her diet. I should try him. What had I to lose?

Gerald was a practitioner of Whole Person Massage. He told me the details of its oriental ancestry but I forgot it at once as I did everything else he said. I always thought of his sessions affectionately as dimly relaxing, painful and soporific by turns with an accompanying commentary of oriental wisdom, analysis and advice. I could recapture the general tone and some of the content – stress levels, vital fluxes and so on – but nothing in detail. It did not seem to matter. Gerald's athletic method had cured me at once. I went back every month out of gratitude.

The ritual was pleasurable in the same way as a visit to the dentist or a haircut – the pleasure of relaxing into an interlude of complete powerlessness. What must happen would happen. I enjoyed being the Stephen Rix that was an object of Gerald's work.

'Great! Stephen! Hi!'

He was standing waiting at the red basement door in his usual track suit, barefooted and beaming. His eyes were lost behind the flashes and reflections of his thick glasses. He beckoned me in. His basement was white and meagrely furnished. Scratchy rugs partly covered the concrete floors and books, balanced on shelves made out of bricks and planks, lined some of the walls.

He followed me as I headed mechanically for his treatment room, a white box decorated with a single, huge poster of the male human body with its meridians, fluxes, nodes and auras, all marked and identified.

'Well! Stephen! How've you been?'

'Fine, fine. Almost nothing. Slight stiffness, occasional twinge.'

'Overworking, I bet,' he said in his usual arch, admonitory tone.

Gerald launched into one of his long explanations involving many fluxes and meridians about why my job and my temperament were particularly bad for backs. As he did so we automatically went into our usual routine – me changing into a vest and track suit trousers that I kept at his place, he fussing about the room.

The first phase was always the most painful. He drove his thumbs into my stomach and leaned heavily to twist and pressure my limbs. While on my back looking at him, it was difficult to avoid conversation. This was mildly recriminatory as it emerged that I had drunk none of the herbal tea he had given me last time.

'It's very important for you,' he explained. 'I can keep your back right, but you need to help me by looking after your whole person. You have a tendency to drive your stress inward. I'm just counteracting that, but I can't correct it. You need to watch your diet and drink that tea, it relaxes and helps you externalize the negative energy. Got that, Stephen?'

'Got it. Externalize the negative energy. Right. I'm sorry, Gerald.'

'You have to start thinking of yourself as a single system. It's very interesting you're an architect. You're used to breaking things down into separate problems. Perhaps it has to be done that way. But the human being is a wholeness. If you have a pain in your back, it's because the whole balance of your life is wrong.'

'I'm convinced you're right. It makes perfect sense. Architects are always breaking things. How is the committee?'

Gerald was the secretary of our neighbourhood Millennium Committee and any reference to its work invariably distracted him from his lifestyle lectures.

'Not all bad. That dotty actress has resigned and we've got some real money coming in now. The street party is paid for and we're working on the memorial column. Of course, that's a lot more expensive, but it might happen. Mrs Rix is being great. I don't know how she finds the time . . . '

'I know, a wonder-worker. Ah!'

Gerald had found a particularly painful node. But soon the pain of his initial attentions began to wane. He had abandoned his pressings and leanings and had now moved into a gentler phase of stretching and pulling. I need do nothing but turn over when he instructed me. I would let him talk. In due course I turned over. Almost at once he stopped both talk and massage and began prodding painfully at a point just below my right shoulder blade.

'Hold on a minute. What's this?'

'What? Tumour or something?'

I thought of my numberless moles.

'No, no, no. What's been happening to you lately? Anything you haven't told me? You haven't been fainting a lot, have you?'

I twisted and stared at him.

'I feel I have a lot of confused energy here. It doesn't know which way to go and I don't know whether it's negative or positive. But it's just locked here. Very unbalancing. I don't think I've ever come across such an extreme case of a blockage.'

To be struck by the startling accuracy and precision of Gerald's words was a new experience for me. He appeared to have found my cathedral in my back.

'What exactly do you think it is, Gerald?'

'Well, I had a case like this – nothing like as strong but a similar conformation – with a woman who had decided to kill herself. She was quite happy and calm about it, but her meridians were fighting with all these conflicting signals. Her nodes were like rocks. And, much weaker but similar, you get this with marriage break-ups, job changes, house moves, the usual. But first impressions here . . . well . . . ' he prodded a little more, 'I can't begin to imagine . . . '

I wondered for a moment why anybody planning a suicide should bother to keep an appointment with Gerald. Perhaps it was a good idea. He had once told me of working on the fluxes of the terminally ill, giving them, I supposed, a positive attitude towards unbeing. Then I sighed and told him all as he prodded. He whistled.

'Wow! That's a first. This could take a lot of massage. Maybe you should come every day. What's going to happen? What are you going to do?'

'I don't know. Build it maybe. And I can't come every day. We'll just stick with the usual system. I'll get back when I can.'

The usual lasted an hour. The second half hour was always spent with me lying prone on the thin, greyish pad that kept me from the cold of his concrete floor. He would work energetically on my back, at the climax placing his big toe into the area of my kidneys and pulling my legs upwards until my face ground into the grey material and my body arched into a position that should have been agonizing. But, by this time, I had always begun to doze. I seemed to be sinking into the floor which, in my almost-dream, became a wall of my church. As I was forced into that curve, I felt my nose flatten against one of

71

its damp walls. I was a whole person. This body was me just as the observing mind was me.

Gerald brushed his palms over my back and announced he was finished. I rose awkwardly on to all fours and then to full height. I smiled weakly at him.

'Best to take a rest if you can.'

He always said this, I never could. I picked up my watch from the floor. I had twenty minutes before I had to meet Orlando and his developer.

'No chance.'

I changed hurriedly, gave Gerald his cheque and we fixed our next appointment. I climbed the steps from his basement and glanced back at him standing in his doorway. He seemed to have forgotten me and was staring vacantly at the sky through his glinting glasses.

'The whole person!' I shouted, clenching my fist in a salute of solidarity. 'Me!'

'That's right!' he cried, snapping out of his daze. 'Go with it! I'm really going to have to think about this cathedral stuff, maybe do some reading.'

I laughed at the idea that he could look it up in some oriental encyclopedia. 'Do that. Tell me what you find – any interesting cathedral cases. Happy New Year, Gerald, only nine months to go.'

'You too, Stephen, not long to go now.'

SIX

Whatever changes were to be required of me, I still felt the car must survive, though not necessarily the large, rugged, orange thing we used for family transport. This awful wagon flaunted its gross practicality as if to demonstrate that everything else on the road was inadequately equipped. Spare tyre, lights on chrome swivels, bulbous handles, mirrors, steps, even a ladder encrusted its exterior, while inside all seven seats offered a fantastic variety of entertainments, comforts and safety measures. The Rix family cruised and bounded over the countryside, smugly embodied as a single, rational, flamboyantly functional, four-wheeled, steel and fleshly soul called, according to the scroll of chamfered chrome that leapt across our rear door, Intruder.

No, the car I must have to journey to whatever came next was the car in which I travelled alone. This was an SL-4X, known to its few devotees and many detractors as a Leopard. Handbuilt by a small company that periodically filed for bankruptcy, always to be saved by some sentimental hoodlum with a yacht and white trousers, Leopards were rare and temperamental. Buying one was not a contract, it was an induction into a new identity. In truth, you could not really be said to buy a Leopard at all, rather you applied to be included in one.

About six months after paying your enormous, initial deposit you were invited to the factory, a dazzling yellow shed in a fold of suburban countryside. There a Mr Dentressangle, a legendary figure, welcomed you with coffee and a monologue about the difficulties of maintaining any degree of individuality in the mass-produced world of today.

'Humanity', I remembered him saying, 'is diminished when a man who can afford something better succumbs to the temptation to buy the sensible car. It is a question of accepting one's true self.'

Then you were shown your half-built car – in my case grandly marked across the windscreen 'Vehicle of Mr Stephen Rix' – and required to sit next to it in a molten white substance which moulded itself to your shape and dried at once. This eloquent effigy of the nearest space that was not you was used to model the seat and ideal driving position. A close and detailed interview about driving habits followed, covering speed, personal preferences, musical taste and the types of road normally covered. From this they built in customized adjustments to performance, suspension, sound systems and the stiffness of control switches – the latter determined by obliging you to drive a car connected to a computer that recorded the strength which you were prepared to devote to, for example, pushing a disc into the player. Mr Dentressangle then gave you another cup of coffee and engaged in a disquisition on the importance of the right car to gentlemen of your quality. Then he shook your hand and nothing happened for a further six months. Finally, without warning, Mr Dentressangle turned up at your home with the car. He did this early in the morning to 'catch you in' and departed having given you an 'owner's compendium' the size of a small suitcase. Thereafter you were regularly harassed by brotherly, enthusiastic mail from the thin ranks of other Leopard owners around the world and by reminders from Mr Dentressangle about the importance of regular services and of little maintenance routines.

'Have you', he wrote, 'remembered to check your windscreen

washer fluid this week? A small but, I'm sure you will agree, important detail.'

As a result of all this, the Leopard was regarded by many as the best car in the world. If it were not, why the effort? It would not have qualified on looks alone – the body was a series of obviously compromised attempts to encase its cabin, fantastically large engine and eccentric drive train into some supposedly nice shape. Bits of chrome were employed to conceal the many sculptural failures of the vehicle as well as a number of strange pleats and darts. Yet, as car rather than sculpture, it was unmatched. Certainly faster than anything else on the road, it had an unparalleled ability to convince the driver that he was one with the machine. You drove round corners as if you were walking round them, so utterly natural was the bodily action involved and so tightly did the tailored interior embed you in the machinery. I called it temperamental, but I had lately begun to realize that the vice was really mine and the car was simply a behavioural mirror.

My Leopard was green and its interior was a pale, sandy colour, a combination, I was assured, that was perfect for the sculptural dynamics of the vehicle. I drove with the roof down in all weather conditions short of actual precipitation and I was routinely jeered at, sneered at and spat at. The sheer bulky ugliness and excess of the machine brought out the worst in people and the terrible, apocalyptic, whining roar of the exhaust rendered them senseless with rage. I played the radio or discs, invariably at full volume, to drown out the abuse. In the Leopard I was somebody else, an untouchable half-machine in a car that was half-man.

I ran back from Gerald's session to change into my weighty, slithery, blue, meeting-a-developer suit, knowing that Orlando would expect nothing less. I heard Jill returning as I was changing.

'I'm late,' I said, passing her in the hall where she was standing, waiting for another opportunity to berate me.

'Try and get it right, Stephen, just do what you are supposed to do.'

'Absolutely! Precisely my intention – to do what I am supposed to do.'

75

I edged the Leopard thunderously out of the garage, a manoeuvre that provoked Dandy to a fit of hysterical barking, his paws scrabbling at the window. I set off for the office with a symphony of Hommelard's grinding, sullen and discordant, from the dashboard. Again I passed the old actress in the hat who had evidently fought through the swirling logic of her madness to make another attempt on the garden. At the sound of the music she flung down her basket and stood to attention, staring after me.

The journey took ten minutes, half a Hommelard movement. I parked in the office basement next to Orlando's grand tourer, an ancient, gleaming, blue Riviera with the downward swept tail of a motor launch.

The firm occupied the fourth floor of a daring, swooping, old office building from the summit of which rose a curved, tapering mast in white concrete, now stained with streaks of rust that bled from its interior, the sleep of a building pricking at its eyes. Nobody used the lift for fear of the stoppage threatened by the continual jolts. I ran up the stairs and pushed, panting, through the double doors of our offices. Late one night these doors had been painted in livid purple and gold by one of our trainees. We had intended to have this removed and the boy sacked until I noticed that he had included two small but perfectly painted figures. Almost hidden in the purple flames, there were Orlando and I. We were appropriately flattered and the painting and the trainee stayed.

Tina was at her desk, holding a mirror and pushing at her hair.

'Morning, Stephen, how you? Just in time. He's not here yet. Orlando's waiting for you.'

She gestured towards his office. I looked around Tina's partition to see, behind the glass, Orlando's bowed head, blue smoke rising about him.

'Great. Thanks Tina.'

I wasted a smile on her inattention and then strode down the open, white space of the office, ignoring the murmurs from the heads bowed over drawing boards, computers or flung back exhaling smoke in long tusks from their nostrils. I waved aside one hand, that of Bernard, raised to try and halt my progress in order to discuss some outstanding difficulty. Orlando rose to meet me, but I ducked away in the other direction into my own office.

I closed the door and stood motionless. There is a fashion for senior architects to work in glass-walled rooms as if they need to appear as operational specimens to their staff. The egalitarian idea was that they should be as assaulted by the daily attentions of others' eyes as was everybody else. The glass walls were only there at all as a gesture to the sensitivities of those outsiders who might expect at least acoustical privacy. Orlando, in spite of his aristocratic impulses, had felt driven to compromise with the style by half-glazing his office so that, when working, his bent head could just be seen. I, however, had chosen complete concealment. My office was a dark blue cube with a single, circular, exterior window over which a blind was more or less permanently drawn. Inside were a desk, a drawing board and an immense computer screen, each awkwardly isolated on a grey floor of ridged steel. For decoration there was a large, predominantly orange, abstract painting and a life-size bronze figure, roughly representing a man. I had no particular affection for these works, but the tone seemed about right, more or less what was expected. Today they disgusted me. I kicked the statue and it rang dully. I opened the blind and looked down into the street. A red car had pulled up outside the building and a curiously shaped man was struggling out. He looked up and down the street, fastening his jacket button with one hand and stroking his hair with the other. Then he came through our front door.

I closed the blind, waited for a few moments and then went to join Orlando. I slipped into his office, sat down and even began idly sketching before allowing myself to meet his eyes. I felt as always that his conspiracy with Jill allowed me a few moments of icy vengeance.

He was leaning across the frosted glass sheet of the table giving me his nervy, urgent, pre-business look.

'Stephen,' he said rapidly, 'let us, for God's sake, make an effort for me, for us, for them maybe. I know you are in a mood. I can tell.'

Had he already spoken to Jill that morning? To make his

point he waved at his half-glazed wall. Beyond sat the two rows of our sad architects, their soft, dishevelled clothes hanging from bony shoulders and their faces pale and fatigued. The sight of those ragged shapes must have made him grateful for my blue suit.

'I suppose I should be pleased that at least today you don't look too odd. Appearances, though deceptive, can be our salvation.'

I followed his gaze out into the office. 'Make your choice, Orlando. God, you or them, which is it to be? Who is it really for?'

'Oh dear, he's going to be difficult. Not cathedrals today, Stephen, OK? Anything but cathedrals.'

As I looked into the office Tina appeared from behind the partition that mercifully concealed her from the rest of the staff. As usual she had decided to add to the mysterious burdens of the pale, young men by clicking down the aisle between their drawing boards, high-heeled and tightly dressed, her curls bobbing. One sad head after another rose in turn to answer the inevitable call of her hips etc. Bernard closed his eyes and sniffed the scented, disturbed air as she passed.

'This way. They're ready for you,' she called without looking back.

She appeared to be talking to empty space. But then a man of absurd proportions appeared from behind the partition and began to pace slowly in Tina's wake. His body flared impossibly in two single parabolas that reached their most distant points at his waist and then tapered smoothly to the crown of his head. The usual articulations of neck, chest, waist and calves were missing. He seemed to have been conceived as a single shape in deliberate defiance of any known ideal. Even his hair, short and spiked, leaned inward to continue the smooth directional flow of his geometry. What should have been his chin was a stubbly discoloration from which projected a cigar clenched ferociously in the gleaming teeth that were now revealed by the immense grin he was dispensing like charity to the gaunt, frustrated figures as he passed. In what must have been a calculated clash with his bodily geometry, the briefcase he carried was small, shiny, hard and rectangular.

Tina clicked on, not noticing that the man behind her had paused to clutch at one bony shoulder, that of Bernard, the fragment of smoking emotional wreckage that had tried to stop me. His hand must have closed on almost nothing but grey shirt and maroon waistcoat, the flesh beneath being so wasted by the austere, disciplined aspirations to non-being of the young and creative. Through the glass screen of the conference room I just caught his words, delivered as he waved with his cigar at Bernard's drawing.

'Like it! Like it! *I* like it! What's your name?'

'Bernard.'

'Bernard, I like it!'

He nodded his thanks through a sudden coughing fit, brought on by the shock. The hand was removed and I noticed dark sweat stains from the man's fingers left behind on the flimsy fabric. Now Bernard was being patted therapeutically on the back. Tina, meanwhile, had stopped clicking as her heels encountered the conference room's grey, flecked carpet.

'Mr David Hirtenstein,' she said, her face slightly flushed by her rapid, unnaturally taut and erect gait. When nothing happened in response to the name, she simply stared without any decipherable emotion at the frozen tableau of Orlando and I facing each other: he imploring, I with my head twisted away from his demand, the better to watch Hirtenstein's approach. The tableau held and then, finally, our visitor elbowed his way past Tina and Orlando broke away to welcome him.

'Dave, it's been so long . . . '

Orlando had risen and become appealingly fulsome, a talent of his whenever confronted by a possible client.

'Right, right,' said Hirtenstein, his smile having weakened fractionally with an instant animal awareness that he was being sold something. He held Orlando's eyes for an unsettling moment and then, as if reluctantly deciding he had nothing to lose, shook his hand.

'Dave, I'd like you to meet Stephen Rix, my partner.'

Hirtenstein swivelled and paced rapidly towards me. Cornered by his purposeful advance, I rose and took the pale white hand. Like the rest of his body it appeared to be a single shape, the surplus flesh smoothing out the contours of the individual fingers. He allowed it to rest in mine without pressure or movement. In silence he held my eyes for even longer than he had Orlando's. He smiled shrewdly.

'You think I'm a fat, ugly bastard, don't you, Steve?'

'Well yes, actually, Dave, I do.'

I was pleased both with the remark and my response. Beyond what would have been Hirtenstein's shoulder, I saw Orlando's eyes close and two fingertips rise to the bridge of his nose.

'You're thinking: this fat, ugly bastard will be dead of a heart attack inside five years. And you've already worked out that whatever I turn out to be like will be some sort of compensatory behaviour for my horrible appearance. And really deep down – I know you won't admit this one – you're thinking nobody this fat and this ugly can be good, not good at work and not good in life. You don't have to say anything, Steve, we understand each other.'

These were slightly more contentious propositions than his first, so I waited, less for thought or to ponder the accuracy of his reading of my mind than to see what he would say next. I had not actually gone as far in my imagination as he had suggested, but the logic seemed plausible enough. He turned away from me and carried on talking as he paced around the room and the frozen figure of Orlando.

'Well you're right about the fat and ugly bit, spot on. But I'm not going to have a heart attack, I don't compensate and I'm not bad. For a start I may be fat, but I'm fit, very fit. Fitter than you, Orlando baby.'

He poked my partner in the stomach and then placed his impractically slim briefcase on the table, his cigar in the ash tray, turned to face the wall, raised his arms in the air, took two paces forward and rolled smoothly over so that he was standing on his hands, the soles of his feet resting on the white wall where they made small, grey, cloud-like scuff marks. His clothing was strangely undisturbed by this procedure; the jacket and trousers crumpled a little and one pocket flap inverted, but otherwise nothing. He continued talking from this position.

'No heart attack, you see. I work out every day. But more to the point . . . ' he now let his feet drift away from the wall and began walking on his hands, ' . . . I'm a fat, ugly bastard who's in control, who knows what he's doing, right?'

He raised one arm off the ground, wobbling, but only slightly.

'Right, Dave,' said Orlando nervously.

'And I'm also a fat ugly bastard who's given himself the chance to make something beautiful and that's why I'm here.'

Orlando laughed with frightened abandon and nodded in enthusiastic agreement with this wisdom while simultaneously directing a pleading expression towards me and applauding softly the gymnastics. A couple of the thin, bony ones in the office outside had stood hesitantly to look over their drawing boards at the sight of these shining black shoes rising above the glass partition. Hirtenstein ignored Orlando and, returning his second hand to the floor, took one swaying hand step closer to me. He was small so his shoes only came up to the middle of my chest. Around my ankles the expression on his face suggested he was about to accuse me of something, though the inversion made it hard to tell. But he said nothing, turned away after a few moments as if having arrived at some conclusion, flipped back to stand on his feet and briskly seated himself at the table, his face reddened. Orlando breathed again and signalled to Tina to bring tea.

'Always unexpected, eh, Dave? Even acrobatics, very impressive. Now, Stephen, David's company Foundations . . . '

'Foundations?'

'Yeah, yeah. Says it all,' breathed Hirtenstein, waving his cigar.

'Of course.'

'Foundations are . . . is looking,' Orlando continued, 'at a number of possible leisure developments. Big leisure developments.'

'Beautiful leisure developments,' added Hirtenstein, 'foundations of the future! Foundations of a new culture!'

Orlando, I consoled myself, must know what he was doing. Ever since our early experience with the weirder end of the spectrum of property developers we had tried to work solely with those with no more than slight eccentricities or minimal megalomania. In our maturity we reasoned that only with the dullest and most reliable partners could we freely indulge our few modest extravagances and keep our youngsters from ultimate despair and unemployment. Hirtenstein appeared to be a throw-back, one of those dangerous temptations from the heady, early days of the partnership, perhaps even from the lime green picnic. They would turn up in exotic, disordered clothes, wave fabulous sums of money before our visionary eyes, talk of art and then vanish leaving us with hundreds of hours' worth of useless drawings of Fun Pavilions, Play Palaces and Urban Experiences. But Orlando was deferring with unusual intensity for this to be simply another crooked, ambitious, rich charlatan. He could, when detecting time wasters, become extraordinarily rude.

'And,' Orlando continued, 'Dave is interested in our approach. He is especially fond of the Soolio Theatre . . . '

'Yeah, I am,' said Dave, 'but that was marking time. Good of its type, but a type whose time has gone. What we want now is a new architectural language for a new age. I want to know if you guys are up to it.'

This wearied me. In spite of the entertaining madness of Hirtenstein, we had begun to go down the familiar route of artistic babble and pompous justifications employed as dressing for the same old compromised tat. Let us just get on with the usual office block or apartment building. On the other hand I, I then remembered, was not the same person who had done this so often in the past.

'Which particular new age would that be exactly?' I asked with a calming note of polite enquiry.

'There's only one and it's coming, Steve, believe me, it's coming.'

'The trouble is,' I began, Orlando spotting at once from this phrase that I was not about to play the game, 'that architecture isn't a language and this age isn't new. Call me a sentimental old fool . . . '

Orlando's features died, the gloss faded.

'I shall *never*', he murmured, 'call you a sentimental old fool.'

Hirtenstein had turned to face me, a neckless movement necessarily involving his entire body. His expression indicated aggression.

'Before there were cities,' he said with an unexpectedly analytical air, 'there was no country. The idea of the rural derives its energy from the idea of the urban. Right?'

He was determined to make it clear that I had misjudged him. Years of suffering veiled contempt for his appearance had written this script as surely as it had written his earlier onslaught. Intending to provoke a philistine builder, he was making it clear that I had encountered a philosopher–constructor.

'I mean,' he continued, 'I've been through all the anti-progressive bit, the communes and so on. Remember Dave the Man Hirtenstein?'

This was directed at Orlando who recovered rapidly to glow with the sudden warm presence of a fond memory.

'Yes . . . yes. Ah yes.' Orlando actually rubbed his hands at this point. I feared for the last remnants of his dignity.

'But I grew up. Now I'm Dave the Developer Hirtenstein. I realized the buildings would happen anyway, progress would go on. The trick was to make it right. Work yourself into the position of the scum-of-the-earth property developer and then go with it. Build the new age, the new cities, the new countryside. It's started already. Look at my Spear Court – nothing like that anywhere in the world. A building to grace the Millennium . . . And the things I've put up under the Open Countryside Scheme in the Rural Beauty Zones. I've changed the idea of the rural.'

I was dimly aware of Spear Court, a vast, green building rising by the river, and of the way Orlando had frequently grown pale and silent when talking of the sums being spent. And we too had been involved in the wave of rural developments following the decision to derestrict planning in the Rural Beauty Zones. More important than silent, pastoral contemplation, it had been decided, was the need to spread the population more evenly across the land.

Tina brought in the tea, smiled at Orlando and glanced through me, apparently at the floor beneath.

'Everything all right?'

'Perfect,' said Orlando with bright irony. 'Milk? Sugar?'

'I have found new reasons for style,' Hirtenstein continued, angered by the interruption, 'new justifications after the death of the Gothic god or the classical *polis*. In the ruins of clapped-out bourgeois humanism, my buildings will raise a new rationality, define a new justice, welcome the new Millennium. Buildings for a species that will have landed on Mars. Mars! That, Steve, will be the big one. Black, please.' He took a small purple tin of artificial sweeteners from his pocket.

It was, I mused to myself, rare to hear such sentiments expressed in the manner of a professional hoodlum's threat of extreme violence. Nevertheless, Hirtenstein was beginning to make some sense. He would have been an eager radical reader of all the right books in his young days, patronized by the likes of Orlando as a marginal clown doomed to hustle for attention at the periphery. Then, in the blinking of an eye, he would have taken on significance. All that earnest learning would become the foundation for a programme of action demanded by the urgency of the age. The fat fool had, all along, been more firmly plugged into history than any of them.

Orlando was now hurrying to salvage the situation, fussing with tea and pouring forth practical explanations for this meeting. Hirtenstein was smiling benignly back, even once shaking his head in my direction in a conspiracy of agreement about poor Orlando's limitations. This must be revenge for the awful power play of their earlier relations when Orlando would have queened, glorious and contemptuous, over the little fat man and his books.

'As I recall,' he was saying, 'you were arguing the last time we met, Dave, that the superfluity of the idea of leisure . . . '

'Freed style, exactly, liberated the architect. Liberated us all. Long live the revolution!'

'Have you considered the possibilities of Gothic?' I asked.

Orlando appeared to be struggling with this, unsure of how far I intended to go with the question and alarmed that it might be all the way.

'Gothic', I continued, 'tells you a story of the earth. It tells you that there is something else apart from this muddy plot. Classical is that something else – completion here on earth. Gothic is incomplete. A pointed arch is not a resolved form. It is broken and only repaired by the sense of its own balance – of counterposing forces held in check. In classical the forces are dissolved, the narrative is over. Gothic is a story, a narrative of significance designed to tell us something that is still happening and in which we, therefore, have a part. Dynamic equilibrium.'

Hirtenstein looked startled and then excited, Orlando weary; he could not see the money at the end of this, only more of Dave's auto-critique.

'Right! Right! I see where you're going, Steve. This would make Gothic the logical leisure architecture. Right?'

'Well, quite the opposite, I would . . . '

'No, no! Dave's quite right,' Orlando burst in, having immediately realized that I was about to sacrifice this one unexpected advantage. 'Gothic would be the new language of leisure.'

'Impossible,' I insisted. 'Pleasure dome – dome, you see. Classical. Nice restful curves . . . All leisure developments have domes . . . or spheres. Mainly spheres, in fact, a few domes. Some spires, I suppose.'

'But this', Dave's whole body had begun rocking slightly, 'is the new dynamic leisure. Endless becoming, not the stasis of eighteenth-century gardens or follies, no more of those phoney globes.'

As he said this a moment of obvious possibility flickered across my mind, an intuition that this preposterous debate might lead somewhere, back to the field maybe, back to the possibility of doing something with my cathedral. My talk of Gothic had been intended as a way of idly toying with Orlando. But now I felt again the pressure of Ralph's message – build it, build it – was Hirtenstein to be the means? Strange messages delivered by stranger messengers.

'Maybe,' I said, picking up a pencil from the conference table and starting a sketch, 'you have a point.'

'Right!' cried Hirtenstein, 'I have a point, a pointed arch!' He glanced at my sketch, the outline of a crocket. 'Wow! You really are into this, aren't you? You really are the man for Gothic. Gothic Steve. Like it. Meet me at my gym tomorrow. Early. Talk to my secretary. We'll take it further. I think I like this. No, no, I'm sure I like it. This could be big. I like your style, Steve.'

And with that he left, this time ignoring everybody in the office except Tina whom he kissed briefly on the lips as he gave her his card and rubbed her thigh. She neither objected nor reacted.

Orlando at once recovered his non-client composure.

'That was a bit quick, but we appear to have achieved something. You appear to have done something, partner, but I shudder to think what. I shudder.'

'You've been talking to Jill again, you bastard.'

He lowered his eyelids in an expression of queenly confidence.

'Of course. Why not? Your state of, I use the word advisedly, mind is of urgent concern to both of us, though I sometimes wonder why you oblige us to spend so much time on the subject. There are, I think, other minds.'

'Sorry to be a bother.'

'There are also practical considerations,' he waved at the bent figures, 'as well as, shall we say, domestic duties, responsibilities. Even without this church, neither seemed to occupy quite the place in your priorities we – Jill and I – might have liked. I suppose you'll be out for the rest of the day . . . it is *that* day isn't it? The day for your bit of stuff.'

'Don't talk to me about practicalities after that little piece of theatre. Look at Hirtenstein. I appear to be just the kind of madman he needs. He likes my style. Being like me can bring in business, Orlando. Funny business, but still business. And, yes, it is *that* day. I'm off.'

I headed back down the office, this time letting Bernard intercept me. He had been working to complete the balcony design I had left unfinished. Orlando had quietly brought my drawings back to the office. Bernard was, predictably, puzzled by the sleight of hand I had stolen from Rizzoli.

'I don't get it. It looks great, but I don't get it.'

I gave him the reference.

'It's all there, Bernard, just lift it.'

'What?'

'Lift it.'

'Oh, thanks, Stephen, thanks . . . Is it all right to do that, to lift it?'

'Yeah, yeah. Absolutely. We're not purists here. It happens all the time. And don't thank me, thank Rizzoli.'

I tried to regain the momentum of my leaving.

'Oh, Stephen,' Bernard called after me, 'why was that guy upside down?'

'Just wish I knew, Bernard, just wish I knew. I think he was making a point.'

I retraced three steps to clutch his shoulder as Hirtenstein had done and then left, swaggering slightly and ignoring Tina before she could ignore me. In the Leopard I changed the music to a monastic chant and headed across town, accompanied by the usual jeers. My head was light with excitement and anticipation of almost everything.

SEVEN

'STEEEPHEN!'

Inside. There had been a sound in the room and now there was a weak longing, a momentary tension of dry lips, a flickering of the eyelids, a long exhalation – clouds and great mists were floating above – at some remote point there was a painful need for tension in the relaxed limbs as if in the bed there was suddenly too much space and the body was too weak to fill it . . .

The sound had been a soft cry. A voice.

'Steeeephen!'

Again. The sound may have been inside – imagined or dreamed. The voice may have called to itself. Or outside. This room was real.

It did not matter for now it was moving away. It had begun to have happened at another place, another time. Here there was only this spreading stairway and these crowds slowly advancing downwards. Murmuring. A great, high coolness.

'Oh Steeeeephen!'

The bed again and now clothes on the floor, tangled like flotsam. And a hand pulling at the arm across the enormous bed. This may still have been inside. But there was an answer anyway, emitted with a slight gasp of effort.

'Yes! Here. Must be here.'

'Hungry baby. Really hungry. Let's eat. Must eat.'

But nothing moved, no more was said and the doze restored itself – moving out, moving in; ebbing, flowing, the stairway now empty but for one woman who asked about the fish and pointed. They lay overlapping on slabs.

Moving outward there was a white cloth on the wall – a cotton banner covered in splashes of paint. A large mirror with a golden frame.

Moving inward again there were now clouds and an underground sea. A beach with more people and some peaceful horned animals.

'Really, really must eat.'

Again it might have been dreamed, but the mirror had come back.

And now the bed creaked and bounced and there was a room again. In the room the presence split and located itself as two. There were two of us. And the other was moving. It had come from outside. She had been speaking.

'Let's go!'

She slapped my face, quite hard. I was back, thinking.

The doze, this was the first regretful thought as I stretched my muscles and compressed my face, is the true condition of the organism, a delicious state in which time drags rather than vanishes as in sleep and the mind still takes in the little intrusions of the world – traffic, the tapping of a blind against an open window, birdsong, the wind, voices from another room, the heavy gyrations of a fly. Yet still you dream – slow fantasies in saturated colour, memories, stories. Water rushed and bubbled in streams that fed that underground sea: in the room as I slipped down into sleep, in my head as I rose to consciousness. The doze crosses back and forth between outer and inner, what might be true and what might not.

' . . . the celebrations which will begin in earnest in the autumn when schoolchildren around the world . . . '

She had turned on the radio.

In the doze hours may seem to pass. But they don't, only

89

moments. The world continues slowly, interrupted by flowing episodes of liquid dream. This dozing is the higher life, the longer life. To doze means that you have kept the lower at bay. The things that make you move and act are disabled. Time slows that it may be examined more closely.

I tugged her back into the bed and tried to re-enfold her into the warmth and the doze. She relaxed and let me, but the tone of her body told me we were getting up, it was time to eat. Now I was irretrievably back in the room.

' . . . said that the Millennium would be the greatest world-wide festival since . . . '

There was no returning, not for now. She kissed me briefly, slapped me again, gentler this time, and pulled herself away.

It was *that* day, as Orlando called it, the day I visited Francesca's flat and her bed, the day for my dozing and the submarine life of the lover Stephen Rix. The time seldom varied, but the encounter always happened as if by accident. She was never fully dressed when I arrived, though I somehow took this to be due to inattention rather than sexual practicality. I had run up the three floors to her flat, still suffused with optimism, still laughing at the idea of Hirtenstein's Gothic. This time she had been wearing a satin dressing gown which she slipped off to welcome me with drowsy enthusiasm.

'Oh, Stephen, hello, lovely Stephen. You've come to be mine for a while. Now get into bed.'

The words 'no problem, no problem' whispered in my mind as I swam peacefully into her arms and sank into the controlling logic of her body.

For there were no demons in the perpetual twilight of her flat, nor in the benign white expanse of that bed. There were no bad dreams. Her rooms were contrived to be indecisive, unclear, seen only through the corner of an eye. Thin white blinds, always drawn, cast a uniform, dusty glow. There were deep shadows and hazy pools of darkness in every room. The furniture was low, amorphous and soft, white lamps stood on the rough beige carpet casting circles of weak, yellow-ish light. Even, I noticed, where the walls met the ceilings the plaster waved and rippled.

The one clarity in this shimmering pond was the organized

ferocity of her reading. In this she was systematic and rapid. She felt compelled to know the contents and preoccupations of all the new novels and biographies. She read with ritual precision, sitting on her sofa, her knees up, in the one hard bright pyramid of light she permitted herself. This spread about her from a black gallows of springs and struts bolted to the undulating wall. They were the only straight lines in her home.

'I read, Stephen,' she would explain, 'because it's better than life.'

Her work, however, was lost in the same fog of imprecision as her furniture. She grew bored, her face compressed with irritation, if asked to explain what she did.

'Oh not now, Stephen, life's too short . . . '

So, over the months, I had assembled little more than a few hints of meetings, telephone calls, the occasional trip and the barest suggestion of some form of research into what people thought and why. Once I was too persistent in pressing for more detail.

'It is not for you, Stephen,' she had snapped. 'You know that. Behave.'

We had met because she had visited the office to question me about my work, opinions, clothes and food. That same day I had taken her to lunch and we had come back to this flat.

'Yes, Stephen, let's go back to my home and make love. That will be so nice. Let me look after you.'

Into this life I plunged, a myopic diver in its blurred depths. I watched her floating before me – the swimmer's body, the long hair, the pale face, the heavy nose and wide mouth. And the water rushed and bubbled from the breathing equipment that I needed and she did not . . . rushed and bubbled inside and out.

I had only once met somebody else from her life – Moira, a friend since school; short-haired, tall and with a glow of fierce common sense in her eyes.

'You're perfect for her,' explained Moira, 'easily dominated. Don't feel bad about the mistress bit. The guilt stuff. You don't have to say you're going to leave your wife. She doesn't want any more of you. She just wants you to turn up and

91

be run by her. And, of course, that's exactly what you really want as well, isn't it, Stephen?'

I had looked at Moira, seeking a clue to the roots of this insight. But her glazed eyes gave me nothing.

'I know her very well,' she added. 'I know exactly what she wants, Stephen. She's perfect. She'll hurt you when the time comes. But, for now, you don't make trouble.'

The closedness, the opacity of this sex. I loved Francesca and the idea of these inner defences, patrolled by Moira, made me jealous, dizzy and sick. I resented the closed certainty of the idea that a man in her life meant a series of episodes made more clearly episodic by the perpetually unresolved fact of adultery. I tried to prise something out of her. But she repeated: 'Not for you, Stephen, not for you . . . ' Perhaps this was what kept me here, the suspicion that there was more to come; as if this secret were the promise of some superbly exotic sexual variation. One day I would be initiated. Before then I was trapped. But, no, there was more. I loved her to the death, my death. And she loved me, but, for her, love had moved on to become a controlled convenience.

The tone of the radio voice had changed. The Mars mission was in some kind of trouble. I quickly tried to grasp the sense.

' . . . may be the result of a computer malfunction that mission control describes as "a cause for concern". The crew have been instructed to get some rest before tackling . . . '

Now she was up, dressing purposefully while I swung to sit on the side of the bed and ground the heels of my hands into my eyes.

'What's happened? Did you hear what they just said? Captain Dale's in trouble.'

'Is he? Oh dear. We must pity the poor captain, mustn't we, Stephen? Boys' games can turn dangerous.'

Perhaps because of Francesca's strict limitations on my knowledge, our conversations were never really about imparting information. The talk was full of incompletion and dislocation. She spoke to me as if from some lofty perspective. But I did not quite feel patronized, rather verbally cuddled, swaddled, bound like a child. Her refusal to allow logical development made being with her unexpected, unplanned, an always random progress through my requirement for a rationality that would allow me to move on to the next thing and hers for an avoidance of final exposure and certainty . . .

'I was dreaming, a perfect dream,' I attempted to explain as I leaned into a standing position and she turned off the radio and danced towards the door, already cloaked in heavy, black woollen triangles. Her clothes followed some alternative, alien fashion injunctions. In everything she operated according to her own laws. Once she was outside none of the calculated haze of her interior would cling to her. Her exteriors were permeated with a bright magic. The world became crystalline and jewel-like as if miniaturized. Surfaces here did not become porous and rough when you looked closer, they really were smooth. Outside and inside, her flexible, expert, inaccessible soul managed the difference without a thought. Once outside I could not bother her with talk of dreams.

So she paid no attention and waited by the open door as I dressed awkwardly in front of the mirror. I felt humid and heavy and I thought of Captain Dale. I was frustrated not to know what was the matter. Were they going to die? A bad start for the new Millennium. At last we clattered down the stairs and into the street, the cold sunlight bursting into yellow spears about my head and a small figure with dry, grey hair and shawls tugging at my sleeve.

'Hello, dear, buy some lucky heather for the young lady . . . ' I pulled my sleeve away. 'Suit yourself, I hope she dies of it.'

Francesca, holding my hand, pulled me along at a speed that made me, still in semi-doze, feel the air was as thick as water parting before me. Her long hair trailed and danced.

This world was hers, not mine, clear and imbued with a toy-like contingency. It was bright, cold and clear. Birds pecked and bobbed on cobble stones. We raced through a square with a market that seemed to have been flung together by a child. The stalls were covered with red and white plastic awnings flapping gaily in a breeze that had sprung up since this morning. The remains of some baroque arcading that must have once surrounded the square had been glazed over. They were filled self-consciously with tables, each covered with

93

paper tablecloths of acidic blue. I looked through the glass at the tables and a scattering of people peering into the flat, round pools spread before them. A waitress was tugging at the brown plastic tray beneath one man's coffee and sandwich. He stared uncomprehendingly at her and then back at the blue.

A man wearing dazzling white overalls, a thick, orange scarf covering his mouth and black shoes walked by, nursing under each arm a comically enlarged plastic bottle of water.

We found ourselves behind two men in tight, dark overcoats. They walked slowly, but, for the moment, we were unable to pass because of the crowd.

'I'd just tell him because it's costing me money,' said one. 'There can't be any problem. It's all in the same batch.'

'The guy who's with Jimmy,' said the other, 'who is he?'

'Don't worry. Jimmy knows his stuff.'

'Sure, Jimmy knows his stuff.'

'I don't want to spend my mornings down here. You know what I mean – I've got things to do.'

'Captain Dale's in trouble.'

'Yeah, I heard.'

By skipping briefly off the pavement into the gutter, they deliberately disturbed a flock of pigeons that was feeding on some bread thrown from a café table. The birds were suddenly everywhere, the wings creaking and rasping at the air as they stood up into the breeze and twisted desperately to be off.

Then we dived downwards into the black lacquered basement that was Francesca's favourite restaurant. The air turned from rushing cold to steady warmth. Waiters in striped waistcoats, menus. Music was playing, tinkling and warbling. On each table a silk flower in a slender blue glass vase. She ordered for us both. They recognized us.

'Nice to see you again, madame, sir.'

Our silk flower was replaced with a bunch of real, pink carnations.

'Only for our regulars, you understand.'

There was a still silence until the food came. I looked at her across the table, moving aside the flowers to see her better. She was preoccupied with assessing and reorganizing the contents of her plate. Looking more closely, I saw she was separating out

the water chestnuts. She glanced up and smiled, slightly embarrassed about the childishness of the act. She had long passed out
of our earlier daze, a condition in which embarrassment would
not have been possible, and into our afternoon mode of more
definite consciousness. By the evening she would almost be in
my world of real work and bared souls. Sometimes, late in the
day, I had almost been able to see her as just another person,
somebody good or bad at her job, more or less acceptable to
my friends, somebody I could assess instead of this fabulous,
guarded mystery. But then, always, she would see the danger,
turn and rush away until my next day.

But had everything now changed? Had I lost the world that
made me a visitor in Francesca's? Seeing cathedrals did not fit,
it was a greater mystery. So what next? Could I continue with
this benign arrangement? I sensed now that it might only work
because of the contrast: my work and love – her reticence
and indulgence. If I had slipped out of my world, perhaps
I had also slipped out of hers.

'I *love* water chestnuts, don't you, Stephen?'

I felt a familiar, though always shocking, hollow in my
stomach. This time it was at the moment of her closing her
eyes on the word 'love'. I swallowed slightly and looked down
to conceal the passing weakness. She thought I was searching
for water chestnuts on my plate and reached across to help me
find some.

'There!'

She found one, picked it up with her fingers, pushed it
sloppily into my mouth and then patted my cheek.

'Eat up, Stephen. Delicious, aren't they?'

'Perfect. Heaven.'

I looked back to catch her eye so that we could play with the
possibilities of the metaphor. But she had returned to truffling
through her own brown and green collation.

'She's a bright girl who needs pushing. And now I've got
everybody concentrating on their goals, I feel really on top of
things.'

It was the voice of a young and raw-faced company man,
having lunch at the next table with a more quietly spoken
friend.

'We're going to pull through on this one. That book, it works. Management Targets, that's the secret.'

And, as I looked, I knew that my cathedral did not separate us. I knew that it meant we had to be together. Raw-face rambled on.

'It's back to: you can handle what people say about you, but you can't handle what people say about other people. I know full well that of all the gossip sources, she would be number one.'

'I think it actually frightens me how different you are from Jill. It says something nasty about things.'

Somebody else seemed to have spoken the words. They did not come from my thoughts. Francesca's eyes narrowed. Such conversations would invariably sharpen her wits. Relationships, psychology, this was home territory to her. I was trespassing. These were not 'soft' subjects, they were hard, tough, real. In this, I supposed, she would have agreed with Jill. But Francesca's research was more thorough. She had actually lived for some years with a psychologist. After they separated, she had been misdiagnosed as having some terminal illness. This misunderstanding, the failure of communication, the fact that she had somehow given the doctors the wrong signals, the fact that she had appeared to flirt with oblivion without ever really doing so all fitted the Francesca of the mornings perfectly. She had told the psychologist.

'OK, I'm not interested for now,' he had said, 'but I want to be at the death bed scene.'

Perhaps he had been expecting something like this crisis, aware, as I and probably most of her lovers had become, of the way she would always appear to be on the edge of being somewhere quite different.

Nevertheless his attitude appalled me. Of course, she had quite liked it, deriving some degree of icy reassurance from the possibility of such detachment. She had, however, admitted it was a relief to return to the normal responses of other men after he emigrated. I smiled to find myself in such a category. 'Normal' naturally meant 'controllable'. But the whole affair had left her with a startling, analytical harshness when it came to 'relating'. It was in this realm that she was most passionately involved, it was here that her reactions suggested that she thought she was living her real life. Her language instantly hardened.

'You mean it implies you are capricious and inconsistent – one of us *must* be the wrong person for you, but you are too weak to work out which. Is that right, Stephen? Is that what you are trying to say?'

'No, no. Nothing so specific. It's just that if people are *that* different, how does the language work at all? It's a miracle we can agree that the sky is blue, that up is up and down down. Fixing lunch is a triumph of the imagination and an absurd act of faith that all the basics are agreed.'

This dandyish conceit had moved us safely out of the landscape of the psychological into that of the philosophical: my place. She relaxed – this was not urgent, this was 'soft' – and turned again to her food. Her long dark hair shaded her face. She always looked as if she had just come in from the rain, faintly bedraggled.

'Well, *our* lunches are like that anyway.' She spoke suddenly and without interrupting her increasingly unproductive search for water chestnuts.

'Sorry?'

'Lunch – a triumph of the imagination, absurd act of faith. So's fucking. Fucking you is fucking fantastic, Stephen.'

She smiled at me with languid, superior affection, loosening every nerve in my body and making me wonder why we were bothering with this business of eating.

'Well, of course, that's all right for us. But it's not really a programme for living. Men should have children and dogs, a role in life, status, not just this . . . indulgence.'

'Oh, forget all that crap. What it's all about is loving and being loved and you take that where you find it. Anybody who tells you different is a liar! You just don't like things being that obvious, it's too simple, you want interesting complications. But it's not necessary. This might just be the boring old love for which we were made. Can't take that, eh, Stephen?'

Well, of course, but if that's all *this* is about, what's all *that* about? I couldn't just love and be loved and walk away from my church. The response seemed feebly inadequate. I was stung by the rebuke of her purism and the soft lash of her mild sneer. I felt

97

myself sliding resentfully into disclosure. We ate silently for a few moments. Then my hunger left me as I decided to speak.

'There's something rather big I haven't told you.'

She looked up, suddenly alert, her face composing itself into coldness against the news she most expected – goodbye. But, instead, I smiled soothingly and told her about the church. This time I was able to include the Hirtenstein development as a curious, realistic twist.

'You mean he'll build it? Stephen, are you sure?'

'No, I'm not sure. I haven't even told him about it yet, not specifically. But he might. Anyway, I would have thought it's a small step from walking on your hands to building a Gothic cathedral.'

'And you've already walked through it. It was – sort of – built.'

'Not sort of, completely. It was there, it just isn't now. Come up. I'll show you where.'

'To your country place? I've told you, Stephen . . . '

'Yes, to the country place.'

It was too direct an invitation into that other life. She had always accepted adultery as the condition of our love. She had not seemed to want more and she despised the role of demanding lover, preferring potent mistress. 'She knows', Moira had said, '*precisely* what she is doing.' Going to the country with me had always been too much, a crossing of some line. But now I saw that matters had to be resolved, cleared up, and I suddenly knew how.

'This is all new, a different world. There is no pretending this didn't happen. I've been called or I've called myself. I've been told to stop messing about with all these compromises. We're a compromise. I don't want that any more. I want to be with you for a long time, perhaps for ever. I am going to stay up there, sort this out . . . maybe. I think you sort me out. But anyway I want you there with me. It could be . . . heaven.

'And,' I added anti-climactically, 'you could meet this guy Ralph.'

I felt breathless, shocked at myself and suddenly dizzy. I looked and looked at her and saw . . .

'I think I've cracked it this time,' Raw-face exploded enthusiastically. 'I really think I've cracked it. High performance stuff, well inside budget. Oh, yeah, have you heard about the Mars mission? Big problems. Some kind of explosion. Checkout time for Captain Dale McCluskey.'

I turned to snarl at the next table, but Francesca's voice cut through my anger.

'OK, Stephen, you want us to leave then?'

'What here? I've not finished.'

'No. Leave. Go and try your plan. Stay down there. Leave – live, you know. If you are expecting me to change my life, you could concentrate, Stephen.'

She looked and looked at me, thinking; her lower lip caught between her teeth for a moment giving her a worried look. But her eyes were steady. What was I? How much of her was I worth? It would be over one day, like everything else. Nothing is for ever or, rather, nothing *is* for ever. Just that, nothing else. And, of course, Moira would disapprove, considering this elopement a betrayal of her power.

'For good? Is that what you mean, Stephen, for good?'

'Or ill.'

'Oh stop it, Stephen, you mean permanently.'

'Yes. Why not? You've nothing to keep you here.'

'I have a job, remember, and, anyway, you have – job, children, wife, everything . . . '

A waiter had appeared, his striped waistcoat hovering and strobing like an optical illusion at the corner of my vision. He knew us well and would normally shake hands and talk. This time he saw we were too engrossed for all that.

'Everything all right, sir . . . madame?'

'Fine, absolutely fine. Could I have some water?'

'Only tap water, sir. Our delivery has not come today. Ah, wait a minute, he has just arrived!'

He gestured triumphantly at the door. A man in dazzling white overalls, an orange scarf and black shoes nursing a huge plastic bottle of mineral water under his arm was pushing his way through.

'Water man!'

The water man strode into the restaurant, swaying and

banging noisily against a table. Finally he reached the bar and, placing one hand on the bottle's neck and the other flat on its base, he swung it up on to the zinc surface where it landed with a metallic, dimly resonating thud.

'Let's just say for now that I shall come and see the site. I am curious. This *is* different. I shall visit. I shall simply visit you. No obligation. And, if . . . when I decide to leave, you will not object. You will not be permitted to object. Do you understand?' Francesca said.

I jumped to my feet, scattering money on the table. We were leaving.

'Yes, yes, I understand. Right, let's go.'

I pushed my way past the waiter, the figures rising from the next table. This was it.

'Steeeeephen!'

EIGHT

UNCERTAIN OF BEING able to find Hirtenstein's gym in time for the early appointment, I had taken a taxi instead of the Leopard. The office block he had named to Tina turned out, surprisingly, to have a charcoal-grey, austere, classical façade. It was set back from the street behind a courtyard and massive iron railings topped with fearful spear heads. At the centre were two heavy, square, blocked columns surmounted by lions resting their front paws on stone shields. The columns supported two iron gates, flung wide open, and a high arch of wrought iron at the apex of which stood a crowned eagle. At the dead centre of all this barbaric drama stood Orlando in his long, green coat, smoking a cigar and peering into the sky with absolute concentration. He could see nothing, I knew, but was concerned to avoid an appearance of loitering. I joined him after paying off the cab. He did not acknowledge me, so I simply stood by him and stared upwards at the same patch of blue sky.

'Chilly,' I said after a long silence, 'but, in the event, it does not look like rain.'

Orlando started slightly, pretending to be caught unawares by my arrival. He slowly lowered his head, looked at me and then turned back to gaze at the sky before replying.

'Sweet of you to come. What with all that cathedral stuff on your mind. And how is the dear Francesca? Yes, I think the rain will hold off.'

'Possibly a shower later. It is that sort of weather. And, yes, sweet certainly. The dear Francesca is well, thank you. But I must say that yesterday's meeting rather raised my hopes that this *was* the cathedral stuff. Are you sure we have the right place?'

'No mistake. Smith House. Neo-classical. Redeveloped. Botched by Sinton, rebotched by Goldrings and, doubtless, superbotched by the designers of Hirtenstein's gym thing. At least they kept the gates.'

He shrugged himself into purposefulness and flicked away his half-smoked cigar. 'Not allowed here, I assume.'

'Frowned on at the very least, I'm sure. A matter of hygiene.'

'More likely a matter of the usual high-minded prigs wanting to live for ever. The best of us simply have to die young. And the very best don't feel the urge to reproduce. This has terrible evolutionary implications for the human – what's the word? – stock.'

'Awful. We are a dying breed, Orlando, entirely because of the diligence with which we go about our dying.'

'After you, brother.'

'Yours at the gates of hell.'

Together, with something of our old heroic disdain, we walked through the thunderous gateway and across a newly cobbled courtyard, arbitrarily partitioned with iron posts and chains. Just before the portico and its embracing steps was a discreetly small metal sign, decorated with pastel stars and bearing the word 'Alive!' A curving, aluminium arrow pointed to a ramp that dipped along the front of the façade.

'I think', said Orlando, 'they are trying to tell us something.'

The heavy, rusticated stone of the building gave way, below ground, to bland, yellow brickwork. Orlando grimaced. 'The great achievement of the modern world has been to stand archaeology on its head. These days it is the past that is above ground, the present beneath.'

The ramp took us down to a depth of about twelve feet and around the corner of the building. There we found two glass doors surmounted by a turquoise pastiche of the pediment of the main building. Across the glass in pink imitation of a casual scrawl was, again, the word 'Alive!' An eau-de-nil streak underlining the word rose to transform itself into a naked, leaping girl, her hair coiling back to form the exclamation mark.

Orlando paused before the doors.

'Now, Stephen . . . '

'I know, I know.'

'There is a remote chance that you may have made some kind of breakthrough with this Hirtenstein. I think he likes you – God knows we should be grateful for that . . . Even if we do have to come to places like this. Sometimes I think I have no pride.'

'Thanks for the credit and, of course, you have none.'

'All I want to say is . . . '

'Try not to mess it up.'

'Quite.'

'Quite.'

We turned on our heels like some venerable theatrical double act. Our entry – one to each door – divorced 'Al' from 'ive!' but they were at once reconciled with a soft whoosh. We stopped. On our left was a curving desk in light wood and, before us, two further doors, this time in opaque white glass with a small, round, transparent section in each. From behind the desk we were assessed by a thin teenager with short greased hair and wearing a T-shirt decorated with the Alive! logo. A badge indicated he was called Cliff. Passing rapidly over me, he lingered on Orlando knowingly. Orlando responded by allowing his lids to hood his eyes and raising a faint half-smile. He took two paces over to the desk.

'Ah, Cliff, Mr Hirtenstein is expecting us,' he said, allowing his hand to fall gently on the wood on the exact beat of the last word. He paused, but not long enough for Cliff to respond.

'Through here?' Orlando's hand rose and moved to push the white doors.

'One moment, sir. Mr Rix and,' he flicked through some papers, 'Mr Cum . . . cum . . . cum . . . ah yes, Cummings?'

'Exactly,' I agreed, following Orlando through the doors.

'Little tarts', Orlando was murmuring, 'everywhere you go. Euuurgh!'

He was exclaiming at the sour smell that was not adequately disguised by a chemical, floral breeze. The light was pinkish and subdued. We were standing at the end of a curving walkway of polished wood with steel cabling on either side. This bisected a large, high, square room. Narrow, horizontal windows ran in a band just below the level of the ceiling, filling the upper air with hazy light. The concave side of the walkway defined the perimeter of a restaurant. With their black curved backs, steel chairs embraced tables covered with white cloths and laid with angular cutlery. In the centre of each was a chrome sculpture of the Alive! sign and the leaping girl. In this incarnation she also held a slender, horn-shaped vase from which sprang a single white lily.

The convex side of the walkway swung out over the gym itself. The floor level was perhaps eight feet lower than that of the restaurant. Dark-grey machines with occasional flashes of chrome were arranged in ranks. They were indecipherable, some with the air of crouched and waiting creatures, others with the smug intent of operating tables. More familiarly there were dumbbells, weights lined on racks and an immense clock whose face was swept by a red second hand that quivered with the onward jolt of each passing second. Soft violin music was playing.

The place at first appeared empty. But then my eyes began to distinguish human flesh from the machinery in which it was entrapped. The first man I spotted appeared to have ground to a halt in the midst of a network of rods, beams, wires and padded plastic. Another, seated, was engaged in desperate motions of his arms that caused cables and pulleys to move with sighs and whistles about his straining form. Something about the facial skin, the haircuts and, of course, the club itself, suggested wealth. But the pale, soft bodies and immobile eyes suggested only the usual, ugly, bare, dying people.

Hirtenstein was on a machine that clearly, for all its immobility, evoked the concept 'bicycle'. In silence but for a slight hiss, he was pedalling without obvious effort, his arms folded and his eyes closed. Sweat gleamed on his face and marked his white T-shirt, though there was no sign of a gasp or struggle. His body still looked merely fat and as absurdly proportioned as ever, but, in these clothes and in this place, it displayed a certain respectable tautness.

We moved to the centre of the walkway by the entrance to the restaurant – a couple of steel steps downwards through a gap in the railing. There was no visible way into the gym, a feature that gave the spectacle the air of an exhibit, a working model or experiment, isolated from chance variables and interventions. There must be some kind of door beneath us leading to changing rooms. I was beginning to like the enfolded logic of the place, it told you what to do. You exercised, you changed and you ate. Each activity was implicated in the others, they flowed through the crossroads of your body.

Orlando stood uncertainly for a moment, watching Hirtenstein with an embarrassed air. He appeared to be seeking the correct protocol. Meanwhile, I found myself suddenly confused by the position of the walkway and its fancy geometry. I felt caught in the steel and wood as the gymnasts were caught in their machines. There was a moment of vertigo and the possibility of an awkwardly timed and dangerously placed faint. I swayed towards the cables of the handrail. As my hip caught them, they gave and rattled against their tubular guides. All the gymnasts except Hirtenstein looked up. I smiled apologetically, having inconsiderately dragged them back to their souls. The smile was dying and the gymnasts were lowering their eyes again by the time Hirtenstein opened his.

He continued to pedal, raising his hand in greeting, an immobile gesture comically at odds with the rapid whirling of his legs. Orlando raised his in reply. Hirtenstein glanced down at a black panel in front of him which, I now realized, provided in red, glowing figures the details of his performance. He raised three fingers to indicate, I assumed, the number of minutes he was still obliged to complete and waved us backwards into the restaurant.

We retreated awkwardly and sat down. Without any order from us, we were at once served coffee by a waitress with pink lipstick. A leaping girl brooch on her blouse said her name was Sal. My dizziness had, at last, passed.

'Little tarts,' I murmured as Sal left us, 'everywhere you go.'

'I never felt the need for all this myself.' Orlando waved his arm around us. 'I have, I suppose, inner beauty. Nothing like yours, of course, nothing so grand. But enough.'

'It would be pointless for you to dream of exerting yourself, quite superfluous under the circumstances.'

'*You*, of course, have no need because of your increasingly widely known contact with a higher realm.'

'Quite. Much higher.'

Orlando had put a cigar in his mouth, forgetting his earlier awareness of the likely rules of the club. Sal appeared at once.

'You cannot be serious,' she said, pointing at Orlando, shaking her head and tightening her lips in an expression of exaggerated anger. 'Here!'

'Of course. You are right. I *cannot* be serious here. How could I be?'

He removed the cigar, causing a tiny mountain of membrane to rise from his dry lip and then fall. Hirtenstein suddenly appeared in a black track suit, a white towel around his neck like some specialized ecclesiastical garment. He just heard Orlando's whispered, 'Little bitch!' and noted quickly the cigar he was now dropping into the vase, the brief hiss as it was extinguished underlining the venom of his words.

'Give the girl a break, Orlando. This is a health club. What do you expect?'

'I know, Dave, a slip. I apologize.'

Sal looked round at Hirtenstein, thought for a moment, probably of pursuing the abuse of the vase, then smiled and left the situation in his hands. But, as she turned, he caught her wrist.

'No, no. Hang on. Two continentals, darling. Decaff, fruit and yoghurt for me. OK? Oh and honey.'

'Yes, dear?'

'No, no. I mean I want some honey. That all right, boys?'

We nodded. Hirtenstein smiled and released Sal. A man in shorts and a T-shirt appeared. Hirtenstein twisted to greet him.

'Hey, Joe! Looked at my card recently? Strength to strength, my man, strength to strength.'

The man was young, crop-headed and hesitant. He wrung his hands and flexed his legs slightly as if in urgent need of dissipating surplus energy. He glowed so absurdly with health that I found I had to look away in embarrassment as if he were deformed or scarred.

'Joe', explained Hirtenstein, 'is my personal health counsellor. Think you could do anything with these two, Joe?'

He smiled shyly. Orlando tried to look amused to conceal his obvious interest in the shiny flexings of Joe.

'Naw, you're right, Joe,' continued Hirtenstein without waiting for an answer, 'they're hopeless cases.'

'Mr Hirtenstein, I just wanted to say it's time for your next reassessment, sir.'

'Ready when you are, counsellor.'

'Tomorrow at nine OK, sir?'

'Fine. You'll find I've entered a whole new phase. I am more than a new man. I am a new *type* of man. We are talking phase transitions here.'

Joe smiled uncertainly, nodded uncomprehendingly and walked off, followed by Orlando's eyes.

'Bad day, eh, Orlando?' said Hirtenstein. 'Don't tell me, you don't exactly feel at home here. Not your kind of place at all.'

'No. I'm afraid not.'

'Steve, on the other hand . . . '

'Me neither,' I said rapidly, not wishing to collude too easily with the man. 'I find these places pointless in all the obvious ways.'

'Right, maybe, pointless. Not Gothic at all.' He laughed and slapped me on the knee. 'Not Gothic – no points. But however bad it gets, remember it's worse up there,' he pointed upwards. We looked puzzled.

'You know. Those boys flying to Mars. Big trouble. They may just flip out and die slowly, drifting out into space . . . The slow death of Captain Dale McCluskey.'

'Yes, bad way to go,' I agreed. 'A lot of time to think about it. And I suppose we'd have to listen to them . . . Er, Dave, why do you do all this exercise stuff?'

'This? Simple. Live longer. OK, it doesn't seem to make me

107

prettier or thinner, just makes the fat harder. Been doing it for years too.'

'Living longer would be a curse in a doomed spaceship.'

He smiled uncertainly – had this been a put-down of some kind? I looked at his face as he studied mine and noticed for the first time a certain tightness and smoothness about his features. Fat people are generalized in my mind. I take for granted their enlarged pores, slackness, an appearance as of the flesh coming away from the bones, never to return. The possibility of hard, smooth fat intrigued me so much that I reached out to touch his cheek. It was cold from showering and, yes, hard. Orlando looked shocked.

'See,' grinned Hirtenstein, always able to read my mind on the subject of himself, 'not fat like you expect, not the flabby stuff. The point is to live longer. What other game is there? Life is all you've got, so prolong it. The best information we have is that exercise should do that. And I always go with the best information.'

Orlando twitched slightly, suspecting the businessman's wisdom might signal that the conversation was about to become relevant.

'Do you always go with the best information, Orlando?'

'When I can get it, Dave, when I can get it.'

The food arrived. The waitress bore the lot on a single, large, oval tray which she balanced on a bent-back palm. There was a long interlude of tinkling plates and cutlery which concluded with a hearty valedictory cry from Sal of, 'Enjoy your breakfast!'

'Enjoy your breakfast!' mimed Orlando to me with a sultry hooding of his eyes. Hirtenstein caught it and flicked his gaze between the two of us. Then he looked downwards to a mango that had been helpfully turned inside out, its flesh diced.

'OK, Stephen,' he said, spooning mango, 'tell me about yourself.'

'Myself?'

'Well, I know all about him.'

'Then you know quite a lot about me, we've been together for a long time. Other than that I faint quite a lot, I have a bad back, I'm married with two children . . . er . . . '

'Fainting, eh? Why?'

'I don't know. It's nothing serious.'

'Maybe you're living on the edge. I bet you eat a lot of cold soups – you know, watercress – the house has four storeys, right?'

'It does, but I loathe cold soups.'

'And you have a sports car and a ute.'

'Ute?'

'Utility – country thing, lights, ladders, big tyres . . . '

'Yes, exactly, very good. So I'm a type. A sports, ute, soup type.'

'We're all one type or another. The type is just the thing you get out of the way before getting on to the real man. I'm not insulting you, Steve, I'm just getting all that stuff out of the way. OK?'

'Precisely,' said Orlando and toasted Hirtenstein with his coffee.

'There is something', I said slowly, 'that doesn't fit with the watercress soup and the ute.'

'Tell me.'

'Oh dear,' murmured Orlando. 'Must we . . . now?'

'Tell me,' insisted Hirtenstein, leaning forward to exclude Orlando.

I told him, pointing out for his benefit how the cathedral had led to my fascination with Gothic.

'So you see, Dave,' I concluded, 'it's the soup, the ute and the cathedral. Doesn't really fit, does it?'

He was silent for some time, staring intensely into my eyes.

'Well, no,' he spoke at last, keeping his tone even. 'I can't say I've come across this combination before. But you've always got to be ready for new variations. And maybe the cathedral is the real Steve Rix, your atypicality. Maybe it's just the way you do it, this building thing.'

'Maybe', I agreed, 'it's just the way I do it. Though, I have to say, I have never done it this way before.'

'Stephen', said Orlando as if helpfully trying to affirm the normality of this eccentricity, 'has never been one to do things in the usual way. He likes novelty.'

Hirtenstein was still staring.

'What', he asked, 'does it mean to you?'

'Everything with the proviso that it might mean nothing. I intend, one way or another, to fling my life into it . . . '

'More probably his wife . . . ' said Orlando softly.

' . . . accepting that I may be the victim of a delusion, an illness, a malfunction, whatever.'

Hirtenstein flicked his eyes to Orlando and then back to me. 'Ever since you came up with that Gothic angle, Steve, I've been thinking. Hard. You're on to something, something big, something new. And now the cathedral idea – this is dead right.'

'It was not an idea. It was something that happened to me.'

'Oh yeah? Well, what are ideas if they aren't things that happen to you? And the thing is . . . ' His eyes suddenly lowered and the tone of his voice deepened. ' . . . about this cathedral. It's not impossible. The first point is that I've got a lot of funding in hand just now and a lot of friends in the right places. I hadn't thought of a cathedral until you just said it, but the Gothic thing really got me going.'

Orlando hunched forward, a piece of croissant held elegantly between his thumb and forefinger.

'Of course, on the face of it,' Hirtenstein continued, 'it's crazy to build a cathedral. I mean, think about it. Cathedrals were built like that because they *needed* to be, that was the technology. If we want to enclose large, vertical spaces, we've got steel and concrete. Right?'

'Right!' said Orlando, a little more fervently than he intended. On the one hand he scented business; on the other indulging my visions disgusted him.

'And,' Hirtenstein said, 'if we build a Gothic cathedral using steel and concrete, it's just pastiche, isn't it? We'll be bolting fibreglass stone on to steel beams. Theme-park stuff.'

'I know,' I said, rubbing my eyes at the onset of a sudden weariness, 'I know all this stuff. I don't want to get carried away. Perhaps building it isn't really my point. You need lots of people for a building and this is really only to do with me. Why should everybody else get involved? Maybe I can find another way of dealing with it – building a little one, maybe. A cathedral the size of a garden shed. I could sit in it.'

Hirtenstein raised a hand, a gesture which, combined with

110

the towel, gave him the appearance of a priest in the act of delivering a benediction. 'Hang on, hang on. Let me finish. The fact is theme-park stuff is the name of the game. That's what they want out there in the sticks. They want things to look like other things, things they know. And remember, they've got to build now. All the old planning controls are out of the window. What the government wants now is population dispersal and open countryside – Rural Beauty Zones, all that stuff. But the yokels are so stuck with thinking you can't build anything that they can't figure out what they should build. And even now you can't just stick up a leisure centre in your part of the world, Steve. It needs something more, some kind of packaging . . . '

'Disguise, you mean.'

'Exactly. Disguise. Camouflage. Masking. It has to look like something else, like I said. So, as it happens, yeah, a cathedral is precisely what I could build, a big cathedral just like the one you saw. It fits. It really fits.'

'But what for?'

'As a leisure centre, of course, try and stick with this, Steve. Like I said – packaging.'

'You mean you could build my church as a cover for a leisure centre because they like the look of Gothic cathedrals. Of course! How could I be so blind? That is the only way you could build it today, as a leisure centre. And, of course, the only way you could get permission for a leisure centre is by building a Gothic cathedral. Brilliant.'

I moaned and dropped my forehead into the palm of my hand.

'Exactly. But don't get me wrong, there's nothing to get upset about. I'm all for this church for the same reasons you are – as a vision, Steve, a vision – but it's got to pay for itself, so something's got to happen inside. It can't just be a big sculpture. Now, by a nice coincidence, you just happen to have dreamed up the one way we could build a leisure centre. What's wrong with that? And don't kid me, you don't really just want a cathedral-shaped garden shed.'

Orlando was beaming by this time and eating his croissant with untypical gusto. He looked at me and then raised his eye heavenward in gratitude. The cathedral could be built without indulging me. This way it would be more like a humiliation. Again Hirtenstein watched all this.

'Of course he doesn't,' said Orlando, 'nothing wrong with a leisure centre, nothing whatsoever.'

The idea was certainly monstrous, absurd. Yesterday, as a way of teasing Orlando, I had accepted Hirtenstein's excitement about Gothic. Today I saw its simple logic. My church would pay for itself and give Foundations a way into a piece of countryside from which it would otherwise be excluded. My lovely, inner drama had become the fantasy of a theme-park designer. What would the world know of my turmoil? The scheme and its inspiration would be dismissed as just a smart way for a clapped-out architect to justify selling out. Here was I, the conscience of the partnership, flogging a fibreglass church.

'So,' Orlando continued, 'this is formally a job then?'

Hirtenstein looked at him, knowing that, now, he really was being sold something. He reached inside his tracksuit, took out a cheque book. He called over Sal and borrowed her pen. He wrote a cheque and then passed it to me while staring at Orlando.

'I think', I said, suppressing a gasp, 'it's a job.'

I passed the cheque to Orlando, frightened by the knowledge that, once he had seen it, we would be trapped. He looked at the figure.

'This concept is little short of brilliant,' he cried. 'It really is brilliant! Brilliant! Waitress! Waitress! Er, Sal!'

She came to his elbow uncertainly as if expecting some further dissent from the house rules.

'Do you do champagne? Of course, you do. A bottle of your finest!'

She looked at Hirtenstein who was watching me expressionlessly. Without moving his eyes he reached out automatically and stroked the side of Sal's skirt. She looked down, shrugged and, in the absence of further authority from that source, she accepted that of Orlando and went off to find a bottle. I noticed one of the other gymnasts had sat down in the restaurant and was staring at us. But for the expensive track suit, he was like an old man in the Arches – watery eyes and white skin with raw, reddened patches.

'Does all this worry you, Steve?' Hirtenstein finally asked.

'Of course it does. I go crazy for a while, I see momentous things and all that happens is that we are turned into theme-park hacks. My great truth turns out to be a smart way of exploiting the planning climate.'

'Don't knock it, sunshine,' said Orlando with breathy irony as he slipped the cheque into his inside pocket.

'Look, Steve,' began Hirtenstein, leaning forward, his fore-arms on his thighs and his fingers twisting one of his rings, 'the first thing is that, OK, it will probably be fibreglass, but it will be good. I don't want an approximation of a Gothic cathedral or a parody of one, I want the real thing, close as we can get. And, if we get this through, there'll be plenty of money to do it. The second thing is: what's your big problem? You know you saw this thing. Fine. You feel it should be built. Great. It can be built. And you say you're worried about what other people will think. Come on, Steve! These people are pygmies. You're supposed to be the artist here. Just do it. Go for the burn.'

I looked down at the buttery remains of my continental. This was all, of course, revolting. First the cathedral, then Ralph, messenger of the artistic conscience, now Hirtenstein on How to Build It. I saw the interpretations proliferate like computer-generated chaos. I was mad, the church was real; Ralph was sent, Ralph was an accident; Hirtenstein was talking honest sense, Hirtenstein was corrupting me. The alternatives multi-plied and swirled, spiralling, downwards, the inward curves decorated with little crockets of possibility. I noted, with fleet-ing happiness, an insight that could have made me famous: deterministic chaos was Gothic. Then I sank back into bit-terness. With every movement away from that afternoon in that field, I gained more pressure and lost more sense. With Ralph, building it had been the obvious answer, a drunken, lighthearted thing. But now, with Hirtenstein, I saw what building it really meant. Now it had to be reasonable. Big money was involved and big money required a reason. But there were no reasons for new cathedrals other than to be like other cathedrals, reminders of how strange life used to be.

The champagne arrived and there was more tinkling, this time of glasses and an ice bucket. I watched the film of condensation

113

around this silver cylinder as Orlando opened and poured the champagne. The seething foam rose and fell in the glasses.

'To Stephen's church!' cried Orlando, raising his glass. 'St Stephen's! The Cathedral Church of St Stephen in the Field, leisure centre and existential crisis.'

I could hardly resist on the grounds of idealism. I had no idea what ideals to attach to this thing. And, of course, if the one ideal was to build, what alternatives did I have? Here was Hirtenstein, in Orlando's pocket was his money. If it was all just me, a malfunction, a fantasy, a disorder, then nothing would be lost. If it was not . . . well, how much or what kind of an abuse would this theme park be? Finally there was the astonishing fact that I had seen this cathedral and, within a few days, found somebody to build it. Ralph had been sent, Hirtenstein had been sent. I was doing no more than what I was told and, for once, it was easy. Building the church had become the next thing. Best to get on with it.

Hirtenstein watched me, waiting for my response to the toast. I slowly lifted my glass, keeping my face solemn. I could not resist the requirement of the moment. There was nothing to lose; nothing, at any rate, that I could imagine. I allowed myself to smile.

'St Stephen's in the Field!'

'All right!' cried Hirtenstein. He stood up, drained his glass, wrapped it in one of the linen napkins, twisted the cloth and smashed it against the table edge with a padded crash that once again brought Sal scurrying to our table.

NINE

SHE SAT AMIDST her attributes and attendants. One girl stood
by her, white-coated and bearing a black, plastic tray of imple-
ments. Another, also in a white coat, sat on a low stool and
worked on her nails with stainless steel tools. A young man
combed fiercely at her damp hair so that it formed a glossy
sheet covering one shoulder. The remaining hair was clipped
to one side or, on the top of her head, twisted around regal,
red rollers. Her body was covered with a light blue plastic sheet
from which her face emerged, motionless and intent upon its
image in the mirror. One hand only, that being manicured,
projected. Her feet, bare, rested upon a chromium bar covered
at its centre in black, ribbed rubber. Before her on the counter
lay a magazine, open at a picture of a modern interior in iron
and wood. The discarded shoes, flat-heeled and dark green,
lay on the floor beneath her feet and, alongside them, her
capacious, soft leather bag, a single pink tissue projecting.

The chair was of chrome and thickly padded black leather.
It ended in the middle of her back to leave room for the cutting.
Above, a jointed metal arm held an umbrella-shaped array of
infra-red lights and, above that, a thin wire provided both

support and power for a row of small but intense spotlights that pointed randomly about the room, casting bluish pools of illumination.

The mirror was a large rectangle with one corner sliced off. This appeared to be no more than a device to allow room for the dryer arm to be attached to the wall, but, in fact, the pattern of the clipped rectangle was a theme, repeated all over the shop as well as on the signs and cards scattered about the place. The name of the shop was Clipped.

Her chair was concealed from the others by white panels attached to the floor and ceiling by thin, steel rods. There was a gap of about a foot from the floor to allow for the sweeping away of hair cuttings. The booth formed by these panels permitted just enough concentration and privacy. By depriving her of any easy excuse to look away from the mirror and increasing the intimacy of the contact with her attendants, she was persuaded of the authority and seriousness of what was taking place.

All conversational eye lines were maintained through the mirror. She did not turn to speak to her cutter, she gazed at his reflection and, to respond to her words, he dipped his head alongside hers and gazed back. He was animated, she impassive, mildly ironic. They lived through the mirror; they had to look away from each other in order to look at each other. And, for their reflected selves, the contact was franker, easier and the gaze held longer than for ordinary people.

I stood at the threshold of Clipped, just inside the sickly blast of hot air which acted as an invisible door. I felt absurdly dark, prominent and clumsy in this gleaming haze of metallic brightness and clarity. Pungent smells agitated my nostrils, their impact heightened rather than softened by the perfumes added to the mixtures to disguise their corrosive, burning, distilled potency. The air seemed plasticized and corrupted. You cannot separate a smell from the air which bears it, the smell becomes the air, the air the smell. These people lived in this man-made medium, so much thicker and sweeter than ordinary air. Perhaps, over time, their bodies suffered from numberless, poisonous effects, which, because of their slow insidiousness, were concealed among the many processes of ageing.

It had been a day of drink. Beginning with the champagne at the Alive! breakfast, I had moved on to wine at lunch with Orlando, the morning having passed in desultory jokes and discussions about the right people to form an office team that would unburden me of the details of my church. Orlando had finally abandoned the attempt and taken me out. The drink had combined and conspired to daze and dehydrate me. A thin, skin-deep heat prickled at my face and a steady, cold sickness afflicted my stomach. The outlying perimeters of my body felt uncoordinated and beyond control. My being tried to shrink away from these surfaces, only to find it could not.

I crossed the inner threshold of Clipped. I feared I would slip on the white tiles of the floor or sway and crash against the machinery and the trolleys carrying combs, brushes and bottles. Everything was on castors, all possible supports would simply roll away at my first grasp.

My eye was caught by a row of glass cylinders, each filled with turquoise liquid and capped with a chromium dome. Every one was labelled with a name – Bob, Sandra, Del, Bea, Zad. Inside were combs and scissors being sterilized, burnt into harmless purity. These tools could be lifted out by raising a plunger that terminated in a small sphere on top of the dome. One dome was leaning to one side leaving the cylinder half uncovered. There seemed to be an obsessive, leaning asymmetry about this place.

Finally, having survived the passage from the door, I stood behind Jill, just outside the immediate aura of her ritual but almost fully present in her mirror, only my feet were excluded by the angle of the reflection. For a while I was unnoticed. My position was beyond the haze of more intense light so a casual glance in the mirror might only reveal a deepening of the outer shadow. A closer look might show a hovering, ectoplasmic shade, pale and sickened.

Then Jill saw me. She squinted briefly and raised her head to silence her cutter. I felt he must have been saying something she did not wish me to hear. He obeyed and stood upright, scissors dangling from one hand and comb gripped in the other.

'Stephen! What are you doing here?'

I stepped forward.

'I came to see you.'

All the attendants had now paused to stare at me. There were no welcoming smiles; I had clumsily broken the clicking rhythm of their work. They took the cue for their response from the edge of irritation in Jill's voice. Her face was now flattened with impatience and resignation.

'Why?'

I realized she was now thinking that I had come here to break some bad news – I'm leaving you, Dandy is dead. Everybody seemed to expect this of me all the time, people lived in fear of what my appearances might mean. I was a baleful portent, a comet, a supernova.

But I realized also that I was not quite sure why I had come. I had simply wandered from Orlando's lunch with the idea fixed in my mind of seeing Jill. I had not questioned this idea as I had walked, gloomy, fatigued and flustered, through the streets. Even the complication of remembering she was having her hair done at this hour had not made me pause and examine my motives.

'I don't know. Loose end. Insecure. Do I need a reason? I suppose I do. Oh and Hirtenstein's going to build it.'

Of course, that was why. In the silly warmth of the wine I had embraced the consoling thought that, however grotesque the church scheme had now become, at least its practical, commercial vindication would be a satisfying rebuke to Jill's scepticism. I had been quietly and unconsciously cuddling that thought as if it were some new soft toy.

'Build what?'

'My cathedral. What else?'

'This is a joke, I take it.' She smiled at the cutter who sought out her expression in the glass and then smiled back. 'Who's Hirtenstein?'

He had told her everything but the name, a small advantage for me.

'Orlando's friendly developer or developer friend, whatever. Dave the Developer Hirtenstein. The one we saw yesterday, we saw him again today. At his gym, very nice place. Perhaps we should join. You would like it.'

She turned away from the mirror to stare directly at me. The move broke the paralysis of her attendants and the cutter, seeing that I was staying, suddenly moved to wheel in an extra chair for me to sit down. The manicurist rose and offered to fetch me coffee.

A few moments of reorganization passed and once again the scene was stabilized. I was seated symmetrically across from the manicurist sipping coffee, nervous of the destructive power of my elbows. The low chairs made the girl and I look like two respectful, heraldic lions at the feet of Jill.

'Let me get this clear – this Hirtenstein actually plans to build your damn church. That is what you are saying. The church you saw in that field.'

I explained, able from this position to talk almost directly to her face without distracting her concentration from the mirror. I ran through the exquisitely fortuitous interlockings of the elements of my vision, Hirtenstein's leisure centre and the aesthetic prejudices of local government. I summarized new central government policies concerning the countryside. I laughed gaily at the steel, concrete and fibreglass compromise, at the irony of it all, but also how, in the end, it made a kind of sense. Somehow Jill always inspired in me this need to make my world of work appear light, refreshing and logical. I wished to laugh it all off, to give her what she wanted and get on with the next thing.

'Are you absolutely sure this is not a joke?'

Orlando, in his euphoria, had evidently failed to call her that morning and had missed her after lunch.

'Could be. Jokes at my expense I often find hard to detect. But he seemed serious. And Orlando believes him, that is what counts.'

This last thought was designed to suggest a certain sly bitterness at their perpetual plots against me. Now I had broken the alliance. Orlando was obliged to be on my side. I was no longer on the defensive. After the gym meeting and the, as he called it, 'profoundly human and moving' cheque, he had been buoyant. Even the mess of the working morning failed to depress his spirits. Finally, he had bought me that expensive lunch consisting mainly of rare salad leaves and some bizarre bread filled with obscure kernels. Orlando insisted proudly that, in spite of appearances, it was all desperately unhealthy.

'Just because that man is giving us a great deal of money,' he had explained, 'does not mean I have to share his unpleasant obsession with longevity.'

The burden of my inconvenient madness had been lifted from his shoulders. Suddenly it was not madness, not even inconvenience, it was an opportunity. Suddenly he saw me as saved by my vision, saved for the real, the profit-making world. At a stroke the need to sustain our pretensions had gone. We would be said to be selling out, of course, but it was the decision of Stephen Rix, the partnership's conscience. He had breezily sent me on my way. He did not care that he would see me no more that day. I had done more than enough.

'It just goes to show,' he had said warmly. 'It just goes to show.'

'What? What does it just go to show, Orlando?'

'That one should never be too blindly practical.'

'That even Mad Stephen has his uses?'

'Exactly. You have your uses.'

He had roared with laughter and ordered more dark yellow wine.

'Then you have both gone mad,' said Jill.

The manicurist looked shocked, the girl with the tray smiled and the cutter yet again sought to establish Jill's expression in the mirror, trying to assess whether laughter was appropriate.

'Well, maybe. But what can I do? It's all going ahead. Hirtenstein wants drawings – real drawings. It's out of my hands.'

The expression pleased me: out of my hands, building this pastiche was a way of being free of it.

'He is paying for these drawings?'

'He *has paid* for these drawings. Handsomely.'

'That's some small relief.'

She caught the cutter's eyes and rolled her own upwards to indicate the madness she had to endure outside the salon. Here, in contrast, was reason, calm, the cultivation of the outer self, a certain customary sanity. I thought of the white, dissolving calm of Francesca's rooms. The cutter raised his eyebrows in reply.

'My husband', Jill explained slowly, 'wants to build a church.'

'A cathedral,' I corrected her.

'A very big church,' she conceded.

The cutter nodded reasonably as if understanding both our positions on the matter.

'A big church, how nice. I think we all feel the need of something like that just now.'

'Something like what?' I asked curiously.

'Like . . . a big church.'

'Why now?'

'Well, the New Year, those poor people stuck in that space-ship. So much sort of . . . big . . . seems to be happening, don't you think?'

'He wants to build this . . . cathedral in the middle of a field in the middle of nowhere — just behind our country place as a matter of fact.'

'Unusual. I bet your country place is wonderful. Does it have rutted tracks that freeze in the winter?'

'He has been *told* to build this church.'

'Anybody I know?'

'Well, God, I suppose. Who else would tell him to build a church? It came to him in a vision.'

The cutter curved his lips downward to suggest either that he was surprised or impressed.

'Well, if he's got the money, why not? We all deserve a bit of luxury once in a while. Personally if I had that kind of cash I would go for surgery, whatever God said. I do love frozen, rutted tracks.'

'Surgery?' I asked.

'You know, plastic surgery.'

'Oh . . . right.'

'Why not? Nothing wrong with looking your best. Silly not to really. Speaking for myself, I could do with some tightening round here.' He indicated the outer corners of his eyes with the end of his comb. 'And a tuck or two here.' He indicated his admittedly swelling jowls.

Jill looked interested.

'What about me?'

The cutter leaned out from behind her hair to study her face in the mirror.

'Well I hardly like . . . '

'No, go on.'

He placed the spread fingertips of his hand on either side of her head and pulled back. Her face rose, tightened and stretched backwards, her eyes narrowed. I was reminded of a film I had once seen of a man's face distorted by the effect of extreme acceleration.

'Just a little pull back here. No real local problems – just a general tightening up to hold back the years.'

'The ears?'

'The *years*.'

She grinned gleefully. This startled me as I did not expect such an idea to accord with Jill's general outlook. Looks were essential, of course, but, in this, there was vulgarity.

'What a good idea! Don't you think so, Stephen?'

Of course. It would be one more way of being inappropriately glamorous, baffling people by caring too much about the superficial while evidently caring so much about the profound.

'It's expensive. But I do know a good man. The best.'

'Stephen will pay. Whatever it costs will be a small price to shut me up about this church.'

I stared at her, but her eyes remained fixed on her lifted face in the mirror.

'I think it is my turn to ask if *you* are serious.'

'Completely.'

'Seems like a wonderful deal to me,' said the cutter with horrible innocence. 'She gets her facelift, you get your church.'

'I see – my church for your facelift.'

'Clearly, thanks to this Hirtenstein, you could have the church anyway. But this way it will be easier. Like falling off a log, in fact, no real opposition. Peace and quiet.'

Suddenly, in spite of the obvious way in which Jill felt she had turned the tables, the arbitrary symmetry pleased me. How strange the way this church made everything fall into place: the messengers, Ralph and Hirtenstein, and now this deal, another sign. This thing worked.

'OK, let's do it. Your face, my cathedral.'

'I don't think I want to end up with quite the same amount of surface detail.'

The cutter laughed.

'No, none of those terrible holes and spikes. What a disaster that would be. But, believe me, you'll love it. The surgeon's name is Wolfson. I'll give you his number. I've cut his hair once or twice.'

'I would have thought he would do his own.'

I laughed feebly then rubbed my eyes to cover my embarrassment at this unfocused joke. At once the western façade flicked into view. I had not seen this before, though I felt I knew its immense doors, its mighty rose, gable and twin towers. The image held, but then began to change. The rose split into two, the doors widened. Eyes and a mouth. It was a face, Jill's face. Details of the façade were smoothed out as her features were lifted by great hands placed either side of her head. The features stretched backwards as if from the force of extreme acceleration.

I turned to look in the mirror, expecting to see the reflection of my west front. But it was simply Jill, motionless again amid her attributes and attendants.

TEN

ABOVE ROSE THE high vault and the delicate, intense sculpture of the crossing. From this cascaded arch upon arch, responds, shafts, piers, all the lithe, dancing machinery of a great Gothic interior space. The eye swooped in ecstasy, finding in its flight a thousand bevelled angularities, a million clenched, incidental spaces. And yet the whole was one, a unity of containment in which each incident acknowledged every other. Everything and yet nothing was superfluous.

The crowds and the air flowed easily through this luminous vessel, tracing its refined logic with gentle, guided precision. There was a sanctity in the movements defined by the building, a rigid, loving orthodoxy. Murmurs and cries echoed off the vaulting, raced down the galleries and rumbled in the belly of the nave. Children chased each other round the columns, their rubber shoes skidding and squeaking.

And there, where the altar should have been, rising in triple-tiered majesty of golden and white light, pink clouds of marble, gleaming lines of brass and shadowy, nested voids and niches, was our local branch of Gabriels, the Department Store with a Difference.

Oh, how their world conspired to mock me and my cathedral! We were lampooned and abused at every turn. That day we were destined to suffer the games of the fabricators of this weatherproof paradise. Gothic to them was just one more colour from their flashy palette to be dabbed on to the sullen canvas of an indoor shopping centre, a 'mall'? High spaces, galleries, transepts, crossings – of course, let's make it Gothic! Well, Gothicky, Gothickish. Instead of stone, gloom and shafts of light they used painted steel and glass to form this shining, undemanding space. Instead of arcade, triforium and clerestory they had jumbled decks of shops rising to a glass roof filigreed with steel decoration derived from the ironwork of the railway age.

Of course, nobody was meant to walk this nave, this choir, these aisles and transepts alone. There were no plans for Stephen Rix to creep in, soaked and breathless, at night. He would be caught at once by those security guards with their olive uniforms, shield-shaped badges and microwave intruder-detectors. Neither were there plans for contemplation, prayer or worship. Benches, wooden and rustic, were provided, but only for the relief of mindless fatigue. Yet still it was a church, a model of heaven with many lodgings, shrines and altars, choirs and celebrants.

And there was even a Chapter House, craftily adapted for modern purposes and called, with the literalness required by fashion, Screens. It was only a sixteen-screen cinema complex, but here too this greedy Gothic had invaded to provide Screens with the right sort of conical roof to rise, green, above its grey, steel walls and peek invitingly above the glass vault of the nave. The whole jolly conceit was topped with a simple, golden ball, speared by a tapering bronze shaft. Did this, to the excited designers, signify light? Was this an emblematic sun? Why not? The light once pierced stained glass to reach our hearts as it now pierces celluloid to reach the screen and then our hearts.

The mall's muted railway theme, quietly touched in for the connoisseur in the roofing, was clamorously slapped on for the masses in the Grand Railroad Cafeteria and Diner towards whose cream, blue and maroon façade I was now being dragged. Within an hour or so Screens would be showing *Rudy the Robot* and Tom and Elizabeth did not want to miss it. But neither did they want to miss lunch at the Grand Railroad.

'Come on, Dad,' pleaded Tom. 'We'll be late if we don't eat now. Come on!'

'My name', I announced with infuriatingly slow solemnity, 'is Daddy.'

He rolled his eyes in the direction of the vaulting and pulled one of my arms, Elizabeth copied his expression of frustration and began pulling the other.

'Come on, Daddy!' she cried.

A passing matron hauling a tartan shopping trolley smiled sympathetically at my plight and nudged her pale, thin companion to draw her attention to this homely scene of demanding kids and smiling, tolerant, tweedy, lumpy papa. The thin one fixed me with a blank, cadaverous stare, looked puzzled for a moment and then began to whisper urgently in the matron's eager ear, making rapid, ritualistic movements with one hand. Did she have the power of insight and, seeing the signs, know at once that I was a dabbler in the darker arts?

The children's dragging made me stumble and I looked away from the women to find that we were at the door of the restaurant. The Grand Railroad's amiable conceit was that we were in a railway carriage. Its frontage was decorated with antique insignia – lions and wheels with wings as well as, oddly, a draped, broken column. Bogeys were painted at either end with much loving attention to leaf springs and the irregular effects of light on the rims of the wheels. Inside, anybody eager to play the game would be disappointed to find that the illusion faltered slightly because of the restaurant's need for a space wider than any conceivable rail gauge would permit. In real life this fake train would become a monster, a bloated slug writhing across the landscape, rather than the slender, graceful, snaking line of fond memory. But rows of booths, served by waitresses in tight maroon uniforms, rescued some elements of the fiction as did the conscientiously painted *trompe-l'oeil* windows and landscapes on the far wall.

It was, I could not quite stop myself thinking, at least as much to do with a real railway carriage as my leisure centre church was to do with a real cathedral. These things were being sent to teach me something: perhaps, boringly, that we were all victims of the demands of the age. Or, more interestingly, that the age could not cope with our demands for railways and cathedrals. And, if it could not, why should we not howl with frustration and build them anyway? It was plastic fakery but it was built. Who was to say the authentically modern was truer, higher, better? The restaurant stylist was my brother. I imagined him, wracked with doubt, waking one night to find a train in his garden and seeing at once what he must do. But then he had done it and simply moved on to the next thing. In the end, presumably, so would I.

We took a booth and ordered from the huge, flopping, engine-shaped menus. Having decided, we simply pressed the right buttons on a pad by each table and, moments later, a maroon waitress arrived with a loaded tray. The food was what the food always is at the places where children especially want to eat – runny, melty, crispy, meaty and salty – the only variation being the menu titles ascribed to the combinations. Here the crisp, runny and meaty might be a Midnight Express, while the salty and melty could be a Slow Train to the Deep South and a meaty and melty was a City Slicker.

The children seriously and silently ate their way through the chosen 'platters', struggling with the mountains of 'garnish' and occasionally breaking off to share some aspect of *Rudy the Robot* for which advance publicity had prepared them. They finished too quickly, gulping and wiping yellow fragments from around their mouths with paper napkins and noisily sucking up the last sluicings of their drinks from beneath the impacted chips of ice. I made them wait and watch with mounting rage and occasional hiccups as I slowly sipped a cup of coffee. But the process was an unbearable drama of fidgeting and muttered complaints and we had, finally, to make our way to Screens, a three-minute walk for which we still had twenty minutes.

I filled the time successfully by distracting them with the shops we passed on the way – funny greetings cards, electronic black boxes with flashes of red and green lights, extravagant shoes – 'Would Mummy like those?' At one shop a huge poster announced that the game Captain Dale's Red Rider would be in next week. Tom punched me to remind me of a promise I had not made. But, best of all, was a model shop.

'Look at those cars, Tom! Wonderful cars!'

'Oh, Dad!'

He turned sulkily back for the fifth time to stare uneasily into the window. At once his anxiety about the time faded as he became engrossed with the ranks of models in seductive red, gold, silver and black. He grabbed a dubious and still-anxious Elizabeth and drew her back to explain and identify the ships, planes, cars and guns.

I leaned against a metal column painted deep green and waited while the minutes were consumed. People passed and repassed, obedient to their allocated spaces. Small bands of teenagers, tense and malodorous, swirled about each other like planetary systems while edging nervously and self-consciously through the crowd, their eyes flicking warily to detect significant contact. Couples wheeling babies clattered purposefully by. Then there were the middle-aged and the old, dressed with aggressively casual taste, some clinging on to each other, others marching in thin-lipped, mute separation divided by the rancour of a sudden row or, more probably, by a long, unexamined indifference. Finally the old women, survivors, alone, wheeling trolleys or sitting waiting, some muttering, all still, even in their last days, unthinkingly trapped in the perpetual festival of The Shop.

'Dad! One of yours, a Leopard!'

'Daddy. It is Daddy. Dad is without meaning for me. I do not respond to Dad.'

'Daddy, I've found a Leopard.'

Elizabeth jumped excitedly.

'The right colour too. Just like yours. Let's buy it! Yes. Yes. Oooo please!'

Rudy the Robot had slipped from their minds in the thrill of finding a part of ourselves replicated in the distant fantasy of the shop window. The existence of the model in this public place granted us some strange kind of fame, the one virtue of which they were always confident.

We went inside and found another Leopard which we could study more closely. It was an expensive, metal model with

128

elaborate detailing of the interior and the engine. Still killing time, I let them grow yet more frantic, unsure whether it was to be bought, while I wandered round the shop. There were ranks of cars, some containing plastic drivers with strange, blurred features. There were ships – long-nosed grey battleships and curved, bulbous galleons – and a prickly array of green artillery pieces. Finally, at the furthest, darkest end of the shop where the mounted, raked shelves had succeeded in blocking out even the superfluity of light designed in by the architects of the mall, there were people: a few women – elaborately clad courtesans – but mainly men, most of them fighting men. There were soldiers in khaki, sailors, infantrymen in red coats and high hats, knights in gleaming, plastic armour, legionnaires and even a caveman wielding a club. The eyes were all staring and blue.

Elizabeth had followed me into these depths, probably sent with instructions by a cunning and ruthless Tom.

'Please, Daddy, can we buy your car?'

'It's very expensive.'

'Yes, but it is *your* car.'

'Let me have another look. I'm not sure I have enough money.'

'Oh, please.'

Tom was waiting for us, holding the Leopard like an exhibit for my inspection. I took it and pretended to check the quality of its detailing. Finally I reached for my wallet, a gesture that elicited an immediate and simultaneous 'Yes!' from the children.

I removed the car from the box as we walked away from the shop, throwing the cardboard and polystyrene into the gaping maw of a cartoon ape that camouflaged one of the capacious rubbish bins at the centre of the nave. I raised the replica to my eye level. Tom was leaping to hold it and Elizabeth was already growing sulky, convinced it should have been for her. But as I looked, I found I could not release the toy. Suddenly it was like being confronted with an unexpected photograph of myself. The size and the accuracy of the imitation disturbed and pressed insistently on some nerve. It felt like a premonition.

At last the spell broke and I gave the model to Elizabeth who cooed and then whimpered when Tom scrambled it out of her grasp. By this time, though, we were in the foyer of the cinema and the imminence of the film took both their minds off the car. We were in a frenetically decorated octagon that filled the ground floor of Screens. Food and drink sales occupied three sides with massive rectangular tanks in which popcorn popped, banks of stainless steel rollers that heated and revolved pale, smooth sausages, stately, cruciform racks of taps that gushed fizzy drinks and steeply raked display cases of boxes and bags of sweets. The ticket office with microphones and loudspeakers for communication with the customers occupied a further side. Wide doorways accounted for two further sides and the two remaining, opposing sides were filled with a three-dimensional cardboard display of men with guns and a hologram of an actress wearing only a shirt advertising films soon to be shown. In between the three food counters rose stairways over which arched electronic signs directed us in words made of glowing red dots to the sixteen films currently playing.

Rudy the Robot was showing on the topmost 'screen'. We climbed four flights of stairs between dark, carpeted walls that felt damp and matted from the daily pressure of people bearing their huge paper cups of iced drinks, tubs of popcorn and bags of sweets. I thought of the stones of the entrance to my cathedral, polished by crowds pressing forward into that interior. Inside I was disappointed to discover that the architect had missed the opportunity to extend the ceiling of the auditorium into the heights of the conical roof. He could have done, executing a toy vault with perhaps a chandelier hanging from the central boss. But, instead, there was just a mute flatness, sloping down towards the curtains, interrupted only by the odd baffle, suggesting the fake science of acoustics was to blame for his timidity.

The lights dimmed, the curtains opened in immediate affirmation of the quality of my timing. Tom and Elizabeth ate popcorn as they watched the screen, sitting rigid and consumed with fascination by the profligacy of detail in every frame of every advertisement, trailer and in the film itself. Drinking something sweet, cold, watery and fizzy through a straw jammed into the plastic lid of a white paper cup, I gradually slipped into the same hypnosis. All films were always irresistible. All films made you lose yourself.

We were in a small town where Brad, an early teenager with a lick of greasy hair and effeminate brown eyes, was being rejected as a swot by his buddies at school. He spent his waking hours, when not in the shining, clattering savagery of the classroom and corridors, in his cramped bedroom amid computers and arcane technological literature. His sister, Zeta, thought he was wet and his parents, Dave and Janet, despaired because he showed no healthy interest in girls. They would call anxiously and feebly up the stairs to Brad, but he would deflect their queries with lame excuses and they felt bound to respect his privacy, taking the view that he was of an age where he needed his own emotional space. They consulted counsellors and psychiatrists recommended by the school. Brad was examined by these experts, but they could find nothing wrong, nothing they could treat anyway, and assured Dave and Janet that it was just a teenage phase. He had, they said, his own agenda.

How right they were! Brad's mind was on higher things. He wanted to build a robot and he thought he could do it. He was a teenager possessed. The action now became concentrated in the dark confusion of his bedroom. The tension mounted and the music accelerated as the film led us to its first climax – the revelation of what was actually going on inside Brad's computers. The camera closed in on one of his screens, passing over his shoulder. Now *our* screen was filled with the dazzling, coloured abstractions of Brad's designs. For several minutes we raced through bundles of circuitry, down electronic pathways. Sometimes we glimpsed a finger or an eye. Then a torso with a huge bull's-eye navel formed before our eyes and the film cut to Brad's face. The torso was projected on to his enraptured features. The cutting back and forth between screen and face increased in speed. The computer images and Brad's ecstatic gaze became mingled and then, suddenly, there was an explosion, a white flash, and a deep bass rumble. The screen cleared to reveal the words RUDY ONE in massive green letters. The words were on the computer screen and this degree of enlargement made them appear to seethe and crackle with electronic life.

They disappeared and were replaced by an image of Rudy, complete at last. He was upright, his legs apart and his arms hanging down but projecting outwards slightly. Finally Brad, over a period of months, conveyed by a rapid series of scenes of frantic activity in the bedroom, built Rudy. He lay inert on Brad's bed. Then, with the flipping of a switch and a crackling net of blue lightning around the bed, Brad brought him to life.

Rudy was a kindly, well-meaning robot. But there was a problem. He acted with naïve literalness, causing accidents and subverting Brad's attempts to keep him hidden. Finally the secret began to get out. Malicious schoolfriends spread the story. The psychiatrists believed it was a defensive fantasy and tried to persuade Brad that Rudy did not exist. But, one day, Rudy, anxious to tell Brad of some new discovery he had made – that, in fact, butter spreads more easily if it is left out of the fridge overnight – rushed unthinkingly into the school. The authorities and the press heard about it and descended upon Brad and his family. He escaped with Rudy into the woods.

Finally, Rudy, now possessed of human emotions, realized that, for Brad's sake, he must leave. His inner thoughts were conveyed by computerized words flashed on to the screen. Brad fell asleep in the woods and Rudy crept off after applying a cold, metal kiss to his cheek. The last we saw of Rudy was a distant shot of him wending his way through the immense trunks of the ancient trees. He was lost, finally, amidst an entanglement of shafts of sunlight. Bird calls and animal sounds were amplified. Creatures peered between the trees after this strange metal man. The sun rose above the canopy of the wood.

As usual my eyes were embarrassingly damp and, as usual, Tom and Elizabeth were babbling with dried-eyed enthusiasm, occasionally turning to me to demand which was my favourite scene or character.

'Baxendorf,' I replied for the character; he had been one of the psychiatrists. 'When Rudy comes alive,' was my choice of scene.

We walked back through the mall, me now silent having bored them with my answers, they chattering. I slowed slightly and let them move ahead and, at once, I felt a great tearing, parting, separating movement within me that made me stop and

132

gasp. The time had come. I was prevaricating with this life. And these children were the real prevarication. The others that held me back were just people, known quantities, and I suspected their commitments were as subtly incomplete as mine, as tainted by secret defences. Children were different, their defences were incomplete, their lives still terrifyingly open to drastic change. I watched them walking away, unaware that I had stopped.

Of course, they had no real need of me, not, at any rate, of the me that walked in phantom cathedrals. We were now discontinuous in our continuity of habits, our films and our shops. Children were different, but they were also different from me. This was an ending, an abandonment for which I would certainly be damned in this world and, perhaps, the next. Tom and Elizabeth were destined to have this severance happen to them. It was just the way of their lives – their father had a big, strange problem and could not grow old walking this mall. Like Rudy he had to walk away. And they understood Rudy.

I caught up with them before they wandered out of sight. It was more crowded now. We had to twist and turn to make our way through the people and, in spite of the certainty of our approaching separation, I felt the familiar panic that the children would be swept away from me and lost. I clasped Elizabeth's hand and she clasped Tom's. The crowds bundled their way past our fragile line, threatening to break it at every turn. They all seemed to be going the other way. We arrived at the car sweating and exhausted. I had grown sick with anticipation of what I was going to do.

Time was passing. Hirtenstein had paid. I had been working on the church, but not effectively. It would soon be spring. I had to move. I had to go now, to get away, back to my church. The conviction came to me as if from outside, from the turquoise ribs and glass webbing of the high vault and from the low, concrete beams of the car park. I looked round at the children, now helplessly strapped into the high back seats of the Intruder. The 'I' that was any good to them had become just a repertoire of old reflexes. I had moved on to some state determined by other demands that could no longer be denied. Fibreglass or not, loved or not, this other I would build it.

'Daddy.'

Elizabeth spoke in her tone of feigned indifference that signalled real concern.

'Yes.'

'Are those spacemen going to die?'

'They might.'

'That's sad. I do like Captain Dale.'

'I think everybody does, he's a hero.'

I would leave with Francesca. Just another marital runaway. But Francesca was a kind of disguise. She provided the acceptable – or at least predictable – public face for my flight. I was really in pursuit of an impossible, unprecedented completion. But I would appear to be in pursuit of the all too feasible, all too common, all too temporary thrill of a new body in bed, a new occasion for tenderness. All true, of course – sweet, cool Francesca – but not the whole truth.

'Home!' I cried, liberating the clattering determination of the Intruder.

'Home to Mummy!' cried Elizabeth.

'Home,' said Tom quietly.

ELEVEN

ON THE MORNING after the Sunday trip to the mall and the adventures of *Rudy the Robot*, I had deliberately risen late while Jill was out taking the children to school. Faking sleep had been a problem; my nerves had kept me awake since dawn and I lay there suffering clammy eternities with every movement of Jill's morning preparations. At least I knew she would not try to wake me, she never did. I used to wonder about this, concluding eventually that unconsciousness was to her an absolute. Asleep I did not exist.

Finally the door slammed and I rang Francesca.

'Yeah . . . hello?' she answered drowsily. In the thickness of her tone, I could sense her body moving in the bed.

'It's me.'

'Hi, Steeeephen. Hello, lover. God, what time is it?'

'It doesn't matter, you don't have to work. I'm going today. I want you to come with me.'

'Sometimes I *do* have to work. Come with you? To the country?'

'Yes. Like we said.'

'Did we?'

135

I felt a familiar anger. So sealed off were our days together that anything said, if referred to later, was usually forgotten, denied or reinterpreted. It was one aspect of her strategy of containment, a way of avoiding awkward spillage. The constant doubt angered me, but the sense of her controlling hand soothed. Her friend, Moira, would smile knowingly.

'For . . . well . . . good?'

'Yes. No. For me yes. For you maybe.'

'But . . . Oh it's too early for this. I really can't sort this out just now. The mornings, Stephen, you know about the mornings. Why do boys never know about mornings? I keep trying to explain . . . '

I heard the bed creak as she fell back on to the pillows in confusion.

'Look, you must, we agreed. I know you can get off whatever you're supposed to be doing. You told me you always can. And don't think of this as running away. Just come for a few days. We must try it. Think of it as an interlude, cut off from everything else. No connections, no implications. Just one of our days, but longer and somewhere else.'

The conversation moved forward falteringly through the mess of her morning discontinuities. At last she succumbed, reserving her position by implying that it was only out of weariness with the discussion.

'All right, all right. An interlude, cut off from everything else. Disconnected. I suppose it would be fun to play for a little longer. But please don't get too serious on me or I'll run.'

She agreed that I would pick her up in two hours.

'This is not a commitment,' she insisted sadly. 'Strictly temporary, strictly . . . well, fun. Fun for me.'

'Strictly fun.'

We hung up and I at once broke the spirit if not the letter of our deal by writing a terminal note to Jill on one of her parchment-coloured sheets of notepaper. The note explained I had left for good. I would be in the country, but she was to make no attempt to visit me as I would be staying there with my new love.

'This is for the best for all of us,' I concluded, 'believe me. Stephen.'

136

Certainty, I mused, was just a case of having a good enough reason to deny ignorance.

I left the note in an envelope projecting like a flag from between two of her box files and, soon afterwards, I was parking the Leopard outside a tall white house, the top floor of which was Francesca's flat. I pressed the buzzer and her voice responded at once through the chromium speaker grille. I offered my customary clownish grin to the security camera whose fisheye lens transmitted a shadowy, monochrome image of me – the head grotesquely enlarged, the tapering, reed-like body swooping away to tiny feet – up to a small, plastic screen in her flat.

'Don't come up. Stay there. I'm ready. I'll be right down.'

This surprised me. I had vaguely expected a couple of hours in her bed. After all, there was no rush, the leaving had all been done. I was free, I could be anywhere. Time and space were mine. But, moments later, she appeared at the door, ready to travel in a long white dress and large blue pullover. She carried a capacious, soft brown bag that seemed only half full. Without a word and with only the briefest glance at me, she slammed the door, walked over to the car and stood patiently by the boot, her head bowed. I followed and opened the boot. She tossed the bag in and, still without a word, climbed into the car and we left.

Her flat was on the wrong side of town so the journey began with an unusually long spell of fighting traffic and enduring the customary abuse and lethally competitive driving inspired by the Leopard. The hood was up in deference to Francesca's nerves. At one point a smartly dressed blond boy crossing the road in front of us, turned briskly and spat directly at Francesca. She flinched, but maintained her silence while my machine coolly washed and wiped the sagging oval of saliva from the windscreen.

Finally the road magically cleared as we reached suburban highways and I over-accelerated in relief, causing Francesca to tense as I swung dangerously close to cars, kerbs and people.

'Stop playing boys' games, Stephen,' she said before falling back into silence.

I slowed obediently and switched on the Traffic Screen. The green web of roads spread and glowed brightly against the

137

dark grey. I called up the code and the route to the house was outlined in red dotted lines running either side of the roads. There were no traffic problems.

The Leopard cut rapidly through rows of trees, past increasingly large houses, then farmland and, finally, we curved over the white arrows on to the clean, black motorway that snaked north-eastwards out of the city. In the hard embrace of the rushing air, the Leopard hummed and sank downwards on to the road. I felt the receding city transformed from an endless net of noise and contact into a bland diagram somewhere behind us. It shrank impotently with the increasing distance, becoming no more than a harmless, grey pattern of haze interrupting the green fields.

Francesca relaxed with the smoothing of the car's movement and slumped down in her seat to become a mound of white cotton and blue wool. Her silence, the misery of the city streets and the time we had taken to get this far had all conspired to fill me with an edgy concern for her state of mind that fought with my desire to smell and taste her skin. I did not dare speak for fear it would precipitate a crisis. I even expected the phone to ring – perhaps Moira, demanding her return. Surreptitiously I turned it off. At any moment, as we had stopped and started, I had felt she might leap out of the door. The motorway made this impossible, but still I was tense with anxiety about what she might say or do.

'We must have music,' she stated.

I put on a tape of some slow, pastoral idyll which I knew she liked. She closed her eyes and eased off her shoes. I suppressed an impulse to touch her. She would not want it. Strange how often women don't.

Motorway time took over. This passes both more slowly and more quickly than ordinary time. In its slow form you are deluded by the fields and towns racing by into thinking that enormous distances are being covered and, consequently, hours are passing. Obsessively, in this phase, I jab at the buttons of the computer in the Leopard only to find that minutes and barely four or five miles have been consumed in what I had taken to be at least half an hour and fifty miles. It does not seem possible that there is so much land,

138

so much space between things. The quicker form of motor-way time is when some train of thought intervenes and you drive as if unconsciously, ignoring the passing incidents of the landscape. Then something – maybe a change in the red and green pattern on the Traffic Screen – draws you back to the process of movement and you find that, now, real time and significant distances have been consumed.

I went through four cycles, peaks and troughs, of motorway time with Francesca apparently asleep and the music automatically repeating itself at least twice, the familiarity becoming hypnotic. Finally, through some reflex, I snapped out of the unconscious, fast mode to turn off the motorway and weave through the narrowing lanes that led to our village, our house and my field. I switched to the radio. Francesca opened her eyes in response to these changes. She gazed out at the passing houses, trees and fields.

'Nearly there?'

The sense of the radio voice resolved briefly to tell us that Captain Dale and the Mars crew were still facing the abyss of deep-space death. The times and distances involved meant that their lives would be in the balance for months.

'Yes.'

When we arrived at the house, I indulged a mindless, proprietorial pleasure in watching her look around. She, however, was uneasy and I made no attempt to act as her guide.

'Oh dear, I really feel I shouldn't be here,' she said, finally. 'This is yours, I mean yours and Jill's. Both your things are everywhere . . . It's really rather tacky, Stephen. Moira warned me I'd hate all this stuff.'

'Forget it. It's more my place than a family place. Now it's totally my place. What you're looking at is the past. And now you're with me.'

She smiled to offer some mild assent to this arrangement, but gave nothing further away. I saw that she had arrived at some private, temporary compromise. It was enough for two nights of languid lovemaking and two days of easy, though cool co-habitation. The atmosphere was consoling and defensive rather than passionate. But, I kept reasoning, this was understandable. She was nervous; it would pass. Soon the house would be turned into a version of the pale bubble of her flat. I encouraged her to move things; I kept the blinds drawn.

Occasionally I worked on fragments of the church and spoke to Tina, through whom I insisted all office messages were to be channelled. Tina was a neutral mechanism and I did not want to suffer from any unnecessary contacts. The room was soon awash with faxes. But paper can easily be burned, conversations are remembered. Meanwhile, Francesca pursued a few minor household tasks, took short walks in the valley or into the village to shop. Most of all, she seemed to be waiting.

This waiting of hers was an active presence in the house; it followed me from room to room. Something was supposed to happen. Doors were ready to open, phones to ring. Once I did hear the phone ring briefly by my drawing board as if she had been talking on the other extension. I asked her about it, but she said she had not used the phone. I accepted this without much thought. The ring had not felt like a human event, more like some manifestation of the field of unfocused expectancy in which we were living.

On the third morning a letter arrived from Jill.

Dear Stephen,

Well I suppose it had to happen. Some fault on both sides is the usual explanation, but, try as I may, I simply cannot help piling all the blame on you. You just pulled out, wrote us off. You just decided something was wrong and that it was too late to do anything to put it right. But you didn't even do anything positive about ending it, until now. You were a coward. All you did was sulk. Even those pathetic affairs were sulks – all the time you sulkily thought those women were showing you what you were missing. But you were too much of a coward either to run or even to fake a happy marriage. Instead you just hung on and tortured me – us, actually, because the children suffered as well. They could both tell your heart wasn't in this household. Oh they adored you for it; children always love the irresponsible one. I loved my father and he left too. But I grew up to

140

hate him when I realized what he had done. I swore I'd never fall for that again. But now I suppose I did. Tom and Elizabeth have begun to understand, and suffer. They will hate you too. My father, like you, refused to supply the boring side of life – the side that makes life work. You thought it could be all rapture, long afternoons in bed with your lovers and then home to us. But you also knew really that if you actually did leave us, you might discover that rapture didn't last. Real, boring stuff would begin to intrude. Well, maybe you'll discover that now – in our country house, the one we bought for the kids. Remember? Now that damned church makes perfect sense to everybody, it's just a way of dramatizing something too ordinary for words – another pissy little affair for another middle-aged man. You really are a pathetic bastard, Stephen.

Regards, Jill.

I did not show it to Francesca, honestly intending to do so later. The envelope had been unmistakable – large and yellow and the address in that tense, formal script, written as if on a ruler. It had arrived before Francesca had risen. I read it standing in the door between the hallway and the living room. Jill wrote with her usual rapid efficiency. How could somebody so full of analysis and theory be so definitively convinced of the virtues of the practical?

'Remember?' she wrote. All that I do remember: love for the impermeable, the blurred, the temporary. And the venom of her closing words. It was, perhaps, only right for such a letter. She would know that and oblige. Such conventions she would be keen to observe.

Each of these nights I had woken early, crept out of bed and walked around the house and grounds. A couple of hours later Francesca would come down to find me sketching.

'Can't you sleep?' she asked on the first morning.

'I always wake early up here. Perhaps it's the silence. I need noises from the street to tell me the time. The birds don't work.'

'Birds never do. Is there something wrong? Don't, please, tell me you are missing something or I shall have to hit you and leave.'

'No, no . . . no. There is nothing wrong. How could there be? This is what I want.'

I pulled her white-shirted hip against my face and sniffed her night scent.

The phone sounded briefly again on the morning of the third day, but again she said she had not made a call. Still I was not exactly suspicious, but uneasy. I concealed Jill's letter with unusual thoroughness. Sensing a mounting airlessness about the household, that day I took her to the Arches in the early evening. A different airlessness. Jack eyed us, smiling.

'You brought a new friend to meet us, Mr Architect Rix. How nice.'

'Yes, this is Francesca. Francesca this is Landlord Jack. He is an old friend.'

She seemed to curl away from his grin like a drying leaf.

'Hello, Francesca.'

'Hello, Jack.'

'Any *friend* of Mr Architect Rix's', he sneered, 'is a friend of mine. Ask anybody.'

'No, Jack, I do not have to ask. I trust you completely.'

We sat and I managed to sustain a jokey monologue about the horrors of Jack and the Arches. Francesca laughed indulgently.

Then Ralph and Sally appeared. It was the first time I had seen her awake. He was in his leather, she in jeans, black jacket and white shirt, a monochrome couple. I felt massively relieved by their presence, stupidly happy to be offered this new, distracting dynamic. I considered that the external pressure of company on Francesca and me might be useful. We introduced each other. Sally looked curiously at me for an uncomfortably long time and then quickly at Francesca.

She turned back to stare at me.

'Ralph told me all about you and how you saw me asleep.'

I noticed the astonishing light greyness of her eyes.

'I did.'

'And he told me all about your church. You must be a strange man. You must tell me about yourself. I'm very interested in people.'

She spoke the words slowly and seriously.

'Then I suppose I must.'

'Sally, dear,' said Francesca, establishing with the 'dear' a certain sisterly authority, 'you are asking for trouble. My friend Moira says never ask any man to tell you about himself, it is quite superfluous.'

Sally gazed at her, the grey eyes now clouded with a sort of disappointment.

'Your friend Moira', said Ralph, 'sounds like a barrel of laughs.'

'She is.'

There was this initial brittleness, but no real pressure. Francesca relaxed into gentle containment of the jibes. We grew drunk under Jack's disdainful glare. Sally lost her somnolent intensity and Ralph lapsed into provincial baiting of Francesca. I found myself wondering what authority I had previously detected in this man. They returned to the house with us. Almost at once Ralph slumped into an armchair, his legs twisted in some semblance of comfort. Sally crumpled into a corner of the sofa and fell asleep. Francesca looked briefly at them and went to make coffee.

I sat down and reread Jill's letter yet again, concealing it in a sheaf of office material that I had picked up from the fax machine. Its vehemence seemed not to quite reach me, as if stopping some distance from the centres of my response. I felt I was reading of some other marriage on this yellow paper. Francesca brought coffee, glanced at me, made a slight sucking noise, presumably disapproving of my involvement with work while we had guests, and wandered off to clutch her mug protectively in her two hands while sitting huddled on the sofa at Sally's feet.

Nothing then happened. This was a difficult interval, filled with Jill's absent presence wreathed about me like smoke.

'Tell me about your work, Ralph darling,' Francesca suddenly demanded.

I assumed she was intending to distract herself from all the remote vibrations that seemed to be filling the silence of the room.

143

The words came out too loudly and caused Sally to stir and convulsively wake. She glanced at Francesca then round the room
to settle on me. She focused and stared fiercely as if angry.

'I know you, don't I?'

She pushed herself upright to lean on her extended left arm.
With her right hand she brushed away a heavy wave of hair
that fell across her face. The terrible, fragile grace of youth, of
childhood.

Ralph looked impatient and twisted to stare irritably at her.

'Of course, he's Stephen. Go back to sleep.'

He turned back to Francesca.

'A sculptor. Stephen's seen the stuff. We can work together.
Lot in common. Must show you the work. It's good, really.'

His anger towards Sally had, however, distracted Francesca.
She looked irritated on her behalf, but Sally merely continued
to gaze. This seemed to frustrate Francesca.

'Do you want some coffee, dear?'

Francesca wanted Sally to be Sister Moira for the night. But
still Sally's stare did not waver from my face.

'I dreamed that you looked different and that you kissed my
eyes.'

The second 'that' felt delicately poetic, a pale marsh light
seemed to hang about her.

'Really? How different?'

'I can't quite say exactly: the same, but different, smaller, I
think. My dreams are usually right.'

So were mine, an alarming thought under the circumstances.
Last night in my brief passage of sleep I had seen bright
lights, glaring and diffused through clouds of smoke that rose
around a heavy, squat building. Windows in this structure were
illuminated by a hard, bluish glare from within and, from its
roof, tiny points of light shone and burst into haloes and spears
as they caught the eyes. At ground level there was an orange
glow through which silhouetted figures, all wearing long coats,
moved with slow gravity. Distant bells rang and sirens blared. I
became aware that I was leaning against some kind of pillar and
a small girl was murmuring at me, her two arms outstretched,
her hair wet and clinging to her face.

'Help me. Help me.'

144

Her face was white and expressionless, not pleading. Her words were flatly stated. Did she want money or something else? She seemed to be acting. An immense anxiety flooded the scene and a man was suddenly whispering in my ear: 'Leave! Leave! Leave now!' But I could not go. I was stuck to the pillar. In panic I tried to pull away. The skin peeled off my back with a damp, ungluing sound. I screamed and woke.

The living room was divided in two. We were sitting at the end nearest the kitchen. At the other end, by the entrance from the hallway, was my work: drawing board, desk and little glowing machines. Unable any longer to cope with Sally's stare now that it had evoked the memory of this dream, I rose, walked into this other zone and began plucking at my papers, drawings, books, yet again concealing Jill's letter among them as I did so. I felt mildly wounded that there seemed no further interest in my church, confused by the drunken drama of the room and uneasy that some new crisis was imminent.

Francesca pressed some coffee on Sally who finally turned away from studying my face and drank from the mug. Ralph stopped reading and walked stiffly over to where I stood inconclusively amid my papers and drawings.

'So you think you're definitely going to build it.'

He looked uncharacteristically purposeful, nodding as if to will me to respond. Work was clearly at stake here. He was pitching for business. I would have preferred something a little more vague and inspiring from my local artist, but he seemed determined to cut through the foggy muddle of the evening. It was his job.

'Well this developer's coming at some point to see the site. There is a kind of weird possibility apparently. It's absurd. But I think now I want it to happen. What else is there to do?'

'Never mind all that. If it's being built, it's being built. Like to work on it – sculpture, whatever. This is right. Said so – about the site.'

I smiled, unsure whether to be touched by this gesture of loyalty or to be adopting a robust business-negotiation attitude. Sally looked up from her coffee.

'What would they use it for?' she asked. 'I don't suppose that many people want to go to church and they don't pay for that, anyway.'

'A leisure centre – like a tasteful theme park. No details yet. That's the only way to get it built.'

'Oh. Isn't that a bit ordinary?'

Francesca smiled slightly at this remark and Ralph snorted and paced impatiently. But Sally was still watching me steadily, expecting an answer.

'Probably. We live in ordinary times. Everybody has to be ordinary. The cathedral must be ordinary and must pay its ordinary way. It doesn't matter what goes on in my head or my field.'

'Why do it then? Why not just stick with what you have got? Some kind of dream. Dreams are fine and they don't have to be ordinary.'

'Because,' said Ralph with the particular mild, drawling, impatient anger he seemed to reserve especially for Sally, 'he wants to build it. No point in being an architect if you don't build things. Anybody can have dreams. The thing is to do something apart from sleep.'

'In any case,' I broke in, embarrassed by his tone, 'it wasn't any kind of dream. That's just what I don't want people to think. It was there. I walked into it. It was as real as you . . . ' I looked at her and we both realized with sudden smiles of intimacy, noted by Ralph, that this was not necessarily the best example, ' . . . or this drawing board.'

I kicked its metal leg illustratively. Absentmindedly I continued with this line of thought: kicking a human wasn't a satisfactory proof of their existence; perhaps you simply had to kick them in the right place. I had often fantasized about kicking people. It was a gesture so unarguable and extreme that I longed to see what would happen. In the midst of the most solemn negotiations I would imagine kicking some client, engineer or accountant on the shin and kicking him again each time he protested.

'And then gone,' said Sally.

'And then, as you say, gone.'

She had stood up and was walking towards me with an awful imploring look in her eyes. I felt that familiar, distant,

146

unresentful yet intense desire to kick her experimentally – my foot would have gone through her barely existent substance or she would simply have crumpled into sleep.

'And not come back?'

'Well not to my knowledge. There may be some crazed shepherds who've always known about it, of course . . . Those guys in the pub, maybe. Perhaps it's just a fact everybody lives with in this place, a well-known local phenomenon.'

'Yes, maybe, but they've never talked about it to us.'

Tiredness swept through me and the energy required for my posturing vanished. I decided to try and say *something*.

'You know the duck–rabbit picture?'

The memory of the old puzzle had surfaced and offered a glimpse of significance. I picked up a pencil and drew it rapidly on the edge of a sketch of a flying buttress that was pinned to my board.

'It is a duck – here is its beak. It's a rabbit – the open beak becomes its ears.'

'Oh, yes.'

'But the thing is: you can't see both at once. Observe yourself switching back and forth – duck–rabbit, duck–rabbit. But it can't be both. No rabbuck emerges, no dubbit.'

Sally stared for a moment and then reeled back, her fingertips pressed into her eyes.

'It hurts me to do that. It makes me dizzy . . . sick.'

'It can do. It's like vertigo. For some reason that's the way I think of my church – church–field, field–church. But never both and you cannot see both an empty field and the church, you cannot see the point of transition. Or perhaps you can see a world without this church, or one with it. But not both and nothing in between. No matter how much you explain it to yourself, you can't see both at once. So, because I now have both, I get this vertigo . . . I faint a lot anyway.'

Ralph was singing softly to himself and suddenly broke off to announce: 'We could have a rabbuck for a gargoyle. Or a dubbit.'

'A non-creature that you cannot see,' I replied, 'and in a high place, very appropriate.'

The tension had gone. We sat, isolated in space, but without

147

anxiety. The rest of the evening passed on the safer territory of old music and eating. Sally and Ralph stayed the night. I rose early as usual, burned Jill's letter in the kitchen stove – a few seconds lying flat on the red coals, then curling, blackening and, at last, blossoming clean, yellow flames. Then, in the cold air of the dawn, I went to see my church.

TWELVE

I WALKED STEADILY towards the cathedral, resisting the encouragement from the gentle downward slope of the pasture
to break into a run. I sensed the need to stay in control, to
discipline the giddy lightness of my head. I wished to impose
my will on this object, to subdue it into stable, recordable
existence.

The sky was just turning blue-black with the onset of dawn
and the stars, earlier so bright and numerous, were fading. The
air was sharp, clear and light with grassy fragrances. There
was no weight of blurring rain or wind to crush my spirit and
distort my vision. The outline of the masonry and even a few
brief passages of glass and tracery rose before me with a new
clarity. Undeniable. Waiting for me.

But there was also no moon and, as yet, no sun, so precise
detail within this outline was impossible to distinguish. I grew
impatient and strained desperately to see more. But the effort
was destructive, the building began to lose its lucid, pristine
immobility. The half-light played tricks with my straining eyes.
Shadowy liquid shapes seemed to be moving over the surface
of the cathedral as if spectral labourers were still working

on its fabric. Pinnacles and parapets were smudged, the few fragments of outlined tracery began to twist and multiply. I struggled to control the pace of my walk, and the over-eagerness of my eyes. I had to restore the calm, effortless presence of these stones and that glass.

It worked. Now, as I walked onwards, the cathedral became as solid and undeniable as it had been before. I started once again to identify what I could of the layered styles of the building. The procedure filled me with a relaxed certainty. I was doing something to deny the enormity of the event, pursuing a professional routine like a soldier under fire, doing what I was paid to do.

Again I was struck by the building's relentless inclusiveness. Its eclectic balance suggested an almost non-committal synthesis: not a cathedral with all its clashing styles and ancient compromises, but *the* completed idea of the cathedral, saying everything and, thereby, nothing. Was it a modern cathedral that knew too much of the official histories, a smart, knowing, studied building? Or perhaps its perfection was real and old. Perhaps my unease was that of a modern man expecting incompletion, imperfect forms, something unresolved. To my tainted eyes the real, realized thing appeared false, phoney. Cathedrals had to be roughened and spoiled by the effort of their construction; Gothic had to fight noisily with itself. But this one possessed an improper poise, an eerie harmony.

Either way, I mused, just right for Hirtenstein's steel and fibreglass. That too would look indecently clean and new and that too would function as a rebuke to my corrupted tastes.

I had been out on one of those pre-dawn walks, familiar to all insomniacs, when at last the hot, black beast of the long night loosens its grip and some faint, refreshing coolness in the air tells you that you will soon be set free to start again. I had been walking aimlessly around the house. Then, on my fourth or fifth lap, I registered a dark flicker in the corner of my eye. I had looked and seen at once the central tower and I had laughed at myself. Wishing, I thought, can be seeing. I had so often looked and expected, hoped, that I was reluctant to believe my eyes when they found what they sought.

But then I took a few paces and looked again. My throat dried and my stomach hollowed. I paused and clenched my fists, summoning up my determination. This time, I told myself, there would be no mistake, I would check everything – the inscriptions, the details, what lay behind the cloth. This time I would bring back evidence.

In this mood, and fighting off all others, I walked down the sloping pasture into the black junction of the nave and south transept. Not only had I been here before, but I had also in my memories relived this sequence of events so often that something in the moment seemed routine. But still I approached the doorway with some trace of the old dread that had succeeded in breaking through my will's noble discipline. And, as I touched the silvered oak of the first door, the familiar sickness returned to overcome all my calm. I felt the black spaces waiting inside to crush me. I paused. Slowly I breathed once, twice and entered through the second door, my eyes closed and my nerves singing with terror.

I opened my eyes as the inner door sighed shut behind me and the dry, cold air of the interior washed over my face. The darkness was at first thick, intense and chilling in spite of the deep, livid blue of the dawn that had now begun to illuminate the tracery and the huge rose window in the north transept. I could taste the dryness of the stone and I remembered the arid, choking taste of the dust from the great cloth. I shuddered and forced saliva into my mouth to rinse away the bitterness.

I could make out little of the nave, the crossing nor even of the transept in which I now stood. But the usual terror of interiors left me impotent, without thought or perception, all bold resolution gone. After a few moments of fearful waiting with a sickeningly thumping heart, I grew aware that there was a silence – no cracking this time, perhaps no cloth. But more likely it was simply still, for, with my reason beginning to function again, I knew that there was no wind in the valley to pierce the gaps in the glass, lead and stone, or to rush through the great gaping space which I had previously tried to convince myself was the only secret concealed by the cloth.

My eyes had at last begun to penetrate the darkness and I could make out the walls of the south transept. There were clusters of shafts joined by a line of blind arcading that rose into fine, slender ogees. At its centre this line was interrupted by a large monument that rose far above the ogees to the level of the triforium. I walked towards it, intending to read the inscription. But after one step I saw, or rather I knew, that it was blank. The monument consisted of a panel of marble, just identifiable by a slight sheen on the white surface with its smoky grey streaks, surrounded by Corinthian columns and surmounted by a pediment. At the base of the columns there were three steps in half-relief with a cloth fashioned from pure white marble falling haphazardly across them from a point behind the panel. It was all new and crisp, apparently waiting for the engraver to come and identify the death owed to these stones.

The classical forms suggested once again the stylistic universality of this place. Elsewhere in the building, I was now convinced, there would be some seventeenth- and eighteenth-century classicism, nineteenth-century stained glass and a spiky twentieth-century sculpture.

I walked on, keeping to the wall. I turned into the nave and, in my eagerness to find more monuments, I forgot, for the moment, to look in the direction of the altar. Instead, finding no further signs of identity, I stared for some time at the labyrinth in the floor at the centre of the crossing. I tried to trace white pathways through the corridors of black stone, then black through white. But the plan defeated me. I was about to kneel and follow the pattern with my finger when, suddenly, I remembered the altar and turned towards it, taking my fears by surprise before they could stop me.

At first I assumed the cloth was still there. The towering blackness suggested as much and the vaulting of the ceiling simply faded into the darkness as it approached the altar end of the nave. But as I stared, unable to move forward, I began to believe that the cloth had gone, that this was some new, more horrible kind of blackness, a blackness of air rather than of fabric.

I edged forward, my legs reluctantly unlocking, passing through the screen into the choir. I moved diagonally to the right and, like a blind man, reached with my arms for the columns of the arcade. At the touch of the first column I pushed myself forward, feeling for the next as soon as I lost contact with the first.

After no more than half a dozen paces I realized that the cloth was still there. A certain shading in the darkness that I had taken to be yet another trick of the light had resolved itself into a long diagonal undulation in the material. The sight made me shudder with the memory of the choking dust in my throat and my entanglement in its reeling cone. Hypnotized, I approached its surface, remembering yet deciding to ignore the fact that I may be about to lose my chance of preserving this new appearance. After all, I calculated, the place could vanish again at any moment whether I approached the cloth or not. I had no certain hold on this building; in an instant I could find myself waking in the vacant pasture, without evidence, as mad as ever. Yet, as soon as I thought this, I felt the stronger conviction that the church would be there for as long as it took me to do whatever I was intended or intending to do. It was there for me.

And still there was no noise. As I moved into the centre of the choir to stare at the full expanse of the cloth, this silence suddenly became dreadful. The shock of it assaulted me like a crash of thunder. It was a rushing, threatening, engulfing presence hurtling down the nave towards me. I spun around only to see a quiet, empty vessel of air.

I turned and walked rapidly to the right-hand side of the cloth. I stopped when I was within touching distance. Into this instant crowded all the anguish I had ever felt at confronting large interior spaces, the sum of the sicknesses of opening the door of every cathedral, castle or great chapel I had ever explored. Again I found myself raiding the defences of my fears; to draw back now, I screamed in my mind, was to die.

The cloth was thick and its weight formidable. Its inertia overcame my first efforts. I had begun experimentally by pushing violently at the surface near the corner, but it barely gave and did not even send a ripple across the black expanse. I realized I was avoiding the inevitable. I was acting like a bullied child, afraid of full retaliation and, instead, pushing impotently at his persecutor. I must grow up.

153

So, with two hands, I reached down, slid my hands between the stones and the edge of the cloth and pulled at the corner. It rose sluggishly. I pulled harder, my arms aching with the effort, and then crouched down and pushed my head underneath. Beyond this awning I at first saw only more awful darkness and I again felt the dry choking sensation of the dust in my throat. I took one crouching step forward, rose to my full height and slowly allowed the cloth to slip down my back. Its weight, massive and insistent, pushed me onward. Finally, I was inside the terrible space and the cloth had returned to its natural position. I looked upward, a movement that caused me to become briefly dizzy and stumble. Then, as my balance returned, I saw the outline of immense windows, their topmost tracery dark against the blue outside. At their base I could discern the darkness of the hills, a range of humped curves behind the rising mullions. Most of the glass appeared to be clear, but the angle was too acute to make out the contents of any colouring in the highest tracery.

I stood for some time on that spot staring upwards. Finally, I allowed my eyes to follow the central mullions downwards to where they met the points of the arcade arches. Below this the rising light now revealed an ambulatory with what I assumed were clustered chapels running around the end of the church and beyond the margin marked by the high east windows. I could now identify the familiar clutter of columns defining the curvature of the passage and rising into the ribs of its vaulting. The pattern of these columns was, as it always is, bewildering from this perspective. But, in plan, I knew a rigid, mathematical logic would be revealed.

Then, close to me, I saw what must have been some form of altar. Something, however, was wrong. There was a table, certainly, but from its surface rose an outline too complex and too large to be the usual cross, crucifix or tabernacle. I edged closer with some fear since the floor remained still gloomy and I was stepping into wells of darkness. But the surface was flat until I reached a step, then another and finally the table itself. Now I saw what stood upon it – a perfect wooden model of the cathedral. It was immense. I moved slowly round the table and reached out to feel the model's surface. The wood was polished and hard and the detailing sharp and new. I moved further along towards the west front which, at that moment, I realized I had never seen, only imagined. But as I allowed my eyes to follow the logic of the building round to the façade, I was distracted by the sudden, familiar sight of the south transept where I had entered. I made out the door, clad with ironwork like the real thing. And then, suddenly, absurdly, I saw a tiny model figure that could only be myself, standing, the legs slightly apart, the arms crooked and the fists clenched before the chest, steeling myself to enter like the brave boy in some child's illustrated adventure story.

I leaned forward and picked myself up. I turned my back to the model so that the figure would be illuminated by the light from the east windows. It could only be me – the clothes were mine, the long brown hair was mine and, staring at the tiny face, even the thick eyebrows, one unsymmetrically arched, were mine. At once I thrust the figure into my pocket, not so much to save it as to get it out of my sight.

I began shaking violently and turned again to face the model. I felt fear, certainly, but also a terrible pressure, a narrowing, a constriction like dying. I was trapped in this. In what? An idea made me go back to the east end and look through the model's version of the windows beneath which I now stood. It was a mad, awful idea, but its logic gave me some slight feeling of power. I was right – inside the model was the table at which I now stood and yet another perfect model of the entire building and, as pathetic specks that could almost be dust, there I was again, this time twice – once standing by the table and once in the south transept.

Hours may have passed as I leaned, my hands grasping the cold edge of the table. My eyes were fixed on the smaller model inside the larger, but I saw nothing, I only imagined an endless recession of interiors, countless versions of me standing before an infinity of doors. My hands grew cold and then numb. A steely emptiness filled my body and then that too vanished. Finally my vision doubled and the twin linked images from each eye began to drift, detaching themselves from their objects.

An instant of panic, of vertigo, brought me to my senses. I pushed myself away from the table and closed my eyes tightly in an attempt to restore my normal vision. For a moment it worked. I looked at the chapels and columns beyond the altar. I could see the dull sheen on the floor of the ambulatory and the elaborate bases of the columns. The interiors of the chapels were also growing visible in the dawn light. I took two paces eastward, down the steps of the altar, and then froze as I saw a movement amidst the columns. A silhouette of a man had flickered against the illumination from one of the chapel windows to my right. I stared hard at the place. The figure had disappeared behind a column but had not reappeared on the far side. Then it did, flickering to life again. Now I raced after it, reaching the point of the last sighting in a few paces. But the figure had moved. I could see it now winding between the far columns. I ran again, but stopped when I lost all sense of the position of that last sighting. I did not know whether it was in front of or behind me. The curved passage and the forest of columns offered no clues. I looked round but now could see nothing clearly except for the rhythm of light and shade that suffused the ambulatory with the full onset of dawn.

Suddenly I was overwhelmed by this succession of shocks. A sickness tore through me; I staggered, the columns rolled upwards as if I were falling away in a long, backward curve. The great east windows stretched to the sky, becoming slender shafts of light.

I came to yet again lying prone in that same field, the cathedral gone. By a touch of warmth on the back of my head I knew that the sun was now well up in the sky, a soft breeze was rustling the grass, some sheep were calling in ludicrously plaintive anger across the pasture and, from the far side of the valley, came the sound of distant shots. Crows were being slaughtered, or rabbits. A few minutes passed. I kept my eyes closed and allowed the sun slowly to warm me. I did not wish to think, only to feel; I did not wish to see, only to be there alone.

Then there was a voice calling. I tried to resist the sound, pushing it away to the edge of my senses. But the shouted name became steadily clearer, too obviously mine, and I could no longer ignore the urgency of the tone. I raised myself unsteadily to a sitting position and saw, at last, Francesca running towards me. Somebody was walking behind her.

'Stephen, Stephen. Are you OK? Where have you been? I thought . . . '

'I'm fine. I'm fine. Really. Just another episode. What did you think?'

'What? An episode!'

Awkwardly I struggled with my trouser pocket and managed to find the figure. I stared at it for a moment and burst into uncontrollable, agonizing laughter, my head sinking between my knees as Francesca stood over me, baffled and hurt.

For a moment she appeared to consider anger, but then changed her mind and, with an air of resignation, she sat down beside me and rested her head on my shoulder. I put my arm around her and buried my mouth in her hair.

'Oh Stephen, Steeeephen!' she whispered. It sounded like pity, but then it sounded like regret.

It was Ralph who had been following her. His appearance now made me yelp with idiot happiness. I had news for him.

'Ralph!'

'Hi, Stephen. Don't tell, let's guess. You've been cathedral spotting again.'

'Exactly. And look at this.'

I gave him the figure. He turned it over in his pale, tattooed hands. 'It's you,' he said with no sign of surprise and handed the figure to Francesca who took it without raising her head from my shoulder.

'Quite. Quite. It's me.'

I laughed again causing Francesca to jerk upright.

'Very nice, very pretty. But, Stephen, we have had a few moments of anxiety. I've been running around the place looking for you. I've had Ralph and Sally out searching as well.'

'They won't mind, they're getting used to me. Did you see anything?'

'What do you mean?'

'Did you see the cathedral?'

'No, of course not.'

'Ah.'

'Who did this anyway?'

'No idea. I found it in the cathedral.'

157

'Of course he did,' said Ralph calmly. 'Don't you see? It's come again. That's where he's been.'

Francesca looked at me in dismay. I saw that my previous sighting had been no more than a symbol to her, a gesture encompassing all that was involved in my flight from home. She had not expected this. She turned the figure in her hand. I leaned over and held her for a moment.

'Sorry,' I said. 'I'm sorry for all this. I did try to explain.'

She shrugged and I felt a moment of panic as her expression turned to one of defeat.

'I'm not sure I can take all this, it's all too messy,' she said slowly. 'Come on. Let's get some coffee.'

She stood up and tossed the figure into the air. Alarmed, I watched it rise, pause and start to fall. Somehow I feared it might disappear in mid-flight. Its existence was so precariously and improbably established by . . . what? It had no right to be here. It should have vanished with the cathedral, but instead it was falling directly towards my face. I reached up and caught it, feeling its hardness, the sharp points of my hands pressing into my palm. Then I rose stiffly and followed Francesca and Ralph back to the house as more shots echoed across the valley. I had my evidence, evidence of me.

THIRTEEN

THERE WAS THE warble of a car horn: loud, close and piercingly high-pitched. The room was convulsed. Sally woke, Francesca started and turned, Ralph jumped to his feet and I rose stiffly from my stool, twisting to evade the malevolent stabbings of my back. The sound had been such a gross, improbable insult that, but for all these reactions, I would have been certain that I had imagined it. On returning from the field we had been overcome by immobility and silence. We were exhausted by circumstances. I had possessed and paralysed them all with the second appearance of my church. Once again I was a wild, wandering creature to be brought in from the fields. But the sound brought relief. Something had happened to lift the weight of my spell. I headed for the front door, elated and grateful.

A scarlet hull was parked, its nose facing the front door. The car's opaque black windows revealed nothing of the occupants and there was, for the moment, no sign of anybody getting out. The object appeared to have arrived under its own guidance and was now simply waiting for a human command.

'Hello,' I offered experimentally from the doorway. Nothing. I stepped outside to study it. This silent visitor and the increasingly familiar act of walking and wondering around enigmatic objects made me fear that this may be some new vision. Perhaps inside this car I would find myself in replica yet again. What could be made of that? It would seem derisive; a car is not a cathedral. This one was a low, smooth thing, immaculate but for the sprays of drying mud behind each wheel. It radiated warmth and emitted the random tickings of contracting metal. On the front wing was an icon of a spiked creature breathing fire and, along its tail, the word 'Dragon' in a dramatic, racing, italic script.

'Hello, Dragon.'

This time there seemed to be a response. There were muffled voices and thuds from the interior. People were trying to get out. Perhaps there was some danger, they were running out of air or the car was primed to explode. Feeling something was required of me, I stepped forward and depressed a square red button in the side beneath one black window. The entire door and window dropped downwards, vanishing into the bodywork to reveal a tall man in jeans and a long, black velvet jacket in the passenger seat, the top of his head brushing the black cloth of the roof. He had been struggling with something, possibly a seat-belt, and now froze to stare at me in shock as if I had discovered him naked. On the far side in the driver's seat was Hirtenstein, wearing a lavishly colourful pullover and lurid green corduroy trousers, evidently his country clothes. He was poking at the dashboard which responded by flickering at him in orange and green. He glanced at me and then back at the flickering.

'Steve, hi! Be with you in a second. This machine has a mind of its own. Well, three minds really.'

He poked for a little while longer, the lights replied angrily and then finally died to leave a black, featureless sweep of plastic.

'Great! Three computers. You turn it off and at least two of them won't believe you. We wanna stay on, we wanna stay on!'

He slammed his hand against his door, apparently at random, and that too dropped out of sight. They both emerged. Hirtenstein pressed a small box held in his palm and both doors leapt back up with a hiss and a velvety thud. A coquettish female voice simultaneously murmured, 'Armed', apparently from beneath the car. Hirtenstein smiled in satisfaction and strode round his Dragon to greet me, as he did so his arms made embracing gestures at the valleys and hills.

'My man, Steve! What a place! What . . . a . . . place!'

'Hello, Dave, glad you could make it. Nice car.'

'Wouldn't miss it for anything. Yeah, a Dragon, not many of them on the roads. God! A Leopard! Is that yours, Steven?'

'Er, yes.'

'Not what I would have expected, not what I would have expected at all. You must have met Dentressangle.'

'I did.'

'That's a strange man . . . and, talking of strange men, Steve, I want you to meet Lionel. Lionel the Night Tripper.'

He gestured at the tall man who was now standing awkwardly before us. He had long hair, a fringe, a massive, drooping moustache and an air of profound gloom. He held out his right hand while brushing something from his jacket with his left. He nodded as he did so and smiled, his teeth appearing startlingly white behind the thick, wet lips that dampened the lower fringes of the moustache. Amidst all this casual softness, his eyes, wide and intense, came as a shock.

'He's my engineer, best in the business, a genius. Plays the guitar too, could have been right up there, eh, Lionel? But music didn't do for him what engineering did. Remember the space frame at Spear Court? Lionel's. He's got concrete for blood and steel for bones. Lionel, this is Steve Rix, my man with a vision. He's got soul. And a Leopard.'

'Hello,' Lionel acknowledged me with a raised hand. 'Do you mind if I take some pictures?'

He pulled a small camera out of his pocket and waved it at me as if uncertain that I would grasp his words. I had been surprised by the quiet, deep neutrality of his voice.

'Not at all.'

'Good. Thanks. I like to try and remember everything, you see. It's a habit.'

'For work, you mean?'

161

'No, for everything, wherever I go I do this. It's important to try and remember. If you think how extraordinary it is to have cameras at all, it's madness not to use them for this.'

'It's a good idea. If you take enough pictures you could become immortal.'

'Not quite. But I do have a terrible memory. But, of course, that means I really do remember things. People who have good memories never really remember anything. It's all just there in front of them. They're not remembering, they're seeing. Do you understand me? I take pictures everywhere I go and then I remember. It comes back to me. That's real remembering.'

He spoke slowly with an air of a man who seriously wanted to impart all of his wisdom at once. And he wanted it to be right. He would argue, I knew, with my most casual asides.

'Kind of a diary.'

'It's not quite a diary. That's not quite right. More a history really, my history. I don't feel I can understand anything unless I understand everything and that means having everything available to remind me.'

'The quandary of the metaphysician.'

'Yes, metaphysics. That's my problem.'

Then, quickly, he backed away, put the camera to his eye so that both his sharp elbows projected at shoulder height and took a picture of Hirtenstein and me by the car.

'Thanks. I'll just go and . . . ' he waved the camera in the direction he intended to go and then walked off around the house, signalling his presence by an occasional click. A moment later he reappeared, frowning in irritation with himself. He had forgotten something. He smiled apologetically, took a picture of the Leopard and then returned to the back of the house.

'An artist of technology, a loner, a saint, a truth-teller,' explained Hirtenstein. 'He *eats* differently from us. Born a hundred years too late, of course. Should have been an Arden or a Smythe driving railways through mountains or bridging great estuaries. Now . . . well, you know as well as I do, Steve, it's different. Everybody's got the technology. But I know Lionel's special. Give this man the materials and he could engineer an entire galaxy. I sometimes think that's what he really wants to do. But Gothic cathedrals – hah! Nothing to him.'

'Probably nothing to me either.'

'Don't start that, Steve. Don't go negative on me. Cathedrals – definitely the next best thing to galaxies. Nice place this. Secluded. Tough to find. But worth it.'

I did not respond, allowing an awkward silence to develop.

'You don't look so good, Steve, been working too hard? I know what you need. Have some Dip. Grade A stuff. Imperial. The works.'

Out of his trouser pocket he slid a small, round, silver box with curious writing engraved on the lid which, after some thought, I realized spelled 'Imperial Dip'. He removed the lid to reveal an inner container of blue glass. Attached to the silver lid was a small spoon. He took this and seemed to press some kind of catch. The blue glass sprang open. He rapidly dipped the spoon inside to coat the bowl with a thick, blue syrup. He slipped this into his mouth, drawing the spoon slowly and greedily between his tightened lips so that it emerged perfectly clean. As a final precaution he ran his tongue over his teeth and lips.

'Grade A!'

I recalled reading of this fabulously expensive drug, available only to the wealthy few. There had been police raids in fashionable areas, television pictures of stainless steel drums of the blue syrup, thinly but expensively dressed women dragged protesting into the night.

'What does it do?'

Hirtenstein laughed as his fat fingers delicately replaced the spoon and closed the box.

'Everything, everything! It makes me the man I am. Without Dip I would be another Dave the Man Hirtenstein. Dip is totally harmless but totally effective. The healthy high. Comes from a jungle plant they discovered a couple of years ago. Grows way up in the canopy. Try it. The planet will love you for it and I know you will love the planet.'

'Maybe some other time.'

'Any time you need it, Steve, any time. And I think you will. I think you will very soon.'

I led him inside, fearful of the demands the chemical might place on his behaviour. Francesca and Sally were now together on the sofa and Ralph was by the drawing board.

'Folks!' cried Hirtenstein, rubbing one eye violently with his fist. 'Great to see you here.'

I introduced them all and explained about Lionel who could be seen outside taking pictures and, just at that moment, wetting his index finger and then holding it upright, apparently to test the wind direction. I had been expecting Hirtenstein, but he had not specified a time and he had not mentioned Lionel. I felt raw and unprepared for this confusion of new reactions. The room had become dangerously unstable. But the other three seemed unshocked by the fat, round man and his lanky photographer. Lionel was now peering in through the window, his hands shading his eyes against the daylight so that he could see the interior. Perhaps they accepted such interventions as normal in my abnormal orbit. There was some flustered rearranging of roles. Hirtenstein shook hands, massaged shoulders and generally displayed intense enthusiasm for everybody in the room. He talked noisily and quickly.

'Now, what's everybody got planned for the New Year? Come on now. Remember this is the big one.'

This was the standard small talk of the time. For Hirtenstein it seemed to be a kind of break-the-ice party game. But the response was no more than a few distracted murmurs.

'Come on! Once in a thousand years – you can't pass on this one. No time to stay at home with the telly or the VR. You've got to plan. Well, I'll tell you my plan, maybe that'll get you going. Yeah, listen to this one. This is one great plan. I'm going to build a church. Steve's church. Good one, eh, beat that.'

He patted my back, grinned ferociously and looked expectantly round at the others. He had offered me up as a dynamic protagonist rather than a case, a patient or a hazard. He saved me from doubt. Real work was afoot; Hirtenstein's bustling presence proved it. But still he could not quite command the room. They, after all, knew one big thing that he did not.

'Oh, yes, the church,' said Sally. 'He saw that again this morning.'

Hirtenstein's bustling ceased.

164

'What? Run that past me one more time.'

'He saw it again this morning. He's seen it before, he saw it again.'

I picked up my figure from the marble table. He spun round at the movement as if I had cocked a gun.

'What's that?'

'I found it this morning. It's me.'

'Yeah, it's him,' confirmed Ralph with breezy satisfaction.

Hirtenstein glanced at Ralph in a way intended to subdue him and bent closer to my hand. He looked as if he were feeding or engaged in some secret act of obeisance.

'It *is* you! Who made it?'

'I don't know. I found it in the cathedral. It was there this morning.'

Hirtenstein rotated slowly upwards to stare at me.

'So. You saw it again.'

'Yes. I think I would prefer to say it was there again. "Saw" is a bit subjective.'

I realized that Hirtenstein might by now have crossed some decisive line with this project. Now it was real, he would not wish to hear of more visions. They would get in the way.

'Steve, what is going on here?' Had he previously taken my story as merely a colourful way of putting forward a scheme? If so, then insisting on another sighting must be unnecessary and potentially insane. He was going to build it, what more did I want? 'OK, OK. Let's get this straight. You saw this church again, you walked into it and you found this dummy of you inside. Right?'

'Exactly. But it's more of a maquette really, don't you think?'

I saw that now was not the time to explain the precise circumstances – the cloth, model, the altar.

'This is really . . . '

'Weird,' suggested Ralph with happy enthusiasm.

'Look, Dave, I saw it once, now I've seen it twice. For me this alters nothing. For you, maybe it does. Pull out now, cut your losses, I'm crazy . . . '

'There is', he said with awestruck grandeur, one hand raised as if in benediction, 'no way I'm going to pull out of this one. I'm still in even if you start clucking like a chicken and barking like a dog. Got that, Steve?'

'Cluck, cluck,' I said. 'Woof, woof.'

'Could you, er, like hold it up?'

Lionel had come into the room. He wanted to photograph me with my figure. He was looking at me through his viewfinder. There was a sliding sound and a little flashgun extended from the side of his camera. Hirtenstein seized the moment, hugged me to his side, beamed and held the figure aloft between us. The flash exploded, bluish white, to fill the room with dancing bulbosities, impossible creatures feeding on air. I looked around, but the flash had momentarily blinded me to the feebler light. As the shapes began to fade I saw the other faces, pale in the shadows, turned towards me. Francesca, Ralph, Sally – a line of faint ovals.

Then the ovals moved. Francesca and Sally had decided to go into the kitchen to make lunch, primarily, I suspected, to escape from the pressure of Hirtenstein's presence. They both went through the kitchen door, but then I saw Francesca hug Sally, nod reassuringly and push her away. Sally walked across the room, passing us without acknowledgement and slowly climbed the stairs. Francesca busied herself with plates and bowls.

Lionel sat down on the sofa and, slowly, balletically, we three managed to sit down as well. It had become a meeting and Hirtenstein at once became chairman.

'We are here to build a cathedral,' he announced as if addressing an enormous rally. It shocked me slightly. I felt dizzy and uncertain that these things were happening, these people talking because of me and my church.

'Ralph, incidentally,' I said quickly, grateful to be able to make a friendly gesture, 'is my man to be in charge of sculptures.'

'Fine. I'll check out his work.'

We all noted that Hirtenstein had made the decision his, not mine. Ralph's lips tightened. Lionel studied Ralph for a moment and then rapidly took a photograph.

'I want to worry about precise use, planning permission and so on later. This is one of the rare occasions in a developer's

166

life where the shape, texture, style of the building come first. Right, Stevie?'

'Inevitably, I suppose, David,' I tried for a bluff tone to maintain my style of competence and cool. 'Hard to think of any kind of planning or use rationale for building a Gothic cathedral – structurally it's unnecessary, stylistically it can no longer mean what it was meant to mean . . . and so on.'

'Exactly. Exactly. All our rationalizations will have to be post-rationalizations. That's how I like them. And, let's cut the crap, that's what all rationalizations are. But, Stevie . . . and it's a big But . . . people feel something special about these buildings, these great churches. They feel they are part of what they are. This is not a replica, a pastiche, a reproduction, a parody. This is not a slavish tribute to history because we are too cowardly to cope with the present. This is a monument to our imaginations, our memories . . . We're not playing at history, we're making it.'

The precarious calm I had been clutching since being brought back from the field had now entirely vanished. With these words I felt the nausea of extreme acceleration, of being engaged with some fatal madness. Hirtenstein had grabbed my church and was racing away with it. He was rushing to monuments, great public works, and yet the whole scheme was predicated on me. It was out of control, but, then again, it was controlling me.

'I think Stephen is aware that there is a small matter of truth to be considered here.' This was Lionel, who was now staring at Hirtenstein, his moustache jutting with the threat of awkwardness.

'Truth!' exclaimed Hirtenstein. 'Truth! What kind of truth? Quantum mechanical? Religious? Emotional? What about imaginative truth? You're going to tell us it's somehow untrue to build a Gothic building. Well . . . History is truth, and this is history!'

'No, I meant structural truth. Cathedrals are the way they are because of the sort of way they were built. Making internal spaces that big with that amount of glass, with pointed arches to avoid different vault heights and so on, they needed all that stuff, all of what we call Gothic. We don't. We *could* still build following their techniques, but it would be crazy – expensive and pointless. We can do anything, we don't need any particular style to glorify necessary structure.'

'Why pointless?' Ralph asked.

'Because it would be no more than reproduction. We can build a perfect replica using a steel frame with stone or plastic as cladding rather than structural support. But if we insisted on the original techniques we would only be proving something to ourselves. Spending crazy money for the sake of being crazy, being very crazy.'

'Seems fair enough,' said Ralph. 'Let's be crazy.'

It was a remark that pained Hirtenstein who had grown instantly impatient with his genius's objections.

'I do not intend to be crazy,' he said contemptuously to Ralph before turning to Lionel.

'So what you are saying, Lionel, is that this structural truth is not actually a practical problem, right? We can go with the lies. It's cheaper.'

'No. It's not a problem in that practical sense. Only in this other sense. And it would be a lot cheaper. I was just worried . . . '

'So,' Hirtenstein repeated slowly, 'your precious structural truth is not a problem, right?'

'No, of course not. But there is a problem about what's right.'

Lionel looked at me. I knew the expression: an awareness that structural truth was precisely the kind of thing an architect should insist on, especially an architect who spent his time walking around non-existent buildings. I had to be some kind of idealist. I felt both that I wished to calm his doubts and that I had no time for any of this. I was not any kind of idealist. I stared back at him for a moment, trying to construct a reply, fighting against my mind's sick desire to wander off, to be somewhere else, moving on to the next thing.

For a moment I lost the fight. My mind did wander as if in sleep to Jill's dressing table: its curious, familiar collection of bottles, a hairbrush, a small pink hippo, two belts, a scarf, a bowl filled with hair clips, bands, complex spring-loaded devices, a box of pearls, tapes of Vogel's concertos, four novels. The details had always repelled and lured me. There they always were, witnesses to the accumulating disillusions or comforts, gestures of the familiar. Upon these she leaned – each to hand, locatable if the lights went out, if she was struck blind or if I left. Emblems of boredom, not of suffering – and, hanging from the angle of the mirror, a thin gold chain with, at its end, a harlequin in enamel. Then Lionel was the harlequin, the flecked colours of his shirt . . . And Lionel needed my help.

'No. Don't worry, Lionel. In this case I don't give a damn about structural truth. It's over-rated anyway. Like Dave said, it's all post-rationalization. People build things because they like the look of them and then make up respectable reasons why. It's not bad, everybody does it, even the best. Lies, I'm afraid, are probably the precondition of all good art, so why not tell a few real whoppers? Cheap is good. And, anyway, it's too late now, far too late. Also the thing about lies is they tell you exactly what to do, they control you.'

I gave Lionel what Orlando called my pale, adulterer's smile. But, as I did so, I sensed I had begun to understand something important. Lionel nodded slowly.

'That's one way of looking at it.'

Francesca came in from the kitchen.

'I've made some food – any time you like. It will be delicious. Sally said she was going to have a sleep.'

Ralph leapt up.

'Oh, yeah. She won't eat. She feeds on sleep.'

We followed him slowly into the kitchen as Hirtenstein launched into a standard eulogy about the house, the valley, how wonderful the food looked and so on. We ate and talked with a normality that began to pain me. Led by Hirtenstein, we discussed work and home life, news and opinions. We drank white wine – Francesca slowly, Ralph unconcernedly, Hirtenstein sociably, Lionel voraciously and I to produce some carefreeness and to suppress a growing fear about the continuingly cool and remote state of Francesca's mind.

'It's a trick,' insisted Hirtenstein. 'There's nothing wrong with that ship. They're just saying those guys will drift off into space and die to stir up publicity, a bit of excitement, and keep the money coming in. And look at Captain Dale, straight out of a comic. Dale McCluskey. It can't be his real name.'

'Yeah, maybe,' agreed Ralph.

'A good trick, though,' I said. 'We've all imagined the horror of the slow, distant death. Think of being the last one to go . . .'

Afterwards the usual fatigue threatened us all. For some time we half-dozed and talked desultorily until Hirtenstein insisted on a walk around the site. Reasonably enough, I supposed, that's what he was here for. But the whole affair seemed increasingly invisible, hidden beyond mountain ranges of tiredness and anxiety. I felt little enthusiasm for the project and the second appearance had driven the vision inwards, away from any sense that could be made clearer by the frantic and tortuous processes of a construction project. And there was Francesca. She stayed behind, leaving the four of us to trample the field. Lionel took notes and photographs, Ralph stood on any available mound that he could find, the better to survey the area, and Hirtenstein enthused.

'Lovely site, lovely. Got to get people in, of course, but that shouldn't be too difficult. Few roads, car parks. And what will they *do*? No, no. I mustn't think about that now. Steve, stop me whenever I start getting practical. Look at him!' He gestured at Lionel. 'Having the time of his life. There's a happy man. If he couldn't be building the Millennial Archive or the Villaincourt Bridge, which he can't, then this is the next best thing. Don't let all that structural truth stuff worry you, Steve. It's going to be great.'

Hirtenstein needed to be blind to the problem of Lionel's doubts. Maybe he was right, maybe Lionel was always unsure of the truth of his buildings. Was this one really more of a lie than any other? Could a building lie?

For a long time we were out there, walking, talking and sitting, all of us following Hirtenstein's lead and exuding optimism and enthusiasm. It was simply too exhausting to attempt anything else, I thought, as numberless anxieties and premonitions swelled within me. We sat at last in a mute row, even Hirtenstein's patter having been depleted and the Dip, I assumed, having worn off. We were halfway up the slope of the far side of the valley. Below us the field, the stream, the fences and walls around my site. Almost level with us on the other slope was my house and, above that, the stone walls that formed square fields, each with its own small barn. Distance lent a poignancy to this ancient organization of empty space. The far hill seemed trapped beneath a net of stone which held it down, kept it still for the barns to be built and the sheep to graze. Only the rocks, the caverns, the water beneath this artificial surface were free of us. On the surface nothing was untouched by men and their animals. This place was as replete, crude and vivid as a city, as busy with the past. Yet the landscape of our intervention remained a thin skin. Immediately below and immediately above we barely touched. The theatre of our action was like a painted surface, extension without depth, a stretched membrane . . .

'It's a great site,' said Ralph.

Hirtenstein slapped him on the back.

'You're right, Ralphy, a great site. My Stevie and my Lionel will work wonders. Have some Dip.'

'Wow!' exclaimed Ralph, 'Really? Dip!'

'Never had it, eh? Well now's your chance, Ralphy. Imperial – the best stuff. Just the little finger.'

Hirtenstein was now exerting his control over Ralph, subduing his awkward, cool independence. With the clumsy expertise of the fan who derives his knowledge from reading rather than doing, Ralph wet the end of his little finger and touched the surface of the blue syrup. He then studied the resulting dark, glossy circle before pushing it luxuriously into his mouth.

'Waaah!' he sighed happily.

'Straight through the membrane,' Hirtenstein told me with a pedagogic air. 'Doesn't have to get through the stomach and all that stuff. Instant happiness. Instant totality. Sure you won't have some?'

'Not now, thanks.'

'Waaaah,' moaned Ralph, grinding his fist violently into one eye.

Lionel looked at me, his eyes giving away nothing. Unable to respond, I lay back in the grass and closed my eyes. A soft breeze was blowing and I listened to the birdsong that it seemed to carry across the pastures. The other three were silent again. I thought of us, a motionless tableau on the hillside. My consciousness wandered and slipped into a momentary sleep. I was walking down the three steps of the monument I had examined that morning. Behind me was the blank rectangle of the plaque. I placed one foot on the rippling material that lay there. The shiny surface slithered, carrying my foot off the edge of the step. I fell backwards and, as my head hit the plaque, I jolted awake, sitting up at once and staring across the valley, tense with anxiety.

'Wow! Stevie! Take it easy,' cried Hirtenstein. 'You got a problem of some kind?'

I looked at them quickly. Ralph was now hugging his knees, his head was flung back and his eyes closed.

'Great site,' he was murmuring. 'Great site.'

Then I looked back across the valley. Rising up the far slope along the mud road that led only to my house was a car. Blue and purposeful, it arrowed up the slow incline, glinting as it was caught by the early evening sun. It was Orlando's car. Behind it, pompously bouncing and splashing along the track, was the square orange bulk of the Intruder.

FOURTEEN

'Visitors!' cried Hirtenstein.

'I know ... Orlando ... ' I stood up, muttering, 'among others' to myself.

'Great! Orlando! Couldn't be better. And who are those other guys in the ute? Is this a party? Yeah, Stephen's cathedral party.'

For Hirtenstein, of course, there never could be too many people. A group convinced him that he was functioning properly, a crowd that he was winning. He was struggling to his feet and trying at the same time to heave Lionel up by one thin arm. Lionel was attempting to oblige, but his shoes kept slipping on the grass. Ralph was roused from his dipped bliss and he was now staring, empty-eyed, at the cars.

'Busy, busy,' he said in breathy wonder. 'Things happening. Life ... it goes on. You've got to hand it to life, it just goes on.'

I considered waiting for these people. They seemed sadly helpless and disordered on that hillside. But I was too much in fear of what was going to happen next to delay. The cars were an invasion fleet. I was being raided. There was an old, infantile, guilty liquefaction of my bowels; I had been caught with what I had stolen. I turned and walked rapidly, tripping and stumbling, down the long valley slope.

'See you at the house,' I called back.

I had to hurry, the cars had begun dipping downward towards the trees. My chest was clutched by a desperate, erotic anxiety. My soul was entangled with the musk and the cool, dry slither of Francesca. I had left her unguarded. Suddenly I knew exactly what those brief rings of the telephone had meant. These cars did not carry visitors, they bore sensible executives, rational people rushing to the rescue, delivering justice, restoring harmony. They had come to take her away.

'This cannot happen . . . this cannot happen,' I chanted to myself with each jolting pace down the hill.

It took a painfully long time to reach the house and I was breathless when I arrived. Orlando's car was parked awkwardly at right angles to Hirtenstein's. The two made a lethal steel 'T' in red and blue as if signalling to passing aircraft that this was the right house to bomb. The Intruder was neatly aligned with the Leopard, a pair that dumbly summarized the old balance of my life. The front door was open. I walked straight in like a suicide, charging violently at my fears because of the greater fear that they would hold me back.

'This cannot happen . . . this cannot happen.' Get on to the next thing.

Inside I first saw Orlando standing at the living-room window gazing across the valley. Clearly he had been watching my descent and was now following the less frantic course of the others. On the sofa were Jill and Francesca and, silhouetted against the brighter light emanating from the kitchen, was Tom. Panting, I considered my reactions as the eyes of the room – though not Francesca's – swung towards me.

I was not quite shocked. Orlando and Jill colluded on so much. Now, presumably, they had some plan of salvation, revenge or organization that would neutralize or reverse my flight from Pointed Park. The eyes waited, confident. I felt the soft weight of their gaze and the awful conviction that my body was to be deprived of what it most needed, Francesca's controlling presence.

174

'Dear boy! Nice to see you.'

'Orlando, what a pleasant surprise! *And* you brought the family.'

'Of course. You have been missed. We cannot let you get away that easily. Now catch your breath. You are quite red.'

I looked at Francesca and felt a dome of pressure rising in my chest. I gasped audibly with the effort of preventing the pressure being released as a sob. Francesca raised her eyes. I was about to lurch forward and fall at her feet, but the pause had already been long enough for Hirtenstein, Ralph and Lionel to catch up. The room was filled by a confused crowd. Sally was, I assumed, still upstairs sleeping. That still left eight of us. Hirtenstein was at once happy with this number, the noise and the action, but he understood that here was a crisis. I had told him most of the details in the course of the afternoon. He adopted a solemn expression. But, even as he did so, it became clear that the stimulus of the sheer number of people had overcome any awe that he might have felt before the issues at stake. Presumably also he had taken some more Dip on the way down.

'Wow! This is really a big meeting! Everybody's here! Orlando, glad you could come. We've got a lot done today. We can fill you in. Lots to talk about . . . '

'Hello, Stephen,' said Jill, her voice cutting through every other sound in the room and turning even Hirtenstein into a marginal presence, 'I thought we had better meet. Tom wanted to see you as well, Elizabeth is with the Beatties. Francesca and I have had a very useful talk.'

With that brief list and the cosy menace of that 'useful talk' she subdued the farce of the room into an ordinary, rational, psychological drama, one she had probably witnessed and even staged a dozen times among her friends. This was a generic scene, played daily up and down the land. Hirtenstein, Lionel and Ralph were merely comic adjuncts, light relief from the main action. And the main action was the marriage. In keeping with my role in this new play, I felt myself adopting the pose of manly wrongdoer, phlegmatic in adversity.

'Hello, Jill. Would you excuse me for a moment?'

I walked through to the kitchen and smiled at Tom who turned to follow me. I poured myself a large drink, walked back into the lounge and dandyishly raised my glass in a toast to Orlando who was watching me with a mild, expectant smile. I fought against my awareness of the still figure of Francesca.

'Well, Orlando, you've done your bit. Here's to it. Best have a drink. I would hazard a guess that there is some rough ground to be covered.'

'Thanks, Stephen, ever the gentleman. I'll have a large one.'

A long ballet ensued. Drinks were provided for everybody, temporarily and grotesquely turning the affair into Hirtenstein's party. We shuffled and deferred. I marvelled at the power of the mechanics of civilized behaviour. The dance ended with us all standing. Orlando had his back to the fireplace, his legs slightly apart in the 'warming' position favoured by rural types. I pointed this out to him.

'I know. I know. Something about a fireplace – fire or no fire – that makes me do it. Ancestral memories, I suppose.'

'No, you instinctively go for the spatial focus of the room, the better to dominate.'

Jill was heading towards us.

'Of course, silly of me, the altar of the household gods.'

We were both now watching Jill.

'I'm finding it difficult to reach altars ... though I made some progress this morning.'

She had arrived and was watching us patiently.

'Yes, yes, I know. Gigantic cloths, rain, wind, the Gothic imagination ... Wait a minute, you mean it's come back?'

There was a panicky acceleration in his voice. I detected in this the faint shadow of a previous agreement with Jill to try and play all of that stuff down.

'Afraid so.'

He sighed. The fireplace itself was a reminder – arcades of pointed arches in the surrounding woodwork, two sneering faces to keep the spirits at bay. Orlando followed my eyes.

'Gates of hell, dear boy. Don't let the absence of flames fool you.'

Jill took hold of his elbow. I expected her to address me, but she simply drew Orlando away. Her direct powers were now diluted by the number of people; this was a gathering rather than a meeting. There were conventions to be observed. Nevertheless, she would use her silence towards me as a weapon of intimidation. Without Orlando I suddenly lacked a role. I was isolated in my exposed position, centre-stage by the fire. Presumably that had been her intention. I felt some defeat approaching. More than ever I needed Orlando's chatter, whatever gross conspiracy he had indulged. That was, of course, why she had so artfully taken him away from me. I was obliged to seek other male company. I headed, almost without thinking, for Lionel and Ralph. They were in a corner by the stairs. I arrived as Lionel was demonstrating some structural principle with the palms of his hands. I chose to ignore this and launched into a speech, the style of which I assumed Ralph would recognize and indulge.

'OK,' I began, spreading my hands in counterpoint to Lionel's, 'we say this man is interested in, say, astronomy. We psychoanalyse this interest and come up with psychoanalytical explanations – maybe a mother's blue dress covered in tiny polka-dots drives him to study the night sky for the rest of his life. But it tells us nothing about astronomy.'

Lionel was watching me, his palms still poised in a now redundant demonstration. Across the room the others were talking quietly in a single group. Hirtenstein was standing slightly apart and beginning to look irritated. Tom was reading on the sofa – a book on stars.

'OK, you reply, but the universe is a human construction. Astronomy is only human. It has no autonomous existence. So when studying the human reasons for an interest in astronomy, we study astronomy, such as it is, admittedly reduced. But: that is fine and true, it does not, however, answer the original problem, though it may define the reason for the impulse. Or does it? The psychoanalytical conviction arises from an understanding of *why* we say/do/are things. It misses the point that we are doing it at all . . . '

Lionel nodded slowly, thinking mistakenly that he had missed the reason for this speech. He decided to ignore what I was saying.

'In the future,' he said, 'we are going to have a lot to say to each other, Stephen.'

I stared at him, shocked by the tone and baffled by the forecast. From nowhere Jill appeared.

'Stephen . . . '

But Hirtenstein had also arrived.

'Talking it through are we?' he asked with an unaccountable sneer in his voice. 'Good. Because this is serious. I get the impression around here,' he gestured at the others, 'that some people think this is some kind of *joke*. Well a joke is exactly what it is not. And I would just like to say here and now to you, Steve, that out there in that valley, something happened for me. Now I know for sure that it is not a joke because I began to see something, a bit of your cathedral.'

I stared at him in disbelief.

'Don't look shocked, Steve. I really mean this. There is a magic in that site and I believe you have seen deeper than anyone into that magic. But others can see it too. Maybe not as deep as you but you can't have magic just for one person. I really think I began to see a tower. You know – crenellations and all that.'

'I suppose I find that quite flattering.'

I had spoken quickly and without meaning. I feared Jill's expression that suggested she might lose her social poise in anger at Hirtenstein's confession and simply attack me with the weapon I knew she was concealing – Francesca.

'You saw it,' said Lionel with sceptical wonder. 'You saw his church in that field? Are you quite sure?'

Ralph laughed. This provoked a savage glare from Hirtenstein. I could see that laughter was the worst reply. All his energy sprang from his desire to be taken seriously. He had been a joke once, never again. If he saw the pale, shaking outline of a tower hanging in the air, it was no laughing matter. Jokes were out. Hirtenstein was, after all, a visionary.

'The fact that I saw it tells me something. It tells me there is some buzz, some vibration in this valley. It tells me that Steve is on to something important, universal. You've got to do things that seem right, however crazy. I *feel* this is right. You've been given something, Steve, I don't know how, but it's right. I know because I saw it.'

He was using words designed to subdue all criticism. He was

accustomed to the freedom of expression granted by power. This would, of course, be useless against Jill. I glanced at her, risking contact. I wondered if our plastic surgery deal was off. If she was about to trample upon Hirtenstein, as seemed likely, then she would be effectively breaking her end of the bargain by threatening the project. But then, I supposed, at the time the deal was struck I had failed to mention the flight with Francesca.

'I wish to talk to you, Stephen,' said Jill.

'Ah, one moment. I must just go and talk to Tom about something, something important . . . Tom.'

'Hello, Dad.'

'I was thinking about that film – *Rudy the Robot*.'

'Yes.'

Orlando had joined Hirtenstein. 'So you've seen the church, Dave. Extraordinary. You do have this marvellous reputation for close identification with your schemes.'

'It's what you all want to do, isn't it, all children – build a perfect friend, a friend who really likes you, that you don't have to worry about,' I said to Tom.

'This is going to work, Orlando. Right, Lionel?'

'Well, no reason why not, structurally speaking. It will work. We can build it, we can blow it up, we can do anything. That's the strange thing, we can do anything.'

'Got to work, got to work.'

Voices, voices, let me hide in the voices.

'I suppose so,' said Tom.

'Yes, a perfect friend who will lead you, guide you and tell you what you want to hear. That's what you – we – all want.'

'Yes, but why did you leave us, Dad?'

'Oh, well . . . that's something else entirely.'

I turned slowly from Tom to face Jill. I suspected her face behind my shoulder had provided the cue for Tom's question. He would have been briefed. You have a right, she would have told him, to know. He is your father. Ask him.

'Now I suppose we must talk,' I said to Jill.

'Of course, we must. This is all I have to say: you're making a fool of yourself. What is all this? All these people? It means nothing, exactly nothing. That Hirtenstein is up to something, he's not going to build your church. Even if he was, what on earth is the point? See churches if you like, but why torture everybody with them?'

Tom was staring earnestly at us. I looked at Orlando; he looked at me and then at Francesca who put her hand over her eyes in a delicate, mannered pose. The room's eyes were all closing against me.

'Ralph, Ralph, about these sculptures . . . ' I said desperately.

'Got to work, got to work.'

But Jill had followed me.

'You'll go on because you think everything really means nothing, so why not follow any passing craziness? But that is pathetic – just cheap boys' talk, games, gadgets, wanting to have something new at any cost. Oh, you'll bumble on convincing yourself it's the meaning of life, elevating your own wants and needs to some great system, but never actually getting anything done that involves anybody else.'

Her face was without expression, her voice quite calm.

'I have', I said softly, 'no say in whether these things happen to me. They happen, that's that.'

'So you have to build it – just because it happens. What you should be doing is asking why it happens.'

'No! Why? What on earth is the point of that?'

I had howled this and the silence afterwards was intolerable. I had to escape it. I pushed my way through to the kitchen, stood for a moment and then turned to confront the room. Faces, many faces.

'Francesca . . . '

In my confusion I could not see her.

'Francesca . . . '

There was a dazzle of lines, forms, a flock of shadows. And then her voice.

'Yes, Stephen, I'm going back to town with Jill. It is the right thing to do. Remember our agreement – you will not argue. I have spoken to everybody concerned and I have spoken to Moira. I know you said this was just a visit and it was all voluntary. But I had to get a lift back and I could scarcely

180

ask you. You were in no mood. So I spoke to Orlando.'

'Orlando. Why not Moira?'

'She does not, as you know, have a car.'

'Ah, yes, of course, Moira does not have a car, but Orlando does.'

Now I saw Francesca clearly. I closed my eyes and felt the darkness of her skin, the drowsy welcome of her arms ... Steeeephen!

I slumped heavily against the table and smiled at Orlando.

'You bastard. Why have you done this to me?'

FIFTEEN

THERE WAS A long, embarrassing interlude in which Francesca prepared to leave while the others engaged in a friendly, sensible debate about the journey back to the city. It was as if nothing had happened. That, of course, was the point – once I was discounted, nothing had happened. Consequently I was to be either ignored or treated with distant, proper deference.

'Excuse me a moment, Stephen,' they would say with lowered eyes, 'I just have to get this . . . '

'Yes, yes. Sorry.' Sorry for having happened.

Hirtenstein, who, alone in that room, still seemed to have an investment in my self-esteem and sanity, took me aside to murmur encouragement and practical details. I was aware of the vehemence and precision of his voice – real business was at stake – but I understood nothing. I could only watch people bravely becoming themselves again, solemnly detaching their lives from mine. Jill organized everything and rattled car keys; Francesca was gracefully mute and obedient to the impersonal necessity of a quick exit; Tom ran about the house on useless errands invented by Jill; Sally appeared drowsily from the bedroom and observed the activity from the stairs; Ralph and Lionel talked quietly, occasionally helping; Orlando smoked and watched.

Finally, there was a conclusive assembly, a roaring and a cloud of blue fumes, and the Intruder left, hurling two muddy sprays at the Leopard. Hirtenstein was standing behind me, clutching my arm. The pain of his grip woke me at last to the meaning of his words.

'Remember this, Steve,' he was saying, 'remember. If this is what it costs, this is what it costs. But you still want to buy. You have to know when to pay. Now is when.'

'Ah. Yes. That makes sense. Now is when I pay. And,' I pointed, 'they made a mess of my car.'

'Yeah, but, look, it'll wash off. The thing is: keep at it, Steve. We'll talk. Soon.'

'Right.'

Then, to my surprise, he collected Lionel, disarmed the Dragon and left. I had thought that we still had some unfinished business, but evidently not. As they left, Lionel lowered his window, leaned out and made some hand signal I could not decipher. I stood, forlorn and dazed, at the door and then went back inside. Sally and Ralph looked at each other and also decided, with a regretful smile at me, to leave.

Clearly, I was contagious. They had all edged politely away from me as if by agreement, leaving only Orlando, still leaning against the fireplace, still watching me. His decisive immobility suggested there was some conspiracy at work of which this was the final act. Orlando was to make sure that I was all right or, at least, understood everything that had happened to me – they would all want to be sure I understood.

'You bastard,' I repeated, placing the preceding fuss neatly in the parentheses of my abuse, 'not content with conspiring with my wife, you now conspire with my mistress. Or rather you arrange for her to be kidnapped.'

'Mistress, mmm, quaint word. I take it she told you we had spoken? Told you, that is, before the announcement she just made.'

'No. I worked it out from the coy dings on the telephone extension and from the somewhat disembodied quality of her denials. Though I realize now that one of the dings must have been bloody Moira.'

'Ah. Moira? Bloody Moira?'

'Her friend.'

'Ah. Women always have friends don't they? Unattractive habit.'

'Well, what did you say to her?'

'Surely that is obvious. I told her with worthy, poignant concern that this was good for neither of you, that you were in no condition to make such decisions and the best she could do for you was to let you sort out this crisis alone.'

'Why should you do that?'

'Because I thought . . . think it is true. Face it, Stephen, you may be having some sort of breakdown. The thing is to make these decisions – about Jill and the children – properly, not in the shadow of this bloody church, this job, and certainly not with the easy availability of a comfortable alternative like the darling Francesca. You know I want you to build this thing now. But it's just more architectural stuff, not a life change. I think all this other stuff threatened that. The more you think of this as just work, not a life crisis, the better.'

I sensed a motive I could not fathom. This was too rounded, too perfect. 'I think you should be careful what you say about Francesca . . . '

'Loyal to the last. I meant availability to you, of course.'

'Yes, but this breakdown – correct me if I'm wrong, but don't you approve of its financial implications, the Gothic leisure centre . . . Hirtenstein's business . . . Maybe Francesca, my, mmmm, mistress, had sound, cash flow implications for you.'

He smiled, curving his lips downward. 'I repeat: I don't think so. I think she was in the way, the whole breakdown thing was in the way. As you know, I'm all in favour of getting the work, dear boy. And certainly Hirtenstein has already committed himself – er – seriously . . . In that sense you can't get out of it. It is important for all sorts of reasons that you are unencumbered.'

'So you just want the bit of the crack-up that makes money?'

'I suppose that's right. But that does not preclude me being concerned for whatever suffering you may cause to yourself and others. And, come on, I'm afraid Francesca didn't need much persuasion from me. She told me she had only come for a few days anyway. And surely all *that* was a distraction. Why can't you just stay up here alone and get on with the work? We just put up stuff, nothing to get hysterical about.'

'Because this stuff is different. You cannot consider this cathedral as just another scheme, another fact in the world of facts. Well, perhaps *you* can, but I can't. It is not the same sort of thing. For one thing it is pretty obvious that Rix–Cummings would not be building a Gothic cathedral if I hadn't seen it. This can't be just more stuff.'

We were beginning to talk angrily without the usual camouflage of style. We both noticed it and we were both embarrassed. Orlando made uncomfortable moves to leave. This frightened me. I asked him not to go just yet. I asked him to stay the night. He agreed. We said little more that evening, indulging in a long charade of dinner and drink and both going to bed early, insisting we had reading to do.

The next morning we met silently over coffee. He indicated he had to leave early. We decided upon a quick walk. We chose an undemanding route along the side of the valley, following rather than crossing contours in deference to Orlando's poor physical condition. He was silent until we dutifully paused to admire a view. By now he was red and sweating from the effort of the walk.

'Do you remember that shop?' asked Orlando. 'The Everything Shop.'

'Dimly.'

'We thought it was going to be the biggest job of our lives. Those strange, thin men – the Pameran brothers – wanted us to build them a store that sold everything, absolutely everything in the world. Before we even met them we had drawn fantastic, hundred-acre sheds.'

'I remember. And when we did meet them they just wanted one small, white room, one desk and one chair. Customers would go in and tell them what they wanted and then the Pamerans would hit the phone.'

'It was a lovely, white room. Nice job in its way. I used them once. I wanted an ounce of a herbal aphrodisiac from the Far East, unbelievably rare. But as soon as I mentioned it the Pamerans asked me if I wanted the green or the white. They found me an ounce of both within a week.'

We walked in silence for a while. Orlando appeared to be struggling with something more than just the effort of the walk. He gasped occasionally and emitted the odd opening syllable, but each time he changed his mind and aborted the sentence.

'Forgive me,' I said finally, 'but is there something you wish to say?'

He was irritated by the intrusion, but concealed the fact. 'Nothing at all, dear boy, nothing of substance. Meadow pipit.' He pointed at a small bird swooping low over the grass.

'I'm sorry. You seemed to be trying to speak. And, on the whole, I think you owe me quite a lot of – er – chat.'

'Explanations, you mean? I thought I had explained. I have this simple, practical role in your great, significant life. I am the fat, literal friend of the thin, dreaming idealist, I am sure you have encountered the convention. I may be the last in that honourable line. Perhaps I am here to save your neck.'

He clutched me painfully just above the collar as he said this, squeezed and then pushed me away as if in disgust.

'Well, thinnish. Lark.' He snapped the last word as a bird rose close by, rising as if borne up by the downdraft of its frantic song.

'Yes, perhaps saving my neck is what the world requires of you, Orlando, and there is an awful lot to be said for doing what the world requires of you.'

'You can talk,' he flared grandly. 'You've just stopped doing precisely what the world required of you.'

'Not at all. I'm still being an architect. I'm merely doing what the world would require of me if it were the whole world as it really is. The world can't be simply you, Jill and the children.'

'Yes, but what the world seems especially to require of you seems to make such a mess.' He gestured back at the house.

'I don't really mind, of course. But it's essential to keep the ordinary life ticking over, not to let the magic stuff get out of hand. Curlew.'

A large, pale bird with a long, downward curved beak dived into the valley emitting a sad, warbling, unresolved cry.

'How do you know all this stuff about birds?'

'In a minute, let me just sort out the matter of magic. Apart from anything else, it can blind you to some basic problems of, well, values. It might interest you to know, for example, that Hirtenstein is probably a murderer.'

'Really?'

'There is a lot of talk – substantial talk – about one or two people who've stood in his way mysteriously vanishing. I expect he was wonderfully convincing about why it had to be done. But he is still a gangster.'

'God! How worrying do you find this? You're the one who brought him in. And, anyway, surely you're the big pro-cathedral man these days, the convert to the cause. Why bring up stuff like this?'

'That's my entire point. You've got to see the magic clearly to be able to get on with it at all. I want you to see this as being nothing more than it is – not a drama, not a dream, not a vision of heaven, just more stuff. There's no real problem about Hirtenstein, you always have to deal with the acceptable bits of people and ignore the rest. I just want you to know. And, since you ask, I've always known about birds. My education was one of great breadth.'

'I know. I was there, if you recall, during the great days of your education.' Orlando sneered slightly at this. 'But you can hardly just dismiss the cathedral as magic. Remember I saw it, touched it.'

'I suppose on the positive side we can say it's not involved anybody's death yet, though it will. There is, as you know, a more or less fixed death rate for buildings. People drop off and God knows how many will tumble down your west front or crash from your transepts. But the thing is I don't want it to kill you, it's done some damage already. You've no women left for one thing, you've gone from two to zero rather quickly. And that's not just my fault, you know that perfectly well. You've got to watch this. Believe me, it's just stuff like any other stuff. Let's call it Adulterer's Gothic.'

'Very good. That captures the sexual implications. My church, I meant to say, is male.'

'Some consolation.'

'It's specific, selfish. Men always have their particular problems. They make, for example, lousy friends. They can't talk because they always come back to their answers. Women make good friends because they might be altered by what you say to them. That's what I used to like about them when I had a couple of my own. But nothing can alter the cathedral – so it's male. And, probably, because it kills people. Men do that too.'

'Don't get obsessed with the killing thing. Perhaps I shouldn't have mentioned it, though one hates not to. Also there is such a thing as a good man friend, that's what I am trying to be, not that you would understand. I'm trying to help you.' He had stopped and was looking at me. But I avoided the proffered intensity.

'Oh, yes. Now I understand. Kidnapping a lover is a traditional gesture of friendship in certain rural societies, I believe. Even maybe destroying one's faith in a saviour – Hirtenstein, in my case. Oh, yes, those are the actions of a true friend.'

'Oh, for God's . . . ' He paused, bent down and pulled up a clump of grass as if dissipating the energy of his frustration. 'Think about it, Stephen, think about it.' He was angry, more angry than he should have been.

'Look, there is no point to whatever it is you are trying to do,' I said. 'There's no persuading or explaining to be done. The cathedral stops all that.'

'Yes, yes. You mean it's an absolute. Fair enough. Men are absolute, women relative. I, being a man, live in a world of absolutes.'

'Oh right, that's fine then. So what you are doing is giving me a shot of absolute – get on with the work. I'm all man at last.'

'Plus, thanks to me, you can get on without all that kissy-kissy stuff. Lapwing. Always works,' said Orlando, suddenly expansive, 'the countryside . . . ' A breeze was hissing softly through

188

the grasses and there were more larks, trilling dementedly upwards.

'Yep, suckers you every time. A good place for my work – building a cathedral for a dope-crazed killer.'

'Dope? Oh yes the Dip – I noticed that. I wonder how much he takes.'

'As much as necessary, I'm sure.'

We stood silently for a moment.

'I suppose you want me to see clearly that we are blackguards in collusion with a crook we hate.'

'No, I want you to see much more than that,' said Orlando. I noticed his eyes were damp. I had never seen this before.

'Come on, you don't care, it's just profitable stuff.'

He looked at me in desperation. 'Stephen, why can't you see . . . ?'

But he could not finish the sentence. He swallowed with terrible difficulty. There was nothing more to be said.

Soon afterwards we returned to the house, we shook hands – something we never did – and he left. I stood at the door watching his car pitching and slithering through the mud and rocks of the road and the completion of his sentence came to me – ' . . . that I love you.' The car vanished beyond the trees leaving me connected with nothing.

That was it: jealousy and possessiveness, indulging my church but stripping out of it all that might take me away from him. I tried to face this, but it was no good. The shock waves of my loss were still too strong.

'Can't you get it into your head,' Jill had said as she left, 'that other people have problems. So bloody self-absorbed.'

'But am I? I ask because I really want to know.'

'You are', Orlando had murmured from the shadow of the porch behind me, 'definitely self-absorbed.'

I turned to see his shadow at the door.

'You just work towards neutralizing everybody you meet,' Jill had said, climbing into the car. 'Then, when you have, it's all over for you. Move on to the next person.'

It was sort of true, but what did it mean? It was just a characteristic, it wasn't as much as all of me or as little. Inside the car Francesca had sat in the back seat, her head bowed.

189

Tom was beside her, palely watching me. I raised my hand and held it motionless in valediction. What I really wanted was to be neutralized in return.

Frightened by loneliness after Orlando's departure, I walked into the village to visit Ralph and Sally. Ralph, I told myself, was part of the project, part of work. I was not even avoiding work by such a visit. But I was. Sally answered my knock at the studio door. She looked dishevelled but unusually awake.

'Stephen. Ralph's not here.'

'Oh, well, I . . . '

She ran her hand through her hair, at a loss for a moment. Finally the hand fell awkwardly into a gesture of invitation.

'Sorry. Come in. Have some coffee anyway. You must be feeling very bad, that was some scene. Have they all gone now?'

'Yes. I'm sorry to come down here. I couldn't face things . . . '

I didn't mean to place myself so much in her care, but I knew well enough the motives that had defeated me again. This was a desultory opening for seduction. Look after me, I was saying, stroke me. Please.

'That's OK. Sometimes it's no fun being alone.'

'Where's Ralph?'

'Oh, I can never be certain. He does things – I'm never sure what.'

The last words were thrown as a parenthesis over her shoulder as she turned from me and walked back into the studio. I followed her. The large room was as before but neater. The bed was made and most of the debris had been arranged in piles – metal with metal, wood with wood and so on. The sculptures remained as I had last seen them, except that each was now surrounded by a swirl of imperfectly swept dust. I sat on a low, black, canvas chair as she made coffee in a far corner.

'You're all alone up there now?'

'Yes, as we said . . . '

'Oh yes, you explained.'

'Orlando finally abandoned me today. He's my partner, the big one. You know about the others, they all went yesterday.'

'Yes. Orlando asked us to go. I thought he was being a bit domineering, but he said you two needed to talk. Perhaps it's the best thing for you to be alone.'

190

I looked at her to establish if this was a considered remark or a simple pleasantry. But her back was still turned and her head bowed to the running water. Her right forearm rotated vigorously as she cleaned some mugs.

'I hope so. I suspect at the moment it is the *only* thing.'

This made her look round, a new alertness in her face.

'Yes. It can be quite clear what is right. That's all right. Sometimes you can tell, even though most of the time you can't.'

'Can *you* sometimes tell?'

'Sometimes, very occasionally. Of course, I've never had a cathedral. But there are other things ... things you see, things you know. I usually know when I've finished with somebody, for example, even though I might want to stay. How do you want your coffee?'

'Black, no sugar. I want to stay awake.'

'Coffee doesn't do that for me.'

She brought the drinks over and then sat cross-legged on the floor in front of me, nursing her mug between her cupped hands, her head bowed and her face concealed behind the curtain of hair.

'What do you mean about sometimes you can tell? It sounded as though you had thought a lot about that.' I felt I was talking to some oracle or medium who required gentle, portentous interrogation before she would yield her meanings. I imagined her as a rock or dark pool of water before which I sat in supplication.

'Well it's obvious, surely,' she spoke as if trying to establish whether I knew the password. 'Sometimes you know what to do without actually being able to say *why* you know. That's all. It's not complicated.'

'No, it isn't. I think that's exactly right. Maybe that's the only way you ever really know – without being able to say why. How long have you known Ralph?'

'About a year. We met at some exhibition. He was trying to break bits off the sculptures without anybody seeing. But I saw him at once. I always seem to see things I am not supposed to. I asked him what he was doing and he said he was improving them.'

'Was he?'

191

'Who knows? I think he was really trying to improve himself. I liked that and he looked good. I just wanted to go to bed with him. I don't often get that feeling, but I always act on it. He says he can't just look at things any more, he needs something to happen, something to mark the fact that he has looked at things.'

'He's right about that.'

'Like you, you mean? Getting your cathedral built.'

'I suppose. But he is at least inventing his achievements for himself. I had this cathedral thrust upon me. No effort on my part at all. I didn't have to break off anything. It seems to be just a question of copying it down.'

'Tell me what happened the last time it appeared – when we went looking for you. Nobody talked about it afterwards. That was eerie. I felt sorry for you, you must have needed calming down.'

I described the incident as completely as I could. When I reached the absurdity of the climax, I became self-deprecating, laughing at the infinitely regressing maquettes of myself as they appeared in the narrative. But I could not deflect her purpose with my ironies, she only listened ever more intently. Again this was seduction, I knew perfectly well she would feel obliged to fight my self-dismissals. I stopped at the moment that I was discovered in the field, clutching my poor self. She stood up and walked over to a window carrying her coffee. She gazed into the street without moving and spoke distantly as if not to me.

'I suppose it means you cannot ask any questions.'

'What?'

'Well, when you get past the curtain to the altar it only shows you yourself and the cathedral. There's nothing *behind* it, only the same thing over and over and that's you. So you can't ask it questions like: Should I build you? Or: What do you mean? You just have to deal with what you've got. And that appears to be you.'

'Have you been thinking about this?'

'Not really. I just don't think I've made the mistake of *not* thinking about it while pretending I was. I mean I haven't been thinking about it as part of something else – your life

192

or whatever. It's obvious you have to think of it as something new — not just as more of the same.'

'Exactly what I was trying to explain to Orlando.'

'Can I try something with you?'

I felt a swift, erotic expectation. Women could always convince men that something sexual, something sexual and new, was about to happen. We were victims of our own optimism. But did women know that men always hoped they might mean that?

'Of course. What?'

She turned from the window and walked over to a small cupboard. She took out a red, lacquered box.

'I have this friend. Well, she's a teacher really. But she teaches everything. Not arithmetic and that kind of stuff . . . the forces that lie underneath, the things that make arithmetic and everything else.'

I fought one disappointment only to be confronted with another — she was a sweet, gullible mystic. She sat down on the floor again, opened the box and took out two silver objects from their nest of crumpled silk. At first I thought they were spheres, but, as they caught the light, I saw that they were polyhedrons.

'She taught me this especially.'

'Who is this woman?'

'Who . . . ? Her name is Freya, but asking "Who?" about her seems silly. She knows too much to be a "Who?" Whos don't live for ever, but I think Freya does. She says she doesn't, but I think she does.'

'Oh. Well. What do these do?'

'This is perfect for me and it might be good for you. It's a way of focusing things. These are Talisks. They are solid silver and they have, I think, a hundred and twelve sides. They have been made in the East for thousands of years. Each Talisk is supposed to contain all the others that have ever been made and this concentrates their powers. As history goes on individual Talisks will become more and more powerful. But these are already very strong, even though Freya says we have hardly started.'

'What do you do with them?'

'Just this.'

She cupped a Talisk in each hand and raised them, her arms bent, to shoulder height.

'That's all. But then you have to relax and concentrate. That's difficult. You can only learn it by doing it. But, once you start, you will find the Talisks will lead you on. You should be a good subject.'

She rose, handed me the Talisks and then gently pushed me out of the chair and into the correct cross-legged position. I held them as she showed me and shut my eyes. They were cold and heavy.

'Nothing might happen. Some people have too much resistance. But you shouldn't have. Let your mind settle. Don't force it. Just let the things you are thinking about kind of subside. It should really work for you, Stephen.'

She kept talking in this vein, in the way, I assumed, Freya would have done with her. It was all hypnosis, I supposed, but why not? And how could we know? Maybe it was not *all* hypnosis. I would be a good subject because I saw cathedrals. I was already committed to the underlying forces; I had seen them in action; I was worthy to be initiated.

The pose and the closed eyes made me feel vulnerable. I felt the heavy, threatening presence in the room of Ralph's sculptures as if they might lurch towards me. Some part of me also feared that Sally would suddenly leap forward and tickle me under the armpits, revealing that it had all been a joke. 'You looked so serious, Stephen . . . ' How easily Jill or Francesca could have tricked me like that. I remembered an adolescent party game in which I was blindfolded and a girl had taken hold of my hand, pointing with my finger. She used it to trace around the outline of an imaginary woman, rising, finally, between her legs, higher and higher and then . . . she put my finger in her mouth causing a leap of shock as the woman-drawing momentarily became intimately real.

In my mind I laughed and wondered at this. Then it was as if I dreamed. Sally was still delivering her repeated instructions, but I was in a room with the cloaked man, the cats, the howling creatures.

'These are your dreams,' said Sally, 'but you are not dreaming them, they are being drawn out of you by the Talisks. Dreams

194

do not mean anything as we always like to think. They are just yours. Relax and concentrate.'

Or was she now in the dream, talking to me? I had simply dozed off.

'No you have not. That is how it feels, but you are still here, still awake. Remember these dreams do not mean anything. They are just part of you. That is why I cannot see them.'

Now I was walking across the field. It was light. I looked up to see my church. But it was not there. Hirtenstein was in front of me, looking up at where the west towers would have been. I placed my hand on his shoulder, he shrugged it off angrily . . .

'Ralph's back. We'll have to stop now.'

Rubber soles hissed against the surfaces of the stone steps, the door opened.

'Steve, she's got you at it too. Worked has it? No, of course not.'

Opening my eyes was a colossal effort. Ralph was smiling jeeringly at me. Then he looked at Sally, then back, just long enough to suggest he could suspect infidelity in case it were true. It was a gesture that depressed me, reeking, as it did, of cheap, male games.

'She really goes for this stuff. She really thinks you can get there with some magic, but you can't. There's no short cuts. Only work. It's all work. Well that was an amazing scene yesterday, amazing . . . '

What had fascinated me about this man? He now seemed no more than the route to Sally. Women, women. He was looking impatiently at me for a response. Then he shrugged.

'Oh, OK, tell me: did Sally's magic balls work for you?'

'I don't know . . . I . . . '

'God, you won't leave it alone,' he said to her. 'That bloody Freya, another crazy earth mother. They're all so gullible when somebody has big dresses and dopey eyes. Get somebody in the right mind, you can talk them into anything. As if Steve didn't have enough to deal with.'

Sally had taken back the Talisks and was slowly putting them away.

'Yes,' she murmured. 'You can talk us into anything.'

195

'Were you telling me that I was not dreaming?' I asked rapidly before Ralph could take over the whole room.

'Yes, of course, you weren't dreaming.'

We looked at each other.

'Love's young dream,' sneered Ralph. 'Old silver balls Steve. You'll grow out of it. Everybody does. Look, you have more important things to think about. Been working on the church stuff. Look.'

He strode dramatically across the room and, with a flourish, drew a white cloth off a table to reveal a number of models for gargoyles.

'Look! Come over here.'

I rose painfully from my cross-legged position on the floor and walked to the table.

'Look at the faces.'

He had done me, Orlando, even Sally and himself, all straining outwards, projecting on short stumps of clay. There were also rapid drawings of Jill, Tom, Hirtenstein and Lionel.

'I'm going to get them all in.'

'They're brilliant. You work very quickly.'

'When I've got something to do. I work through the nights.'

'Poor Sally.'

'Don't worry about her. She can sleep through anything. And she's got her balls.'

He dismissed her problems with a backward sweep of his arm. I wondered if she was still with him out of inertia or lust. I searched rapidly for some way of neutralizing Ralph so that Sally and I could continue to talk, so that I could find out what she had done. The women, the women, why did they always do this to me? Why did it always seem different? What good did it do them? This one used magic. But Sally felt no need to keep in touch. She replaced the box, took the evening newspaper Ralph had brought in and lay down on the bed to read it.

'Are these finished?' I gestured at the heads.

'As models yes. We'll need more, of course, but these are as good as they'll get.'

The weight of his work, the responsibility it placed on me, finally swung my concentration from Sally to Ralph. His confidence in the entire project unnerved and embarrassed me almost as much as Hirtenstein's. 'When I've got something to do,' Ralph had said. I had given him a goal in his life. I was a patron, dispensing work to a studio of eager aspirants. He had delivered the message and I had accepted it, signed my assent. Soon my doubts would be overwhelmed by the need to keep them all employed, soon the logic of simply continuing would take over from the unimportant issues of significance. I couldn't, as Sally had pointed out, ask it questions and, soon, I would not be allowed to. Working drawings would be taken from my board to be deciphered sceptically by engineers, builders and labourers, perhaps recruited from the Arches. And all because of this unquestionable entity. Sally was right, the fact that it would speak only of me as well as only to me made it hard and unapproachable. Perhaps her Talisks were more reliable guides. You could only ask the cathedral what it was but not how or why it was. And yet how could I ask anything else? What it was was too easy – a good, Gothic cathedral, a thing with a context, a history, an apparent catalogue of attached meanings. You could *read* about such things, they were a matter of public record. But no index or bibliography would lead me to how or why.

I was suddenly unable to cope with Ralph's expectant pressure. I turned away from his table, and, in my distraction, I walked over to where Sally lay and attempted to continue our conversation.

'That ... what you said earlier ... means I have to build it. I cannot think about it further, there is nothing new to be learned or said, the only additional knowledge available is whatever will be acquired in the process ... That is the message.'

She looked up from the paper, her eyes blurring with impending sleep.

'Right!' cried Ralph, flinging the sheet back over the heads. 'So let's build!'

Sally was looking back at me as if to signal that she had heard my voice and excluded Ralph.

'It's asking a lot,' I said as softly as I dared, 'expecting me to go ahead with something which most people would regard as a clear symptom of madness. And maybe your Talisks . . . '

'Just do it if it seems right,' she said. 'Don't listen to *most* people. What's the point? Life's too short. And the Talisks might help as well. It's the thing about dreaming.'

'Because of life being short you could talk yourself into anything.'

'Or out of it. Anyway you didn't talk your way into this. You said yourself it's not your achievement. And I bet it's too late now. That businessman seemed pretty keen. He could do it without you, couldn't he? Maybe I'll talk to Freya.'

'Well, of course Hirtenstein could. In fact, he'd probably have me killed if I got in the way. But that just means it's better that I do it instead of some hack.'

'Yes.'

'Yes!' called Ralph from the far side of the room where he was making himself some coffee. He had abandoned our conversation in disgust, but was prepared to endorse any positive notes. 'Yes! Fuck Freya! Do it!'

I left them soon afterwards, feeling disconsolate and disorganized by these conversations. Nobody could help me with this, not Sally, not Ralph, not Freya. I walked across the fields, thinking of Sally's sleep. Not carnal, I thought, something else. But that was what I always thought. It was probably lust, finding yet again some transcendent value in the next woman, the next sudden girl. And I wondered about Orlando. What did he want?

I began work again. It was ten twenty-eight the next time I looked. Darkness had fallen unnoticed. I was alone. The night air was still. I felt cold. I hobbled, awkward with the stiffness of my concentration, into the kitchen to find a drink.

These were to be the days of disconnection. Only me alone with what I had seen and what I wanted to do. To most people, I thought in the first flush of confidence from the first swallow of whisky, such days never came. They simply died having been accompanied and connected in everything they did, not being self-absorbed, not being disconnected. But I had joined the aristocracy of absorption, the dynasty of the driven. The trouble was that the choice was not mine. I had been chosen. But, then again, it was all and only me.

I glanced out of the window to where the church would have been, but there was only darkness and no moonlight to silhouette any spires or pinnacles. So? It would come back, even if I had to build it to make it come back. I finished the whisky and went to bed to dream exclusively and endlessly of Francesca while Sally explained to me that I was not dreaming.

SIXTEEN

THE NEXT DAY I began work at once. It was easier than ever before. The lines were calmer and clearer. Through them I could see the stones, or, at least, Lionel's structurally lying substitutes. The drawings had become practical. Now, as I drew, I felt the forms growing outside me instead of bursting from within. I had stepped back, taking, after all, some of Orlando's advice. I still used my first, rapid sketches as guides, but they had lost the excitement that had previously obscured their precise content. Suddenly this was a job, suddenly I was a craftsman engaged by Hirtenstein and preparing for the awful literalness of the build-ing frenzy that was to come. Just work, stuff, that's all it was.

Orlando rang.

'Stephen. What are you doing?'

'What do you think I'm doing? I'm working. That is what, you will recall, I am here for.'

'Of course. Just checking, dear boy. No further symptoms, I trust, nothing unsettling?'

'Orlando, thanks for ringing, but I'm working, that's all you need to know. I think I want all future work traffic to go through Tina.'

'Right. Well, while we are on the subject, could this, ahm, traffic be two-way? I know your romantic exile is paid for and everything, but it would help us no end if we could see something.'

'Of course, I shall send you everything that is remotely definitive.'

I hung up. The burden of madness was being lifted from me. It felt like a betrayal of Francesca. But it was workable, I could function, I could become the job.

Tina rang.

'Hello, Tina.'

'Hello, Stephen. How you?'

'Fine, Tina, fine.'

'Good, a few messages . . . '

She reeled them off. Bernard had asked me to call, he still could not grasp that balcony. There were a few anxious client demands – perhaps they had heard that I had become unreliable. Orlando could handle all that. But Jill had also rung with some studiedly elaborate details involving the children and had even included two painful messages from them.

'Good luck, Daddy,' said Tom's.

'Buy me a bear,' said Elizabeth's.

All designed to damage me, an effect accentuated by the neutrality with which these words would be delivered to me by the exquisitely disengaged Tina. These women. They *thought* about such things. Nothing, however, from Francesca. She would be talking to Moira.

'Thanks, Tina.'

'That's OK, Stephen. Hope it's going well. Anything you need?'

'Time.'

She laughed. I hung up.

Time. A few weeks since this had all begun. Was it spring yet? Robbed of my consolations, I was falling towards the Millennium. In a crippled ship, Captain Dale McCluskey was falling towards Mars. You and me, Captain Dale, in one descending curve.

Outside a fine rain was falling, spring rain, barely wetting the land, though, seen across the breadth of the valley, it formed heavy curtains that declined gracefully into the ground. The phone calls had snapped the thread of work. They had freed my mind to eddy away from the drawing board and drift through those curtains, across those distant surfaces of grass, trees and rocks. Time passed and the falling of the rain engulfed me in a thick, slow tiredness. I slumped into the familiar base condition of my being. I was as if turned down to conserve power. Here nothing happened but the sluggish meanderings of thoughts, disorganized as smoke directed only occasionally by some purposeless, inconsistent breeze. Here it did not matter what or how the world was, the chains of my daily linkage to its demands were fully severed. The ship and gravity would take me to Mars.

Some small physiological jolt, some chance chemical flutter flicked a degree of life back into me. I looked at my latest drawing. The spandrel danced before my eyes, its concave sides detaching themselves from the capital and twisting upwards, flamelike, before falling back, becoming again fine lines of black ink, sharp images whose precision seemed a defence against the future chance distortions of stone or plastic. Outside one of Orlando's curlews cried. Strange hollows pitted my skull and my mouth felt dry. Buy me a bear . . . Good luck, Daddy. Green, chamfered numerals on the black, plastic square attached to my drawing board told me it was eleven thirteen. This clock had no depth, how could it tell the time? It would tell me what came after eleven thirteen, but only when it came. For the moment, however, its message fitted the likely facts – my furies of concentration averaged four hours and I seemed to recall feeling this southern flank of the nave take me over at around seven.

I became aware again of the terrible vacuum of the house, now filled only with the evidence of my work, precisely that which had driven all those people out and exiled my children. The walls of the living room and kitchen were hidden by the drawings I had tacked and taped to each other and to the powdery stone as soon as I had woken. Details, plans, elevations, axonometrics of the cathedral. This was the work of a man alone. The drawings concealed almost all the evidence of a previous life – the pictures and the mirrors, they even spilled out to mask Jill's dark, patterned rugs. So right, I thought, so true; these vaults, these arches, trefoils, clerestories, arcading, these were the stuff of something lasting.

The pomposity of the thought made me laugh at the moment of thinking. Lasting how long? For the moments, perhaps, that they chose to taunt me in that field. Never mind. I had chosen them rather than anything else. Why? Because of some argument. With whom? I don't know, but there is this argument with myself as another. What are *you* doing? What am *I* doing? All an illusion, like feeling a pain and saying: 'I am in pain.' Absurd. There is a pain . . .

There had been this church. Yes. And here it was, so complete now that Hirtenstein could almost start digging. It worked. A vault of 110 feet, high but not a joke, not a theme-park exaggeration intended merely to sting soured, modern palates. Instead the whole formed a subtle confluence of styles, the high summer of Gothic yet freshened by its early spring and even cooled by autumn and intimations of decay. Also, of course, midnight: the finger that raced at you from the altar as you entered from the west front to crush you with the sombre, roaring certainty that You Are Nothing. Men once lived to build such things, for what? For an abstraction that said your petty life, your fears, worries, even your certainties were so much dross unless they were redeemed here. Oh we carved the quaint workmen at their humble tasks, but not because they were who they were. It was the tasks that counted: humble, yes, but, more important, exemplary – gathering wood, picking fruit, who cares? They only gathered or picked for this sublime summation, to be raised to this model heaven. Finally, petrified in limestone – itself the product of countless, silent, pointless, marine lives – and framed in marble, granite, lead, glass, they became their tasks. Names spent, little dramas long gone, words forgotten, they hunched obligingly beneath their parcels of logs or peeped roguishly from the foliage of an apple tree. Or, for my church, Ralph's jut-chinned cast of characters, lacking attributes maybe, but drenched in personality.

But these churches were not made by the little people. Such places were designed by a few crazed, fine-boned intellectuals who saw, for those brief centuries, divinity in a structural necessity. They fingered the sharp bones of their cadaverous cheeks and decided that nothing was not structure. Even the pinnacles, such apparently gratuitous embellishments, were there to counterbalance the thrust of the vault by pressing down upon the buttresses. Because the world was made like this with its leverage, its light, its stones and, above all, its gravity, they had to build like this. Therefore the work was divine, the way the world was and the way that heaven must be. The stress, the effort was an endorsement of this transcendent realism. Classical repose was a denial of the nature of the world, it spoke only of redundant effort, an excess of support. Gothic celebrated the limits, the extremity of circumstance, the freak chance that brought us to life – the strong force, the weak force – such a delicate trick, as fragile as the shafts that rushed upwards and then sprang and splayed into the vaulting. Now we know the universe is like Gothic, straining and creaking, emitting occasional cracks and detonations with the efforts of its own continuance. It could fail at any moment, but it does not. Those intellectuals worked it all out so that their structures shivered with a terrible efficiency on the brink of existence. It cannot be, the coincidence and the effort are too much. And yet it is.

Yes, yes, this was the way to do it. I would work Jill and her contrivances out of my system. 'Buy me a bear.' 'Well, I suppose it had to happen.' It certainly did. Francesca, so long.

Start with the vault, the roof of heaven. This had made sense as a semicircle, a simple, pure form and one believed to be structurally sounder than any other. But semicircular vaults can only cross at the same height, must be of the same width so that the radii of the arcs are identical. Or, of course, you can stilt the lower and narrower, but then you have the ugly transition between different heights of the springing as you turn the corner from nave to transept. The answer is a pointed arch. This allows the vault to spring from the same height with the difference being embodied in the curvature of the vault itself – the narrower the nave or transept, the steeper the incline of the vault. The construction is more complex since wooden centring must be provided for two curves rather than one. But, happily, the idea that semicircular arches are more structurally sound turns out to be an illusion. And the different curvatures solve the aesthetic problem. They leap ahead of the lumpen barrel vault, capturing variation as the quality of a better heaven.

But that is not all. There had been pointed arches before. What was new here was the rib, the raised element that delineates the point and curvature of the vault. Once you have these ribs the entire nature of the building is changed. We are looking not at a two-dimensional structure whose fabric is also its support. Rather we are looking at a rhythm of rib and web — the ribs the frame, the web the infill. Suddenly there is tension, the drama of how much can be held up by how little. This building is not standing up simply because of the redundant massiveness and solidity of its structure; it is standing because of the absolute precision with which the lines of stone have followed the lines of stress. The structural wall becomes a vulgar abomination. Now thrust can shoot up and down columns, shafts and responds. The logic of the vault flows down through the church. And, as we follow it down, the web is replaced by brittle, coloured glass in celebration of our liberation from the wall. Meanwhile, outside, the outward thrust of the vault is caught and conducted downwards to earth by flying buttresses. Again the stone is freed. Even beyond the primary confines of the building, the stones still fly along the lines of force as if the church's logic radiated outward to change the world.

There was no limit to the implications of that ribbed vault. Its logic was pursued downward through tracery and ornament. The buildings angled and twisted their way into ever more astonishing improvisations, ever more devious avoidances of the cool frontality, the severe receding planes of the classical, always aspiring to some ideal of dynamic repose. And that repose would mean the perfect, lucid city had been realized, a city because of its million niches and corners for a million people and perfect because the logic of the rib and the vault had been fulfilled. Then we would see the light at the beginning of the world, the light that came from beyond and pierced these fragile nets of stone, the light that came in intense, sloping shafts, blinding us and thickening the patches and corners of darkness. The light was the justification.

I knew, then, why I wanted this. The style freed me of the responsibility of style. Gothic controlled me, told me what to do, what was the next thing. I was freed of the burden of starting again with every building, the awful openness of being modern. What I had to do was not design a church, but design a *Gothic* church. I belonged to the idea, as safe and secure as those little stooped figures of farmers and peasants. Unknown but recognized, unnamed but identifiable free not to invent rules but free to follow them. Saved by a system that required not Stephen Rix, but an architect.

Then the man in the black cloak was pleading with me in some unknown language, a cat was howling in agony and we all raced together through immensely tall, leaning columns that supported a vault too distant to be glimpsed but whose oppressive, pointed forms seemed clamped to the dome of my skull. The scene was lit as if by a frozen lightning flash that cast silvery-blue rhomboids across the stone floor. Running ahead of us, flitting between those terrible, irrational columns, were, I knew, Tom and Elizabeth. And, above me in the tracery, was a face.

I was woken by a sharp knocking. Sleep, I reflected bitterly, always intervenes to cut off your escape or your happiness and then you are saddled with a new kind of wakefulness. I had slumped on to the drawing board and a small thread of my saliva had stained the spandrel. I shuffled to the door, feeling a certain gratitude, something needed to happen. I had begun to sense the danger of an approaching pause, the danger of being overcome, paralysed by the returning madness of the enterprise. I opened the door to find a man with a gun.

'The postman', he said at once, 'is laid up. He broke his leg. He fell badly from a wall.'

I nodded sympathetically. The postman was an important man up here. He would be one of those carved in wood on a screen or in stone at the apex of an arch, one of the belongers.

'I hope he will be all right.'

'He will. He asked me to give you this.'

Over one arm was crooked a broken shotgun, the other now reaching towards me, offered a letter.

'It's registered, you'll need to sign.'

I took the letter and he pulled a small pad with a pencil attached to it by an elastic band from his pocket. I signed.

'Probably the bank or a parking ticket.' He looked at the Leopard.

'Probably.'

'Anyway, I'll be off.'

He did not move.

'Thanks for bringing it.'

'My pleasure. You're the architect then.'

'That's right. I am an architect.'

'You're going to build a big church here. That's a new one.'

A great weariness overcame me as I realized there would be ever more people demanding explanations. Here, in his boots and coat, was the representative of the locals, concerned not with my vision, Hirtenstein's money nor with Sally's oracular insistence that I go ahead, but with the awful, banal impact on the town, the valley and their lives.

'Oh, you've heard. Well it's early days yet.'

'But that's the plan?'

'Yes. It's a possible scheme.'

He noted with a slight sneer my pedantic modification of his vocabulary.

'A possible scheme then. A possible scheme. What's it for?'

He shifted his gun to his other arm and the fantastic thought crossed my mind that he was actually there to threaten me. Soon I would be crouched naked on the ground, the barrels in my mouth and the surrogate postman demanding that I forgot this cathedral business and left the valley for good.

'It's a kind of landmark, a leisure centre. The developer wants to bring people here – it's so beautiful –' I gestured feebly at the bluish-grey bowl of hills, 'but he thinks it needs something like this as a kind of focus.'

He nodded and said nothing. I carried on recklessly.

'The cathedral was just an idea I had that I happened to tell him about. I never thought . . . I think I just imagined that this place looked as though it was made for a . . . building like that . . .'

'One of these Rural Beauty Zone jobs then?'

'Exactly.'

The phone rang. I looked slightly desperately at the man to

discover what more he might want. Let me just get on to the next thing, please.

'Ah . . . I've just got to get the phone.'

He nodded, leaned his gun against the door frame and crossed his arms.

'I'll wait.'

Then, with some fleeting idea that I might at least separate him from his gun, I invited him in. He followed me as I rushed to the phone. It was, as I had guessed, Hirtenstein. He would not have allowed himself to become traffic for Tina.

'Steve, you OK?'

'Fine, fine, never better. What could possibly be wrong?'

The man was now studying my drawings. He started by peering closely at them, cocking his head from side to side. Then, as if dissatisfied, he swung his body back and squeezed his eyes half-shut, drawing his chin into his throat in what I took to be spinsterish disapproval.

'Working?'

'Yes. Never harder.'

'Great, that's my boy. Well the big thing is that this is going to *happen*. Do you hear me? I've been studying the politics, they look good. Those guys up there want a big building. They're tired of all that small stuff. It's like I always say – there's nothing wrong with big buildings as long as they're done right. Big buildings are good for people.'

The man had now picked up one of my sketchbooks and was studying it. After a few moments he seemed to grow more interested and sat down in an armchair the better to concentrate on what he had discovered. The particular book he had chosen was an early one that included wild drawings of my dreams as well as comic-book retellings of my vision narrative that I had dashed off in a wild, ironic moment. This was not the stuff to show the locals. This was not convincing. Hirtenstein was still talking.

'. . . should be round to see you any time.'

'Sorry, Dave, I didn't catch that last bit.'

'I said this man Greaves want to meet you. They take these things personally round there. He said he'd drop round today. I'm just ringing to make sure you'd be in.'

'Greaves?'

'Steve, focus, focus. I just told you. Greaves of the local council. If he likes it we're laughing. Just impress him. Try and see things through his eyes.'

'What does he look like?'

'How should I know? Apple-cheeks, potato-face, bandy-legged, chewing straw . . . whatever. I've never *seen* the guy. Somebody did say he carries a shotgun everywhere . . . '

I hung up.

'Mr Greaves.'

He raised his head from the sketchbook and lifted his eyebrows in response.

'I wish you had introduced yourself to start with.'

'I don't usually have to bother with introductions. Everybody round here has run into me at one time or another. Mr Greaves, that's what I am. I'm part of the scenery.'

SEVENTEEN

Passing Greaves I descended deep into the nested circles of work, deep into the mire, the morass. The days merged and flowed. Months passed, seasons changed, the broken spaceship dropped towards Mars. I worked alone but for the phones, faxes and mail that signalled other life; alone, therefore, but for all these virtual people that shimmered in and out of my room, borne on waves or by the limping postman. I lived a single fury of process. The cathedral became a normal building with the usual clamour for attention, the suppression of general doubts, the necessity to keep going.

But there were themes that threaded their way through those days, distinctive themes that forced me back to the madness, the absurdity of this desperate attempt to sublimate my visions into this reasonable frenzy. There was, worst of all, the publicity theme, the would-you-believe-it?, strange-but-true story of the crazy architect and his plastic cathedral. It began, as everything now did, with a call from Tina.

'Hello, Stephen. How you?'

'Perfect, Tina, perfect.'

'Just one tiny thing I need to bother you with. There is this man from *The Mentioner*. He wants to talk to you about your building. He says he wants to do a big piece. He sounded quite nice.' I had at that stage rebuffed all the half-hearted approaches of the local press. They had been content to do without me and run the story in an incredulous manner, implying it would never happen. *The Mentioner*, however, was different: national, serious and powerful, it had, in the way of such things, influence.

'Does David know about this?'

'Oh, yes. He thinks it would be great for us.'

'Well, I'd better do it then – if David thinks it would be great for us.'

The man from *The Mentioner* arrived with a small, froglike photographer whose vocation seemed to have wrecked his nerves. While I talked to the writer he emitted groans of frustration as he walked around the house and peered out of the windows in search of a location that, as he explained, 'told this story'. I agreed that it was a difficult one to 'tell'.

The writer was Peter, tall, blond, curly-haired. He was possessed of, to the point of being burdened with, an extraordinary quantity of self-assurance and worldly awareness. The cool disbelief with which he regarded life had permanently hooded the grey eyes and driven them high up the forehead in pursuit of the perpetually raised yellow eyebrows. His mouth, meanwhile, had thinned to an immobile line that extended itself horizontally when called upon to indicate a smile. He recorded our conversation on a tiny, pyramid-shaped machine that presented a black grille to me and a triangle of illuminated, digital information to him. He also took notes in a small, green book with such studied infrequency that, every time he did so, I found myself struggling to work out what in particular had caught his attention. Each time I finished an answer he said nothing for a distinct and, I thought, carefully timed pause during which he fixed his grey-eyed gaze upon me as if waiting for me to crack into some kind of confession. Foolishly I had failed to discuss the interview properly with Hirtenstein, so I began by giving the clear impression that the whole thing was a perfectly normal project, only the style of the building being a little odd. The writer disdainfully allowed me to persist with this for a while before revealing that he knew all about my visions and, therefore, that I was obviously trying to mislead him.

'Mr Rix, what precisely do you take to be the significance of these visions?'

He chose his words with an awful fastidiousness that gave me the fleeting sense of urine splashing into a stainless steel bowl. I returned his stare as blankly as I could while my mind swung helplessly from each of the cruel ropes of his question – 'Mr' . . . 'precisely' . . . 'take' . . . 'significance'. I noticed that his flesh formed a curiously flat plane beneath his elevated eyes.

'Significance. Well, what can I say? Perhaps that is for others to decide. Maybe it's just one way of coming up with an idea for a building.'

'A rather extreme building – one unlike any other . . . '

'Yes . . . well, no in fact, precisely like a large number of others.'

There was nothing in those grey eyes other than a smart sense of the trivial reality of the world. This he could carry with him wherever he went and apply like ointment to whatever threatened to bother him.

The article – under a sketch of the writer with an italic caption that read: 'Peter Lightfoot, En Passant' – appeared with an enormous photograph of me gesturing across the expanse of the valley. I had discreetly avoided showing Lightfoot anything too recognizable as the finished look of the church. But it had been, in the event, a futile delicacy, for another photograph of the site was overlaid with a drawing of the cathedral which was accurate enough to suggest that *The Mentioner* had been helped by Hirtenstein. He had nothing to hide; he wanted the world to know. The words made much of the Hirtenstein connection, implying that my madness had provided a convenient design excuse for a building that was otherwise inconceivable. It was, in short, a handy cover for a famously ruthless property developer.

'Rix,' he wrote, 'an icily amiable and occasionally evasive man, will not be drawn on the significance of his visions, nor will Hirtenstein on their profitability. The locals are not so reticent – they mean big money and a crazy addition to the landscape.' The headline was: 'Theme Park Gothic for a New Age'.

It was to mark the beginning of a rolling, howling tumult of publicity, all of it encouraged by Hirtenstein. He insisted I give more interviews and even gave a few himself. I and my cathedral became an issue. Long, painfully thoughtful articles appeared about the significance of this church.

'How', asked one architectural critic, 'can we condone this slavish essay in repro-Gothic?'

'The Millennium will dawn', wrote another, 'on an unreal nation, stupefied by pastiche and hell-bent on filling its countryside with plastic churches.'

'The Church', lamented one priest, 'can only regard with sadness a project that mocks the familiar imagery of the faith.'

One red-faced Gothic revivalist leapt to my defence: 'The building is a masterpiece, a great, generous, inclusive summary of the greatness of our greatest style. Praise be to Rix! Thank God for Hirtenstein! They have brought us back to our senses.'

A psychoanalyst was called in to unravel my 'hallucinations'. The cathedral, he said, was the body of my mother, my need to build it was my desire to possess her. 'We, the public, must make up our minds how far we feel inclined to indulge this familiar, all too familiar, impulse.'

'Another Gothic revival', wrote a celebrated 'cultural commentator', 'signals the onset of the conclusive phase of that fragmentation that began with the Renaissance under-determination of the image and, I thought, had reached a climax with the arrival of a Virtual Reality machine in every pub. How wrong I was. We still had this final, monstrous step to take before the Apocalypse.'

A literary journal carried an enormous article headlined 'Gothicism and the Divided Self', but I could read no more.

I could only regard Stephen Rix drifting across this grey, mountainous sea of impassioned words. I felt I had pushed him off from the shore and was obliged to watch as he lost control of his vessel. I stood helpless as this other I was tumbled and thrown by the anxieties and imperatives of all these public people. This 'I' had become a name for something that they needed, the representative of some ill-defined cause they could exploit, abuse and conquer.

And the words were followed by pictures, again Hirtenstein insisted. The first television crew filmed me standing in the middle of the site. In my innocence I talked as slowly as I could to avoid misunderstanding and to sabotage any preconceived 'story' that might be in the mind of the fierce woman who interrogated me from behind the red-bearded cameraman. But the effort was futile. This was one story in which the plainest truth was a sensation. Even if they had wished to present me as a judicious, sober luminary, even if the Stephen Rix in the fierce woman's head had been the Stephen Rix I took to be in mine, there was always the moment of transmission when he would become millions of crazed or corrupted Rixes in those massed heads crouched before their screens.

Except, of course, that fierce woman knew a story when she saw one and she had no intention of trusting her cattle-like viewers to make it up for themselves.

'MISter RIX,' she began, unnerving me with her startling tonal variations. 'HOW did the idea for this caTHEDral first COME to you?'

I realized the stressed syllables were being employed as prods or goads, initially to unsettle me and later, on transmission, to jerk the masses out of the mode of sullen inattention or sleep.

I watched her report on some sombre late-night programme a couple of days later. The camera panned across my valley. Pastoral music played. Larks sang, curlews cried, pipits dipped and cheeped.

'THIS', fierce woman began, 'is a VALLey of VISions . . . '

Yet another I appeared, his hair lashed about his features by the wind, his hands in his pockets, his body braced against the steep incline on which they had made him pose.

'Well, yes, as you have clearly heard, I have, in fact, *seen* the building in question.'

'Right here WASn't it?'

'Yes.'

'And you walked THROUGH it?'

'Yes.'

'And THEN it VANished?'

'Yes. Yes.'

Her last question was almost shrieked, probably in incredulity, but, ostensibly, to conquer the noise of the gale.

'Yes, it vanished. As you can see, it's not there now.'

The cattle did not really matter, of course. She had only one audience, the audience of her peers and their Stephen Rix was either mad or the purveyor of a cheap gimmick. She efficiently suggested the first possibility at the beginning of her film with the aid of lies about my eccentric ways from a smirking, confiding Jack at the Arches. But her real conviction was that I was just another huckster and this was the tenor of her conclusion.

'MADman or SMART OPerator, STEPhen Rix is WELL on the WAY to transFORMing this QUIet valley into a TOUrist TRAP, an inTERnational ODDity, a FOLLy for our TIME. HERE he plans to build the FIRST CHURCH of the NEW MillENnium.'

For a few moments I felt sorry for television's version of Stephen Rix, he had been so cruelly used, plundered and mocked. He was not mad, he was simply trapped by a circumstance that happened to be inexplicable in the terms of late-night television. Poor Stephen Rix. And then the phone rang, brutally cracking open my brooding pity.

'God, Steve, did you see that?'

'I did, Dave, I'm sorry. What a mess. Maybe nobody was watching.'

'Sorry? It was fantastic and what a line! The First Church of the New Millennium. That's our name. That line could get this thing built all on its own. Do you think she has copyright? Sorry! God, Steve, you break me up! This is amazing stuff!'

Two days later Hirtenstein's faxes changed. They began to arrive with a heavily patterned letterhead. This was in the form of a decorated Gothic screen, rising and swelling in the centre into the multiple pipes of a church organ topped by trumpeting angels. Laced into the tracery of the screen in thunderous, though not immediately legible Gothic script were the words 'The First Church of the New Millennium'.

But, in the mire, Lionel was the strangest theme of all. Of course, throughout he nagged me with the usual professionalism of an engineer, demanding ever greater degrees of definition and finality from my drawings. In return he faxed me

215

engineering diagrams which were now mounting, unregarded, in the corner of the room immediately behind where I worked. But Lionel's work was personal. He needed to show me his life as well as his art. His communications displayed the hitherto hidden scars of the man. There was an undertone of bewilderment, of anxiety that he ought not to be doing this at all, that it was not right but that he *had* to work for Hirtenstein for reasons, he wrote ominously, which I probably understood.

'For the thing is,' he kept insisting, 'we can do anything now, anything we like. That creates terrible problems.'

The technical details that stuttered out of the fax machine were preceded by personal letters giving me news of himself. His wife, these revealed, was enthusiastic about the project, considering it a liberation from the routine of his usual work. His children – four of them – were also excited, having seen the newspapers and the eldest daughter having been allowed to stay up and see my appearance on television. She thought I was 'really wild' and 'rather hunky'. Lionel himself confessed to a degree of agony. Certainly he could attach the details to the steel frame. But he would lie awake at night wondering by what bizarre historical accident he found himself attaching these buttresses, these arcades, this tracery.

'We are doing something here for which we shall be judged. I do not think these things belong here or now. Perhaps we are not good enough for them.'

At first I ignored these confessions. But, finally, I felt I had to respond. I was causing him to suffer. I wrote back insisting there was something arbitrary in everything we did. All functions could be realized in a multiplicity of ways. We chose particular ones for reasons that owed nothing to function. We made choices in spite of functionality. So why not make choices in spite of all functionality? Yes, of course, he replied, but where was the discipline in that? Certainly function could be arbitrarily realized, but at least the idea of function remained as a discipline. I know, I replied, but Gothic was the form that most aggressively celebrated function. This scheme acquired its discipline from being the most extreme denial in employing the most structurally honest style and realizing it in the most completely dishonest way.

216

The argument was out of focus. I no longer suffered from the sense that the plastic of reality betrayed the stones of my visions. I had been shown a surface and, I now told myself, asked to build it. And I belonged in this surface, it spoke to me, instructed me, controlled me. This was not in the same category as Lionel's doubts. We were at cross purposes.

The fax machine itself seemed to shrug at my sophistries. It was, at least, a conclusive position. Afterwards Lionel's personal messages reverted to tales of the family, of Hirtenstein and of the hours he worked. One day a motor-cycle messenger clad in red leather arrived with a long, cardboard tube. Inside was a huge blow-up of one of Lionel's photographs of the site with his steel skeleton sketched in ink over the field and overlaid with a finer drawing of the finished building. I pinned it to the wall, covering at least three layers of my own papers. Accompanying the picture was a note on blue paper: 'We shall have a lot to say to each other one day. Lionel.' He had not been persuaded of anything. He was biding his time. As I read the note I knew that one day he would be right.

Greaves called again, still carrying his gun. He told me he had written to Hirtenstein and a day had been arranged for an informal meeting with local politicians and civil servants to discuss the scheme. Its chances, he said, looked surprisingly good. But there were problems – local groups objecting to the intrusion, irate farmers, straightforward sceptics and ancient landowners were offended. Even, he pointed out, if it were built and everybody was enthusiastic, there would be the awkward problem of failure. What if nobody came?

'Yes. But I'm not sure I would have much to say about all that. That's Hirtenstein's business.'

'Come on now. You can't get away with that one. I know the architect has a lot to do with it too. It's up to you to design it to work and to put things in it.'

'Yes. Yes. All right. I know. I'll be there.'

Hirtenstein stayed with me on the night before the meeting. He arrived with two black leather folders containing loose, square sheets of thick paper. On each there was a point, a defence that we had somehow to incorporate in whatever we

217

said the next day. The points were printed in huge capital letters so that barely fifty words filled each page. Hirtenstein gave me one folder and we sat late into the night rehearsing and analysing the points on his 'strategy cards'.

'REMEMBER', said one, 'NEVER TO ACKNOWLEDGE THE ELEMENT OF *STRANGENESS* IN THE SCHEME. IT MUST BE SEEN TO MAKE PERFECT SENSE. SO WE DO NOT USE ANY WORDS THAT MIGHT SUGGEST *EXTREMITY, ECCENTRICITY, FANTASY, FOLLY, OB-SESSION, MEGALOMANIA*, ETC. WHAT WE WISH TO CONVEY IS THE *SIMPLE LOGIC* OF THE IDEA. SEE SHEETS 18 TO 21 ON HISTORY, CONTINUITY, CEL-EBRATION ETC.'

'Are you sure this is the right approach?' I asked. 'Oughtn't we to face up to the madness of the thing? Come clean. Tough it out. Appeal to the heroic in them.'

'No, no, Steve. Trust me. That might work with some of them. But those types are always in the minority. And in the end they always cave in. You've got to grab the middle ground. Make it seem as if building the thing is really the only moderate choice. They're all moderates when the heat's on. So we have to stop them thinking that there are only two choices – build or not build. They have to think there's a third – something far worse than either so that building is the easy way out. Look at Sheet 5.' I looked at Sheet 5.

'TURN DOWN THIS OPPORTUNITY AND ONE DAY YOU MIGHT HAVE TO SAY YES TO ANY OLD LEISURE CENTRE TO SAVE THE LOCAL ECONOMY. ONLY THIS SCHEME OFFERS GENUINE ORIGINALITY AND SENSI-TIVITY TO THE LOCAL CONTEXT. SEE SHEET 22.'

'It's like selling,' explained Hirtenstein. 'You've got to narrow down the possibilities until buying or building is the only honest, fair, reasonable or sane thing to do. Look, what we're doing is making them climb a spiral staircase. Right? There are doors that will let them get out of the climb. Our job is to distract them whenever they pass a door until they only notice there are no more doors when it's too late. Or, best of all, they don't notice the doors at all.'

'Can't they just go back down?'

'*That* is exactly what they can't do because we're blocking the staircase.'

He smiled triumphantly, swelled his chest, lit a cigar and poured himself a large brandy.

'You people, you architects, you should get wise to this stuff. The trouble with you lot is you don't have real confidence, confidence in something just because it's what you've chosen to do, not because it's right or wrong. Everything's right, everything's wrong. Worry about that and nothing happens. You've got to go with what you've got because it's you. It's what you do.'

He swallowed the brandy and clenched the cigar between his grinning, confident teeth. He was happy to be passing on his wisdom. It was the secret lore of his craft, of what he was: Hirtenstein the Fixer. Orlando the Partner would have agreed with him, but out of exhaustion rather than conviction. He too would have argued the virtues of getting the work, fixing the deal. But only because he could see no alternative. He would not have Hirtenstein's faith that wanting to do something meant it was justified at any price. I tried to believe that such a faith was monstrous or such exhaustion was cowardice, to feel superior to both of them. But I could scarcely ignore the fact that here I was in this house with Hirtenstein, learning from his big cards.

The meeting was held at some decayed council offices nearby. It was, as everybody kept insisting, informal, a quiet chat. Greaves was accompanied by four men and a woman, all of whose names and functions I missed in the mêlée of introductions. They seemed uncannily similar – all aged about fifty, all respectably well-groomed and all dressed with a definitive, rural correctness. The room was a dusty rectangle with three windows overlooking the street. Heavy, red velvet curtains were tied back with grimy gilt ropes, but they still covered more than half the windows' surfaces and misty smears kept out what remained of the daylight. Thick wallpaper covered the walls with dark red, plush flowers and a carpet covered the floor with seething tendrils and blooms. Greaves's gun was propped in one corner. We sat on metal chairs at a long table surfaced with wood-patterned plastic. Anticipating our arrival there were stacks of cups and saucers and a plate of beige biscuits. The clock on the mantelpiece chimed springily ten times and we began.

Hirtenstein and I sat facing the fifty-year-olds. Their backs were to the windows so the little available light did not reveal details of their features and expressions. I could taste the dust in the air and feel the remnants of the brandy from the night before as a metallic nausea in my head. I felt rather than heard a high-pitched sound as if wind were rushing through a taut, steel cable and I pulled at my ears in the suspicion that it was some mechanical defect.

'Gentlemen,' began Hirtenstein, ' . . . and lady . . . ' he bowed in her direction, 'I think I shall begin . . . '

'I think,' said one of the silhouetted men, '*we* shall begin.'

'Of course,' Hirtenstein raised his hands to indicate his generosity of spirit. 'You're the ones with all the questions. We're here to answer them. That's what we're here for.'

There was a pause, a movement of heads and then the woman leaned forward slightly and spoke into the surface of the table.

'Mr Rix, what is all this about?'

Hirtenstein rested his foot on mine and exerted pressure, a gesture I took to mean 'Steady'.

'I'm sorry?'

'Well, I read', she produced a cutting of Peter Lightfoot, En Passant from a handbag on her lap and smoothed it on the fake wooden surface, 'that this cathedral originates from some kind of dream you had. Is this intended to persuade us of the superior quality and poetic inspiration of this plan? Or was it just . . . well . . . good copy?'

'No, it is the simple truth,' the pressure from Hirtenstein's foot increased. I hurried on.

'But it is not relevant. You have the scheme. If you want to approve it you can do. Its origins do not affect its quality or validity.'

I felt relaxed by the effrontery of this confession to these silhouetted authorities. I was theirs to judge. Hirtenstein removed the sole of his shoe and replaced it with his heel which he dug sharply into my instep.

'No, but if you are making this up, it may tell us something about the kind of people we are dealing with here.'

'It would, but I'm not, so it doesn't. And, in any case, I can think of worse reasons for buildings than somebody seeing them first.'

Hirtenstein raised his heel and spoke quickly.

'Stephen is an unusual man, a gifted man, in my opinion he is a genius. This is a wonderful thing, but it means we must make allowances.'

The remark appeared to signal the abandonment of his attempt to turn me into a salesman. Now I was to be the wayward artist. The woman primly distracted herself by pouring coffee and distributing biscuits. One of the men took up the theme.

'Be that as it may, Mr Hirtenstein, I think my colleague was getting at the fact that we would like to know exactly what we might be being asked to approve here today. It seems to have made a lot of people very cross already.'

From an inside pocket he produced a cutting of the priest's article.

'Father Harrington, for example, says we . . . '

The way the publicity had connected us all — given us so much in common. I saw how those drifting, buffeted Is had become real to these people and how they saw them all in me. Publicity was real, there was no inner place to hide. I was the Stephen Rix in question, wasn't I?

Hirtenstein rose to his feet.

'How would it be', he said slowly, 'if I just put our case first of all and then you tried to shoot us down. At the moment you're just sniping at us on the back of things you've read in the press. Or you're questioning Mr Rix's motives. Let me say what we want to do and then you can say what you like.'

'Sensible suggestion,' said Greaves, slapping the table top. 'Go ahead. Perhaps we'll find this idea isn't so strange after all.'

The sudden Greaves enthusiasm and his use of the word 'strange' startled me. But I had no time to consider what it meant, for already Hirtenstein was leading us up the spiral staircase.

The performance was immaculate, engrossing and breathless.

At one point I actually found myself tapping my foot to the rhythm of this delivery. On the lower steps, where I knew there were still many exits, he charmed us with a hypothesis. Say the church was already built. We were to forget all our reservations, ignore all that we took to be problems for a moment and imagine the completed project. Ignore, in other words, all these silly doors. Suddenly the land was alive with new possibilities. Traffic was being discreetly ducted into a vast underground park. New landscaping in the valley concealed the area around the base of the cathedral so that we saw only the building rising above the hills. At night sound and light shows – soft sound and soft light – drew reverent crowds to the exterior of the building to hear explained the history of cathedral building and its place in our heritage. Inside there were interactive exhibits and even rides – one that swooped high in the vaulting, threaded through the triforium and looped up the central tower, another that plunged below ground, crashing rapidly throught the crypt and into the archaeological depths, down down to iron-age man and then the mammoths, sabre-tooth tigers, the glaciers. Virtual reality rooms allowed visitors to take part in the building of the great cathedrals with the stonemasons, the carpenters and the sculptors or to relive the life of a local saint and his heroic but peaceful resistance to alien invaders. This could not be accomplished, for obvious reasons, with any existing church, we needed to purpose-build. We were well up the staircase now.

The effects on the local community would be galvanic. Traders would benefit from the swarms of new visitors. Employment would soar. Only a couple of doors were left.

And consider this building process. It would be a huge local event. We would consult closely with the community about the most detailed points of the building. The church would belong to the people. The grocer might be realized in stone, Landlord Jack of the Arches immortalized in stained glass, the butcher carved on a misericord and so on. This would be an event that celebrated this place. The communal basis of the entire enterprise would recapture the spirit in which the great Gothic cathedrals of the Middle Ages were once built. This was not just some theme park, tacked on to a convenient location. It was a sign of what you are, a celebration of your past and a statement of faith in your future. We could see the sky above us, it would be madness to climb down now.

But say you decide not to build. So high were we now that the very idea frightened us. He, Hirtenstein, would go elsewhere. Other grocers, other publicans, alien butchers would be immortalized in glass or stone. And what would they do then? They would struggle on with their failing local economy, the dribble of tourists, the low-spending, rambling types and the uneconomic farms. Eventually they would have to do something, but what? Persuade some industry to locate here for a few years and leave, claiming costs were too high? Go for the theme-park business with some bland scheme with the usual roller coasters and plastic castles?

'We are offering you The First Church of the New Millennium, are you going to end up with the last funfair of the old?'

This was the gist of an astonishing forty-minute speech. Hirtenstein paced about the room, diminishing the power of the still, silhouetted committee by the freedom of his movement. At one point he even addressed them from behind, his astounding double-curved figure outlined against the dusty daylight, rising behind the committee like a collective inspiration. By the time he reached his 'What are the alternatives?' demand he was leaning over the table supported on his arms and peering into the eyes of the woman who had started all this with her doubts.

There was complete silence. I wanted to applaud. I had never seen such a performance. There we all stood at the top of the staircase, barely even capable of considering the possibility of being anywhere else. The view was tremendous, the wind whipped at our clothing, the sky was blue and dotted with fluffy white clouds. In the entire speech there was not one moment in which anybody could have believed that Hirtenstein had ever had or would ever have a second's doubt about this scheme. You wished to believe it was an act because you knew that was Hirtenstein's job. But it was impossible to believe. Nobody acted that well. He said this was the building he had waited all his life to build and nobody could seriously doubt him.

After that long silence, Greaves looked at the others, coughed and looked at us.

'Mr Hirtenstein, that was very, very impressive. I have never heard such enthusiasm for a building. You made me feel we should be on that site digging at this moment. And I, for one, think that is exactly where we should be.'

Again I was puzzled to discover that Greaves was so enthusiastically leading the pro-cathedral faction. There was some shuffling. We had all found we had been sitting motionless and tense throughout the speech and now movement was painful. Two of the men came out with roughly pro-cathedral remarks. The woman said something about 'Needs looking at in more detail.' The meeting ended in weak murmurings as if the speech had drained us of all energy. Greaves gathered up a capacious old briefcase and came over to congratulate Hirtenstein on his presentation.

'I think', he whispered, 'it's going to be fine.'

He struggled with his briefcase for a moment and it fell open awkwardly. Inside I saw a black leather folder identical to the ones Hirtenstein and I had employed for a rehearsal the previous night. Then I understood.

Hirtenstein, quivering and speechless, drove us to the Arches. There the lunchtime customers were just arriving. I glanced at Jack who had so blithely questioned my sanity on television. He wiped a glass and smiled broadly. I smiled back. Hirtenstein bought us drinks and gulped down a large whisky. Ralph and Sally were there. Ralph rushed over, pleased to see me. All the cool he had previously exuded before his friends had evaporated. His role was now so locally well-defined that he could not suppress his exultation. He was no longer obliged to be the outsider since he was a celebrity by association with me and my church. I was on TV, I was famous, no matter that I was famous for being mad.

'Steve, some great new work to show you. Can you come back now?'

'Not now, Ralph, I've got to talk to Dave.'

'Right. Right. Later.'

I looked over at Sally. She looked back, half-smiling. She was holding a small glass of orange juice and was surrounded by the young farmers. I imagined her pale body and imagined, as usual, that it would save me. I nodded, she nodded in reply and Hirtenstein and I left.

'Disarmed,' said the Dragon lady as the doors dropped open. They closed, eliminating all outside noise.

'You fixed Greaves then?'

'He certainly seems to have seen the light. And why not? It's a great scheme.'

'He had that folder of strategy sheets in his briefcase.'

'OK, OK. I fixed Greaves. That's the way these things work. And if I don't do some fixing, who will? You let me down. You abandoned the whole plan the moment we got in there. You're lucky I like you, Steve, I could get very angry.'

I thought of the murders, of a call from one of Hirtenstein's assassins. 'Mr Rix?' 'Yes . . . ' 'Mr Stephen Rix?' 'Yes . . . '

'How much?'

'For Greaves? Enough. Look, do you have a problem with this? It's what I said before, you've got to believe in these things beyond right or wrong, you've got to believe because *you're* doing them. And, if you believe that, the odd sweetener is no problem. He's taken money before. Known for it.'

'I know. You're right. It's just such a funny state of affairs. A man being bribed because I saw a church in a field.'

'In that field, Steve, remember you did not just see a church, any church in any field. You saw The First Church of the New Millennium.'

'Ah, yes. Incidentally I've been meaning to ask you, Dave, have you ever killed anybody?'

He looked across at me and smiled gently.

'I bet you got that from Orlando. Real industry chatter that is — how wicked Hirtenstein is in with gangsters who do his dirty work. Look, I don't need it. You saw me in there. I didn't need to kill those people, I just needed to talk to them.'

'Yes, I saw that.'

Back at the house Hirtenstein at once began making himself a sandwich out of any food he could find. He drank several pints of water with noisy desperation. He looked up when he saw I was watching him.

225

'Those presentations take it out of me. I get so psyched up it's unbelievable. I have to keep driving myself or . . . '

'Or what?'

'I would just break down. I'd fall apart. I'd turn back into little David Hirtenstein being bullied by Orlando and his friends. I'm not like that really, I've learned to *will* it. Lucky for you I did. Why wouldn't you stick to the fucking plan?'

'Maybe I just can't do that stuff.'

'I don't believe that. You've made a lot of money, you must have got your hands dirty.'

I had picked up the usual pile of mail and had started sorting through this as we spoke. Two letters stood out – one with Jill's handwriting in her familiar mauve envelope and another in a more anonymous white envelope from Francesca. Neither had written since the big confrontation.

'Darling Stephen,' wrote Francesca, 'I really do hope everything is going well for you. Orlando was tirelessly insistent that you would be at your best alone and he knows you better than anybody. Doesn't he? I hope you don't think we plotted. We just talked. It had to be done. Moira warned me about all this runaway stuff and she was right. She has been so helpful since I came back. Of course, I love you. But, as Moira pointed out, love doesn't necessarily work as a way of life. My love was all about our days. That was how I liked it – having you locked away with me. And that's what you liked really. I think Moira understood you better than I ever did. You couldn't bear having me around all the time. Admit it. Love Francesca.'

'Dear Stephen,' wrote Jill, 'I go into hospital tomorrow. I'm told there is quite a lot of pain involved. I had assumed cosmetic surgery was painless, apparently not. Thank you for sticking to our deal. It's turned into a kind of adventure. It's funny how surprised everybody is that *I* am having this done. Tom and Elizabeth are, as you would expect, wildly excited about all the publicity you've been getting and want to come and see you. I have explained you are too busy. Tina and Orlando have kept me informed of progress. It seems, amazingly enough, that this church is in serious danger of being built. It still seems mad to me. We are managing reasonably well. The children demand to know when you are coming back to Pointed Park. I keep telling them when you are ready. You have a lot of work and a lot to think about, I say. You may be wondering why I am writing. It is not just because of the operation. I have been trying to work things out, to interpret my own feelings. I have been talking to people about this because I think that is the only way. Having to say something is the way to bring things out. And it has certainly brought something out of me that I didn't think was there. I need you, Stephen. How else can I put it? Please come home. Love Jill.'

Both letters shocked me. I was fixed in their minds whether I liked it or not. In Jill's I had even mutated into a Stephen she wanted to come home, her stern solidity had cracked. Or had it? Such wreckage, so much debris for a steel frame, plastic stones, a bribed man, a few thousand jobs and later a handful of inevitable deaths. I noticed the high-pitched noise was still in my ears and again I plucked at them.

Hirtenstein was sitting at the kitchen table eating his enormous sandwich. A quarter of a tomato coated in mayonnaise slithered out of the side as he took a bite. A familiar cold moisture prickled on my skin and the air thinned. The high-pitched whine was joined by a rushing noise, as of water, the room seemed to swing upwards and suddenly I was dreaming that I was walking through a mass of people. They were all facing one way, but they turned as I passed.

I came to with my head cradled by Hirtenstein who, with his other hand, was wiping the mayonnaise from his lips with a large, dark red handkerchief.

'Steve, you all right? That was a hell of a crack when you fell.'

'Yes. Sorry, Dave, this happens from time to time.'

'I know. Orlando told me about it. Was there something in those letters?'

'No, no. Just a long morning, no breakfast, the usual stuff. I'll be fine.'

'It's my fault. I'm laying too much on you, Steve. I know. You can't do this selling stuff, leave that to me, we're nearly there. Take a rest. Take the rest of the day off. Everything can wait. Why not try some of this?'

He handed me a round box, similar to his own.

227

'Dip?'

'Yeah. It works for me.'

He fussed for a while, made me food and, finally, announced he would have to leave. I saw him to the door.

'Remember, take the rest of the day off. Try the Dip. It can't do any harm. You be all right now, Steve?' he called as he lowered himself into the Dragon. And then he answered the question himself.

'Course you will! A great force watches over the architect of the First Church of the New Millennium. Be good!'

EIGHTEEN

TAKE THE REST of the day off. Be good. It was a beautiful, simple idea. All I had needed was permission and now it had been granted. I was to be allowed to walk away from this awful cathedral. I had needed a voice from outside to point out that, if this was just work, then this could be just a holiday. Nobody was being betrayed or abandoned, not even me. I could play at being free as other people were free.

The shock of this liberation coursed through my body like a drug. As soon as Hirtenstein left, I was convulsed with the need to hurry. I ran up the stairs, pulling off my clothes to arrive naked before the mirror in the bathroom. This was clearly still a madman and an appearance of sanity was required. I bathed, washing quickly, and then lunged out of the bath, suppressing the usual moment of airy dizziness. The body was powdered and perfumed, the hair blow-dried into arty waves. Clothes were chosen for their neutral raffishness; I had not worn such things for months. Returning to the mirror, I saw what I wanted to see. The man who stood before me was an urban cruiser, bound for the city lights. He was light, unencumbered, free. He was normal. He did not see cathedrals. Now for the short but intense vacation from the season of solipsism, of private subjugation to the Gothic law.

Downstairs there was Hirtenstein's Dip on the marble table. I slipped it into my pocket. There was also the model of myself. I should have ignored this intrusion, a mad, uncontrolled mystery did not fit with my present camouflage. But I picked it up and slipped that too into my jacket pocket. I had no idea why.

Delicately avoiding muddying my shoes, I dropped into the embrace of the Leopard, put on some sticky, insidious music and headed out. Beyond the immediate lanes and tracks of the valley, the Leopard and I drove east on a winding road through twenty miles of farms and villages. We were driving quickly, but with light-headed, confident ease. We reached the big motorway junction in record time. Going home to Pointed Park, we would turn south here where the countryside faded into mere acreage, but, instead, we turned north-west into the wildness and towards another, closer, stranger city.

On the motorway I allowed the Leopard to fling us both forward. Small cars in the outer lane swerved desperately aside, their drivers shocked by our terrible pace. We were travellers from another, more potent realm, temporarily passing through their little, crowded lives. The fields and houses unrolled. The car sucked up the road and the land as if preparing, with one final surge of acceleration, to fling us out of this fragile, shaking stage set of a world into something harder, colder, grander, better. Even faster. The Leopard pressed itself downwards, the better to grasp at and consume the black surface. The road became a rubbery tape that we were sucking in and blowing out in shreds behind.

It was a late autumn afternoon and the light was failing. The lights of the other cars blinked on to signal their presence, ours had already been continuously employed as a warning. The land darkened beneath the cold grey lid of cloud, buildings became indistinct smudges and fields dissolved into a single, black blanket that rose in folds to meet the sky. Inside the car the lights on the dashboard and the circling music were soothing, assuring me that we could not be invaded by those people, cars, fields or the cold, rushing air, assuring me that I

230

was, once again, functioning within the consoling systems of my life. A red warning light flashed and there was a soft ringing – police radar. I slowed to the legal maximum for a few miles, taking a new pleasure in watching small, identical, tin boxes struggling triumphantly past this monster and, in their little pride, risking capture. But then the light faded and the ringing stopped. I allowed my right foot to drop to the floor and felt my bodyweight sink into the seat. The Leopard ripped onwards, devouring the landscape, shredding the road as if to ensure that we would be the last to use it.

Soon there was a misty, yellow glare rising into the sky from beyond the next hills, the faint halo of the other city. The car followed a final, long, flowing curve of road and then, as we crested the next hill, I saw a huge pool of orange lined with rows of little stalks. The motorway had suddenly acquired lighting. Then the lamp posts were flickering past us and we were arrowing through like a dancer flung from the wings into the all-exposing glare of the stage.

Other roads crossed mine on elegant bridges that picked their way around obstructions on long, slender legs. I saw low ribbons of houses, fragile, static shelters, pathetically woven through these bigger, cleaner necessities of movement. One terraced house was shattered rubble, the nearby motorway fencing was broken and ringed by warning signs and flashing lights. Clearly something had flown off the road and destroyed the house. I imagined that beautiful, curving, silent fall and then the crashing and roaring before the silence was restored.

The motorway surrendered itself to roundabouts, suburban dual carriageways and, finally, the impossible miasma of an inner city road system. With easy satisfaction I passed long queues of stationary cars as people abandoned the centre after work. While stopped at traffic lights, I watched the examining, bitter eyes of these commuters. Some sneered, others just studied me and thought. The thin, high whine was still in my head.

For perhaps half an hour I cruised the streets of the centre. I basked in the luxury of having no need to leave as the shops closed, the parking lots emptied and sad, muffled pedestrians waited for their buses. Heads rose and followed the Leopard

231

as we passed, hearing, as a faint, intimate, bass rhythm, the music from inside. I knew this city well enough and that drive reminded me of the broken grid of its street pattern, the baroque domes and spindly turrets of its buildings, the flapping posters pasted on every wall and the piled, black, shining globes of rubbish sacks, always waiting for collection.

I parked close to a hotel. The high, wide façade was lit from below in pale blue so that projecting signs and details cast long, inverted triangles of shadow, strange, soaring beams of darkness. But at street level there was merely bright light, constant movement and uniformed men. It was a place where the Leopard was unlikely to be assaulted. Also hotels like this had hotel bars.

Hotel bars are all the same and all perfect. In a hotel bar you are expected to be no good, on the make, emitting sexual demands so shrill they can only be felt, not heard. Life has all been lived in a hotel bar. There is no hope of improvement nor prospect of any homecoming. Indeed, the whole point of a hotel bar is that you are not at home. In a hotel bar you must look better than usual but be worse. You are judged by your appearance because there is neither future nor past on which to base any other judgement. Whatever is to happen happens here and now and it happens only to you as you appear to be. A nameless viciousness emanates from the hard, reflective surfaces; some awful treachery is implicit in the heavy ash trays and the abstract prints.

All hotel bars are, in principle, the same, but, in detail, this one was an unusually fine example. It was arranged on several levels which at first seemed to follow no pattern. But closer examination revealed that they formed an arena. To be in the lowest, central levels was to be the most looked at, to be on the higher, outer levels was to be the most looking. Already the few early occupants of the bar had followed the human logic implied by this. Four men were arranged about the outer levels and a group of five women and one man were at the centre. I took a position between the two, spread my arms along the dark blue upholstery and looked up just as the waiter, a silver tray under his arm, looked down.

'A large whisky and water, no ice.'

232

He inclined his head and left to return, moments later, with the drink and a white, segmented plate filled with varieties of nuts and seeds. This, the nonchalant luxury of this plate told me, was a real hotel bar. I drank half the drink and then leaned my head back on the upholstery to dwell on the deep, deep pleasure of being a stranger alone and free in a strange city.

This was why I had come, in search of this preliminary thrill of clean, limitless anticipation. The night would decay, the opportunities narrow, the infinite possibilities would shrink to a few time-wasting inanities. But, for this moment, the unpredictability of a city night lay before me. The chief pleasure lay in watching. In this bar I was implicated, but nobody quite knew how and only I knew that I was pointless and disengaged. If they had known they would have grown uneasy, I would be beyond the discipline of their savagery. But the watching was my only function, I was putting all of myself into the act whereas they only used watching to involve that small part of themselves not employed in the malice and schemes of the moment. So I watched these two groups, the composition of their limbs, torsos and heads, the colour and cut of their clothes, the low intent of their features. More came in and the nervous and deadening effect of my cold gaze was diluted by the confident presence of newcomers to the arena. I drank more; they drank more; we all drank more.

Finally my powers failed. There were too many people and they had drunk enough to regard me with contempt instead of suspicion. I paid off the waiter, leaving an insulting tip. As I returned the change to my pocket I felt Hirtenstein's round box. Of course, here was novelty. I could take some Dip and at once redeem the night from these first portents of its inevitable decay. Whatever it did, everything would be different. What did it do? It made you, Hirtenstein had claimed, more confidently and completely yourself. Perfect.

Amidst the marble and the fronds I found the men's room, a mirrored, stainless steel *salle* with soft music. There was nobody there to trouble me, yet in one mirror I caught my astonishingly furtive manner as I sidled into a cubicle. I opened the box and stirred the Dip experimentally. I knew nothing of dosage or rate of onset. But the method of dispensation meant that any dose would be approximate, so I blithely sucked a stickful. It tasted mildly bitter and dissolved the instant it touched my tongue. I felt a wave of brightness as if filters had been removed from my eyes or more lights had been switched on. I took this to be no more than the effect of my own excitement.

I left the hotel and stood on the cream marble steps of the entrance, watching the now quieter street. Cars of the night people with their different kinds of work had now parked around the Leopard. A hotel doorman stood beside me in his strange light green uniform flecked with jagged darts and decorated with epaulettes and frogging as if he were a senior officer in some alien, pantomime army.

'Taxi, sir?'

I looked at the pale face under the cap. He was a boy.

'No, I'm going to walk because I would like to think.'

'A nice night for it, sir.'

I gave him a brusque smile and set off down the street, watching. I ran into small groups of people, the men in dinner jackets, the women in varieties of tight, glittering dresses. They laughed too loudly to cover their self-consciousness in the street. Some of the women wore the men's jackets over their bare shoulders. Their voices echoed and roared as if poorly amplified and their skins were unnaturally pale, the colour of bone. I looked round to see where they went. They disappeared up the cream steps of the hotel, each group awkwardly saluted by the boy on the door. A nice night for what? Thinking?

Turning right I found myself in a darker street. Scaffolding bridged the pavement and drops of water fell from the ropes, boards and poles. Music came from a place down this street where a blue plane of light fell across the black pavement. It was an amusement arcade with slots, pinball and VR. But the shop window had been designed to conceal what went on inside behind the imagery of a brittle, lacquered respectability. On a black velvet cloth were cheap vases, cut glass bowls, plates and some small porcelain deer, their heads bowed to graze on the black pile. Some local law must demand this masquerade of gentility. I went in, slipped my money into the VR machine, entered the booth and put on the helmet and gloves.

I was standing on a white rocky surface, the sky was black and, rising from the smooth, curved horizon, were bland white blocks indicating a city. I turned full circle, but the entire landscape was featureless, white rock. Looking back towards the city, I discovered the line of a path. I stepped on to the path and began to move forward. The machine translated my slightest movements into giant's leaps. Almost at once a squadron of robot insects were racing at me, firing little bolts of lightning. I drew one of my weapons, dipped down on to one knee and started picking them off. When hit, the insects exploded, sending debris flying past my head. Finally they were all destroyed. Further on a bag lay on the path. I picked it up. Then a tank appeared and its shells began to explode around me. I fired back to no effect. I tried other weapons, but they did not work. The tank was close. I ran around to try and conceal myself in its flanks. Then I remembered the bag. Inside was a grenade. I climbed on to the tank, dropped the grenade in through the hatch and leapt away. The tank exploded. I walked on. Just before I reached the city, I was confronted by three huge metal men. They shouted orders and then they fired at me, I fired back. There was a long, intense fight, but, finally, they were all destroyed. In the city I fought more metal men before forcing my way to the large, square central building. Its windows were illuminated by a hard, bluish glare from within and, from its roof, tiny points of light shone and burst into haloes and spears as they caught the eyes. At ground level there was an orange glow. Inside a glowing bright light indicated the presence of the evil master I had been sent to defeat. He roared out challenges and, moments later, I was killed by the shimmering fireballs that flew from his weapons.

The battle left me sweating and excited. I emerged from the VR into the dark, dancing colours of the arcade. It was a deep, red cave. I returned to the street. The evil master's building had brought back brilliant memories of my cathedral. I chanted Hirtenstein's words to myself: take the day off, be good.

I turned right again and walked straight into the first pub I found. It was warm and crowded, its walls were covered with painted tiles and columns encrusted with plaster mouldings ran the length of the room. There were heavy wooden cubicles with doors and etched glass windows. Four barmen were serving, they wore waistcoats striped in red and grey. I bought another large whisky and walked along the cubicles hoping to find an empty one. To my surprise I did. I sank into the old, buttoned leather bench and regarded my little room with a new, lonely satisfaction, the opposite of the populated satisfaction of the hotel bar. It was still early. Perhaps I should see a film. The idea was attractive, but I knew at once I would not act upon it. The effort of finding times and a cinema was too much and too destructive of the necessary indiscipline of the day. I was swept by a wave of contentment as if I had just remembered some wonderful news. So intense was the feeling that I was convinced for some minutes that there must be some such news. There was nothing, so I just relaxed into the sensation.

But I had brought nothing to read and I knew, even in my contentment, that I was facing the inevitable issue of what, exactly, I was expecting to happen in this city. Somehow, in the first exultation of arrival, I always forgot that this question had no precise answer. The possibilities always seemed to include a sexual adventure, but I never wished to do anything about it. And, without that, without a film, there was only food, drink and more VR. I bought another drink.

Then I was hungry. I left the pub, puzzled that I could detect none of the usual effects of the whisky, and searched for a restaurant. This took some time. I developed a fervour for making the right choice. I rejected several and then walked back to reconsider them. The process left me breathless and anxious. I finally chose a dark place behind a wooden façade covered in a trellis with creepers and flowers. I was welcomed with the usual disdain reserved for those who eat alone and take up tables that could otherwise be sold to two. The food came too quickly, indicating their desire to drive me out. I barely noticed what I ate. I drank a bottle of wine and left after little more than an hour.

The city had taken on the full, windy emptiness of night. There was no movement but for papers blowing along the streets and glowing lights advertising closed shops. The day off was over. I had been good enough. I began to walk back to the car. There was another wave of contentment and then I remembered the Dip. It had simply made me happy to do what I did. It made me happy to be myself. I took the box out of my pocket and sucked the largest dose I could balance on the end of the stick. It would, presumably, make me happy to drive back.

I walked on. Immediately I was lost. The broken grid of the streets had malevolently abandoned its logic as I ate. I walked past warehouses and building sites that I had never seen before. I tried and failed to retrace my steps to the restaurant, now finding myself walking by tall wire fencing running the length of a canal. I turned and turned again. There was nobody to ask directions and, in any case, I realized I could not remember the name of the hotel. After more walking the streets began to make sense again, at least they started looking like city centre streets while still refusing to be specifically familiar to me. Then, among all the closed doors, I came across one that was open. A painted sign lit by a single naked bulb signalled that this was the entrance to Henry's Club. I went in, vaguely thinking I could ask for directions. There were narrow steps downward. Both black walls brushed my shoulders as I descended. At the bottom was a split door with a plastic sign saying: Private Club, Members Only. I knocked and, after a moment, the upper half opened. Muffled talk and slow music came from inside. A fat man confronted me. He was wearing a T-shirt with the words Henry's Club printed on the front in stark, black capitals. The material ran taut over his stomach, flattening and indenting slightly where it stretched over his navel.

'Sorry to bother you, but I'm lost.'

'Where you going?'

'Well I left my car outside some big hotel, but I've forgotten its name. Been wandering around for hours.'

'Probably the Lex.'

He looked me up and down, deciding apparently that I was in no condition to take directions.

'Come in and have a drink.'

'Oh, thanks. Kind of you.'

The invitation struck me as wildly generous and I regarded the fat man with a kind of love. He smiled back and opened the lower door. I followed him between more black walls and then into the club itself. Perhaps twenty people were there. A few women sat on stools at the bar and small mixed groups talked and smoked intently at tables.

'Welcome to Henry's,' said the fat man. 'I'm Henry. Perhaps you'd like to join.'

He gave me a blue card with four dotted lines marked Name, Date, Signature, Reference. I filled it in, putting Orlando down as my referee.

'That's all we need. You're legal. What'll it be?'

'Whisky.'

The 'large' was unnecessary. I watched Henry fetch the drink with grateful, damp-eyed affection. I sat on a stool. The woman next to me turned.

'Nice to have a new member,' she said brightly. 'My name's Courtney.'

'Nice name. Uncommon. Mine's Stephen.'

She wore a short, black dress, black stockings and black high heels. On one ankle was a gold chain. Her face was heavily made-up and ageless. Her hair was long, straight and dyed blonde and her lips heavily reddened. She was an astonishingly concise summary of all the most direct sexual signals, an uncomplicated flowering from the earth of the free, strange city. I bought her a drink – wine – and turned my damp-eyed affection to her.

Courtney came to Henry's regularly to meet people. It was, she said, a friendly place. Henry looked after her, ensuring she did not get into trouble. I nodded to indicate that I understood. She then went to some lengths to establish for my benefit that she was no whore and neither was she 'easy'. But Henry's was a good place to meet people and she did have a weakness for brief flings with the nice men she met at the club.

'Why not?' I said, raising my glass to her. I felt waves of gratitude and respect.

'That's right. Why not?'

She spoke with a slight lisp and her words were punctuated with quick giggles, habits I supposed she had acquired
with the hair colour to complete the character. I looked at
her in wonder. Courtney did all that was required to make
straightforward men with conventional tastes want to go to
bed with her for uncomplicated reasons. Why, as she asked,
not? She lived in a flat near the town centre and worked in
a men's clothes shop. On the manager's instructions she never
got involved with customers, though she was evidently required
as a permanent lure and tease.

'It's funny everything's worked out so well. I've got the job,
the flat, Henry's and all my friends. Everything I ever wanted
really. Everything that's, you know, me. It may not seem much
to you.'

She looked at me, anxious to be sure that I understood
and, I supposed, to draw some sort of answer indicating I
was wealthy. I looked away, but nodded wisely as I did so.

'You're lucky . . . knowing what's, you know, you. It does
seem a very great deal to me.'

She looked concerned. My answer implied that I might not
be so lucky and she asked about my circumstances. I told her
some bare details and invented a meeting that afternoon as
the reason for being in town.

'Married?'

'Yes.'

'Kids?'

'Yes.'

'Nice.'

'Yes.'

On some fleeting impulse I took the model out of my pocket
and placed it on the counter.

'Oh,' cried Courtney, 'a little you! How sweet! Did you have
this made?'

'Yes, I suppose I did.'

I returned it to my pocket. She looked disappointed not to
be told more. Then we drifted into jokes and silly stories
about aeroplane flights and holidays. Henry supplied further
drinks and then told Courtney I had come in looking for the
Lex.

'Well you won't find it here, Steve, but I can take you there! Lovely hotel, lovely rooms.'

'That would be wonderful. But I'm not staying there. It's just that I left my car outside.'

She looked disappointed, but then a flicker across her features indicated she was prepared to make the best of a bad job.

'OK, let's go and find it then.'

Henry reached over from behind the bar to hang a thin black coat from her shoulders, she clutched a glittering handbag under her arm and we stumbled up the stairs giggling. She led me briskly to the hotel, her heel taps on the pavement echoing against the buildings.

'See, that wasn't too far was it? Where's the car?'

I laughed. It was an odd question since only the Leopard was now parked in the street. Perhaps she found it difficult to associate its profligacy with the man she had just picked up in a bar.

'Well, erm, that's it.'

'Oooooo . . . wow! Nice! I thought you said you were just an architect. That car makes it look as though you own a big club or something.'

'Well I build a lot. Can I give you a lift somewhere?'

'You bet! I wouldn't miss this.'

She settled into the car and immediately started flicking through the rack of discs. She picked one and slid it expertly into the dashboard, her long, red fingernails clicking against the varnished wood. I turned on the ignition and the predictable boom-a-boom filled the car. I accelerated away without first asking her where we were going. The surge of power flipped her backwards into her seat.

'God! This car is soooo sexy!'

I laughed again. This is what women should be like, amiable, appreciative life forces. I cruised around the streets. She kneeled on her seat facing backwards and pounded on the headrest in time with the music.

'I love this!'

'Where are we going?'

'Oh, right.'

She directed me through narrow, empty streets to a blank

240

suburb close to the motorways. We passed the house that had been destroyed.

'Terrible that,' she said. 'A baby was killed.'

We stopped at a small brick terraced house whose front door opened directly on to the pavement. The street was illuminated by lamps giving off a thin, silvery light that seemed to intensify rather than disperse the darkness.

'Come on in, you deserve some fun. You and your sad face.' She plucked at my cheek.

Her flat was the upper floor of the house. Its rooms were placed awkwardly off a snaking hallway covered in posters. She sat me in her living room, brought me a drink and vanished. It was like a recently vacated hotel room. There were signs of a life but they were superficial and could be obliterated in moments. I felt a lumpy pity for Courtney's life and wept slightly. She left no traces.

I swallowed the drink and the room reeled as if I had activated all the night's alcohol at once. I lay sideways on the sofa for fear I would fall forwards. A roaring drowned the whining that still afflicted my ears. I may have blacked out for a moment for the next thing I knew Courtney was standing before me wearing only stockings, suspenders and high heels. Her body seemed astonishingly white and smooth. She must be younger than I had assumed.

'Come on then, didn't you hear me call? Falling asleep, I ask you, what's a girl to think?'

I rolled forward to the floor and kissed her shoes. She sighed heavily.

'Oh. That's what you like. God, it's amazing how many of you do. Well so do I. Get undressed then and perhaps I'll give you a good spanking.'

She walked out of the room. I rose cautiously and followed, tugging at my clothes. In the bedroom she helped me undress and then kissed me hard and effectively on the mouth, holding my head still with both her hands. Her aggression filled me with a sense of peace. She pushed me to the floor and stood over me, rubbing the soles of her shoes over my body and forcing me to suck on her high heels. There was a rightness to this. I found myself thinking of what my professional

241

rivals were up to: Hudson lying awake worrying about his millions, Davies sleeping peacefully dreaming of another thermal barrier, Wilson redeeming the city . . . And here was I. Again peace flooded through me.

Shouting her instructions, Courtney told me to bend over the bed and she began to spank me with a hairbrush. I felt remote from the whole scene, I could almost see it from across the room. But I also felt a strange combination of happiness and extreme excitement. The powerlessness was the point. Clearly I did want this. Courtney knew me better than I knew myself. She was wonderful.

She ran through an extraordinary repertoire of beatings, abuse and gentle humiliations. She seemed to be working to a script or at least a regular routine. Either way I found a few trickles of my blood were involved. Finally the mask dropped and murmuring, 'Nice, mmmmm,' she allowed us to slip on to the bed together and into the more familiar ritual. As it ended I passed out.

I woke moments later to find her laughing at me.

'Was I that good?'

'Very, very good,' I mumbled, rising and searching at once for my clothes. Something was wrong now. The whining was louder and Courtney seemed to have become an awful burden.

'God, that's a bit quick.'

'Sorry, sorry. I feel terrible.'

'Surprised yourself, have you? Well, just lie down. You're in no state to drive.'

'No, no. I've got to move. The Dip . . . too much.'

'Oh God, another bloody doper. Sod off then and don't come back.'

She climbed under the sheets, lit a cigarette and flicked on the television with a remote control. A man was smiling so fiercely that it closed his eyes and his face was shot as if through gauze. I left as rapidly as I could, though even that seemed to take embarrassing hours. In the car I leaned for some time against the steering wheel, only starting the engine when I began to fear falling asleep in this street. I drove as cautiously as I could, though I was unable to tell exactly how fast we were going. The speedometer did not seem to correspond with my experience of the car's real movement in the real world. It was neither faster nor slower, it was just disconnected. I had, of course, no idea where we were and no turn I made revealed anything familiar. I was trapped in these terraced streets. And every few moments the returning memory of me bent over the bed or of Courtney's heel being driven into my mouth would cause me to flinch and twist as if trying to escape from being the person who had just done this.

After some time I realized her boom-a-boom music was still playing. I turned it off and the air cleared slightly. I caught a distant view of a high city centre building and managed to turn towards it. The streets began to make more sense. I breathed easier and the speedometer now seemed to be telling the truth. I saw a familiar sign, swung off this street and found myself heading out of town on, miraculously, the right road, past the destroyed house where the baby died and out towards the open country.

In relief I dropped my foot hard on the accelerator and the Leopard surged forward. But, at that moment, Courtney's repertoire of pain raced back again and filled my mind. It was accompanied by an agonizing intensification of the whining sound in my head. My foot remained on the floor even as the familiar rolling visions and thinning air warned me of an approaching faint. I wanted the car and I to race out of myself, down this black road and away from all that.

Again the city gave me what I wanted. We streaked through a tunnel and then, as we emerged, the street lamps curved upwards and over my head, the road dived away, the roaring and whining ceased and I was in a room with a man in a black coat, muttering incantations and then, before I could move, rushing at me with a knife that cut into me with terrible hissing, grinding and screeching noises . . .

Blood and the black, rain-drenched walls dragging before my eyes. I have been torn. The knives have cut deep within. They have cut something out.

Jill's face hung between the two western towers, her hair forming shining curtains about her shoulders. She was speaking.

You build it, Stephen, but come back. I have been thinking. Orlando too. He has been thinking. Perhaps we both need you, Stephen.

Francesca is slapping me. 'Steeephen!' But she is not angry, she is smiling kindly. She says she is helping me. Tina comes in and brings us tea. She watches as Francesca slaps me.

Cold air, flashing lights. Curious how they really revolve but seem to flash. Strange how everything moves because we move. Someone is pulling me by the shoulders. My feet are pointing upwards and I am dropping out of the car door. Everything is upside down. I smile at all the faces, but they avert their eyes.

Orlando, surrounded by a glorious cloud of birds – lapwing, curlew, lark, pipit – is calling to me. 'Stephen! Steeephen!' He is walking about the valley. The birds sing. He looks anxious, even frightened. 'Steeephen!'

Rattling, tubes, a uniformed man sitting by me. He is reading a newspaper. A howling noise. Hirtenstein is cycling, he says he will live for ever. He knows how.

Your children want to see you, Stephen. They are *your* children. They have a right. Francesca was talking. Tom and Elizabeth come in. He holds a car, she a bear. Why did you leave us, Dad? I am Dad. I left them.

There is a black tunnel. What is me happens when the tunnel stops and there are lights and noises. Waking and sleeping down the tunnel. The tunnel is me and not me. I is what conforms to its shape and follows its commands.

The great cloth, sweeping and cracking. And, inlaid in black and white, the constructor's labyrinth. Above the censer, hanging from its massive chain. I could push it and it would swing, the air rushing and whistling through its niches and voids. Swinging further and wider, out out into the transepts, the racing air fanning its fires. Interleaved arcs of fragrant smoke sink into a veil of mist. Pierced by shafts of sunlight.

I want to lie here, but I cannot. They are calling me.

In a great room a great silence, not of emptiness but of many people being silent, waiting.

NINETEEN

STEPHEN RIX FOUND himself facing the west front. Soaring into the bright sky above him were the two west towers, the gallery, tabernacles and rose window of the façade. He shaded his eyes and seemed to be trying to decipher the details of the upper stages of the towers. But the sunlight was hot, white and dazzling, it made him sweat and must have dissolved the heights of the towers into liquid shadows against the sky. After a few moments he abandoned the attempt and stepped forward into the shade. He looked up again at the curved showers of angels and saints and the blank stone of the empty tympanum at the summit of the great portal.

Finally, with a sudden, self-persuasive nod of his head, he decided something. He took a breath, stepped forward, twisted the iron handle and pushed at the small, silvery oak door that was set into one of the two huge west doors. Lean-ing with his shoulder, he opened it just enough to admit his body and, with a brief sideways step, he was inside. The door creaked shut behind him. Again he paused, this time before the spectacle of the nave. He hesitated, apparently unable to interpret what he saw. He closed his eyes, massaged them with the thumb and forefinger of his right hand and then looked again.

The nave was filled with two huge rectangular blocks of people. They were standing in disciplined ranks and files facing east. Nobody moved and, from where Stephen stood, he would have heard no sound. He looked about as if seeking some explanation in the arcades, in the tall, wooden font cover, in the vaulting. But the building was as mute as ever. He stared again at the people, or rather at their backs. They were dressed with all the usual colourful, sloppy variety of the crowds in the streets. There were adults, children and babies in arms, all silent, motionless and gazing steadily to the east. Stephen followed the line of all these eyes. But he would have seen nothing for the rising sun was blazing through the glass of the choir. Everything beyond the crossing was a dusty, hazy obscurity behind great, slanting bars of light. At least this sight must have told him that the black cloth had gone.

Once more he looked about him and swayed as if about to faint with bewilderment or shock. He walked unsteadily to his left, reaching out his hand to support himself against the first column of the north arcade. He sat down slowly, steadying himself by sliding his back down the column. He tilted his head backwards against the stone and then dipped it forward between his knees and interlaced his hands behind his neck.

Minutes passed in still silence. The air drifted and eddied. The crowd was waiting. Then Stephen rose carefully as if fearful of injury, pushing himself upright by pressing his hands downwards upon his knees. Without looking up from the floor, he turned into the north aisle and began to walk steadily eastward towards the crossing. After passing about ten rows of the congregation he glanced at their faces but he would find nothing there. They were people, that was all, just people, and they appeared to be taking no notice of him. He smiled strangely and seemed to lose interest in his forward movement. Instead, he began studying the building again: the vaulting of the aisle, the columns and the tripartite windows surmounted by their complex cusped *oculi*. He stopped at a monument between two columns of the arcade. Inside a black iron cage and canopy, decorated with black shields, was a heavy marble sarcophagus.

247

It was unmarked. On top lay a painted wooden figure, a thin, bearded man clad in black robes. His bony, veined feet projected from the cloth and rested on a carved cushion. Above the figure rose another canopy of delicately carved white marble.

Stephen smiled again and looked around as if for confirmation of some insight. He took a few steps further and he stopped to examine a grey plaque on the outer wall of the aisle. He stared closely at the marks on the stone. They represented the dancing script and the leaping girl of the Alive! gym sign. Evidently shocked, he began to look more closely at the stones about him. A few moments later at his feet he discovered a large, flat, polished stone showed a running leopard and a drawing of his car. Next to it another stone carried the rough pub sign of the Arches.

Stephen began to rush back and forth in some excitement. He discovered an engraving of the metal insignia that Ralph had worn at their first meeting, the clipped rectangle of the hairdresser's shop, the façade of Gabriels department store. Carved into the surface of one of the arcade columns was an image of Rudy the Robot. A diamond-shaped stained glass window advertised Henry's Club. A small, stone bowl of water cut into the aisle wall bore a transparent pool upon which floated in oily rainbows the smiling face of Jill.

He spun round to face the congregation. But his excitement died at the sight of their still unconcerned faces. Then he seemed to remember the need to continue eastwards. He carefully centred himself in the aisle and began to walk forward. Approaching the crossing he stepped into one of the shafts of sunlight and stopped to look up at its source amongst the choir windows. But the light still dazzled and obscured. Again he tried to look forward, still nothing. Then, with one further step that brought him to the very end of the arcade, he would have heard the low murmur of the litany. A man's voice, barely audible from here, came from the direction of the high altar.

Stephen moved quickly forward to stand in the labyrinth at the centre of the crossing. He looked rapidly about the transepts, they were empty, and then eastwards. The choir stalls were full of gowned choristers who, like the rest of the congregation, were turned to face the altar. Slowly he raised his eyes to face the eastern end.

The tall, slender clerestory windows were no longer covered and the sunlight streaming through cast deep shadows about the choir. He blinked and followed the line of the tracery downwards. His gaze came upon a deep band with quatrefoil decoration and then to the point of a gable from which sprang the centre line of the clerestory tracery. Crockets twisted from the sides of the gable which met the rising shafts of the vault just above the springing of the central arch of the ambulatory.

In front of this arch were the black marble steps of the altar leading up to a heavy table of beige stone. A white-gowned figure was bent over this table and it was his voice intoning the incomprehensible phrases.

Stephen rushed forwards. The choristers paid no attention. He leapt the three marble steps and reached out just as the celebrant turned to face him. Stephen froze, his hand outstretched.

'Hello, Stephen, we've been expecting you.' He took the reaching right hand and clasped it between his palms.

'Expecting me?' Stephen was laughing but appeared frightened. 'Who are you? What is all this? A dream? Virtual reality?'

'Oh, no, not that,' he smiled, looking around as if to encourage the others to join in, 'but a dream, if you like. Yes, probably that's best, a dream.'

He wore glasses and his face was round, fat and smiling. Light glinted from the glasses and gleamed on the swollen cheeks. The head seemed to float in a cradle of air and light.

'But it's not really a dream is it?'

'No, it's not really a dream. Nothing's ever *really* a dream.'

'What is it then?'

'Difficult to say exactly. Best for you to think of it as a kind of question.'

'What question?'

'Ah, perhaps, What if . . . ?'

'What if this were all true or real?'

'Something like that.'

'Or meaningful?'

'Or meaningful.'

'And is it?'

249

'Well that's the question in question, isn't it? Perhaps you would feel better if you thought of it as an architectural question.'

He laughed happily, still clasping Stephen's hand. Stephen now released himself and turned to look back, westwards, down the church. The choristers and congregation were staring directly at him. Many were now smiling, some nodding. He turned again to the celebrant.

'What do you mean you were expecting me? Were they all expecting me?'

'Oh yes I think so. They certainly seem pleased to see you. I mean it's your question. You're the point of the whole exercise.'

'I thought so. That's what I always felt. But I never knew if I was right to try and build it.'

The celebrant laughed again, loudly this time.

'Oh, that hardly matters for the moment. But you will work it out in time, when it matters.'

'So it will matter?'

'Of course.'

'Why did I find that model, those figures of me?'

'Same question really – What if . . . ?'

'What if they were me?'

'Exactly.'

Stephen looked down at the heavy brown shoes beneath the white robe.

'But why am I being asked? And why in this bizarre way? It seems so crude.'

'Same question. Same architectural question. It is pretty crude, I'll grant you that. But it would be, wouldn't it? Crude and funny. How else would it be? People always expect things to be subtle and serious, but there's no reason why they should be. And, if you think about it, there isn't time. Enough questions. We must get on. They're calling us.'

'Who?'

'Oh, you'll know soon enough. They're calling you too.' He laughed again.

'What about Orlando and all those people . . . and my family?'

He stopped laughing and smiled questioningly.

250

'There are these people too. There are always people. You can't really get away from that. Nobody can.'

He gestured at the congregation and turned once again to face the east. Stephen waited and then walked slowly round behind the altar and down into the ambulatory. There he appeared to the watching choristers to be entangled in shafts of sunlight and the baffling syncopations of the columns as they curved and wove their way about the chapels at the eastern end of his cathedral. Finally, they could not see at all amidst those apparently random columns which, in plan, as Stephen well knew, revealed an alignment of the strictest mathematical regularity.

TWENTY

LATER WE ALL met for the opening of The First Church of the
New Millennium.

The cathedral was finished. Clean and pale and perfect, it
was a phenomenon of air, too fine, too light to be anchored
in earth. It seemed rather to rest on its site, gently borne
by blades of compliant grass.

The ceremony was held on midsummer day. It was warm
and dry with deep shadows and brilliant air, brilliant light.
Inside the nave there would be intense, angled shafts of this
light, slanting from the east in the late morning, cutting through
that sculpted vessel of still space. Outside on the sloping and
cobbled close with its walls, battlements, banked flower beds
and gift shops a great crowd had gathered. An orchestra played
and flags waved in the breeze. There was a fairground with
stalls and a Big Wheel. Scaffolding stands supported camera
crews and reporters. Sudden local outbreaks of applause and
cheering signalled the presence of acrobats, magicians, clowns,
puppet shows and comedians. Every few moments there would
be booming loudspeaker announcements giving details of the
approaching ceremony, pointing out notable celebrities who

had arrived for the occasion or describing lost property or children. Above huge, silver airships drifted, carrying politicians and diplomats high over the crowd to survey the glistening, waiting cathedral. Above them, tremendously high, there was a spreading, dappled vapour trail in the cloudless blue. In front of the great west doors on a high purple-clad platform from which the ceremony would be conducted, I sat, dribbling slightly.

Around me they chattered and laughed, leaning down a little too frequently to ensure that I was comfortable or to ask if I needed anything. Happiness, I had often observed in the years of my new condition, always brought out the most meddlesome variety of compassion.

'Fine, thanks, fine,' I replied in the friendly, condescending, not quite native tones hard-wired into my computer.

'Isn't it lovely?' cried Jill into my ear, the brim of her enormous hat bending against my head. She still shouted when talking to me; it was, I concluded, her way of advertising the fact that, yes, she owned the cripple.

'Lovely, lovely.'

My voice machinery makes repetition easier than elaboration. After an initial irritation, this had come as a great relief.

Jill was so happy now with her new face, the cathedral – a huge success in spite of everything – and with me paralysed and speechless. She was so happy I barely recognized her these days. But I did not mind. Being noisily and fussily cared for by this new Jill had become one of the more intense, most exquisitely incomplete pleasures provided by my new condition.

And now here we all were on the platform: Hirtenstein and Lionel, Orlando, Tom and Elizabeth, Greaves, the entire committee of fifty-year-olds, Sally and Ralph, now married, Jack the landlord who hated me, the still limping postman, Tina, Gerald, Joe and countless others. Only, I reflected, Francesca was missing, but, long ago, she had emigrated to some frozen, northern country from where she occasionally wrote letters as cool and barren as the climate. 'Dear Stephen,' began one, 'The ice-strewn seas . . . '

There was a smell of cigar smoke and Hirtenstein was clutching my shoulder.

'You are looking great, Steve, great. You've done it. At last you're the star you ought to be. Look at them! They love you. What did I say? Trust Dave the Developer Hirtenstein. That's what I said. Remember?'

Greaves, in a shining suit and a golden, gun-shaped tie-pin, reached down and clasped my hand.

'You should be a very proud man. You dreamed all this up. This is your vision.'

Yes, I had dreamed for a while and then, one night in a city, given my body to the church, or, at any rate, the animating principle of my body. I had known that it had left me as the Leopard screeched and tore and felt no surprise when, weeks later, the doctors confirmed it. 'No more back problems now,' I had written on my yellow pad, smiling, anxious to relieve them of their burden of anxiety. But even they had been puzzled by the loss of speech. For months it was diagnosed as some kind of temporary, hysterical aphasia, but finally they had to conclude it was either physical or the hysteria was permanent. I could not tell, the words just would not come, only formless grunts and whines. Still I could dream of interiors and I did. But, should it ever happen again, I would no longer be able to walk through the visions or feel the walls against which, in dreams, I leaned my face or trailed my fingers.

The ceremony was to be roughly modelled on some medieval pageantry. Hirtenstein had insisted on something authentic, Orlando had conducted some supposedly thorough research, Lionel had provided the hardware and an appropriately re-gional poet had provided the appropriately regional words. The dignitaries would approach, the words would be spoken, the doors flung open. The interior would be empty but for one last evil spirit to be exorcised. This was to be played by a robot called Nick. Devised by Lionel, Nick was an angular, lurching metal mechanism clad in ripped shreds of black cloth and cobwebs. Toy versions of Nick had already been a great success in the shops and there was talk of a Nick film. For the purposes of this ceremony he would, on cue, wave his arms, scream in anguish, howl at the good people outside and then, as the final words of exorcism were spoken, he would rise and race, shrieking, out of the doors, around the platform and then plunge, in a holocaust of flames and black smoke, into a pit in front of the crowds. A thousand white doves would be released and a flight of three aircraft would swoop low into the valley, trailing coloured, sweet-scented smoke. Then the cathedral, cleansed of its last evil, would be entered by a great procession. In the course of the day all of the 50,000 crowd would file through its nave to be presented, on their exit from the south transept, with a scroll signifying their presence at the opening of the First Church of the New Millennium.

Orlando in a white suit and straw hat approached me. He stood before me for a moment, gazing at the crowd, and then plucked at his trouser legs and crouched down so that his eyes were level with mine.

'It's a nice, last bit of stuff, a great valedictory to the architecture business. Kind of, "Sod you, if this is what you want . . . " I like to see it as the far end of an arc of work that began with the lime green picnic. The logic is there for those who care to look.'

'A nice idea,' said my machine, 'both ceremonies of summer. You are leaving tomorrow?'

'Yes, the east beckons. I shall sink into undignified old age on some plantation. I cannot refuse. I've had enough of doing things. Doing anything means being haunted by jerks like Hirtenstein. Anyway, as we know, there's nothing to be done really. I will miss you, Stephen.'

'I shall miss you, Orlando. Orlando.'

Sometimes the machine just repeats itself.

'You can carry on being a star, I suppose. Gothic Rix, the hero of the Rural Beauty Zones.'

'It will pass the time. That Lightfoot has offered to manage my public affairs. I can hardly build anything after this.'

Hirtenstein had overheard. Judging volume on the machine had always been a problem.

'He will, he will.' He strode springily towards us, rubbing his hands. 'I'm working on it. This is just the beginning. This is the *first* church, remember?'

'Ah yes,' said Orlando, 'of course . . . But remember also there is no Rix–Cummings.'

'I only need Steve, Orlando, he's the genius round here. And I'm working on him.'

Orlando flared slightly at the insult. It was true, he had been working on me, encouraging me to think in terms of mosques, an Egyptian stadium, baroque sports centres, classical railway stations.

'But there are no trains,' I had protested.

'Give me a break, Steve, you just designed a cathedral.'

'I think, Dave,' Orlando was now looking contemptuously at Hirtenstein, 'that I was right about you the first time round.'

'You probably were, you fat queen.'

Tina edged through the crowd, taking a tissue from her handbag. She gently wiped my dribbling mouth. I savoured her scent.

'OK, Stephen?'

'Yes, thank you, thank you, Tina.'

Jill pushed Tom and Elizabeth into view. He was now awkward with adolescence and she had developed a withdrawn, cautious look about her eyes.

'Today you should be very proud of your father.'

'We are,' said Tom too hurriedly. Elizabeth smiled. I knew they did not really believe that the dribbling, paralysed, broken doll in the wheelchair was anything to do with the man who had once taken them to see films and bought them toys. I remembered the childhood certainty that whatever looked disgusting was disgusting.

Nevertheless, on Jill's instructions, Tom shook my hand and Elizabeth kissed me. Jill loved all this. I looked at her surgically lifted features. She was, no doubt about it, a new woman. The hard, independent pose had gone. Now she was the loyal wife of a success, a star. The church had changed her.

For my cathedral had become an entirely respectable success. As soon as the first hole had been dug, the public meaning of this building had been transformed. In part this was simple popular excitement at the absurd grandiosity of the idea. But also powerful forces, identifying new self-interests, had intervened to endorse the scheme. The First Church of the New Millennium became a policy. It was, it transpired, an exemplary intervention in the countryside, a triumphant flagship for the Rural Beauty Zones, a magnet to draw people out of the rotting cities. In corridors and restaurants clever people explained to the slightly less clever what a good idea it was and they obediently went off to explain why to the completely stupid. By the time the ultra-lead roof had begun to conceal Lionel's stupendous, raking beams of post-tensioned concrete, the cathedral had become an emblem of national pride. They, the powerful ones, would all be at the opening. It had become too much, too official for Jill to resist, so she did not.

'This is so exciting,' she cried. 'Sooo exciting! Look!'

The airships had landed and the important passengers were making their way, talking earnestly in deference to public expectations, along the white path leading to their special stand to the right of the platform.

The concealing of the structure by fake Gothicry had been painful, even to me. Lionel, in answer to his private needs, had produced an extraordinary concrete creature, standing on high, tense legs that would form armatures for the columns of the nave and choir. The west towers were held by beams raking inwards behind the façade and backwards above the vaulting. At the crossing were four more of these raking beams, joined 150 feet above the labyrinth and sloping downwards to meet the primary concrete skeleton of the building. He had worked neurotically and with immense wastage of time to perfect this structure. Hirtenstein had grown angry – 'What is it with you? Nobody's going to see this stuff.' But Lionel resisted all pressure, insisting on the unity and integrity of the structure and baffling Dave with his reasons. He baffled me too. I could see Dave's point; it would all be lost under the cladding, there could be no possible reason. But, I assumed, this was his way of making the building 'good'.

There were stirrings in the crowd.

'I think it's time,' said Jill, organizing the children.

'It is, it is!' cried Tina, jumping slightly.

The crowd on the platform began shifting and organizing themselves. The files of important people had appeared and were now seated in their stand. Tina wheeled me to my spot at the very front of the platform. I was ludicrously exposed. This, I had noticed, was always felt to be the right thing to do with the handicapped – hold them out like trophies, the spoils of your compassion. A master of ceremonies in a check suit appeared on the platform to delirious applause from the crowd. He told jokes, did impersonations, even lampooning some of the important people in the stand, rolled his eyes and then, after a delicate pause, he slipped into a lachrymose speech about this being, above all, a local church, a thing of the land, a celebration of this valley and these people.

'Very sincerely, folks, this is a very, very big day for us all, for all the world. I am humbled to be here.'

Then he introduced an enormous squad of local country dancers, covered in sashes and bells and carrying ribboned sticks. In their hundreds they jumped, jangled, clattered and tinkled through routines claimed to date back to the first age of Gothic. At last they tinkled to a conclusive formation and filed off to the right. The MC reappeared to introduce Hirtenstein – 'a big man in every sense.' Big Developer Dave gave a characteristically brilliant speech. He spoke about himself, his boyhood ambitions.

'I', he admitted, 'was the fat boy at school. And I'm still the fat boy . . . ' laughter, 'but I can do amazing things.' He flipped over on to his hands, his shiny shoes waving in the air. The crowd roared. The MC leapt to the front of the stage, applauding wildly. Hirtenstein flipped back.

'But I knew', he continued, 'there was one amazing thing I had to do. I didn't quite know what it was . . . until . . . one day . . . I met . . . Steeeephen Rix!'

He turned suddenly in my direction, his arms outstretched.

'The man who dreamed the dream.'

There was applause and cheering. It went on for a long time, I was, after all, in a wheelchair. Some people on the platform fired paper ribbons over me from little guns. I was covered like some decorated tribal fetish.

Next was some politician who said the scheme was a 'brilliant, bold yet historically appropriate way of revitalizing the countryside.'

'This cathedral', he said, 'tells the world that we are a nation returning to the land, embodying its past in a vision of the future.'

Lionel had risen from his seat suddenly and walked across the platform to take an empty chair a few feet from me.

'Lionel,' said my machine, a little too loudly, 'can you get these bloody ribbons off me?'

There was a small, local ripple of laughter and a nearby woman in a pink suit rose and began helpfully pulling at the ribbons.

'Thanks. Thanks.'

Then there was to be a big surprise. This was not on the programme, explained the Master of Ceremonies, because it was just too big and too good. The orchestra had begun a low, premonitory rumble. Somebody had come to the opening whom, he knew, they would all want to see. He was the most famous man in the world, the hero of Mars Mission 2000. The man who saved his ship from disaster, completed the landing and returned to earth. The man who, on planting his foot on the red dust of the red planet, had said: 'Humanity, humanity. Limitless vision. A step into the great beyond.'

'Look what I've got for you,' cried the MC. 'Let's hear it for Captain Dale McCluskey!'

The orchestra surged into a brilliant, high, brassy anthem and, wearing a silver suit and cap, Captain Dale leapt up the steps at the back of the platform and raised both hands to acknowledge the yells, gasps and cheers of the crowd. He reeled back to indicate modest surprise at the noise, levelled his arms and made patting movements with his palms to call for quiet. There was, finally, an obedient silence but for a few male whistles and whoops and female screams.

'Thank you, thank you,' said Captain Dale. 'You know I'm just here to see this amazing thing you've built. I'm not the star of this show . . .'

'There is something wrong here, Stephen. We cannot live for ever with this – these jokes, gags . . .'

The voice seemed to be inside my head, but then I realized that Lionel had moved next to me and was now whispering urgently in my ear

'Think how awful this really is. Think of it, Stephen.'

I felt the brush of his moustache and the heat of his breath. What had happened to him? The words came with a shocking, fierce intensity.

'I mean what is this robot talking about? These are words, Stephen, he's just chucking them around.'

He paused to allow me to sample more of the Captain's speech.

'This building moves me deeply, ladies and gentlemen, deeply. It is an immense gesture of faith, of faith in the deep roots of our history and, most important of all, of faith in our future. See how it soars cleanly into the sky. I walked on Mars, sure, and nobody here can say the same. But my proudest boast is that I walked on the earth, I shared this planet with people who build great, soaring churches. People who are building The New Millennium.'

I caught a glimpse of Tom and Elizabeth, their eyes worshipping the Captain.

'This is a terrible thing, Stephen, a terrible thing.'

I replied using only the screen of my computer. Lionel read the words.

'It was a mistake, a bad mistake. I know. It was the women, Lionel, always the women.'

'No, it was not a mistake and it was not the women.'

'But what was I to do? I saw the bloody thing. You know that. I really saw it.'

'I know. But I also know why you saw it. You saw it because you had to build it because of what you have to do next.'

The Captain was concluding.

'What you people have done with this church is very like what we did on Mars Mission 2000. We ushered in the new age. We took hold of history and made it new. Long live the First Church of the New Millennium! Long live history! Let the ceremony commence!'

'What? What? Do next? Do next? Next. Next.'

I had lost control of the machine. The words were scrolling frantically across the screen.

'We have to get rid of it. No, I mean *you* have to get rid of it. You have to make the decision.'

I employed the painful, jerking movement which was all that I had left to shift the weight of my head. I was now facing Lionel. He was staring at me, expressionless. An instinctive perversity had prepared me to hear his words. This fuss, this ceremony, this noise had already turned me, half-consciously, away from the cathedral in disgust. I had always loathed the warm, affirming pressure of agreement and celebration. I always wished to explain that it was more complicated than that, nothing can be that easy. Such bloated ceremonial had to be wrong. But what was next?

The formal proceedings were about to begin. Figures clad in absurd red robes, designed especially for the occasion, were gathering in front of the platform. The orchestra was playing The Anthem for the First Church of the New Millennium. The composer had aimed for rousing but jagged, popular but new, with appropriate overtones of lute and sackbut.

Lionel, of course, was saying much more than this. Lionel was not perverse. He was saying it was wrong from the first, not just because of this grotesque carnival. Its falsity was real falsity, absolute falsity.

'Look at it!' he hissed.

Flags had been raised by a semicircle of, I supposed, heralds. Each bore a device representing the trades that had built the cathedral: architect, engineer, steelworkers, carpenters, press and public relations, the last symbolized by two shaking hands from which sprang a luxuriant tree. As the red-robed celebrants mounted the platform I saw that these devices were repeated on their backs. A chant was now going up.

'In the name of the New Millennium, to the honour of the people, to the glory of the land . . . '

Four giant screens positioned around the close were showing the ceremony in massive detail.

'In the name of the New Millennium, to the honour of the people, to the glory of the land . . . '

All the screens suddenly cut to a close-up of my face with Lionel's lips, moustache and nose jutting into the shot. I looked at my slumped features with pity, the gaping mouth, the crooked head. That poor man, I thought, that poor man. I noticed Lionel's lips were moving on the screen fractionally before I was able to take in his next words.

' . . . layers and layers. They put these layers over everything, layers of invented ceremonies, layers of fake history, layers of plastic over the concrete.'

And then, I completed the thought in my mind, all that is left are the layers. We would drift endlessly through these laminations, all different and all the same. But who would we be, what would we do? How would we be serious?'

'It must be stopped.'

'How? How?' Again the words scrolled crazily about the screen.

'There is a reason for that structure. It all leans on the four beams of the crossing. They're post-tensioned. Think about it.'

I scarcely needed to. I knew what came next and, at once, I knew why Lionel had fussed so endlessly over his invisible structure.

'There are small charges in each of those beams. Once they blow the post-tensioning will do the rest.'

The beams would explode from the release of their own tensioning. I pictured the structure in my mind to imagine what would follow. The central tower would drop downwards, pulling the concrete arches of the nave and choir inward. What had appeared in the structure to be a way of holding the nave up was, in reality, a mechanism for pulling it down. The building would collapse upon itself, each part tugging the next down into dust. Finally the west front would fall backwards, away from the platform.

'I get it. I get it.'

'It's safe. Only the robot gets killed. Remember I designed all this celebration stuff as well, everybody is far enough away.'

'You're right, but it's too awful. It's too awful now. Doing it to these people . . . '

The music had grown louder and one of the robed figures had raised some kind of spiky stick into the air with which he was challenging the evil within to emerge in the name of peace, happiness and prosperity. A group of dancers in tight, white clothes flung themselves about before the platform in a frenzied evocation of the good. I remember the dance was called The Midsummer Rite of Perfect Virtue.

'It's up to you. The charges can be fired by a signal from your computer. You type the code, send it as if you were saying it through the voice box and they blow. It is up to you, only you. It's your church.'

'What's the code?'

'The Last Church of the New Millennium.'

'Nice, very nice, Lionel.'

I had the screen under control at last.

'Out, out, you spirit of darkness and solitude! Begone from within our midst, abandon ye our great First Church of the New Millennium, O thing of darkness!'

Automatically I entered the phrase, 'The Last Church of the New Millennium' and stared fondly at the blue letters glowing on the screen. I had not done anything yet, I was just thinking, the computer entry was as harmless, as powerless as a thought. In fact, it was just like a thought: a few micro-electronic shufflings . . . But, of course, this thought was now outside in the world and only one movement lay between me and the decision, a fractional roll of the heel of my right hand on to the grey, concave 'send' button. Lionel was right, of course, but how right? Right enough to smash this people's party? And I had, after all, seen this thing, surely that meant something, surely that justified this pale, pristine, finished object in spite of Captain Dale, the MC and the country dancers. Something had intervened from outside. A message had been sent. But then it had become this, neutralized into a new deception, a new version of the old message, that there was nothing to do, nothing to be done but whirl madly through the layers of a sterilised past, through the superfine laminations of the present time.

A slight boom signalled that the west doors were beginning to open. Awkwardly I manoeuvred my chair round to watch. I could only see the upper half of the façade above the heads of the packed ranks on the platform. Now I could hear the screaming of Nick, but I could not see him.

'Out! Out! That the good people may live in peace and prosperity!'

Nick howled in anguish as if the words were burning his flesh.

'He's coming! He's coming!'

Elizabeth was shouting and pointing. Greaves lifted her up and balanced her on his shoulders so she could see the emerging evil.

Nick, I knew, would be stalking horribly down the nave

from the crossing. Most of the crowd would not be able to see him, but it had been felt that the noise of his progress would be the most dramatically effective prelude to his appearance. There would be minutes of suspense. His individual movements were rapid but he was programmed to lurch, falter and howl for maximum impact, so I knew that his forward progress would be slow.

'See, he comes, the Evil One.'

'Come, come and be cast into the flames!' cried another red-robed celebrant.

Lionel was now crouching before me, fixing my eyes. I looked down again at the message on my screen. The Last Church of the New Millennium. I allowed my hand to depress the 'send' button just to the point where a fractional increase in its resistance signalled that it was about to activate. I looked back at Lionel. His face was immobile; he knew where I was, he wanted to know who I was. I felt a sudden, potent wave of affection for him. He was, as I had always known, the best. Stay with the best, do what they ask. I allowed my hand to roll under the pressure of its own weight. I felt the click. In its tones of supremely deferential warmth, my machine voice said, 'The Last Church of the New Millennium' and then said it again. It was just loud enough to be heard above the screeching and intoning by a few people nearby. One or two turned round in surprise and one woman laughed nervously as if afraid of the words.

Then there was nothing, a pause of beautiful, fragile intensity; then there was a series of echoing cracks; then nothing; then there was a terrible, slow, rolling detonation; then a shudder ran through the ground and the people on the platform clutched at each other in shock. I looked up to the topmost stage and spire of the central tower, rising above the gable of the façade. Miraculously it appeared to be stable, yet I knew that all strength had now gone from its supporting structure. I felt it was held there by a kind of disbelief, a refusal to accept the horror, the sudden engineering void below. Lionel had risen to his feet and was now shading his eyes, gazing like me at the central tower. Still the robot was screaming and moving down the nave, but now the crowd were shouting and pointing instead of jeering at his cries of anguish. Some had begun to clamber down the front of the platform in terror and a few children were crying.

'It was too much,' I heard one man shout. 'We tried to do too much, too big, too much . . . '

'It's an earthquake!'

The central tower shuddered and began to descend into the crossing. At first the movement was almost undetectably slow, but then there was an awful acceleration and plumes of dust emerged from the tower's base. With this sign that the collapse of the cathedral could no longer be denied, a great panic swept through the crowd. Some froze in shock, a few, strangely, ran towards the building, but most turned to escape from the confines of the close, funnelling desperately into the narrow exit gates. Many more were now jumping from the platform and one celebrant, tangled in his red robes, fell noisily to the ground. I could not see Jill, Tom or Elizabeth.

Lionel turned to me and, as if following a plan, began tightening my seatbelts and forcing my head into the hard foam rubber ring that held it in place when I was to be moved. He called on Hirtenstein and Orlando to help him. But Dave was too shocked to be of any use. The tightness had gone from his skin. He moved jerkily about, clutching people by the arm, demanding to know what was happening. Orlando was staring at the collapsing church, one hand over his mouth, one pressing his hat to his head as if there were a high wind. He heard Lionel's call and came over to help. Suddenly I saw Jill pushing the children away.

Lionel and Orlando had begun to manoeuvre me to the end of the platform where I could be lifted down some steps. Ralph and Sally appeared. Ralph was shouting desperately.

'What is this? What is this?'

Sally looked hard at me.

Then the nave began its steady collapse. I could hear the great arches leaning and cracking as they began to slip into the boiling clouds of dust around the crossing. They were about to start lifting me down. Desperately I entered words into the computer and hit 'send'.

'No, no! I must see. I must see.'

Lionel looked at Orlando and said softly, 'We'll be OK.' Orlando nodded slowly as if understanding far too much. The wave of destruction reached the point at which the raking beams of the façade joined the nave. There were two further detonations as the tension in the concrete was explosively released. The whole façade seemed to wave and then began to lean backwards. The realism of Lionel's stone made the way it held together seem implausible, surely it should be fragmenting under its own weight. But it held, falling further and further with a tumult of sharp, cracking noises as the thousands of secondary elements of the structure, robbed of their primary supports, gave way.

Then Nick emerged wailing and shrieking, his thin metal arms flailing amid the destruction and his rags flapping. It was like some elegantly crafted gag from a silent film for he had reached the end of the nave just at the moment when he would be saved from being crushed by the opening of the west doors. In complete ignorance of the catastrophe, yet seeming now to be its harbinger, he lurched out of the imploding building and around the platform just below us. He reached the circular metal plate that was his destination, howled for a few more seconds and then fell downwards as the aperture irised open and he dropped into the flames and smoke of hell. Goodbye, Thing of Evil.

The closing iris automatically triggered the opening of the cage of doves and suddenly the birds were thrashing and clambering at the air and darting above the heads of the crowd. There was a further roar and the three aircraft appeared over the far ridge of the valley, dipped and raced on a course that would bring them down what had been the centre line of the cathedral. They turned on their celebratory smoke as if they had noticed nothing wrong. Pink, blue, green and orange trails sprayed from their wings. Almost at once they were overhead and then they were gone. There was a fresh scent in the air and the plumes of smoke were now forming slowly sinking veils above the wreckage of The First and Last Church of the New Millennium.

We watched the rehearsed workings of this unshakeable programme in wonder. There was a pause after the jets had vanished and then, silently, Orlando and Lionel began to edge me down the steps from the platform. The panic about us made this a difficult operation. The sanctity of my handicap was now disregarded in the race for what the crowd thought was survival. I was pushed and buffeted by people struggling to get past us. Orlando swore at them, but Lionel remained silent. He had been expecting all of this and worked steadily at what he must do. We reached the ground to be surrounded by Jill, the children and Hirtenstein. Dave was babbling absurdly, demanding explanations.

'What is this? What is this? Lionel, you bastard, you fucked up, you fucked up. Or maybe a bomb. Do you think it was a bomb? What do you think, Orlando?'

Then I became aware of an immense clattering noise above us. Four helicopters were descending into the close. Huge, black and encrusted with sinister equipment, they howled and swayed in the seething wind and dust. From loudspeakers slung under their bodies voices bawled orders at the crowd to clear the central area and allow them to land. But the crowd, now so pounded and terrorized by events, could not understand what was required. Desperately they tried to obey, but nobody could work out what space to clear. Finally, impatiently, the helicopters landed. Armed men in black jumped out of the doors and fanned out, pushing people away and clearing a circle around the aircraft. Shots were fired in the air and hundreds dropped to the floor. A separate party of soldiers forced a corridor through to where the politicians and diplomats had been seated. Rapidly they collected those who had not fled and ushered them back to one of the helicopters, their heads dipped to evade the rushing wind of the rotors. Clumsily they climbed on board. It took off. The remaining soldiers backed slowly into the other two aircraft and then they were all gone.

'God, God, God!' screamed Hirtenstein. 'Were they expecting this or what? What is going on here?'

'Shut up, Dave!' shouted Orlando. 'It's just security. Let's move now.'

'What happened? What happened?'

'Let's just assume,' said Orlando angrily, 'it was a bomb, a big bomb. At this moment it just doesn't fucking matter.'

They began to push me across the uneven ground of the

close, towards the main entrance, still packed with people. I was breathing very quickly and being jolted horribly by the speed of the movement. My head seemed to be clamped tighter and tighter in the grip of the rubber hoop. Lionel had done something wrong. I could feel its metal frame cutting through the foam, forming an indented circle of pain around my head. Meanwhile my body was being thrown helplessly about and dreadful, stinging, shooting pains darted up my neck and flashed like sparks about the dome of my skull. I could not signal my distress, the jolting prevented me from using the computer.

We entered the funnel of people escaping through the main entrance to the close. Some looked at me curiously, but most were too anxious to escape. Lionel was now pushing me while Orlando fought to clear a path ahead. The crush grew worse, intensifying the terrible constriction I felt. At last we were under the arch of the gate. Then we were through. Lionel, with extraordinary strength, accelerated. The path was smoother now and I was able to input a sentence which I then delivered at maximum volume.

'Up the hill, take me up the hill.'

'OK, Stephen, OK.'

He swerved off the path and across the smooth, mown grass. We rose up the gentle mound that sloped gracefully down to the main gate. We reached the top.

'Take me out of the chair. Lie me down.'

Lionel began to unfasten me. Jill appeared.

'What are you doing? Stop it.'

'He wants to lie down. I think he's in some trouble.'

'No, you mustn't.'

Jill tried to interfere but Lionel pushed her roughly away. He raised the hoop from my head and then, with perfect tenderness, lifted me and laid me on the grass. I could say nothing now. But Lionel had read my wishes. I was lying on quite a steep slope so that, by looking down the length of my body, I could survey the entire scene.

On the broad slope of grass hundreds of people were lying, sitting or standing in little groups. Some seemed to be bleeding and all had torn clothes. Children were crying but otherwise there was an extraordinary silence as the people looked back at the scene below. The cathedral was now an immense heap of rubble with random concrete and steel projections. Dust still rose and billowed, but the destruction, as Lionel had planned, was entirely contained within its boundaries. The platform, now empty, was unaffected and, but for the rubbish left behind by the crowd's flight and a few broken and twisted stalls, the whole area of the close was entirely unaffected. More helicopters were approaching from the far end of the valley and sirens were wailing as police cars closed in on the scene.

My breathing had become easier and the flashes of deathly panic had subsided. One by one the others were arriving and sitting, exhausted and shocked, around me: Ralph and Sally, Hirtenstein, Tina, Greaves, Tom and Elizabeth. Orlando, now hatless, was sitting, his arms crossed on his upraised knees. Lionel was unfixing my computer panel from the chair. He then laid it on my stomach, picked up my hands and placed them over the control surfaces. I looked at him as he leaned over me.

'Is there anything you want to say?'

I managed to throw my head from side to side. No, not yet. I remembered, long ago, sitting on the side of the valley with Ralph, Hirtenstein and Lionel, watching until those two cars had suddenly appeared to take away Francesca. Lionel finally sat down beside me.

'It was right,' he whispered. 'This is best. It could not go on. We could not be a part of that. Something has to be real.'

The sun still shone, the breeze blew and birds sang in casual defiance of the chaos below. Above the rubble my watering eyes told me I could see the outlines of the undamaged cathedral as if its extinction had been so sudden that something of its essence still hung in the warm air. I could see it in the same way that I could sometimes feel my body, as a phantom, a memory.

Hirtenstein was now crying, but the rest of us were silent. The helicopters were landing and fleets of ambulances, police cars and vans were swinging on to the roads that encircled the close. I looked fondly for a moment at the cleared area, now smoothly grassed over, where our house had been demolished to make way for the project. Jill had bought something much grander, of course, but, for now, even that phantom seemed solid and real, its old stones still raised against the wind.

I grunted to indicate to Lionel that I wished to speak. He lifted the panel so that I could see the screen. Slowly, because of the awkwardness of the angle, I entered the words, 'Let the dog see the rabbit.'

I pressed the 'send' button. The voice spoke and at once I realized I had made a mistake.

'Let the duck see the rabbit,' it said. I fiddled with the panel, but the discomfort made me clumsier than usual. The words scrolled and flashed. I could not get it right and, letting my head fall back, I surrendered to the errors, rolling my hand on to the 'send' button.

'Duck rabbit,' it said. 'Duck rabbit, duck rabbit, duck rabbit.'

Lionel laughed, Orlando laughed and so did I, but, of course, no-one could hear me.